D0485647

the enemy between us

OTHER BOOKS AND AUDIOBOOKS
BY MELINDA SUE SANCHEZ

The Fisherman's Daughter

the enemy between us

A HISTORICAL ROMANCE

MELINDA SUE SANCHEZ

Covenant
Covenant Communications, Inc.

To my incredible children. You make me want to burst into song.

Cover image: *Wartime Couple Embracing in Street* © CollaborationJS / Trevillion Images; *Stamp* by swarog, courtesy istockphoto.com; *Blank Franked Feldpost Envelope 194*1 by whitemay, courtesy istockphoto.com.

Cover design copyright © 2020 by Covenant Communications, Inc.

Published by Covenant Communications, Inc.
American Fork, Utah

Copyright © 2020 by Melinda Sue Sanchez
All rights reserved. No part of this book may be reproduced in any format or in any medium without the written permission of the publisher, Covenant Communications, Inc., P.O. Box 416, American Fork, UT 84003. The views expressed within this work are the sole responsibility of the author and do not necessarily reflect the position of Covenant Communications, Inc., or any other entity.

This is a work of fiction. The characters, names, incidents, places, and dialogue are either products of the author's imagination, and are not to be construed as real, or are used fictitiously.

Printed in the United States of America
First Printing: July 2020

27 26 25 24 23 22 21 20   10 9 8 7 6 5 4 3 2 1

ISBN 978-1-52441-346-0

ACKNOWLEDGMENTS

The Enemy between Us has been a labor of love in many ways: first, because of my love of Italy and respect for the pain the people there went through during WWII and, second, because of my gratitude and love for those who overcome bias and bitterness to love unconditionally once again.

The biggest thank-you, hugs, and eternal *baci* go to my amazing husband, Fernando, for his never-ending faith in me and unconditional love. A huge thank-you to my beautiful daughters, Morena and Siciley, once again for being my writing partners, consultants, and cheerleaders. A big shout-out to my handsome sons, Roman, Nico, and Gabriel, for being so much like Peter Weimer. I had plenty of examples to draw on.

A big thank-you to my editor, Ashley Gebert, my publicist, Amy Parker, and the rest of the wonderful staff at Covenant. Special acknowledgements and love to Kathy Jenkins, Pam Goodfellow, The WIPs, The DIPs, fellow friends and authors in ANWA, my wonderful readers, relatives, and friends across the globe!

PRAISE FOR MELINDA SUE SANCHEZ

"The Fisherman's Daughter is a powerful story with strong, convincing characters . . . Careful research is revealed in the timeline of the story and ties in well with the plot arc. The author reveals a convincing familiarity with the coastal cities and rural stretches of Sicily as well as the harbors and markets. The author shows real skill in tying a compelling story to historic facts."

—Meridian Magazine

"This is a World War II book with a plot unlike any I've ever seen... The plot includes plenty of action, and danger for the characters and that really was fabulous. If you're a fan of World War II books, you really should read this one!"

—Mybookaday.com

"A well-written story with plenty of suspense, danger and heart. Massimo and Marianna make excellent characters for this pleasing story. While there are many mentions of war and killing, the descriptive nature is general and not graphic. There is a fair amount of tension between certain characters, but nothing that would create distress for readers."

—Deseret News

Awards for *The Fisherman's Daughter*

—*The Fisherman's Daughter* 2018 Foreword INDIES finalist for romance

—Storymakers First Chapter 2nd place winner for historical fiction

CHAPTER ONE

Peter

September 4, 1943

THE YOUNG WOMAN ROCKED LIKE a spinning top just before it tumbles, her dark hair tangled in ropes over her face and down her back. Blood oozed from the crown of her head as flickering torches caught the sheen of sweat on her skin.

Dank air heavy on my chest, my feet moving against my will, I entered the cavern, stepped around the injured young woman, snapped to a stop before my superiors with the *Heil Hitler* I had come to despise, and swallowed the fire that made its way up my throat.

Lieutenant Keillor sat next to one of his minions behind a crooked table, the narrow glint in his eyes a familiar sight. "Such a pleasure to see you under my command today, Sergeant Weimer."

He pointed at the tottering girl behind me. Her eyes rolled back in her head as she fought to keep her balance, and her teeth chattered so hard the sound echoed off the cratered walls.

"We have an important assignment for you."

There was no need to listen to his pompous voice; I knew what I would be commanded to do the minute I'd heard about this prisoner. Whispers and smirks from the soldiers leaning against the walls told me they knew what was coming as well. I glared at the men who were supposed to be my honorable comrades. My hands balled into fists.

I glanced at the girl, again taking in her gaunt appearance. I'd heard talk of her weeks before, an Italian partisan codenamed *Siara*. Keillor was obsessed with her because the messages she delivered kept sabotaging his plans to attack and spy on the Allies since they'd invaded Sicily and overthrown the Germans. Siara had even sliced Keillor's ankle open and stolen his truck on one of her missions outside of Siracusa. Good for her.

Keillor did not seek information from this woman; he sought revenge. And for me, he sought the ultimate destruction by forcing me to perform the torture he knew I abhorred and found morally repugnant. He stared me down, his face purple with the pomp of victory. Saliva pooled on his lower lip in anticipation.

The girl staggered again, and I questioned how she stayed standing.

Keillor watched Siara, his gaze roving up and down her shaking body. His mouth hung like a panting dog. He pointed at the girl, licking his wet lips. "Our soldier here needs to learn that the führer does not tolerate weak men. Sergeant Weimer will see just how pleasurable torturing a woman can be. He will also give you a sampling of what tomorrow may bring. Who knows, you may even like it."

My gut burned. I had endured Keillor's merciless retaliations against me countless times—endless assignments to the frontlines, cut rations, punishments for crimes I did not commit, and even beatings and threats on my life. But his revenge had never been this personal before, this perfectly aligned with his savagery.

Reality knocked me in the chest and my breath blew hot from my nostrils. A new crossroads loomed before me—the choice between evil and defying my commanders. I shook as if I stood before God, with my hand gripped around my rifle and a helpless young woman staggering before me. She had to be the same age as my sister, Bettina—maybe nineteen years old. I'd saluted evil men in order to protect my family and friends from Nazi retaliation. But Nazis had also done this, reduced a young woman to a near corpse in a cursed cave and ordered me to steal the last bit of humanity she had left.

Keillor would never forget what had happened between us before the war; he would never stop trying to kill me, one slice at a time.

Bile burned on the back of my tongue. Chortles rippled across the room, and I jerked my chin up. "Sir, this girl has nothing to do with what happened—"

Keillor glowered and screeched, "*Schweigen!* You are an affront to the strength and honor of this army. You will obey this order or be shot for subversion."

His lip twitched, and my muscles tightened into knots as sweat rolled down my back. If I took one step in Keillor's direction, I could reach out and snap his neck . . .

The ping of dripping water echoed from somewhere deep in the catacombs as the laughter faded and Keillor's sweaty neck taunted me. He still outranked me, had hated me for years, and now he'd found the way to finally destroy me—ordering me to assault this young woman under his usual guise of trying to get information; an order to force me to be as animalistic as Keillor himself.

It was almost a game to him: bring me in under his command for obliterating his pride and exposing his depravity and force me to debase myself to his level in a room full of witnesses.

He was a fiend who had owned my obedience. But after years of enduring his debauchery, I stared into his bloodshot eyes and decided, once and for all, who would own my soul. It would never be Vasyl Keillor. It would no longer be the Nazi army.

I had mere seconds to find a way out and save the girl from the other soldiers, if that was even possible. The repercussions for disobedience were real; if I could not escape, Keillor would have me shot. Or worse yet, he'd have his chance to finally torture me to death.

Keillor smirked, unable to hide the thrill behind his lidded eyes. He swept his open hand broadly toward the floor in front of him as if it were a stage and it was time for my performance.

I feigned compliance with a nod of my head as my thoughts raced for an answer.

Voices grew louder from another adjoining passageway on the other side of the cavern where two more prisoners, a man and a woman, were being shoved our way. The male prisoner grabbed a knife from his boot, twisted around, and lunged into the soldier behind him. The woman leapt back against her captor, knocking him off his feet and into the last soldier behind them. She scrabbled and grasped for their pistols, and Keillor came to his feet, grimacing with anger. He pulled out a pistol and stomped toward the fighting group.

I took advantage of the distraction.

I picked up a torch from the wall, aware that the last few soldiers in the back of the cavern may still be watching me. I poked the injured girl in the back with the end of my rifle with an urgent command for her to "move it" down the hall toward the labyrinth of the catacombs.

A couple of soldiers made lewd comments as we exited the cavern, but they did not follow.

Siara stumbled, and I forced her up on her feet as we passed the dark doorways of caverns, small caves, and ancient tombs. She cried out, and I placed my hand over her mouth. "No, shhh, you must be quiet, signorina; you must hurry."

Shouting and the sounds of gunfire still came from the cavern we'd left and gave me hope that Keillor and the others remained distracted by the other prisoners, but time was short.

I strapped my rifle onto my shoulder and tried to keep Siara moving. She crumpled onto the rocky floor, and I grabbed my canteen, pressing it to her cracked lips. She tried to slap at me until she recognized my gesture and gulped the water. Blood had caked and dried on her knees and down her calves. Her eyes rolled in her head between consciousness and death.

Seconds ticked by, and sweat trickled like icy fingers down my face and neck. I had come across a hidden cave in the weeks since Keillor had kept me and my fellow soldiers living like rats in these catacombs. Instinct had told me I may need a secret cave someday, and that day had arrived—I could hide the girl there if only we could reach it in time.

I shook Siara gently to get her attention.

"Signorina, I do not want to see you die, but I cannot get you out of here; there are many armed guards in front of the only doorway out. There is a small cave through a hole in the ceiling inside one of the tombs. I can help you climb up to hide, but I cannot come back. God must help you from there."

I leaned the torch against a wall, placed one hand behind her back and the other under her knees, and lifted her into my arms.

She slumped against my chest, and I shook her. "Do not faint again. Hold on to me while I reach for the torch."

She clasped her raw hands around my neck, and I grabbed the torch and ran through a maze of passageways until I found the right tomb and ducked inside.

Siara was a rag doll, but she'd managed to keep her hands locked around my neck, so I knew she was conscious. I took a deep breath. "I will boost you into the cave where you can hide up above. Quickly now. You have to move no matter the pain."

I lifted her by the waist onto a stone coffin that sat beneath the cave in the ceiling. "Reach above you and search inside the opening for a ledge. It turns to the side and you can lay down in there. It is small. Duck your head and crawl or you will hit the top."

I raised her higher, and she somehow managed to slowly scoot herself inside. At one point, she kicked her feet in a panic and tried to scoot out, but I could not let her. I pushed at her feet. "No, no, you must stay here, or they will kill you. I am sorry; this is all I can do. I have to escape now myself. I cannot come back. I will try to send someone to get you."

There was not much time. Keillor and the soldiers could be on their way to find me by now.

I gave Siara my flashlight and canteen of water with instructions that she was not to move. She whimpered and tried to argue, but I had no choice right now but to hide her; the guards would never let me outside with a prisoner.

At last, Siara inched far enough inside the cave. "I will send someone to find you," I promised, ignoring her cries of pain. I hurried as quietly and quickly as possible back down the passageway.

"I am on lookout duty near the city limit," I lied to the guard at the catacomb exit. He let me pass, and when I had turned a corner, I bolted into the thickness of night.

CHAPTER TWO

Franca

September 5, 1943

My forehead pressed against the side of the cow as I grimaced and squeezed milk from her plump udder. Sweat beaded on my nose, and I wiped at it with my sleeve, ignoring the grime it left behind.

Wet manure and musty cowhide emitted an aroma that leached into my skin and clothes as I tugged at the cow's teats, pinching at the tips for more. I let out an exasperated grunt when a mere dribble trickled into the bucket.

"*Dammi la pazienza,*" I muttered to myself and swiped at the hair that hung in my eyes, careful not to touch my face with the fingers that had just handled the underbelly of an animal.

The cow stomped her foot and slapped me across the cheek with her tail. I cursed under my breath and tried again. By the time I gave up my efforts, my collar was damp, and the day had not even warmed.

I wiped my hands down my skirt and blouse—the same clothes I'd worn for days—and picked up the bucket with the pittance of milk.

If we had stayed hidden at our villa, I could have browsed through my wardrobe for clothes I might sacrifice for work, skipping over the lace collars, linens, and silks to settle on a cotton blouse and skirt I'd sewn myself.

Or maybe I would have sacrificed the satin gown I had designed for the dance just a few months ago—the dance where I'd twirled across the floor in the arms of not one but both of the Orlandini twins, one right after the other. The dance where the Nazis pushed their way into the great hall, tore down our Italian flag, and held their rifles against our heads.

The memory deepened, and I curled my toes in the work boots I'd found in the barn, their stiff leather angles showing no mercy to my chafed skin.

A breeze cooled my neck as I headed to the house. Sunrise winked over the hills, shooting pink and gold through the trees where birds chimed like miniature church bells.

My brother-in-law, Bruno, sat on a chair by the chicken coop, his crutch propped beside him and a brood of chickens gathered at his feet.

Another day to scatter feed for fussy hens and outmaneuver a rooster that charged me like a bull.

Bruno looked up as I drew near. "*Buona mattina,* Franca."

I frowned. "You are not strong enough to be out so early."

He held up a can of dried corn. "I thought I would help you with the chickens." His smile slid into a smirk. "The rooster does not attack me as he does you."

The guilty fowl hunted and pecked at the ground, oblivious to my presence. I glared at Bruno and tsked. "That is a *diavolo* rooster. Only a devil goes after the one who feeds him."

"Stop waving your apron at him and calling him names. Maybe he will see your charming side."

"I flap my apron like he flaps his wings at me so he will see who is in charge."

"And is it working?" Bruno tossed more feed.

I pursed my lips. "Well . . . someday he will see."

Bruno chuckled before worry creased his brow again.

I set the milk bucket on a bench. "You watch the roads *troppo* carefully. The Nazis ran to the mainland like the ground was on fire when the Allies landed. We are safe, no?"

He shrugged, and I stared him down.

"I am an adult, Bruno, not just Laura's little sister. Tell me why you always seem so nervous."

He glanced at my filthy clothes. "You have enough to worry about."

I rolled my eyes at the sky in frustration and shook my hand at Bruno. "It only worries me more for you to hide things from me."

The hens clucked and feathers flew as they stomped and pecked at one another in a scramble for the last kernels of corn. They gathered in front of Bruno to beg for more. The rooster stood a head taller than the rest and fixed his beady, black eyes on me. I took a step backward before Bruno answered.

"*Va bene*, I suppose you are right. There are rumors that some of the German soldiers remained here on Sicily as spies or that they may escape the prison camps and head for the countryside. Some are stealing and such as they go. I am just being careful."

He leaned back in the wooden chair and yawned as if bored with the subject. Bruno was never that relaxed.

I squinted and scanned the yard and the long, winding road leading up to the farm. The trees and bushes cast shadows and could provide cover for someone. A chill inched its way across my skin. "I saw a rifle in the closet in the room where I am staying. Maybe you could keep that close by as well."

"That may be a good idea," he said, and then jumped up when baby Luca's cries came from the house. "Ah, the real duty calls." He stood on one foot and used his crutch to compensate for the other foot he had lost in battle. "I am coming, *bambino mio*," he called toward the upstairs window.

I took the can of dried corn from Bruno's hand as he passed. "Is that why we cannot go back to Siracusa, because of hiding Nazis?"

He hobbled toward the house and called back over his shoulder. "Yes, I am sure that is why. Just be patient, Franca. Soon now."

I'd grown to loathe the word *patience*.

The minute Bruno went inside, I searched the yard for any movement or anything out of place.

The farmhouse stood peacefully still, and the sunrise cast a pink glow on the pale stones. Trees circled the perimeter of the land like a ring of soldiers standing at attention, with long, bushy branches and thickset trunks.

I held the can of corn tightly and tossed the rest of its contents up in the air all at once, convinced that Bruno had not told me everything. The kernels bounced as they landed on the lawn, and the rooster and chickens squawked and scurried to get their fill. An ache grew inside my chest as I watched them eagerly grab every morsel they could, scratch at the soil for remnants, and look up at the sky, desperate for more.

My best friend, Marianna De'Angelis, never waited for handouts, miracles, or manna. She saw the pain and injustice from the war and jumped in to help where she could. I, on the other hand, could hardly make myself touch the udder of a cow.

Marianna had cleared the paths we needed, and I'd stayed faithfully beside her to help, but she'd left with my father to work in the hospital a few weeks ago. I had to stay behind with the rest of my family. She marched onward while we stayed tucked away from the front lines and scraped food together to keep my sister, Laura, her baby, and her injured husband alive.

Stepping-stones paved the way to the house through nodding flowers and shoots of grass. Vines and green clover won more battles against the rock-strewn soil in Sortino. Near our villa, the winds from Africa sometimes whistled over the sea, mixed with our salty air, and speckled the shores with a layer of dusty chalk. We were only one or two hours away from home by automobile now, but although the Allies had driven the Nazis off Sicily, our father had instructed us we were to stay hidden here in Sortino.

Until the war began four years ago, life had moved slow and steady for most of my eighteen years on our island of Sicily—like one long afternoon lounging on a blanket under a crisp, yellow sun with only occasional cloud cover.

My papa, Paolo Chessari, was a wealthy vintner and could clear any inclement weather in our lives. And my gentle English mother, Elisa, looked like the women in the fashion magazines Papa brought me when he returned from our vineyard up north. While I was a child, my parents seemed invincible—Hitler's poison had proven that no one was.

I carried the bucket of milk into the kitchen and set it on the long, wooden table before I went back outside.

When the rooster had his back to me, I hurried to the chicken roosts and picked up the eggs from the nests, the smooth caramel-colored shells warm against my palms. I filled the skirt of an old apron I'd grabbed by the back door with the eggs.

Someone came whistling around the corner, and I recognized the hired hand, Giacomo, with a wide basket and a few wrinkled vegetables gripped in his arms.

"*Buongiorno,* signorina Franca. I thought you may need help finding the vegetables *sta mattina*. I found some peppers and a few shriveled zucchini."

Even as he spoke, I could see him staring at my dirty clothes.

"*Che cose?* What are you looking at, Giacomo?"

The old man raised one eyebrow and then shook his head back and forth with a sad expression. "You work too hard, signorina. It is dirty work. And you have smooth hands, city hands. I see how much you try and work hard, but this is *impossibile*—no servants to help is no good for you or for your dear mama."

I wiped at the grime on my face with the back of my hand. "I grew up on a vineyard, not in a city, Giacomo."

But my voice trailed off as I stared at the black hole in the front of the old man's mouth—in all the weeks we'd been hiding at this farm in Sortino, I'd never noticed that one of Giacomo's front teeth was missing. Maybe because my brothers had done the milking and other chores with him when we'd first arrived, and my mother directed them all, and I had been too busy since.

Giacomo's pink tongue poked through the gap as he grinned and held out the vegetables for my approval.

I smiled back and lifted my apron full of eggs to his view, and two of them rolled out the side and landed with a *thwack* on the cobbled ground. I stared up at the sky with a sigh of frustration before I answered Giacomo. "*Grazie tanto.* I am learning. Can you bring the basket into the house?"

The robust *Siciliano* bobbed his head with gusto as if nothing would give him more pleasure. A stray yellow cat rounded the corner, meowing loudly. It licked at the broken eggs, and Giacomo grinned again.

"*Va bene*, signorina, maybe it is no *problema.* Even the cat is helping you." He turned for the house before I could answer, his stout legs propelling him forward while he held his back and upper body stiff and the basket snug against his chest.

I walked behind him and interrupted his whistling before we got to the house. "I never asked, why is your back so stiff, Giacomo?"

He slowed to walk beside me. "I fell off a horse many years ago. It was not so bad at first, but now that I am getting old, my bones are crunchy."

"I am so sorry. Do not worry. I will keep milking the cow. Contrary to your belief, I see I am actually doing better. This morning I can fill Luca's bottle and maybe have some left for Laura."

He tsked his tongue and shook his head. "You must get more milk, or her bag will go dry. You still pull too hard at the teat. I tell you many times that you must not pinch or tug too hard. Be gentle or she will refuse you milk. You must run your fingers down *cosi*; play it like an arpeggio on an accordion." He held his thick hand up in the air and squeezed his fingers one at a time against his thumb in quick succession.

I tsked in return. "I tell you that does not work. I must pull hard at the end or I get nothing."

He stopped walking, rubbed his hand over his brow, and then opened his palm to me. "Does she kick the bucket or slap you with her tail?"

I hesitated. "A few times . . ."

"*Ecco.* You see, I tell you she does not give you all her milk. You pinch, she kicks. It goes together."

I bit the inside of my cheek and closed my eyes. "*Va bene,* Giacomo. I am not accustomed to touching the underbelly parts of a cow. It seems inappropriate somehow. But I will practice arpeggios on the cow."

I opened my eyes as he shook his finger. "Not on 'the cow,' signorina. Remember her name is Rosella, and she likes when you use her name. And she does not mind if you use her teats to get her milk. That is what they are made for."

My face warmed by his brash use of language, and the eggs in my apron grew heavier. "I will call the cow anything you say to make the job easier."

He grinned. "You can just say Rosa if Rosella is too much. Signore De'Angelis let me name her for my grandmother."

I sighed. "Rosa it is."

We made it to the kitchen, where I placed the eggs in a bowl and took the basket of vegetables from Giacomo. He put his hands in his pockets and looked around the room as if in thought.

"Did you have a question, Giacomo?"

He shrugged and pursed his lips. "Ehhh . . . no . . . *pero*, perhaps—"

"Perhaps what?"

He held his hands out, palms up, as he shrugged in what I could tell was a forced nonchalance. "It is wartime. Perhaps it would be better if you did not go far from the house alone anymore, signorina."

"*Perche?*"

"Eh, it is better that we take precautions."

He smiled, but this time, the wrinkles around his mouth looked tight and his eyes did not sparkle.

I lifted my brows. "Giacomo, do you sense danger, that perhaps Nazis are still lurking around?"

"No, no, no, signorina. No one said that to me." He opened the back door, and a couple of chickens squawked as he pushed them out of his way to get outside. "Just . . . be very cautious. A war is very fickle. I am sure all is well, so do not worry yourself."

As if there was any way to stop incessant worries. There had been no word from Marianna for weeks; Laura, who had been born with a weak heart, had not stopped heavily bleeding since her baby was born almost two months ago; my father was gone with no word once again. The list burned behind my eyes all day and all night.

CHAPTER THREE

Peter

I SLIPPED LIKE A CAT around corners and down the narrow cobblestone alleys of Siracusa. The city was packed with soldiers bent on keeping control of Sicily and watching for an enemy like me. I'd severed my alliance to the Nazis when I defied my commander and walked out of the catacombs, and the chances of hiding out on my own for the rest of the war without detection were nil. My only hope for a semblance of safety and to send rescue for Siara was to find the Allied army prison camp and report Keillor's diabolical doings in the catacombs.

The antique city slept under a bright-eyed moon that helped me see my way but also exposed me to soldiers who would shoot before I had a chance to surrender.

My pulse pounded in my head when I spotted the coiled barbed-wire fence that wrapped around an old church courtyard and served as a prison camp for Axis soldiers. Within minutes, I would lose my freedom but also become freer than I had been in a long time.

The American soldiers at the camp entrance pointed their rifles at my chest, their foreheads creased in deep frowns as I walked carefully toward them. They refrained from shooting as I approached and raised my hands to the sky.

I kept my eyes locked on the American soldier who wore the shiny name badge, Lieutenant Jenkins. He loomed over me as I repeated myself for the hundredth time, speaking slowly because his understanding of German seemed spotty. "I am telling you all I know. There is a young woman, a partisan woman hiding from a few Nazi soldiers who are holed up in catacombs under the old broken-down church outside of town. The girl is seriously wounded and needs help right away. Take all the passages to the right and look for a hollow in the ceiling above a stone tomb."

Jenkins scribbled on a piece of paper and set the note on a desk behind him. I watched that paper, hopeful that it was a note to send someone to help the girl but doubtful that this Siara held any real importance to him. The war had started four years ago. Every soldier I knew had seen death and the dying dozens of times.

Two more prison guards came into the tent and sat in the chairs across from me as if they were there to watch my interrogation for fun. One of them looked at the note on the desk, crumpled it up, and tossed it in a garbage can. He smacked and popped his gum like a kid and even winked at me a couple times. "Hey, Jerry," he said, using the typical derogative term for Germans. "Just tell Jenkins here where to find Hitler so we can go kill him, and then we can all go home."

My English was very limited, but I knew the names *Jerry* and *Hitler* and the words *kill* and *home* plenty well.

Jenkins looked over at the guy. "Shut up or get out!"

I questioned if I had done the right thing by turning myself in to these soldiers. The oath of fidelity I'd sworn to my army constricted like a vice around my chest as I prompted these Allies to go find and attack my fellow Germans. But Keillor and his men did not represent the Germany I'd grown up in and knew or any respectable army I would be a part of. Keillor and his men were an abomination, and Hitler and Mussolini had spread their evil and destruction across nations.

I opened and closed my hands into fists over and over, but I gave the Allies the directions to the catacombs and the cave where I'd hidden Siara.

"How many soldiers are hiding there?" Jenkins asked.

"Ten? Maybe a dozen? You should be able to get past them and find the girl very quickly," I urged again.

"What are the soldiers' names?"

I had no problem naming Keillor. But while the other soldiers were foul, they had never attacked me personally, and I hesitated to name fellow Germans. "The lieutenant is Vasyl Keillor," I answered again in frustration. "I do not know the others. I have told you all I know. That is all I can say."

"You will say what we order you to say. You will tell us all that you know." The soldier's questions continued, his eyes glaring into mine, the rifles of his guards aiming at my chest in case I moved in the wrong direction.

The truth was still hard to swallow; the leader was interested enough in my report about the pocket of Nazis but seemed merely curious about Siara. I could only hope that she was alive and that Keillor's men had not found her.

At last, the Americans shoved me out of their tent and into the crowd of German prisoners. I fell on my back, arms and legs sprawled out, sure that exhaustion would sink me into the rocky ground. The moon had ascended high into a sky that swallowed the stars. I stayed on the ground and locked my gaze on the empty void above me and soon it seemed to swoop down and swallow me as well. I'd turned my back on my country—walked away from my duty, my honor, and, most of all, my friends, who were somewhere on the Italian mainland where the battles raged.

The Allies had invaded and taken over Sicily, and the German army had been given no choice but to flee to the mainland. Vasyl Keillor had been ordered to secretly remain on Sicily to spy and had held me in his grip too long.

No one but the two of us knew the real reason Keillor had requested that I stay under his command—about the history of his hatred for me that started in our youth, when I'd reported him to the school authorities for hanging kittens by their necks from a tree in back of the schoolyard and for hurting the girls. And about the time when he was a soldier and I'd pulled him off my sister, Bettina, and shown him how I felt about him with my fists. He'd crawled away, beaten and bloody, and yelled out the window of his car before he drove away, "I will smash you with my heel for this, Weimer. Someday I will outrank you, and you will curse the day you were born."

Rumors of the assaults Keillor committed or tried on other young women grew while he and others from our city were in boot camp, and when I heard of a sixteen-year-old girl who'd gone missing after she'd been seen dancing all night with Keillor at a club, I reported my suspicions to our commander. The impending war kept everyone too overwrought with other worries to take real notice of a missing girl, but Keillor saw my name on the report, and his hatred for me escalated to a burning inferno.

Keillor's predisposition for violence and ruthlessness made him a pristine candidate for Hitler's army. His talent for getting results from interrogations had him quickly climbing the ranks.

The war brought us back together again, and when his position gave him the opportunity to pay me back, Keillor took it with the vengeance he had promised.

CHAPTER FOUR

Franca

Hiding outside Sortino gave my twelve-year-old twin brothers plenty to do to stay busy. There were so many needy families in the area. Widows, wives whose husbands were gone to war, and whole communities hurting for help to produce the food to sustain them until life could someday go back to normal. The boys went from house to house, villa to villa, farm to farm to help where they could; a godsend for those in need.

They had gotten so tall—both of them sprouting like giant sunflowers with heads too big for their gangly frames that hadn't had time to grow muscles as fast as their elongating bones.

They were almost identical too. Dominic kept his hair full and curly as a poodle on top, so he seemed taller than Damiano. But both were more like puppies full of boundless energy.

They often worked outdoors with the hired hands at our vineyard in Siracusa and even helped our housemaid, Alma, with the cooking. They dug a fort beyond the vineyard, helped our workers butcher chickens and cows because they found it fascinating, and helped with the wine presses. When harvest time arrived for the grapes, they were right in the thick of it and only missed the harvest when they had school lessons.

I missed them during the day when they were gone helping others. Their cheerful moods lifted the clouds of worry that hung over all of us, and I missed their help with the farm. But since we had Giacomo and Bruno, though Bruno was limited on what he could do with his amputated foot, we lost out on daily help as my brothers loped down the long roads every morning to help the desperate neighbors.

A soft knock echoed from the front door one evening. My brothers and I looked back and forth at one another in alarm. No one traveled at night these days, and this old farm was at least three kilometers from the next house. Papa had warned us before he left for up north that no one must open the door once the sun had set.

The knock came again, a bit louder this time. Dominic grabbed the rifle behind the sofa. Damiano put his hand in his pocket where he kept a pocketknife. My brothers had instantly changed from carefree puppies to young men, armed and ready to wield a weapon—or to have a weapon wielded at them. Were I not so startled by the presence of strangers at the door, I would have sunk into despair.

Bruno must have opened a window upstairs and looked down in the courtyard. "*Ci sonno una donna e bambini.* Go ahead and open the door," he called from the top of the stairs.

I eased the door open to three dirty children, who clung to a woman dressed in tatty clothes, a baby propped on her hip with eyes weak and weepy, mucus caked under its nose and its hand clinging to the front of the mother's shirt. The woman looked too young to have such a nest of children already. She stared at us through hollowed eyes, and her chin quivered before she could speak.

"*Per favore*, help me please. *Mi chiama* Nina Costa. I have no help to provide for my *bambini.* My sister and her children, they live with me and my mother. Our husbands went to war and the army—" She choked back a sob. "They sent a letter that both of our husbands were killed."

She gave way to more weeping, and my mother stepped through the doorway and put her arm around the woman. "Come, come inside, Nina."

The children held to their mother's skirt as they entered the house, and she explained their plight. "I am the only one who can do all the chores. My sister is very ill, and my mother is old. I cannot care for our animals. Some of them must be butchered. Our garden is running out of food, and it is all I can do to feed my children and my sister's children every day. We live maybe ten kilometers from here, but we heard that you have sons who help people and we—"

Mama finally held up her hand to stop the woman from gushing and begging. "There is no need to say anything more. I am sure our Dominic and Damiano will be happy to help you all they can." She looked at my brothers. "Boys, go pack some clothes and any supplies you want. You will need to stay with this family for a while until their crisis passes."

The boy's eyes opened wide as they gazed over the sad state of the mother and children.

They vaulted upstairs, and my mother patted the woman on her thin shoulders and ushered her and her children into the kitchen. We fed them *pasta al latte* and carrots and gave her milk for her baby after Mama had cleaned its nose and hands. The babe still whined and squirmed, and the children sat along the wooden bench at the table, pressed tightly against their mother in silence as they nibbled their food.

Despite their tall, lanky frames, my brothers were only twelve years old. It was scary enough to live with the enemy sitting on your shoulder. Having Dominic and Damiano at the farm each night with their contagious zest for life kept us afloat. They wrestled, played with tiny Luca, told funny stories with their curly haired heads thrown back in laughter, or talked over the top of one another as they spewed the plans of espionage they had conjured up to end the war.

I hugged them goodbye when the moment came, biting my lip to keep myself from protesting or weeping. Dominic smiled with a nonchalant wave and Damiano promised they would check in with us every few days.

Giacomo hitched the wagon and took the woman, her children, and my brothers down the road. I held my hand over my throat as I watched them leave. The plodding of the horse's hooves grew softer and softer until the darkness engulfed them.

My mother had not cried when she embraced the boys, but I saw her wipe at her eyes a couple of times as they rode away.

Mama's reserve had always been somewhat of a mystery to me amidst the bubbling and vivid displays of emotion of most people I knew. She'd never altered from the reserve of her English background. But I knew she'd suffered loss before. She rarely spoke of her family in England, since they had disowned her for marrying a foreigner of no rank or nobility. My father had made us wealthy, but either my grandparents did not know of his success or they did not care.

I put my arm around my mother, knowing the tears that escaped down her cheeks came from a heart flooded with sadness and worry. A semblance of safety came in snatches as we clung to one another.

I stood in the courtyard after Mama had gone inside, listening to the solitary hoot of an owl and letting the evening breeze stir my hair with its ghostlike fingers. The farmhouse loomed like a prison in the moonlight, and the knot in my throat grew tighter.

CHAPTER FIVE

Peter

September 9, 1943

THE SUN AND MOON TRADED places at an unnervingly slow pace. I spent most of my time swatting flies and mosquitos or playing cards. Everyone longed for food and water. A few of the prisoners marched and paced the parameters of our enclosure. Some robbed, harassed, or pestered each other just to fill the hours. I watched my comrades, sure that if they turned my way and looked into my eyes long enough, they would know I had betrayed and exposed some of our fellow Germans. I wouldn't live long if my actions were discovered. But even though I tossed and turned with guilt in the night, I knew when I'd hid the young woman, Siara, in the cave in the catacombs that I could not stay silent. She had been near death, was thin and helpless, and could not be more than nineteen or twenty years old. I'd had to send someone to help her, even if her rescuers were my enemies.

Keillor and his band of bullies had no true interest in serving Germany. Power and evil possessed them, and word among the men was that more and more of their prisoners were young women who were never released alive.

The prisoners who did odd jobs for the Allied officers usually overheard tidbits of military intelligence that they then spread like honey through the information-starved prison camp. But a few days passed with no word of a raid at the catacombs. The silence was deafening.

A water truck arrived, and a soldier rolled a barrelful of water into the middle of the yard. We could smell the moisture in the air and gathered, tin cups in hands, like starved cattle at a trough, praying that the water would last long enough to get our fill. I gulped cup after cup, the cold water sloshing in my empty belly, and then I rested against a back wall, grateful that the stomach pangs had subsided for at least a few moments.

Five days into my time at the camp, a young Italian man came barreling toward me, anger and panic in his eyes, like a bomb ready to detonate. The prisoners around me scattered as three other men strode up with the angry Italian. He stopped right in front of me, his face just inches from mine and stared me down. "Weimer?" he asked.

My muscles tightened. "Yes, I am Weimer."

The man growled, grabbed me by the front of my shirt, and slammed me up against a brick wall. The air popped from my lungs, and I gasped for breath.

One of his men put a hand on the Italian's shoulder as if to calm him. "Easy, Massimo. We will not find Siara if he is not alive or willing to answer questions."

I jumped to attention when he said the name Siara and sucked in air as quickly as I could. "I speak *Italiano.* The signorina? You want to find the signorina I told the guards about? I . . . I did not hurt her. I helped her."

He loosened his grip on my shirt and set me back on my feet. "Tell me exactly where she is," he demanded.

"The catacombs . . . I hid her. I did not harm her," I answered. I darted my eyes to the side, relieved to see that the other prisoners had stayed back beyond earshot.

Massimo's eyes were narrow slits of suspicion and fury. "Why the catacombs? What was she doing there?"

"A group of Nazis has been hiding there since the Allied occupation of Siracusa. They send out spies and capture people right under the Americans' noses and bring them back to do their interrogations. I was supposed to—to hurt the girl and tie her up by herself in a tomb so they could torture her the next day, but I did not do it."

I noticed Massimo tense when I said the word *torture* and thought he might grab me again or try to shoot me. His fists pumped at his sides, and I could hear his breath seething through his teeth.

His comrade stepped up and looked me in the eye. "Is she alive?"

I shook my head. "I do not know if she is alive . . . I hid her a few days ago. I refused to carry on for the Nazis anymore and surrendered to the Allies."

The man looked at me suspiciously. "Why? You German soldiers are all killers. Why would you help her?" He looked over at his comrades. "This is probably a trap."

They lifted their pistols, and I tensed, ready for the impact of bullets as I stuttered for words. "I could not harm the girl. I have a sister."

Another of the men beside him scoffed. "Ha—most of the men here have sisters. You are a liar." He spit on the ground and glanced at his friend. "It is a trap. We might as well shoot him now."

Sweat ran down my spine as I locked my shoulders and looked him straight in the eye. "I am not lying. I saved the young woman. I did not harm her."

The prison yard had gone quiet, and I was sure some of the other prisoners had inched their way close enough to hear me expose fellow soldiers.

The sun stopped in place while the men decided if I would live or die.

I had saved Siara to the best of my ability, and if I died for it, at least it was for the helpless young woman, a far better cause than this godforsaken war. I thought of my mother and sister waiting for word of my safety and whereabouts. My mother had already lost too much, but my fate was not in my hands now.

Massimo seemed to calm a bit and took a step back. "How many soldiers are in the catacombs, Weimer?"

"Maybe a dozen."

"You are taking us in there to find her."

I knew what my fate would be if I crossed paths with Keillor. "They will kill me if they see me there. They'll know I exposed them," I said.

"Was she hurt?" the friend asked.

"She had a bad wound on her head. The men who brought her in thought she was dead or dying and put her in a tomb for two days, but she woke up."

Massimo's nostrils flared. "You left her there for two days without help? You did not check or try to help her?"

"I was not in there the first two days," I said. "I had been assigned to hide on the outside and watch for the Allies. I was on guard duty. Until—until the young lady you are looking for was captured. My commanding officer thought I was too soft and brought me inside to force me to be brutal. I had seen what they did to women, so when I came upon a hidden cave in the catacombs, I knew I could hide someone there if I needed—one of the women if I had a chance. When your Siara woke up, the soldiers came to get me from my post outside. They threatened me. They wanted me to harm her, but I did not; I did not touch her."

Massimo had not loosened his grip on his pistol. "Why did you just hide her? Why did you not take her with you?"

"She could barely walk; I had to carry her. And the guards would have killed both of us if I had tried to leave with her. She was too wounded, and I had nowhere to take her."

"Why could she not walk?" Massimo asked with a catch in his voice.

"I only saw the lump and the blood on her head, and she had blood on her knees and legs as if she had fallen down. I gave her water. I carried her. I swear to you, it was all I could do. It would have done no good to try to take her out of there. They would have killed us both."

My life lay on a chopping block. The German prisoners who watched me from the sides and this group of partisans both had the power to swing the axe. "The city is full of Allies, so I came here." I lowered my voice, hoping my fellow prisoners would not hear what I said next. "When I surrendered to the Americans, I told them about this girl so she could be helped. But it has been days. No one has asked me about her again until now."

The man, Massimo, turned to his men. "Go see if anyone from Ivana's group is available to help us. The more numbers we have, the better. Meet us back at the guard tower in one hour, fully loaded. We are going in."

The two men took off at a run, and I looked at Massimo, my pulse pounding like a runaway metronome. He could kill me for not bringing Siara out of the catacombs, or if he left me here and the other prisoners had heard that I gave away the location of the hideout in the catacombs, I would get my throat slit in my sleep.

I looked him in the eye. "What will you have me do?"

"You have to come with us, or we will never find her." He took a deep breath and placed his pistol back in the harness at his side. He gestured at my cheek. "That scar looks fresh."

I reached up and touched the long, purple line. "No one displeases the Nazis without paying the price. If you can possibly keep them from capturing or killing me, I would like to see my family again someday."

"You did the right thing to try to save . . . Siara. We will see if we can assist you." I could see that it cost him to speak kindly to me.

I bowed my head, "Thank you."

Massimo reached into a bag one of his men had been holding. He pulled out a set of civilian clothes. "Put these on so you will not be recognized as German right away."

I was more than willing to go incognito. I stripped down right there in the yard, put on the clothes, and folded my uniform, carrying it with me. The pants came up short on my ankles, but they would have to do.

"How far back in the caves did you hide Siara? Can you find it right away once we take care of the soldiers and guards?" Massimo asked.

"Yes—" I blurted to reassure him. "She is in there quite deep, in a small cave in the ceiling inside one of the tombs."

We made our way to the guards at the front, and Massimo showed them papers. "I have permission to take this man with us on an Allied-approved mission." The guards stepped back out of our way, and Massimo turned to me. "Every one of us will be watching you. Do not try to escape. Let's go, Weimer."

I headed out right beside them, relieved, at least temporarily, to escape my death in the prison camp and with a prayer that Siara was somehow still alive and that these men would not kill me.

CHAPTER SIX
Peter

"SHE IS NOT HERE," I said. Dread and fear for Siara sunk in my chest. I delayed looking at Massimo and his men, sure that I would see their weapons pointed at me again.

Massimo jumped up on the stone coffin beside me and reached inside the cavity in the ceiling where I had hidden Siara. It was empty. His breath came fast and furious, and I jumped off the coffin to get out of his way.

The man they called Ronaldo stepped closer. "Massimo, if they had killed her, then her body would be with the others. Davide and James checked, and she is not there. Maybe somebody—"

"Where? Where would they take her?" Massimo interrupted and stared at me, his voice echoing off the cave walls.

I wiped the sweat from my forehead. "Maybe she escaped. Or maybe the Allied soldiers who raided this place found her and took her to the hospital."

It appeared that the Americans had taken me at my word when I'd surrendered and told them about Keillor and his men hiding here. Maybe they'd found Siara hidden in the cave. But there was no sign of her now.

"I had given her a flashlight and a canteen, as I told you. They are both gone. She must have climbed down and escaped," I reassured the men.

The air was suffocating as we searched every nook, every inch of the catacombs, until we found the flashlight and canteen that I recognized as mine inside a cavern close to the entrance. "These are definitely mine. Siara made it at least this far. Perhaps she was able to find help."

Massimo's every movement and word were quick. "James, you find our American military contact. We need to know who attacked and wiped out these caves. Andrea, you and Lello go to Lieutenant Bianco and see what our other contacts may know. Meet us at the Santa Lucia hospital."

The men dispersed and ran, and I made sure to keep pace with Massimo. No one paid attention to me or voiced any other plans for me, so I kept my head low and the tension that hummed in my ears at bay. Massimo jumped into their jeep, and I leapt in behind him. He called out to the rest of the men before they drove away. "No more than two hours before we meet again. *Sbrigatevi!* Move quickly!"

It was strange to see the wounded soldiers in the halls of the Santa Lucia hospital when we arrived. Perhaps I had taken part in the exchange of fire that had caused these wounds. I'd pulled the triggers on my weapons and tossed grenades like everyone else, after all, but I pushed the images of the consequences from my mind. I steeled myself against the guilt pressing down on my shoulders. In my youth, when I had hunted deer, I avoided looking them in the eye once I'd brought them down. We had needed the food, but I had no desire to see the light in the creature's eyes go out.

The groans of pain and stench of rotting flesh diffused through every room of the hospital. Several of the patients stared at me, their eyes wide with suspicion. No doubt my very blond hair and pale complexion was out of place, and they had pegged me as an enemy. I clutched my hat tightly in my hands and watched carefully in case the nurses let the men keep weapons beside them.

I helped search the entire hospital, sticking close behind Massimo's men. I'd been tempted to grab a loaf of the bread laid out on long, marble counters in the hospital kitchen. I could not remember the last time I had eaten, and my stomach gnawed and cramped with hunger.

One of the men who had met us here rushed up. "Wait, Massimo, wait . . . I may be able to ask someone for information." He bolted back toward an office we had not searched. The rest of us followed behind.

A woman, her black hair pulled up in a nurse's cap, sat at a desk, her head bowed over a pile of papers. The young man marched up and shook her hand. "*Ciao,* Donnatella. So very nice to see you."

She glanced over us, her teeth locked in a grimace. "You know I only work in the hospital. Leave me out of whatever this is, Lello."

He laid his other hand on top of hers. "We are looking for Siara, Donnatella. You must know she was captured."

Tears filled the woman's eyes, but she looked down. "I know. She has been gone for days, almost a week."

Lello let go of her hand and stepped around the desk beside her. She turned the other way, and he gripped her by the shoulders. "I know you resent our intrusion. We ask only for information. We know she was taken to the catacombs and hidden there. The Allies just gutted it. Have you heard anything at all?"

Her shoulders relaxed, and Lello took a step back. Massimo reached out his hand to Donnatella again. "Please, this young woman . . . Siara, we must find her."

She blinked back the moisture in her eyes. "I know of that raid; two male survivors were brought in by Father Conforte but no women. I would know her."

Massimo slapped the desktop with his hand in frustration. I had eased my way behind the men, hoping the woman would not be curious about who I was.

Donnatella sat up straighter and held up her finger. "Wait. Father Conforte always helps with the wounded after raids and brings us soldiers, but he never brings any women here. If he found Siara, he would have taken her to the Santa Domenica church outside of town where they shelter only women."

Lello gave Donnatella a quick kiss on the cheek, but Massimo had already dashed for the door.

Massimo stared ahead in silence at the bumpy road as we drove down the coast to the Santa Domenica church. Lello passed me a canteen, and I looked at him in surprise. "*Grazie,*" I finally said. The cool water quenched the thirst that had left my tongue dry for hours. I gulped it down, savoring the cold rush as it passed down my parched throat and into my empty belly.

I'd picked up on the names of the men as they discussed their situation and plans, but except for with Lello, I did not attempt any conversation. I had seen the rage behind the fear in Massimo's eyes, but he'd glanced my way more than once with a nod of recognition as if to show gratitude. Davide, James, and Andrea stayed focused on the search for Siara and let Massimo dictate what they would do with me. My breath stayed locked in my chest; if we never found Siara or we found her dead, I could still be shot or hung in retaliation. I may never see Bettina or my mother again.

I urged the truck to go faster in my mind, willing the tires to spin as fast as my thoughts. Trees whipped past the truck, but fishing boats rose and fell on the slow pulse of the Mediterranean as if peace encompassed the world—as if a young woman's life did not hang in the balance. Seagulls swarmed and dive-bombed the fishermen's catch and escaped with helpless fish clinched in their orange beaks. I had to look away.

The church appeared, and I held my breath as we pulled to a stop and all the men jumped out. James looked at me, his expression grim. "Stay right behind us."

I would have thought the men could see I had no intention of running away by now, but the war had obliterated trust. I'd done nothing but strive to be trustworthy since I was a young boy, but the war had rendered those virtues invisible and suspect. Forced to take orders from men who were obsessed with omnipotence and driven by evil, my patience for the power-hungry had thinned to transparency. But these men had trusted my story about saving Siara.

My head ached with hunger. My bones ached with fatigue. But I matched their steps as we ran up to the church doors, willing them open and that we would find Siara inside.

I watched as Massimo begged the wrinkle-faced man called Father Conforte to let him go inside the church hospital and search for Siara. The priest shook his head no for the hundredth time, and Massimo pulled a blue cameo from his pocket. "I am telling you that I am sincere. I know this woman, but she could be going by the name Siara or Marianna. You will see the name is etched on the back."

"We do not allow men in our sanctuary unless they are a father or a brother to our patients. We have promised them safety and protection, and you are not even sure of the name of the young lady you seek. You will not enter," the priest said.

"I told you, Father, she is in the resistance army, so she used a different name."

"*Mi dispiace.* I am sorry, but you are not family."

"Father, I beseech you, if you will just take this necklace and ask the women there if they recognize it. If you find her or she ever comes here, tell Siara my name. Tell her that Massimo has come for her. I am not married, and I will never stop looking for her."

The priest took the necklace but locked the door behind him as he turned us away for the final time. I clenched my hands into fists and fought the urge to push through the door myself. The priest's brows had lifted when Massimo told him Siara had been in the resistance. He may be more willing to help partisans than he was letting on.

We waited, staring at the door—willing it to open. Ronaldo finally spoke to Massimo, who had not stopped pacing since the priest had locked us out. "Massimo, if this priest had rescued Marianna, he should have told you. I will return later to ask for the necklace. We can see if any more hospitals are nearby."

"Did you see how stern he looked? He sees us as enemies or *ragazzacci*. He would not tell us anything," said Massimo.

Ronaldo patted Massimo's shoulder. "We can all come back and ask the priest if any of the women knows anything and retrieve the necklace. Maybe I can find a sister who will talk to us."

"We should take our time before we leave. I saw something in that priest's eyes when you said Siara was in the resistance. He may actually look for her among the women," I said.

Davide grabbed me by the front of my shirt and grimaced. "No one gave you permission to speak. What would a filthy murderer, a Nazi, know about priests?" He yanked on my shirt again and shot daggers with his eyes into mine.

I should have looked down or away, but I met his hateful gaze. "I want to find the girl as much as you do."

"You want to save your own skin."

Spittle spewed from his mouth and landed on my chin as Massimo walked up. "Not now, Davide." Massimo glanced at me, his eyes guarded. "It will take us a few moments to get to the jeep. We will see if the priest comes back."

We had parked down the road so the nuns would not be frightened by our approach. No one said anything more to the brooding Massimo as we walked away. I trudged behind the others. Davide stomped right beside me, and I was unsure if I would live five more minutes.

CHAPTER SEVEN

Peter

We were almost to the truck when a small voice called out from the churchyard, and Massimo spun around. He paused for one second, then started running back to the church. He ran toward a young woman, who stood in front of the entry gates in a long, white nightgown, her dark hair now clean and long, her skin pale, and her voice calling out Massimo's name. The girl I'd carried through the catacombs, the one I'd feared dead for days, the Siara who I now realized was really named Marianna. She half-ran and half-hobbled toward Massimo until they met, and Massimo swept her up in his arms.

The other men and I took our time but made our way back to Massimo and Marianna. I tried not to stare at their passionate reunion—the kisses, the tears of joy, but my own tears brimmed as I watched them. My efforts had not been in vain.

The other men each kissed Marianna on the cheek before they slowly stepped back. Marianna gasped when she saw me, and tears burned behind my eyelids again when she reached up and pressed her bandaged hand to my cheek.

Massimo still held his arm around her. "Marianna, this is Peter Weimer."

She cried again as she looked at me in earnest. "My savior. Thank you. Thank you, Peter Weimer, for risking your life for me."

"You were well worth any risk, signorina. Be safe and well now." It was all I could say past the knot in my throat.

She smiled at me, her eyes still weak. "I will be both now that I am with Massimo again. But I owe you *la mia vita,* Peter Weimer. My entire life." She looked at Massimo. "We both do."

After a long time of clinging to one another, Massimo carried Marianna inside the church, and the other men followed. Not knowing what else to do, I'd moved to the back of the group, ready to make my way around a corner so the nuns and priests would not recognize me as German.

Marianna made Massimo turn her around to find me. "Do not worry, Peter. You are here under our protection and are not to leave. You will stay with us until we find the safest place possible for you."

I could only nod my head again, and I stepped hesitantly behind a pillar inside the church while Massimo and Marianna spoke with Father Conforte.

I knew they would have to take me back to the prison camp now. There was nowhere else for me to go, but I would have the memory of seeing Marianna safe with Massimo when I returned to the prison camp and confronted the other men who must have heard me expose the soldiers in the catacombs. They would laugh as they each took turns beating me. They would tear my skin from my bones and brag about it.

But instead of taking me away, the other men and I were ushered into a small room with a long, dark table and benches where the nuns fed us pasta and bread on wooden plates. I could hardly keep myself from stuffing the food all at once into my mouth. I had not feasted like this for months and filled up far too soon, but the food slipped like manna down my throat. We stayed in the room, and I gazed at a painting of an angel holding a suffering Jesus in her arms until exhaustion overcame me and I fell asleep with my head resting on the table.

Evening came, and a young nun lead us back into a cavernous chapel filled with dozens of luminous candles, their waxy odor filling my nostrils, while the glow and warmth of their flames illuminated the gold-and-silver saints painted on the ceilings.

The sister gestured for me to sit in the front pew with the other men, but I hesitated and finally took my place on the row behind them.

If the priest and nuns expected me to genuflect or recite a prayer, I was lost and was sure to offend; I had been taught faith and prayer in my youth but not Catholicism. The nun who'd seated us smiled as if to reassure me as I sat stiffly on a wooden pew. No one said anything. No one else came into the chapel for several minutes. The men in front of me whispered to one another but mostly kept their heads bowed. I willed myself invisible.

The air was damp and cool, but I began to sweat. I did not belong here, and that priest who had forbidden access to Massimo and the others would surely recognize me as German. I pressed my hands along the wrinkled fabric of the shirt and pants Massimo had given me to wear. I looked like a pauper who lived in one pair of clothes. At least I was not in uniform, but the Nazi swastika seemed stamped on my forehead. I wiped my hand across my brow.

Doors opened in the back, organ music played, and Massimo and Marianna came up the middle aisle together, Massimo's arm firm around Marianna's waist. She was dressed like a bride. They moved slowly, like they savored every step, and I realized they were going to be married. My shock changed quickly to awe.

The nuns must have found Marianna her simple white gown and the sheer veil that covered her hair and draped down her back. I remembered the girl who staggered, covered in blood in the catacombs, her whimpers of pain, the way she had clung to me as I carried her down the hallway to hide her. Now she took trembling steps to become a bride, still pale, still bruised, but smiling. My throat choked up, and tears stung behind my eyelids. I bowed my head to wipe them away.

I had risked everything to save her, a young battered girl who stirred the memories of my sister but, most of all, made me reclaim my humanity. I would risk it all again to see this quivering sweet bride who clung to her groom and carefully made her way down the aisle. They had wasted no time to be married. The war made every need and every emotion imminent, urgent, desperate.

Father Conforte performed the rites, and when they were pronounced husband and wife, Massimo lifted Marianna into his arms before he kissed her, and they wept together.

Massimo sat down on a bench with Marianna still on his lap. The men patted their leader on the back and kissed the tearful but glowing bride on her cheek.

Andrea grinned. "I thought we were trying to rescue Marianna today, and now I see Massimo just needed a ride to his wedding."

"I have been late for my wedding for too long. We may be called back to duty as soon as tomorrow. I am not going to risk anything coming between me and Marianna ever again," Massimo said.

Marianna leaned her head against Massimo's. "That is right. No more separations."

"You speak of duty, but after that passionate display of kisses outside, you were just afraid Father Conforte would lock Marianna away from you again if you did not marry her," Andrea said. The whole group laughed.

"Did you know that the partisans executed Barberi?" Davide asked Marianna.

"Massimo just told me today." She wrapped her arms around Massimo even tighter. "At last we know we are free from his threats."

Lello grinned at the new couple. "Where will you go for a honeymoon?"

"We are going to stay in an apartment that is part of the church for a few days until Marianna is stronger, and then we will go find her family," Massimo answered. His eyes grew serious. "Every one of you; Davide, James, Andrea, Ronaldo, and Lello, I cannot express enough gratitude for your help today. Marianna and I owe you everything."

"*Siete I miei eroi,* my true heroes," Marianna said as tears trickled down her cheeks. She looked at me. "And today would not have been possible were it not for Peter."

I nodded quickly and looked down at the floor, avoiding the eyes of the men who looked at me as Marianna spoke. For a few moments, I had forgotten all about the war and the threats that followed my every step and let myself taste of the happiness these friends and the new couple basked in. But as the men and Marianna said their goodbyes, I stepped toward the back of the chapel. It looked like the partisans would be the ones to return me to the prison camp. Maybe I could convince them to let me leave on my own so I could make a run for it, though I had no idea where I would go.

Sweat soaked my collar and eased its way down my back. Every person I would encounter on the island of Sicily would want me dead. The Allies and Italians because I was German, the Germans because I had deserted and helped Marianna. If not for these strange circumstances, these partisans would seek to kill me most of all. I had saved Marianna, but I was still their enemy. I hoped their gratitude toward me would last.

Davide and Lello walked over to me when Massimo and Marianna had left the chapel, and we went outside.

Davide sneered and clamped a set of handcuffs on my wrists. "Massimo said you are to stay with us. We'll be camping nearby," Davide grunted without looking me in the eye. "I am happy we found Marianna. But we could have done it without help from a Kraut. Never forget that we are all armed. If you try any tricks, we will shoot you."

Davide trudged off, but Lello remained. "Davide's brother was killed in battle just a few weeks ago, so just lay low around him. "

"You can take me back to the prison camp or let me go and I'll find my way," I suggested.

Lello tsked his tongue. "*Impossibile.* Marianna gave absolute orders that you were not going to the prison camp and that we had to babysit you until further instruction. Massimo agreed because right now anything she says goes."

"What threat did this Barberi pose to try to keep them apart?"

"He was a Nazi general who tried to blackmail Massimo into marrying his ugly daughter. For a while, Marianna believed that Massimo had married the girl, and until today, Massimo believed Marianna had been killed the night the Allies invaded. I guess they married immediately to add a legal bond to their reunion—no more dividing them."

"Except a war."

"They are resistance fighters, *Partigiani*, partisans who will fight the war together."

I had heard of Barberi; every German soldier had. He was known for extreme control tactics and retaliation. It was no loss to my country that one more fanatical Nazi was dead. He had spread evil wherever he went. Sorrow fell with dead weight on my chest again. My country had been so beautiful, so clean, full of music and tradition. Hitler's evil had thrown a bomb on my entire world.

The partisans found a dilapidated building that looked like the rib cage of a barn just a couple kilometers from the church. The sun was going down, and Lello tossed me a blanket from his backpack. "Just sleep close to the campfire where we can see you. You'll be fine."

Three days of tedium and boredom passed before the partisans packed up the camp. "Massimo said to give Mari three days to rest. We have other work to do and will check in with him before we go. We'll find out what they mean to do with you when we get there," Andrea told me.

Except for Davide, the men had been polite to me and even let me help cook and sit at the campfire with them, but I would not be going with them to join the rest of the partisans.

When we met up with Massimo and Marianna at the church, I waited, handcuffed in the truck while they talked inside the church doors. My stomach had turned inside out by the time they emerged. The men all embraced Massimo and Marianna and kissed each of them on the cheek to say goodbye before they loaded into their truck.

"You stay here, Weimer. Massimo will give you orders," Davide snapped.

Each of the others shook my hand. Lello actually embraced me and then stood up in back as they drove off and waved in my direction. "*Nella boca del lupo,* my German friend. In the mouth of the wolf!" he yelled.

Rocks pinged in the wheel wells and flew out behind the truck as they drove away.

Marianna cried as the men left. She was pale and still bruised and bandaged, but her eyes were brighter. She beckoned me closer. "We are going into the countryside to find my family members, my mother and brother, Bruno, and his wife and baby. My closest friend, Franca, is there as well . . . and we would like you to come with us, Peter."

Massimo's brows lowered, but he unlocked the handcuffs from my wrists.

I looked at Marianna. "I am grateful, signorina, but it is extremely dangerous for you to have a German soldier with you."

"I am a signora now." She smiled at Massimo before she continued. "And I would rather have my life in danger than to see you locked up and possibly killed after you risked your life for me."

"As I said, I am very grateful, but this is not just one neighbor repaying a favor. Other groups of partisans and Italian citizens may shoot you for helping me."

"This is not open for discussion. Should anyone ask, you are our prisoner. And you may even be able to help us in the future."

My other options were much more bleak. "Very well," I finally answered. "But if I may say so, it may be best if I stay hidden, at least until we get out of town."

Massimo lifted his head. "Definitely."

There were no motorized vehicles at the church. The nuns found a wagon and one horse, and we started for the countryside.

For most of the day, I spent time in a large trunk in the back of the wagon so people coming up the road would not see me. Or I lay under blankets, supplies, and luggage, wondering where this journey would take me and what fate had in store. The helplessness ate at my nerves but was better than being penned up day after day with other prisoners of war.

The next day, we arrived at a farmhouse that Marianna said belonged to her late aunt and uncle. Her mother and other family members were there, so I had to jump out of the wagon and hide in a large group of bushes until Massimo could tell me where to go.

I watched from behind a copse of bushes as a young woman came at a run down the road, her dark hair flying and a brilliant smile on her face as she and Marianna embraced. I had not seen such unmitigated joy between friends or family for years and watched mesmerized. The woman spun around to see Massimo and I caught a clearer view. Friend or family, whoever she was, there was no denying the olive skin and striking features on this young woman were unequivocally beautiful. Nothing but the ugly brutality of war had filled my vision for months at a time, so the sight of pure beauty was a punch to the belly that left an ache in its wake.

CHAPTER EIGHT

Franca

September 13, 1943

We were two weeks into September, and the war had been raging for four years. It was difficult to remember the world before madness had taken over. I lay on a blanket under a tree beside baby Luca. He would soon be two months old and had learned to smile. I enjoyed a moment of happiness and nuzzled his soft, chubby neck. Luca's fist got tangled in my hair, and when I leaned up on my elbow to untangle it, I spied a horse and wagon as it came around the bend. Soldiers did not usually use a horse and wagon, but I called to the men. "Bruno, Giacomo, someone is coming up the front road."

Signora De'Angelis came outside and took Luca from my arms. I blocked the glare of the sun with my hand as the wagon came closer.

A man, a woman . . . I let out a cry of delight. "Marianna." Much to my surprise, Massimo Scalvone was with her.

I ran all the way to the wagon and wrapped my arms around my lifelong friend and kissed her on each cheek. I stepped back, still holding her hands. "Thank goodness you came back." Joy overwhelmed me until I noticed how frail she appeared. "You look so pale, Mari, and you have bruises that are frightening. What has happened to you?"

She smiled weakly, and Massimo put his arm around her. "She was captured by a secret pocket of Nazis and is still very weak. We need to get her inside to rest."

Marianna took me by the hand. "I will be fine."

I put my arms around her again. The flood of elation mixed with the worry over her battered condition.

"I have other important things to tell you, but I agree with Massimo. I can say things much better after I have rested," she reassured me.

Marianna's mother came down the road, and I took Luca and stepped back so she could greet her daughter. Sobs shook signora De'Angelis's shoulders as they held onto each other, and I had to keep wiping at my tears while holding Luca. Bruno waited by the house, and the same joy erupted between him and Marianna when the wagon pulled up front. Massimo carried Marianna into the house, and we all gathered in the parlor to rejoice at their return.

I was in awe after Mari shared her story. She'd bandaged horrific wounds on soldiers in the hospital, ran messages between groups of rebel partisans, stolen a German truck, and shot at the enemy. Worst of all, she had been seriously wounded when captured by a band of Nazi spies, then rescued and hidden in the catacombs by a German soldier with a conscience. After being told Marianna was captured, Massimo finally found her convalescing in a nunnery hospital through no less than fate and miracles.

Mari's eyes were shadowed with fatigue but followed Massimo's every move and word when he spoke. Her hand never let go of his.

She had looked back and forth between me and her mother. "I had thought Massimo was in a forced marriage, and he believed me dead. But none of the dangerous or frightening things are important anymore because the beautiful news is that Massimo and I were married the very day that he found me. We would not risk ever being parted again."

I wept with joy, pressing my cheek against Marianna's after her mother embraced her. She had found completeness in a world shot with holes, peace and hope in the midst of chaos, and it radiated from her even in her weakened state.

Marianna and I had worn matching braids all through our young years. We'd fancied the same boys and rode our bicycles and horses up and down sloping hills and over the cobblestone streets of Siracusa. We'd hardly had time to embrace our adulthood before war sliced our world down the middle. Now we spoke of attacks, rebels, weapons, capture, and torture.

I carried a full pitcher of water into the room with a clean cloth and bar of soap and set it on the dresser for Marianna's toiletries when she woke the next morning. Massimo had already dressed and gone outside somewhere with Bruno.

I pushed the curtains back at the window, exposing a view of the side property where a cloister of olive trees basked in the sun. A cool breeze floated its way through the room when I cracked a window.

Mari sat up in bed, pushing the feathered comforter to the side and her white nightgown down over her legs. I grinned at her, my heart bursting with joy at her presence before I sat on the edge of her bed. "You are really here. The weeks since you left have moved like a broken wheel. How long can you stay?"

She squeezed my hands in hers and then lowered her dark brows. "Word from our leader is that we can have a few days' rest, but we need to be in Foggia as soon as possible."

"What leader said this? You are not well, Marianna, so thin and weak. Who would call you up for service in such a state?"

A veil passed over her eyes before she answered. "Massimo is needed. I will convalesce before I consider helping again."

"Travel is exhausting. Stay and rest here to gain strength for at least a week or two," I pleaded.

"Being with Massimo is the strongest healing balm in the world. I may never be of use to the partisans again, but I would flounder and weaken if Massimo left without me now. We will stop and rest many times on the way."

I pressed my hand over my heart. "It is like a miracle to see the two of you together. *Bellissimo.* So right and meant to be."

"When I saw him outside the nunnery in Siracusa, I was sure I had died in the catacombs and he was greeting me in heaven. I did not know there could be such happiness."

"You earned that joy and have done your part. Can your leader not appreciate that?"

She picked at the fringe on the edge of the bedspread.

"Why won't you look at me, Mari? Is there more you need to tell me?"

The bedframe squeaked as she climbed carefully off the side, pulled a pale-green dress from her bag, and began to dress. "There are more details, but none that are important right now."

"Right now? Does that mean you will tell me someday or that I will have to find out on my own?"

"It means . . ." She spoke slowly, taking inventory of her words as she went and fiddling with the buttons on the front of the dress. She pushed long strands of her hair out of the way. The dress hung loose on her shoulders. "It means that I do not have all the answers or the reasons any more than anyone else in the middle of war. But we have a good leader we can trust who works directly with the American OSS."

"What is his name?"

"I am not sure I can say."

"Mari, will you look at me? You cannot tell me who you serve under? Your mother and brother are here, all of us—your family. What if we need to contact you?"

"That is true," she said, finishing with the buttons on her dress and finally meeting my gaze.

"What is true? That you cannot tell me who you serve under or that we are your family?"

"Do not worry. The leader's name is Lieutenant Bianco—will you brush my hair for me? It's a mess this morning," she said, straightening her shoulders.

"*Certo,*" I assured her.

I swallowed my frustration and hugged my beloved friend carefully again, squeezing my eyes shut against the terror she'd just been through and the emptiness her departure would leave behind.

But tension ticked like a clock in the room. There was a secret behind that veil in Marianna's eyes, and it frightened me.

A deep melancholy had consumed Mari's mother, signora De'Angelis, since her husband had died. When it was time for Marianna and Massimo to leave a few days later, they took Marianna's mother with them to give her new surroundings. My mother wept beside me as we watched their wagon disappear down the road.

The wind cried a lonely tune through the trees that evening. As much as I cherished my family, I longed for the freedom Mari had to escape this isolated place.

I wished I had been there to see Marianna and Massimo get married. Mari and I had dreamed about our beautiful weddings; I was to design our dresses, and Mari would arrange the flowers.

I climbed the stairs to my room. My paper canvasses and array of pencils and paints were all left behind at our villa, but I had found some parchment and a pen in a desk drawer. I lit an extra candle, soothed by the waxy fragrance and yellow glow, and drew a young woman in a bridal gown of satin and lace that flowed behind her as she walked down the aisle.

Worry rolled like a prickly ball in my belly. Marianna's manner was strange—she was keeping a secret, and there was guilt behind it. I could not fathom the reason why. Exhaustion got the best of me, however, and my head fell back against the pillow as the night drew to a close.

CHAPTER NINE

Franca

October 6, 1943

THREE WEEKS PASSED UNEVENTFULLY AS we settled into a new routine, and I grew more accustomed to the constant fatigue of farm life.

Another dawn arrived, and I dragged myself up and dressed in an old yellow blouse and brown skirt I'd found in an armoire. We'd had to leave our home too quickly when we came here, and I'd had no time to pack enough of my own clothes.

The white plaster walls of the kitchen were too bright for my half-opened eyes. I'd expected to see my mother, her pale hands with long, slender fingers at work kneading bread or rolling dough for pasta, but the kitchen was empty.

Giacomo shuffled through the kitchen door, mumbling to himself and rubbing his hand on the thick whiskers of his jaw like he was deep in thought.

"*Buongiorno,*" I muttered as I bit down on a piece of bread and rested my elbows on the table.

He jerked his head up. "*Buongiorno.*"

It was difficult to swallow my breakfast when I noticed Giacomo's nervous worry. Marianna's ordeal was terrifying, and I'd seen the enemy soldiers attack her and our friends right in front of me when we were just trying to deliver food and water to the needy. The ground had rumbled under my feet numerous times as powerful tanks and trucks passed me in the streets of Siracusa, and I lived underground for weeks while men blew each other to pieces in battle and destroyed Marianna's property and home. With those memories fresh in my mind, Giacomo's worry heightened my own.

Giacomo went back out the door, and I wondered again where my mother was. No doubt she would be in the garden or with Laura. I washed my hands, grabbed the bread and cheese, and carried them to the marble counter. I put on an apron, pulled off a hunk of the bread, and sliced the round of cheese before I laid some on a plate for Laura.

I found Laura sitting propped up in her bed in a long, blue nightgown, clicking her knitting needles together in a rapid rhythm, yellow yarn draped across her lap. I tried to brush off the bluish tint in her lips when she smiled as I entered her room or, at least, the room she and Bruno used for now.

Bruno's aunt and uncle had owned this farm until they died in a crossfire between the Germans and the Allies. The jolly Uncle Mimmo and cautious Aunt Pasqualina watched us from their faded wedding photograph that stood on the fireplace mantle across the room.

Laura laid her knitting to the side and reached for the plate of food and glass of milk. "You work so hard, Franca, and I am nothing but a burden, a nuisance."

I kissed her cheek. "Did I not tell you that I always dreamed of being a farmer and a cook? Just look at these." I held out my hands to show her my new calluses.

She shook her head. "Ha. You dream of being a clothing designer just like you should." She touched my cheek with her finger. "You will be, Francesca. Someday you will go to Milano to the fashion school you used to dream about when we were younger."

I swallowed the pinch in my throat that her words had created and watched my sister eat. Laura had inherited the lighter hair and elegance of our mother, but the angle-softening effect of our English ancestry had skipped me entirely. When I'd turned twelve and the neighboring boys became visible, I'd wished I could use the file for our horses' hooves on my nose to lessen its prominence. And my curly dark hair refused to obey the hairpins and stay rolled in place. Only my eyes and lips gave me hope to be one of the women in the fashion magazines. I'd focused my passion on drawing and clothing design, but it all floated on a cloud somewhere, blown away by the winds of war.

I looked down at the apron that hung like a sack on my thinning frame. I'd lost too much weight. But that was the least of my concerns every day. I longed to be at our vineyard in Siracusa and not here at this deserted farm that belonged to ghosts. If danger came, I could run between the grapevines and hide, or I could dart back to our hidden cellar under the winepresses.

Laura took my hand. "I can see your doubts, Franca. But before this horrible war took over our lives, you had such plans. Do not let this mess take that away."

I sat beside her. "At least we are on the right side now. Perhaps we will win since Mussolini has been captured."

She took a swallow of milk and grimaced in distaste before she answered. "Oh, I hate being weak and drinking milk like a baby." She handed me the cup. "They say Mussolini escaped and is working for the Nazis somewhere in northern Italy."

I gasped. "*Da vero?* Is that true? Who said that?"

"I heard Bruno telling Mama a couple of weeks ago after Marianna and the others had left."

A wave of nostalgia swept over me when she said Marianna's name. I missed her terribly and wished again that I had some of her freedom and bravery.

"Why did no one tell me?"

Laura sighed as she chewed on a piece of cheese. "It is difficult to make Bruno tell me anything. He only let it slip one day."

Laura took a bite of bread and a swallow of milk. Her face and lips hardly held any color. I patted her hand. "Do not concern yourself with Mussolini—the Allies or partisans will recapture him. You have to get well and take care of Luca. Where are Luca and Bruno?"

She answered between bites of bread and cheese. "Bruno took him outside to find Mama. He has learned how to carry Luca and use his crutch for balance."

I had looked out the kitchen window for our mother before I brought the food to Laura. I did not see her or anyone else. It was obvious Bruno and Giacomo were nervous or at least extra cautious. There had to be a reason. If I should not go far from the house, then my mother should not either.

Bruno still struggled to walk with his crutch because of his missing foot—he could not go far carrying a baby. I stood quickly and headed for the door. "Perhaps Mama is in the garden. I had better check on them. I will be back in a bit for your plate. Do not get up; you know it makes the bleeding worse."

I hurried my steps. It was cool in this house and a chill ran up my arms. The thickness of the brick walls kept the heat at bay, especially now that October had arrived. Sunlight strained through a tree and into the window at the end of the hallway, but it was not enough. The chill spread clear down my back. I called out to Bruno in case he'd stopped somewhere inside, but no one answered.

By now, I should have seen or heard my mother come back inside, but not a sound had echoed through the house. Sometimes she spent time in her room. I headed up the stairs. "Mama?" Only my voice echoed back.

Outside, I checked the garden first. In some places, grass and weeds spread like spider webs over the tops of rotting vegetables. By the time we had run from the coast of Siracusa to the low hills of this farm, this garden had gone much too long without tending. Zucchini and cantaloupe had bruised and shriveled like the skin of an old crone. I should have already churned the dying crops under like our gardeners had always done. They would have planted seeds for the winter crops before the end of September.

My mother was not in the garden. The strands of dead grass waved at me in a silent breeze. I shivered and hurried to look out at the pastures. Giacomo's words came back again—I'd gone too far. My throat went dry, and my heart beat faster as I called to Bruno and my mother. No one answered. I scurried to the barn and yanked the doors open. "Giacomo?" I called. Nothing.

I rushed back to the front courtyard and looked down the road that Bruno had been watching. The road stood empty. Cold shivers spread from my arms to the middle of my back.

I jumped with surprise when Luca's cries rang from the house. Maybe they had gone inside the back door as I exited into the front courtyard. Confused, I hurried back inside the front entry. "Bruno? Mama?" No one answered.

Luca's fussing escalated to screams of distress. The screams came from the kitchen in the back. I ran.

I rounded the corner through the kitchen doorway, and my eyes filled with flashes of light as my feet flew out from under me. I slammed down flat on my back on the floor. My head swam and throbbed like I'd been hit with a shovel, and I had to gasp for air. I wiped my bleeding nose with the back of my hand and stared up at the Nazi who had delivered the blow that knocked me to the floor. He stood over me and glared. He held a rifle in his hands, and I'd received the butt of it when he knocked me down. He grimaced like an angry ape I'd seen at the zoo and grunted in German, his rifle aimed at my chest.

My head throbbed and burned like it was on fire. I wiped the blood on my apron and looked through blurred eyes at Mama, Laura, Bruno, and Giacomo all sitting on the benches in the opposite corner of the kitchen. The soldiers must have herded them into the kitchen while I was outside or on the other side of the house. A second Nazi soldier stood pointing a pistol at the group of them. Laura held Luca tightly and whispered in his ear to quiet his cries.

I eased myself to a sitting position and more blood poured from my nose. My mother tried to get up to help me, but the soldier with the pistol yelled in German and lifted his foot to kick her. She sat back down, a look of terror in her eyes as Luca's cries grew louder and the soldier shook his gun at Laura. He pointed at the baby and growled.

We'd been stopped on the road and questioned by Nazis several times since the war began, but never had I seen the hatred I saw in the eyes of these two soldiers. They did not just look like enemy soldiers; they glared like dangerous criminals.

Tears streamed down Laura's face. My mother pointed at Luca's bottle that had fallen to the floor and rolled behind the soldier. The soldier glowered and shook his head no. Mama grabbed a dish cloth from the table beside her and handed it to Laura. Laura draped it over her shoulder to shield herself and put Luca to her breast. But Luca refused to be comforted. He squirmed and shrieked as the pressure in the room grew.

Every time I tried to move, the Nazi with the rifle pointed it at my head. He looked at Bruno and spoke in very broken Italian. "Tell me where radio is."

Bruno shook his head no. "No radios here." The Nazi with the pistol belted him across the face, whipping Bruno's head to the side.

Laura cried out, but the soldier ignored her and raised his hand to hit Bruno again. "Tell us now. We heard German on radio."

Bruno spoke through gritted teeth. "No radio. No Germans here."

The soldier growled and pointed his pistol at baby Luca's head. Laura screamed, and Bruno jumped from the bench, his head bowed and body aimed straight into the soldier's stomach.

Mama leaped to her feet. "No!"

Bruno slammed himself into the soldier and knocked him off his feet. The soldier landed on the floor, Bruno on top of him. The two of them wrestled for an instant before Bruno wrenched the pistol from his hand.

Giacomo scrambled toward the other soldier who held the rifle on me. The soldier turned toward him, and the horrible blast of gunfire exploded in the room. Giacomo buckled to the floor.

Bruno aimed the pistol at the soldier who had shot Giacomo and shot him in the middle of his chest. He fell backward and did not move.

The soldier beneath Bruno knocked him back and scrambled to his feet. He pulled a second pistol from inside the front of his uniform. Bruno turned to shoot at him, but the soldier had pulled Laura from the bench and grabbed her around the neck with his free hand. He pulled her in front of him. Luca started slipping from Laura's arms.

Mama cried out and reached out to catch the baby, and the soldier pointed the pistol straight at her. She lunged for Luca, and another blast of gunfire exploded in the room. My mother flew back onto the bench like she'd been shot from a cannon—her eyes opened wide in shock. A red stain appeared on her side, the crimson edges spreading like a poisonous flower on her dress. I screamed.

The soldier walked backward, dragging Laura with him and stepping between me and the dead Nazi. He held his pistol pointed at Laura's head.

Bruno dropped his pistol and held his hands out to his sides away from his body in surrender. He pointed at me and then at the tiny baby still dangling from Laura's arms, and spoke under his breath. "Franca, get Luca. Now."

I scrambled over on my hands and knees, hoping the soldier would realize I was only after the baby. Nausea rolled in waves from the blow to my head, and terror drenched me in sweat. I slipped Luca from Laura's arms as the soldier pulled her outside.

Bruno grabbed his crutch and followed them out the door while I spun around to my mother. She'd grabbed the dishcloth Laura had used and held it to her side, her face as white as the tile behind her—the towel turning deep red.

I ran to the parlor next to the kitchen where we kept a bassinet for the baby and laid him inside before I dashed back to my mother. She had fallen from the bench onto the floor and didn't move. A sob escaped my lips as I ran to her.

Giacomo lay unmoving, facedown on the floor a few feet away. I turned my mother over on her back and cried out Giacomo's name, praying for a response as I grabbed the soaked towel and pressed it over the bloodiest spot on Mama's blouse.

Giacomo moaned and lifted his head. He looked at my mother and then at me. "Check her breathing."

I pulled my mother's blouse from inside the waistband of her skirt and popped the buttons off to see her wound.

A deep hole looked like someone had plunged a knife rather than a bullet into my mother's stomach just below her ribs. Blood oozed up like an overflowing well, but her chest still rose and fell. "She's breathing," I called out to Giacomo.

Giacomo still lay on his stomach and scooted himself over to my mother, leaving a bloody trail behind him. He lifted one hand high enough to hold the cloth on my mother. "Go see if the other soldier is gone." His voice quivered. "You must . . . get your mother to hospital, *subito.*"

"We must put pressure on your wound, Giacomo. There is too much blood."

"Get Bruno first," he argued.

I grabbed an extra apron and wiped it across my forehead to stop the flow of blood that ran from my forehead into my eyes. The soldier on the floor lay unseeing, with his eyes and mouth wide open as if still in shock that he'd been shot. I grabbed his rifle and fled out the back door.

The Nazi soldier stood on the path that led to the barn and still held my sister tightly with one arm across her chest, while his other hand held the point of his gun against her head. I tossed the rifle toward Bruno, and it landed in the grass just a few feet away from him.

Another Nazi had arrived. He stood behind the soldier holding Laura—a long rusted scythe gripped in his hand. His hair was so blond it was almost white. A long, thin scar ran down the length of his left cheek. Bruno stood twenty feet away in front of them, one hand gripped on his crutch, the other raised in the air in surrender to the two armed men.

Laura's eyes were closed, and her hands shook down by her sides. Bruno raised his arm even higher as he spoke to the men. "I will back away. You can let her go and leave. We will not follow you. You are free to go. Just leave the woman with me and go."

The German holding Laura laughed. "You are not in charge here, you *stupido* Italian. That is why our führer had to send us here in the first place—to give you people some kind of strength and respect, and all you did was stab us in the back. You have no brains." He looked down at Laura and sniffed closely at her neck. "Although I can see why you like your women. I will be taking this one with me."

Bruno took a step forward and slowly shook his head back and forth. "Franca, get back in the house. Now." I started to run but froze in place. The blond soldier behind Laura and her captor raised the bladed end of the scythe higher, and the trill of the cicadas in the trees screamed like a siren.

CHAPTER TEN

Franca

BRUNO POINTED HIS FINGER AT me without looking away from Laura and the soldiers. "Run back in the house, Franca. Go take care of the others, *subito.*"

The soldier with the scythe stood at the ready, and I backed my way toward the kitchen door, my legs heavy and my breath stalled in my throat. Just as I reached the door, Laura used her right hand to ease a knitting needle from the pocket of her house robe. She gripped it in her fist, raised it, and stabbed the soldier in his leg. He yelled and lost his grip on Laura to grab the metal needle wedged in his thigh.

"Laura, run!" Bruno yelled as he lunged for the rifle in the grass. He rolled up on one knee and fired the weapon. The injured German slumped to the ground. The third soldier dropped the scythe and leaned down to check on his comrade.

I ran toward Laura, grabbed her around the waist, and helped her into the parlor, where the baby lay in the bassinet. "There is still a third German. Stay here with Luca until Bruno says it's all clear."

I ran to my mother and Giacomo, where they lay on the kitchen floor. Giacomo had lost consciousness and lay facedown. I pulled him over to check his wound and gasped at the wide pool of blood beneath him. I stuffed towels under his belt to hold pressure on his belly.

My mother looked like a statue carved in chalk. I knelt beside her. The towel was soaked, but the bleeding had slowed at her wound, and her chest rose and fell in a slow but steady rhythm. I pressed a clean cloth over her side with shaky hands. "Mama? Mama, can you hear me?" She gave no response.

Bruno stumbled through the door on his crutch, his eyes wide. "Where is Laura? We have to get your mother and Giacomo to the hospital."

"What about the soldiers? Are they both dead? The one with the scythe, is he still out there?"

"The one I shot is dead. The one with the scythe ran off."

Laura came around the corner and fell into Bruno's arms, sobbing into his neck. He held her close with his free arm, kissing her as if they'd been parted for years. Laura's knees dipped, and I led her back to rest on the settee by Luca.

Bruno followed behind us and helped Laura settle. He gripped me by the arm. "Can you drive an automobile?"

I shook my head no, and his jaw tightened. "I will have to teach you. I cannot drive with my missing foot, and Laura is too weak. We'll put a mattress in the back of the truck for Giacomo and secure your mother in the cab." He looked down at his foot, shook his head, and muttered a mild curse. "I am useless. You'll have to run upstairs and pull a mattress and sheet off the bed. Throw them out the balcony window, and I will get Laura back to bed if she can still walk."

"What about the dead soldiers? What if the other soldier comes back?"

"I will take care of them and be on watch after you go."

I averted my eyes from the dead soldier on the floor and checked on my mother and Giacomo again. As soon as I'd reassured myself that she and Giacomo were still breathing, I rushed for the stairs.

CHAPTER ELEVEN

Franca

"LOOK, WATCH HOW I SHIFT this gear stick so you can get the truck going. There are three movements you must do . . ."

I heard Bruno's words, but the panic that rang through my ears kept their meaning at bay. I knew I could never drive the truck no matter what he said or showed me; I had only driven the horses and wagon a few times when our hired men were too busy. I berated myself for letting the servants and my family pamper me. I sat in the driver's seat of the truck like a helpless child. My head throbbed, and my breath still came so fast and loud from loading my mother and Giacomo in the truck that I could barely hear my thoughts.

I had an urge to grab Bruno's arm and beg him to come with me. I wanted my father—he would fix everything, and he would never let my mother die. I lamented, like so many times before, that my father had to stay up north at our other vineyard and had only appeared in short visits since the war began. We needed him desperately.

Bruno moved the stick that was attached to the floor back and forth while he talked, and I bit my lip to keep it from quivering. His words and instructions barely penetrated my conscience. I nodded to give him hope and repeated his instructions to make him believe I understood.

He had me sit in the seat at the steering wheel and reviewed the movement my feet would have to coordinate with the gear shift. Sweat ran down the side of his face as my feet failed over and over to work in order. At last I championed two tries in shifting through the second gear.

Bruno wiped his brow on his sleeve and stayed at the open door of the truck.

I shoved the stick from one position to another over and over while moving my feet back and forth until my left leg quivered on the stiff clutch pedal. The instructions had finally infiltrated to my memory, but my feet and hands struggled to stay in sync. I glanced at my mother to be sure she still breathed. The stench of blood hung in the air despite the bandaging we had thrown together.

We'd taken a long strip from a sheet and wrapped it around her seat, then tied it to hold her firmly in place. Her head hung to the side as if she were asleep, but I knew she was unconscious. I pressed one hand over the ache and queasiness in my own belly.

Bruno looked at me solemnly. "Do not stop to check on your mother. You will not be able to do anything even if it seems she isn't breathing. The only thing you can do is get her to the hospital as fast as you can, Giacomo too. I tied him to the mattress in the back so he doesn't slide off on the curves or bumps. Try to go around the big holes in the road if you can."

Bruno shut the truck door and stood at the open window beside me. I grabbed his hand through the window and tried to force my shaky voice to a whisper. "I cannot do it, Bruno. Please. Please come with us. I know you cannot push on the gas. I will squeeze between you and Mama where I can reach the gas pedal or curl up on the floor and push the pedal when you tell me to."

He shook his head. "I got Laura to the bed." He took a quick, deep breath. "But she is bleeding so much I am afraid . . . afraid." He cleared his throat. "We cannot leave Laura alone with the baby. She is so weak she cannot move."

My eyes must have reflected my blinding panic. Bruno patted my hand that still clung onto his. "You will make it. It is only thirty-five kilometers. Concentrate on driving. Look at the road. Get the speed up to at least thirty if that is all you can do and keep it steady all the way in without stopping."

As Bruno rushed into the house, I pushed the left pedal with my foot all the way to the floor and started the truck. I moved the stick to what I hoped was the right position and pressed on the gas while pulling my left foot back. The truck lurched forward and jerked so hard my head snapped like a whip and I bit my tongue. The truck stalled. I wiped at the angry tears that flooded my eyes and started the process again. This time we made it ten feet before it stalled again. I cursed. I would not let my inept driving cause my mother's or Giacomo's death. I placed my feet in position again and turned the key.

The truck groaned as I let out the clutch. At last we made it down the road to the first turn. I kept the gas pedal down as far as my toes could reach—until a deep rut in the road caught the tires on one side. We jerked to the right and my foot slipped from the gas pedal. The truck coughed and sputtered like an old man before we shuddered to a pitiful stop.

I checked my unconscious mother, worried that my fumbling had caused her neck to snap, then stared at the road for mere seconds before I gritted my teeth. I would get her to the hospital, even if I had to get out and push the truck. I turned the key and the truck groaned but would not start. I looked back toward the house for Bruno, but there was no sign of him. After several minutes and failed attempts to start the truck, I pounded on the steering wheel and bit my lip to keep myself from screaming.

Someone reached through the side window and put their hand on my shoulder. I shrieked in alarm and looked up, straight into the eyes of the German soldier who had held the scythe behind my sister. I screamed again. He must have waited until Bruno wasn't looking, then ran up behind us.

The soldier opened the truck door, and I reached out, with both hands punching and slapping him with all of my might while I screamed. He finally caught hold of my hands and held them in his grip.

I tried to move my legs around to kick him. "No, no, no!" I yelled. I screamed as loud as I could, hoping Bruno would hear me and come with the rifle.

The soldier pushed both of my legs to one side while still holding my wrists with his other hand, and my shoulders slacked in defeat.

"Please, do not hurt us. You can have the truck. Just let us be. Let us go."

The German held both of my hands in one of his and pressed the pointer finger of his other hand firmly against my lips. "Shhh, signorina. I will not harm you. I am a friend, not your adversary. I will help you. Move now. Move over and let me drive."

I struggled to gain control before I burst into tears. "*Per favore,* my mother may die. Take the truck if you must, but please let us go."

My hands shook so hard in his grip I could not hit him again even if he let go of me. I sat on the seat of the truck like a cornered animal and waited for his answer.

He let go of my hands and startled me further when he crouched down beside me. "You are Francesca, no? You use Franca for your name? I am . . . a friend. I will help you."

I gasped. "How do you know my name?"

"I know your family. I am a friend. We do not have much time. I will tell you more as we go, but we must hurry. I will take you to the hospital because it is so difficult for you to drive."

I had never met a kind or helpful Nazi—but the soldier was not going to let us go, and my mother and Giacomo could be dying. If he was running away or stealing the truck, maybe he would at least get us closer to town, and I could convince him to take us to the hospital. I scooted over tightly against my mother and had to tuck my legs as far over as I could from the gear shift to let the soldier drive as we pulled out of the ditch and headed to town.

The closeness in the cab kept me up against the soldier no matter how hard I pressed myself to my mother's side. I wrapped my arms around Mama. And then the reality sank in—even as I'd fought him I had noticed something different about the soldier; he wasn't in a Nazi uniform anymore. He was wearing Bruno's clothes. I gasped again and heard my voice speak through a darkening fog. "Did you kill him? Did you kill Bruno and steal his clothes?"

I looked over my shoulder at the man who held our lives in his hands—the long, thin, purple scar that ran from below his left eye clear down his cheek, the bright blue eyes of so many German soldiers who could easily fake sincerity and innocence, the strong set of his jaw I'd learned to fear in the Nazis. We were moving faster now, smoothly passing fields and pastures.

The soldier finally looked back at me. "Listen to me, *per favore.* I did not kill or harm Bruno. I left the Nazis because they are bad. I am not a Nazi, just a German. I helped Bruno's sister—your friend, Marianna, when she was in the catacombs in trouble, and that is why I am here. Marianna and her husband, Massimo, brought me to her uncle's farm so I would not have to go to the prison camp again."

"You are lying. Marianna would have told me. She and Massimo left three weeks ago, and you are still here. I would have seen you."

I knew the dedication and determination that drove my best friend, Marianna, when she decided to help someone. But perhaps this was an imposter. This may be the soldier who had hidden her in the cave, but we did not know all the reasons why, and even Mari could be deceived. I took a deep breath. "Where? Where could you have possibly hidden?"

"In the barn."

Disbelief made a full circle in my thoughts again before panic gripped at my stomach—a Nazi right beneath our feet, all this time.

"My family would never keep that secret from me."

He glanced at me. "They would if they thought it would keep you safe. You can be shot by your own neighbor or the Allies for harboring a German, or the Nazi army would shoot you for helping me desert. If the property were searched or you were questioned by the Nazis or the Allies, it is important that you did not know about me."

My cheeks and neck grew warm. My mother must have known about this soldier. Maybe everyone did. Everyone except me. The flush in my face turned hot. What a fool I had been. I was the same age as Marianna but a little child in a world of adults who all knew the truth. I thought of the times over the past few weeks, morning and night, that I milked the cow. Alone in the barn. With a Nazi.

A Nazi with a scythe at his disposal.

The wound on my forehead throbbed with a vengeance. "Wait . . . I saw you holding a scythe over my sister's head. You were going to kill her."

"No. No, signorina, I held the scythe over the head of the German who was holding your sister captive. If she had not stabbed him with the needle, I would have stopped him with the scythe."

My thoughts swirled like a whirlpool. If he had been hiding in the barn, he could have used the scythe on me every time my back was turned as I coaxed the cow to give me her milk. But he had not harmed me. And now he was driving us, possibly at great risk to himself, to the hospital—but perhaps it was just a plan to get his hands on the truck.

Yet if he had been there so long, since Marianna had returned, then he could have stolen the truck many times.

"If Bruno trusts you to drive us to the hospital, then why did he take the time to teach me to drive? He could have told me who you were and let you drive us to the hospital or let you drive them yourself from the beginning."

The soldier took a deep breath. "There were two dead Germans at that house, one of them right in the middle of the kitchen. Someone had to dispose of their bodies right away in case others were coming. Your brother-in-law is not able because he is on crutches. And we have tried to keep me from detection. If I had driven and showed up at the hospital with your mother, then your family would be connected to a German and could be accused of harboring the enemy. Bruno hoped you could drive, but when I returned from disposing of the bodies, you were stuck in a ditch, and we knew you had to have help."

My face burned in humiliation once again.

I checked Mama's breathing to keep from looking at the soldier. Her head tipped back against the seat, and her hair flew about her face in the windy truck. I leaned her toward me, let her head rest against my shoulder, and squeezed my eyes shut against the tears that stung behind my eyelids. Mama's and Giacomo's lives had depended on me, and I was nothing but an oblivious, clumsy juvenile.

But maybe the soldier lied. All Nazis lied. And killed. And fought for the power to take my country away.

"Where did you dispose of the bodies?"

He stared straight ahead, his expression stoic. "I set them on fire in a ravine behind the property. I'll bury the remains when we return."

My stomach roiled. I had no more questions.

The city of Siracusa grew larger on the horizon, and I glanced at the soldier. "I just want my mother and Giacomo saved."

The soldier looked back at me. "I agree. But if I go all the way through town and am spotted, then I am sure I will be captured by the Allies. And as I said, you could be arrested or worse for harboring a German. Could you make the drive the rest of the way if you drop me off outside the city?"

The towel on mama's stomach had not seeped through. I looked at the soldier out of the corner of my eye. His expression was serious. The orange sunset had turned a deep purple, and I couldn't see the soldier's eyes clearly. I bit my lip. "I can try."

"Do you remember the sequence for the gears?"

I'd been terrified when the soldier ran up to the truck, but now I wanted to beg him to drive the rest of the way to the hospital. My eyes burned as I stared at the gearshift.

The soldier climbed out of the truck next to a copse of trees outside Siracusa and leaned down at the window before I started away. "Signorina Franca, would you be willing to come back here for me when you leave the hospital?"

I closed my eyes and bit my lip until I tasted blood, but I nodded in agreement, and the soldier sprinted toward the trees.

I put the gear stick and my feet on the pedals into proper position. The war had pounded my faith into dust, but I said a quick prayer, eased my left foot back, and pressed on the gas.

CHAPTER TWELVE

Franca

The truck ground and groaned its way, but we made it into town and stopped in front of a church that had been converted to a hospital. I checked my mother and Giacomo for signs of life and was sure I still detected a breath coming from each. Then I ran up the endless steps to the church doors.

Stench swirled like a cloud over the main room full of rows of wounded soldiers. The hospitals had been taken over by the Canadians and Americans. I spoke very little English and while we were grateful the Allies had freed us from the Germans, the new president of Italy had not officially chosen to side with them against Hitler. I may find help for my mother and Giacomo, or I could be taken prisoner on a soldier's whim.

A tall red-haired man in a white coat stood next to a bed and scribbled on a chart.

I called out to him for help. "*Aiuto per favore!* I need help, signore!"

The man looked right at me, and I grasped the grain of hope. "My mother and our worker were shot by German soldiers, and they might die. They are in the truck outside. Please, come with me to get them. Please, please come help me."

I walked over beside him and reached for the man's arm to pull him with me, but he jerked his arm back and frowned. "What your name is, signorina?"

"Francesca Chessari."

"Soldiers here only. Clinic in Ortigia for you."

"No, no, no! Signore, *Dottore,* they will die."

He continued to shake his head, and I gulped for air to keep myself from crying.

A thin, dark-haired nurse heard us speaking and walked up beside the doctor. She looked at me. "What did you say your name was, and who is injured?"

I calmed my breathing. "I am Francesca Chessari. It is my mother, Elisa Chessari, and our hired man. They could be dying. Please help us."

"What is your father's name?"

I looked at her, puzzled. "My father?"

She pursed her lips.

"Paulo Chessari."

She turned toward the doctor and whispered in his ear. The doctor nodded, and the nurse looked back at me. "Yes, take me to them. Quickly."

She motioned to a couple of men who looked like assistants, and we all raced out the door to the truck.

A few hours later, I fell asleep, my forehead throbbing each time my head bobbed down in exhaustion and I jerked it back up. But my mother had survived her surgery, and I sat in a chair beside her. I would not let go of her hand. I longed to rest my cheek against her hand, but although a nurse had given me a wet towel to wipe the blood from my forehead and nose, my wound still seeped.

Mother's breathing was steady. Her cheeks, while still pale, had a hint of color. Giacomo rested in a smaller room away from the Allied soldiers. The nurse, who had told the doctor to treat Mama and Giacomo, shook my shoulder, and I jumped to my feet.

"Signorina Chessari, let me bandage your head. Your mother will sleep for a long time. The bullet did not hit the main organs. But your hired man is gravely injured and may not live. You need to rest so you do not become ill yourself. I will watch over your family members."

I dabbed at the sticky blood with the towel as she spoke but was sure I looked a sight with a seeping knot below my hairline.

"*Grazie tantissimo.* I do not know how to tell you how grateful I am. You saved my mother and our friend. What is your name?"

"Donatella."

Donatella applied salve and a thick bandage to my wound.

The hospital had grown quieter as the night inched past midnight; the moaning and cries for help from the soldiers eased. The metal whir of fans lent a calming effect, and the lighting had dimmed to an amber glow. The suffering of the men had unnerved me, and I was astounded that Marianna withstood it when she worked as a volunteer.

"My friend worked at a hospital here in Siracusa. Did you know a young woman named Marianna De'Angelis?" I asked Donatella.

"No, I have never heard of your friend," she answered without hesitation.

"But are there many hospitals here?" I asked, trying not to wince as she taped the bandage in place.

"In wartime there are many. Especially since the Allies arrived."

"But I was sure she—"

"Your bandage is all finished. I will be happy to give you medicine for the pain if you would like."

My head throbbed intensely and made my stomach roil, but Donatella's manner had become stiff, so I hesitated to take more of her time. "I will be fine. *Grazie,* Donatella."

"*Prego,* signorina."

She checked Mama's pulse and wound and bid me a quick farewell.

My mother had medical attention and help here at the hospital, but the worry over my family members tugged on my thoughts.

And I had to make a big decision on the way back to the farm.

I kissed my mother's soft cheek. "*Ti voglio bene.*" I whispered before I let go of her hand.

Giacomo slept just three beds down from the doorway of his room, his skin a pale gray. I patted his hand and wished I knew where any of his family might be.

It was a relief to leave the stench of blood and infected wounds behind as I exited the hospital, but part of me remained behind, pulled by the fear and worry over Mama.

Dogs barked, and the groan of truck engines in the distance resonated through the black night with a melancholy echo. The danger of being out at night had lightened since the Nazis had retreated for the mainland; while they dominated our country, a strict curfew had been in place, and I may have been arrested for being out.

The truck sat where I had left it in the shadows at the bottom of the steps.

CHAPTER THIRTEEN
Peter

THE WIND WHIPPED AROUND THE trees with a low, lonely moan and stirred a percussion of restless leaves and creaking branches. And I was locked in fear—Franca Chessari still had not returned. Perhaps she never would. I could not blame her for not trusting me. She may even despise me. I may have saved Marianna and driven Franca to Siracusa to save her mother and hired man, but I was still the dreaded German.

The hours had trudged by. I wondered if signora Chessari was alive, but I had little hope. Few could survive the loss of so much blood. And the wounded Giacomo was too old to survive such a blow. Two more casualties. God must have lost count of all the dead by now.

I'd contributed to that count out in the trenches. I had seen the terror in a man's eyes right before he dies. The Allies's blood had splattered on my face and hands in the thick of battle. I held rags over the wounds of my comrades and saw the trust in their eyes before the dim light dulled to black.

The waves were ruthless—the swells of guilt and confusion that pulled me into a riptide and made me sweat head to toe. Before Massimo and Marianna left, I agreed to help their resistance army stop Hitler. The Nazis had to be stopped at all cost. But not all Germans in battle were Nazi or chose to fight the war—my lifelong friends, Dieter and August, had been pulled into battle just like me.

The ties that held me to my comrades were severed the day I turned myself into the Allies and trapped myself in a land where I had no footing. I'd been hiding in a barn between bales of hay for hours on end for more than three weeks now and had climbed up a terrace or stairs to listen in on a radio and translate German to help the partisans who fought the Axis—who fought to stop Adolf Hitler.

I sweated in my sleep every night, blanketed in guilt that I am tucked in a barn while my friends are in the throes of hell and locked in fear that my actions may only cause those who do not deserve it more harm.

I stretched out on the scratchy soil and looked up at the stars that watched my every move. They winked at me as if they knew I slipped between worlds that collided and exploded—sanity versus evil—good versus insanity.

The rocks and tufts of grass dug at my back, and I relished the punishment as I endured another wave of anxiety. I'd lied to Francesca. I am the enemy—a traitor to my own country—a friend with a smile on my face and a knife in the backs of my comrades—the ones I swore to fight beside, to sacrifice my life for.

I squeezed my hand around a rock until the muscles in my arm trembled. Had I not walked away that day in the catacombs, had I followed orders and brutalized Marianna De'Angelis, I would have been an obedient soldier and a man whose soul had plummeted to the depths of hell.

Perhaps I'd lost my soul before Keillor even ordered me to the catacombs. I'd marched off to war and riddled strangers with bullets that will have my name etched on them for eternity. But no matter who I'd had to eliminate in battle, I'd reached my limit that day in the catacombs.

I'd decided in that moment that Marianna would live, even if I had to die in her place.

I may have been fighting against Nazism now, against evil, but I deserved no more majesty than my friends who were still trapped by Hitler and dying in his godforsaken war. Axis or not, if Dieter and August were reduced to ashes, they would still belong to the heavens when they reached the skies. As for me, a deserter holds no place in God's halls of glory, but I would fight Adolf Hitler just the same.

The sun would be up in a couple hours. I crouched behind a rock until my legs numbed. "Come on, Franca. Come back. Trust me even though I do not deserve it. Drive that truck around the corner and show me your beautiful face and how brave you are," I whispered to the deaf wind.

CHAPTER FOURTEEN

Franca

THE ROADS WERE EERILY QUIET, the high-pitched cry of the truck engine echoing off the walls of the buildings on each side of the dark, narrow streets as I passed. I stared through the dim tunnel of light that the headlights of the truck provided through the blackness of the night, my head pounding.

Without the panic of earlier, my thoughts came more clearly, and I'd managed to get the truck moving after a couple of false attempts. I slid around corners, the tires vibrating over the cobblestones at too fast a speed, so I would not have to stop and start the truck in motion again, and I found my way out of Siracusa.

Now I had to decide if I would return and pick up the German soldier. He may be waiting in the grove of trees where I'd dropped him off on the way to the hospital. The closer I got, the more convinced I became that he must have run away. There was nothing to hold him to our family. No reason why he wouldn't run for cover or freedom or whatever a Nazi soldier might seek.

I spotted the group of trees and doubted until the last moment that I would have the courage to stop. Enemy or not, if it had not been for him, Marianna would not be alive and I would not have made it to the hospital. I let off the gas and let the truck roll to a stop next to a tree. My foot stretched to the tip of my toe to press the clutch far enough toward the floor.

I watched for the soldier in the headlights, but he came up from behind to my window and tapped on the glass. I jumped in surprise and lost my footing on the pedals. The truck jerked forward as if it had been kicked. I rolled the window down a small amount when the soldier caught up again and stared forward as I spoke. "*Per favore,* do not sneak up on me again."

He placed his hands in his pockets. I flinched and prayed he did not have a gun hidden inside. I'd been a fool to come back for him.

He bent down to speak through the window. "I apologize, signorina; it was not my intention to frighten you. I was over that rise just behind the trees, behind the truck."

I still stared straight ahead into the darkness. I had no desire to battle the pedals and stick shift in front of the soldier. I willed the tears in my eyes to ebb before I scrambled out of the safety of the truck into the dark night. "It makes the most sense for you to drive. I will sit on the mattress in the back."

The soldier stepped out of the way and watched me climb in the truck bed. Giacomo's injury had left a wide pool of blood in the middle of the mattress. I sat on the edge and tucked my skirt around my legs while the soldier watched me.

"Signorina Chessari, I cannot leave you back here. I give you my oath I will not touch or harm you. Please come to the front."

I hugged my arms around my legs to stop them from shaking and averted my eyes from his stare. Minutes clicked by, and the soldier did not give up his stance. I sighed. "What is your name?"

"Peter Weimer."

"And your rank?"

"Sergeant. But I prefer to be called Peter now."

"Sergeant Peter Weimer, you say you know my family." I tucked my skirt around my legs again. "But you are still my enemy."

"If I were your enemy, your mother and worker would not be at the hospital and you would be captured or dead by now."

I glanced at him from the corner of my eye, and he rolled his. "I have explained. I have shown you. You can trust that I will get you safely back to your family, or you can leave me here and drive this truck like a hopping rabbit all the way back to the farm."

I stiffened my shoulders and stood up, careful how I placed my feet as I climbed out of the truck so I would not fall in front of him. I turned his direction and stared at a tree over his shoulder. "*Va bene,* please do not harm me."

I got inside, pressing up against the passenger door.

By the time we returned an hour later, my leg had bruised against the door handle, but I could not make myself move any closer to the soldier. Thankfully, he remained silent until the truck came to a halt in front of the De'Angelis's home.

"I must put the truck in the barn. Would you like to get out here?"

The house stood like a black mausoleum against the sky, as if the dark spirit of the Nazis that had attacked my family still possessed it or were hiding inside. I cleared my throat, suddenly hesitant to leave the truck.

The soldier looked out the front window as he waited. "Would you like me to come inside with you to be sure your family is safe?"

I grabbed onto the door handle but did not pull it back. "No. No, I was just making sure that the truck was completely stopped."

"Signorina, would you like me to come inside?"

I hugged my free arm around my waist. "No."

"But you are afraid."

"I am not . . . well, of course I am afraid. Are you happy I said it? I am not used to seeing my family . . ." I paused and laid my hand carefully over my forehead. Every time I frowned, the wound throbbed so hard my teeth ached. ". . . attacked and seeing my mother shot."

The soldier cleared his throat. "I am also very upset about your mother and worker." His words were kind, but his tone had become less patient. Another minute passed. "So you would like me to check the house for Nazis? The two from earlier are both dead. I will finish burying the bodies tomorrow."

The abruptness in his tone and casual mention of bodies stiffened my back. Maybe he was like the Nazis after all.

"I will be fine." I threw the truck door open and jumped out, shutting the door behind me.

"I am willing to help you," he called out the window.

I forced myself to walk straight for the house without looking back. The truck rumbled as the soldier headed for the barn.

No candles or lanterns were lit inside the kitchen. I knew a box of matches sat on the windowsill next to the door and reached for it in the darkness. It hissed like a snake when I struck it against the top of the stove. The yellow glow exposed no Nazis, but I saw Bruno asleep, his head resting on the kitchen table. My questions and frustration over the German soldier burned in my stomach, but I had to be sure that Laura was alive and stable. I lit a candle and shook Bruno by the shoulder. He raised his head, the shadows under his eyes sunken deep and hollow. "Bruno, are you alright? How is Laura? Luca?"

"They are sleeping."

Relief flickered in my chest for a moment before frustration took over. "Tell me if you knew there was a German soldier that calls himself Peter Weimer hiding here."

He frowned. "Your mother and Giacomo, did they make it? Did Peter help you get there?"

Peter. He called a German by his first name as if they were friends. I headed toward the hallway but turned to answer him. "Yes, they made it. A nurse made the doctor help them. They say Mama will live, but Giacomo is not so good." Marianna would have crossed herself as she said those words, but frustration had taken over my faith at the moment, and I had no inclination to lift my hand.

Bruno's eyes teared up, and he crossed himself. "*Grazie a Dio* your mother made it safely. And I hope Giacomo can hold on. He is a kind man."

Tears flooded my eyes. "Yes. I am so thankful." I turned to go but my angst bubbled up. "So you knew. You knew about an enemy soldier hiding here?" I blurted.

"Yes, I knew. He helped Marianna and left the Nazis. Do not worry about him." Bruno rubbed his eyes. "Were they able to get the bullets out and give them medication?"

"Yes, they did. But Giacomo lost so much blood. My mother may be all right like I said." Anger burned behind my eyes. He'd brushed away my shock and fear over the soldier like they held no significance. I sniffed. "Maybe your Nazi comrade can answer the rest of your questions tomorrow."

"No more anger tonight, Franca. I would not have let him go with you if I did not trust him."

"You are patronizing me?" My voice quivered. "You knew you could trust him. I did not. I thought he was going to kill us."

I almost screamed the words at Bruno but was too worried about Laura to risk waking her. I headed down the hall without another word to check on my sister before I fell on my bed upstairs and sobbed.

I awoke sometime later, drenched in sweat in the midst of nightmares. My mother could die. Another Nazi could come and kill us all. The night air chilled the sweat on my skin, and I shook until my teeth chattered. I curled into a ball beneath the quilt.

CHAPTER FIFTEEN

Franca

THE SUN ROSE, AND MEMORIES of the night before shot through a crack in the curtains with the first rays. I bolted up and shivered as I walked into the kitchen.

Bruno sat at the table, his eyes bloodshot but more awake than he'd been in the middle of the night. Steam rose off the cup of coffee in front of him. I poured my own cup from the pot on the stove and almost startled myself with the loud smack of it as I set the cup with deliberate force on the table. Bruno did not look up, and I slammed my cup onto the table once again to get his attention. Half of the coffee spilled in a wave over the side.

I sat down and stared at my brother-in-law. "So all along you knew, you helped hide him, a man—the enemy—a Nazi soldier—here." I threw my hands up. "How could you keep such a thing a secret?"

Bruno pushed his hair back with his hand and lowered his brow. "What good would it have done to tell you?" he almost shouted. "If you had ever been questioned, it would have put you in danger. He is not a Nazi. He saved Marianna when she was almost dead. It was very brave. It could be extremely dangerous for anyone to know that Peter is here. The Nazis could capture him, and he is also a personal enemy to an SS leader and to every Italian in our country. He can be of great help to the partisans, but we had to and still must keep him out of sight. Do not be afraid."

I bit my lip. I had far too many experiences and nightmares with Nazis to instantly turn off my fears. "Does Laura know about him?"

"Yes, she is my wife. I tell her everything."

I raised my voice. "And she is my sister. We used to tell each other everything."

I hesitated with my next question, but I had to know. "Was Marianna the one who wanted to keep the soldier a secret?"

"No. No, she was not. She was upset about the idea and wanted to tell you. It was your father who insisted. He did not want you having any information in case of questions and threats by the Axis or even the Allies."

My chest eased with relief. It was no surprise that my father would be overprotective. But Marianna and I never kept secrets from one another, so if she had been in favor of this secrecy, the sting would have been so much worse. Still, my questions and anxiety would not let up.

"And Giacomo?"

Bruno hesitated. "Yes, Giacomo knew, but only because he works so much in the barn, and we knew he may see him and try to shoot him." He rubbed his hands over his eyes.

"Giacomo and not me? Do I not *work* in the barn? Milking the cow. That is not working in the barn with an enemy right beside me? I deserved no warning, no respect?"

I suddenly remembered the numerous times I had talked to the cow while I tried to milk her. Times I had coaxed her and cursed in frustration. The solider had been there and heard me all along. My ears burned with humiliation.

"All of you have treated me like a child. I am nothing but a fool." I opened my mouth to protest further but noticed how haggard Bruno's face appeared. He'd grown quiet and stared out the window as if any thought of the soldier seemed a thousand kilometers away. Tears brimmed over his red-rimmed eyes.

"Remember the years before the war, Franca? We laughed . . . all the time. Laura danced even when it made her breathless. We dreamed of owning our own vineyard. She longed for a baby. Even with the dangers of the war and her heart weakness, she wanted a baby."

Nostalgia tugged at the angst that had knotted my stomach. How I longed for those happy days.

"This war may take Laura," Bruno continued. "Her fear yesterday took almost all of her remaining strength. She can barely move." Bruno gripped a napkin in his hand and buried his face in it to wipe his tears. "I do not know if I can bear to lose her, Franca."

Fear stole my nostalgia and my breath. "I may have to take her to the hospital, Bruno. She is too weak, and we do not have anything to help her."

"You know the hospitals will not take sick patients now, only the wounded or soldiers. There are outbreaks of typhus, and everyone fears an epidemic. They act more afraid of the sickness than bullets and grenades."

The white wall behind him illuminated the faint yellow pallor of hepatitis still lingering in Bruno's skin. I laid my hand over one of his. "I will go to Laura. Rest, Bruno. I will take care of it all."

"She is asleep. She is so weak this morning she cannot stand."

He wiped his tears, stood, and pushed the kitchen table to the side. I looked at him in confusion but helped him roll back the rug beneath it where the edges of a trap door were cut into the wood.

"Why are we opening the old cellar? There is no food down there."

"Just help me lift it, and I will explain."

The hinges fought back as we pulled up on the wide handle carved in the door. I gazed down into the dark pit.

The German soldier stood holding a lantern at the base of steep stairs. He looked up at me, his blue eyes turned black by the shadows. "*Buona mattina,* signorina."

I stepped back, my hand over my heart. "*Come mai?* We are not keeping him in the house, no?" I whispered to Bruno. "If he is in the barn, we can claim we had no idea he was there. But if the American soldiers find him in the house, they may take us all away. And the partisans would hang us for harboring an enemy faster than the Allies."

"Peter stayed here in the cellar last night in case those soldiers had others with them. Since we have the main cellar right outside the door, they are less likely to suspect we'd have a second one. Peter has hidden in here a few times when we've thought a threat was nearby. Since we were just attacked, he may need to hide out here more often in case those two Nazis had connections to others who will be looking for them. I give him food, and he hands out the trash if he's down here long. It's only been once or twice."

The soldier still watched us. I took another step back, the front of my blouse still knotted in my hand.

"I'll be back in a moment to let you go to the barn," Bruno told the soldier.

Burno grabbed the last loaf of bread from the table and tossed it down. The soldier uttered a quiet thank-you before Bruno closed the trap door, and we covered it with the rug again.

I breathed easier and sat back down at the table, resting my head in my hands to gather my thoughts.

"Now that you know about Peter, you can help," Bruno said as if that were good news.

My head weighed a hundred pounds in my hands. "Why are we still here in Sortino, Bruno? We must go back to my family's villa in Siracusa."

"Perhaps we can go back. I will see what I can find out today."

I lifted my head in surprise. "What do you mean? How can you find out anything about safety at our villa today?"

And then another reality hit me like a tidal wave. "Wait a minute. You said my father insisted that we keep the German soldier a secret. How did he even know about him? He is up north at our other vineyard."

"Come upstairs with me, Franca. There is more you need to know."

CHAPTER SIXTEEN
Franca

THE STEPS CREAKED AS I climbed to the upstairs bedroom behind Bruno. It took a long time to ease himself up one step at a time with his crutch while he clung to the wrought-iron handrail for balance. The war had taken so much away. But war was not a living entity—it was men who did this damage to my brother-in-law. German men.

Blue flowered curtains filtered the light in the bedroom as we entered. A dresser covered in photos next to a cast-iron bed had a space cleared where my mother had set her hairbrush and pearl earrings. I rubbed my fingers over the smooth surface of the delicate pearls.

Bruno sat down at a table next to a second window. A table that held a black box plugged with wires and what looked like a mouthpiece or microphone. A bulky set of black earphones lay next to it.

I took a step closer. "It is a radio, no? A military device?"

"Yes, it is a radio, one that your mother and I use for listening to German or Axis activity in the area. We keep tabs on the military moves and radio signals and report anything suspicious to a group of partisan fighters that work with the Allies."

I sat in a chair next to Bruno, the air knocked from my chest. "You must be *pazzo.* My mother, a spy against the Germans? A *partigiana?*"

The image of the ragamuffin partisan members I'd seen flashed before me. And the idea of my mother in front of a military radio with earphones pressed over her carefully groomed hair seemed impossible. She had proven her forte many times throughout our lives, but her family in England was aristocrats—I could never imagine her involved in the grittiness of war.

Bruno pulled back the curtains and looked out the window, then sat back with ease like one accustomed to spying on the enemy. "You could call her a partisan. She would probably refer to herself as merely doing her part to help."

"It is not just doing her part to help—it is a huge risk. How long has she been involved? Does she communicate with my father through this radio?"

"Your mother has been doing this for a while now. She communicates to others with radios, who then send the message to another and another until it reaches your father, so that is why she was up here so much of the time before the attack yesterday. Now, until she can return, I need to be here so I can pass warnings or information to the partisans who work with the Allies. I had to report the attack last night. There are still spies for the Axis here, attempts to take Sicily back from the Allies and Nazi stragglers trying to pull tricks."

"Pull tricks? Like the ones who came here? That was hardly a trick. You knew there was a risk of Nazis coming here?"

"We are at war, Franca. Of course there was and is risk. But we had no idea those Nazis were coming here. I told you we had to be very careful."

I frowned at him, and he spoke more quickly.

"We meant to keep everyone safe. No one was trying to keep you ignorant on purpose."

I looked my brother-in-law in the eye. "It seems that no one needed to try. I have been ignorant enough for everyone's convenience." I squeezed my hands into fists so tightly my fingernails dug into my palms. "Apparently it is time for the little sister to grow up and see the secret world she has been living in."

"Nobody sees you as a child, Franca."

I raised my hands, palms up toward the ceiling. "No. Just a pampered girl trying to milk a *stupida* cow or change a baby's diaper or drive a truck without landing in a ditch."

"You are much more than that. We wanted to protect you."

I stood up. "Did you worry about my safety when I was alone in the barn twice a day with an enemy soldier hiding behind bales of hay?"

"He is not our enemy."

I could not get my breath quickly enough. "He is a Nazi, a German. I needed to know. To be warned, to be trusted." I steadied my voice. "I am finished with being protected. I am going to check on Luca and Laura. Then you are going to tell me every single thing you know." I pointed at the black box. "And you will show me how to use this radio."

I headed for the door, and Bruno's chair scraped against the floor as he stood. "I radioed the hospital, Franca. Your mother is still alive and stable. She is still sleeping."

I spun around, my whole body limp with relief. "She just . . . she has to survive. And I had no idea that hospitals have radios. One more thing I did not know."

"But you know now."

"I need to know everything. Everything, or else I will explode like the bombs falling on our heads."

Bruno's voice was gentle. "*Va bene,* no more secrets."

"And Giacomo? How is he?" I asked.

The shadows under Bruno's eyes made him look ten years older. "He did not make it, Franca. His wound was too serious."

Giacomo's huge grin flashed before my eyes; his jolly demeanor and patience as he showed me how to milk a cow. I covered my eyes with my arm and fell against the wall, crying. I used my apron to wipe my eyes and remembered the eggs I'd filled it with and how Giacomo had grinned at me with his missing tooth when two of the eggs fell.

Bruno had quietly slipped downstairs to let me have my cry. Laura called my name. I had not even started all the chores that had to be done so we could eat and drink one more day. I wiped the tears from my cheeks and ran down the steps.

CHAPTER SEVENTEEN

Franca

The next morning, I arose before the rooster trumpeted his wake-up call. I dressed quickly, hardly recognizing myself anymore in Aunt Pasqualina's old clothes and aprons. The eighteen-year-old Franca, who'd dreamed of working in the fashion houses of France, no longer looked back from the mirror.

Dread pressed on my shoulders—I needed to milk Rosa, but the soldier, Peter Weimer, could be back in the barn.

Armed with a bucket and lantern, I slipped outside the kitchen, surprised that the ground was soaking wet, and a drizzle of rain spattered in puddles. I'd slept so deeply I hadn't even heard a storm move in. My shoulders were wet and made me shiver by the time I reached the barn, but the scent of thirst-quenched earth and dewy air replenished my strength.

My sense of impropriety and awkwardness over handling the underparts of a cow had improved bit by bit each day, but now I was aware of the audience tucked away somewhere behind the fort of hay beyond the cow stalls. My cheeks flushed hot. Perhaps I should utter a greeting in case the soldier had heard me come in the barn, but my words stayed locked in my throat.

Luca's cries echoed from the house. Laura and Bruno would awaken, but Laura had very little milk. We needed Rosa to produce the rest. I sat on the milking stool and rolled up my sleeves.

My back had bruised badly when the German monster had knocked me off my feet and I'd slammed down on the floor. My muscles ached and cramped until I could hardly reach under the cow to milk her. I sat back for a moment, willing Luca to go back to sleep for just a few more minutes. The lump on my forehead had not gone down, and a glance in the mirror after I'd dressed told me the wound was swollen with deep purple bruises that extended beyond the bandage.

I squeezed my eyes closed each time my mind flashed back to the evil faces and uniforms of the Nazis who'd attacked us in the kitchen; the explosion of gunfire and the pool of blood on the kitchen floor as it poured from my mother's and Giacomo's wounds.

Pain pounded my head like a hammer to an anvil and the confusion and worry about my mother and my father's absence stayed wrapped like a tourniquet around my chest. I let a few tears drop to the straw at my feet, and they pooled on top of the woody pieces and just sat there without soaking in.

A crack of thunder startled the cow, and she stomped her feet before she stepped back in place. I crossed myself before I began. "Please, give me your milk." My family was in crisis, yet my attempts at prayer were addressed to a cow. If I stopped to admit it, she did seem *simpatica,* as if she knew she needed to be extra patient for me. Giacomo had said I needed to talk to her, so I patted her side. "*Ciao* . . . eh . . . Rosa. I know you are nervous with me, and I am sorry that Giacomo is not here to get your milk. I will try my best to do a good job."

My fingers still hesitated to grab hold of the teats, but in time, I managed to fill half of the bucket with milk.

The stench of dung filled my nostrils. The barn needed to be mucked out and fresh hay laid down, but I could not fathom finding the time to do it.

The squawking and fluttering of the chickens outside lifted the silence as the first hints of a gray dawn edged its way through the clouds and the slats of the barn wall.

Luca's cries carried across the lawn from the house, his sobs lower and shakier. I had been out here too long, and sweet Luca needed me. I wiped my hands on my dirty apron. I had to find time to bathe and do laundry today.

I let Rosa out to pasture and scattered scratch for the chickens before the rooster could come charging.

Rain sprinkled and mixed with the dew in the tall grass, making the ground slick beneath my feet and dampening my legs and skirt as I passed. No cries echoed from the bedroom as I entered the kitchen, and I almost wept with relief; perhaps Luca had cried himself back to sleep. My heart ached at the thought of him falling asleep in hungry exhaustion.

I rounded the corner by the parlor to listen more carefully, the bucket of milk still in my hand. "I am sorry, *bambino mio.* I am coming," I whispered.

The yellow glow of a candle in the corner of the dim parlor caught me by surprise, and I started when the image cleared; the German soldier, Peter Weimer, sat in the big rocking chair with a sleeping Luca bundled in his arms.

I jolted at the sight of the helpless baby in the arms of a German. I stared at him in silence before the soldier stood and walked up to me. He looked down into the bucket that held the half ration of milk.

"She can do better than that." The soldier handed me the baby and took the bucket from my hand before I could manage a reply. Luca squirmed, and I held him closer as the soldier walked out the kitchen door, sunrise peeking its way through the clouds before him.

I sat in the rocker to calm my heartbeat and catch the breath I'd been holding, unsure I could survive the constant shock of a Nazi in close proximity. Memories of the horrible soldiers shooting my mother and Giacomo came up like the ghosts of demons for the hundredth time.

My father had always spoken openly about the evil of Nazism and swore that Hitler was determined to wipe God himself out of the skies. Our dinners around the kitchen table for years had turned sour more than once with Papa's tales of Nazi threats. Mama would lay her hand over my father's when Laura and our brothers and I had gone pale with fear.

Now one of the Germans I'd learned to dread was here, where we were supposed to be safe.

And then a thought occurred to me. Maybe Peter Weimer had no intention of going to the barn for more milk. Bruno must have kept him in the cellar overnight or he would not have been in the house. This could be his plan to get himself out of the cellar and the house and back to the truck. I saw the vision as if I witnessed it—the milk bucket tossed under a bush, the soldier driving down the road as fast as he could to get away. I took a deep breath of relief at the thought of him leaving.

Bruno seemed to trust him as if he were a tragic hero. But we knew nothing of the soldier's true motives. Maybe he was a war criminal on the run. Or maybe he was too afraid to fight, so he'd left his army. As grateful as I was for his help taking my mother and Giacomo to the hospital, and for Marianna's safety, it did not make this Nazi a good man.

Luca sucked at his lower lip in his sleep as I carried him into my sister's bedroom. Bruno lay staring at the ceiling next to a sleeping Laura. At least Laura's cheeks were a bit rosy, and she breathed even and quietly.

I stood right next to the bed so Bruno could hear me whispering. "How did that soldier get out of the cellar?"

Bruno exhaled sharply. "I let him out last night, and he came in before dawn to listen on the radio. He translates any transmissions in German for us. And we need to talk."

"Talk about what?" I asked, swaying back and forth to keep Luca soothed.

"About arrangements and Peter's help. We are desperate for help with the radio and the chores. I am too weak to milk and you work like a slave all day, even before we lost Giacomo and the twins left. You need help."

My spine straightened. "Have you even considered that no matter the things he's helped us with, this soldier is still a Nazi? Maybe he did not help Marianna that much, or maybe he is a spy." I was sure of it now. "Yes, he could be a spy. Have you not questioned why those Nazi soldiers came here out in the middle of nowhere?" I could barely keep my voice at a whisper.

Bruno closed his eyes and sighed in exasperation. "So you think Peter stays here so that he can report to the führer about a sick woman and her crippled husband?"

I tsked my tongue and shook one hand at him. "I see that he has helped us. But how do we know it is sincere? What could you possibly know about him and his past? Is he a criminal? A murderer? Does he have a family? Is he Catholic?"

Bruno rolled his eyes. "He is not a criminal, except to his army. He refused to torture women when they ordered him to. He saved Marianna, deserted, and turned himself in to the Allies as I told you. I do not know if he has a family, and as for religion, I have no idea. I may have seen him praying once when I took food to him in the barn."

"A religious Nazi? They do not even allow religion." I practically hissed the words, and Luca squirmed. The wood floor softly creaked as I turned my swaying into pacing back and forth.

"Yes, they do. Hitler is their god." Bruno pressed his hands together, palm to palm as if in prayer and tipped them forward, up and down. "*Madonna mia,* when did you become worried about religion? And your voice is growing louder by the moment. Do you want to wake Laura too? Have you even noticed that she looks better? Her face is flushed, not white. Thank God for that if you want to be religious."

Frustration pressed like a tidal wave against my temples, but I bit my lip. None of this was Laura's or Luca's fault. Bruno tried to stand up, but I used one hand to press down on his shoulder. "No, stay here on the bed next to Laura. I am sorry if I am upsetting you." I handed him a glass of water. "I will let you rest."

Once I'd laid Luca in his crib, I strode from the room and into the kitchen. The back door opened, and the soldier walked in, a full bucket of milk in his hand. I blushed at the blaring comparison to my endeavors. Francesca Chessari shamed and humiliated by a cow. All the refinement my mother had taught me, all the dance lessons, piano and art and etiquette, seemed so insignificant now. I could not even milk a stubborn cow.

Necessity demanded that I lay that all aside. All that mattered was that Luca would at last have the soothed belly that he needed. I made myself nod my head to thank the soldier, but I could not meet his eyes.

He sat the bucket on the table. "I am sorry to hear of your sister's illness. I can help you with your chores since your hired man is injured and your brother-in-law is crippled."

A sob cracked in my throat. "Our hired man is dead." Warm tears flooded my cheeks.

"I am most sorry to hear that. He was kind to me and always said hello when I was in the barn."

In the barn. The reminder that everyone had known this soldier since Marianna left more than three weeks ago kicked me in the gut. I stiffened as he took a step toward me, and he stopped. "Those Nazis that were here are the worst of men. I hope you will come to trust that I am not like them."

There was no way to answer that, so I just wiped at my tears with my apron. "I do . . . thank you for getting us to the hospital. It saved my mother's life." I looked over at the bucket. "And thank you for the milk. But we've had enough help for now."

I slipped from the room before he could answer. After a few minutes, I went back in the kitchen and pretended I did not see the soldier still standing there. I walked to the cupboard and reached for a bottle to fill for Luca. The bottle slipped in my hand, but I caught it before it could fall and shatter. I tightened my grip to hide the shaking in my hands, aware that the soldier may be watching me. I'd ladled the bottle halfway with milk before I forced myself to look at the soldier from the corner of my eye. "Like I said, I appreciate your help but . . ."

The soldier leaned against the kitchen sink as he waited quietly for me to finish my sentence. I scratched at a phantom itch on the back of my neck and set the bottle down. "*Comunque,* thank you. You can go back to hiding now."

Peter took the bottle, finished filling it, and attached the long, brown nipple to the top before he handed it back to me. "You do not want to accept the help of a German."

"Yes." I could barely speak through the knot in my throat. Maybe I would never be as trusting or as brave as Marianna.

The soldier's eyes had been fixed on me the whole time I was speaking, their bright-blue color reminding me of where he came from. He cleared his throat. "I do understand." He opened the kitchen door.

My face burned like wildfire. "Wait. It is only that I cannot stop reliving the memory of the soldiers who came here, shot my mother, and killed Giacomo. And there have been so many other times of attacks and threats." New tears burned behind my eyelids. "I know you helped me, I mean *us,* but you are still—"

"German. I know, signorina. Do not worry."

I looked down the long marble countertop that ran the length of the wall beneath the biggest window. A deep sink sat in the middle, and a basket of fruit had been placed beside it. I grabbed a couple of peaches, the fuzzy texture as soft as the top of Luca's tiny head, and it dawned on me that I had not picked these peaches. The soldier must have done it before or after milking the cow. The fire reignited under my skin as I held them out to the soldier. "Here, you can take some of the fruit."

He held the door open and pressed his lips together. The steady tick of Aunt Pasqualina's clock on the windowsill counted several seconds before he bowed slightly. "Thank you. I am not hungry."

CHAPTER EIGHTEEN

Franca

THE MAN WOULD STARVE TO death if I did not at least throw him scraps from the table. But the kick in my stomach every time I saw Peter Weimer convinced me that after the horrifying attack on my family, I could not, would not, look at him or any German ever again without panic. Those light-colored eyes seemed to pierce my core, and I had no strength to support it. If I looked at him, the fear could make me topple like a sapling in the wind.

I left a tin of food for the soldier inside the barn door without calling out or speaking to him. My mother would never have done this, acted so distant and unfriendly when delivering a meal. And Marianna would have been much braver and waited for the soldier to come for the plate. She and Massimo had even traveled with him to bring him to Sortino. But I was none of them. The war had left me balanced somewhere between a quivering rabbit and a fox caught in a trap.

I spent the next few days caring for my sister, too worried to dwell on a radio or to leave her side except to do the many chores. Bruno used the radio and made contact with a group of partisans who checked and reported on our mother. A miracle had occurred. Although she had lost a lot of blood, she had improved. It looked as if she would survive.

I carried Luca into Laura's bedroom and told her the good news about our mother. She smiled, her lips almost as pale as her teeth. "Franca, you are better than the *santi* to our *famiglia*. You saved Mama." She grasped my hand in hers. "And you save me every day."

Laura had the maturity of an older sister, but her delicate health always had me on watch to help her. She'd been born too early—two months early. It had been a miracle that she lived. All our lives she got out of breath too easily and had to lie down before dinnertime every day. But that had never hindered her enthusiasm for Bruno De'Angelis.

As little girls, Laura and I played with dolls in our bedrooms or parlor and pretended we were wives and mothers. We had make-believe husbands, and I enjoyed a full menagerie of names and types to choose from in my imagination, but from five years old, Laura always picked the young Bruno De'Angelis.

Bruno didn't hear about Laura's choice until they were eight years old, and Laura and I had been in an argument. I blurted out her secret crush by way of retaliation, and she screamed to try to cover my words. But Bruno had heard me. He'd looked at the two of us with a wide-eyed stare and then threw his glass of water at the both of us before he took off at a run.

But his repulsion only lasted a short while. Within a month, short notes and wildflowers were left on Laura's windowsill, and on her tenth birthday, Bruno gave her a little pearl ring.

"Do you remember the first time Bruno kissed you, Laura?" I asked her one morning.

Laura smiled and leaned back on her pillows. "We were twelve years old, and he jumped out from behind the shed and almost knocked me over. When he grabbed my arm to help me keep my balance, he pulled me in and stole a kiss before I realized what he was up to."

"You would've let him kiss you anyway."

She laughed again. "Probably. I never could resist him." She pulled her fingers through her tangled hair. "What made you ask me that?"

"By the time you ran to my room to tell me about it, your face was bright red and you could barely breathe."

"And for once it was for a good reason and not just because I've always just been weak as a kitten." She frowned. "Do I look bad now?"

I looked at her flushed face and the dark circles under her eyes. "Oh no, not bad. I was just missing old times."

"Ah yes. Would you like me to braid your hair? We could pretend we are at our villa," she asked through pale-blue lips.

The familiar punch in the belly from looking at my fading sister caught me again. "Maybe just one in the back, if you are strong enough. It is embarrassing when my hair flies around my face." I brushed through my tangles and sat down in front of my sister with a sigh. "Although there is no one that would notice my hair either way. It's more that it gets in my eyes when I do the chores."

"There are at least three of us who see your hair, and it is full, curly, and striking. I would bet it could reach your waist if you pulled the curls straight down."

I laughed. "I have not brushed my hair in front of a mirror in so long I have no idea."

"How is it going with the soldier, Peter? Is he very helpful with the chores?"

"He is always in the cellar or the barn."

"Always? What do you mean? He stays in there all the time?"

"I do not see or speak to him when I leave him food in the barn, and I keep the cellar door covered with the big rug and table."

Laura inhaled sharply, and I jumped in. "I have to know we are all safe." Tears stung behind my eyes.

"We are safe, Franca. He has saved our family more than once. You must let him help us—let him help you. Are you more upset that Peter is a German or that everyone kept him a secret from you?"

"I cannot look at that blond hair without getting nauseous. All I see is blood and threats, our mother on the floor, Giacomo dying."

"You have to block that out, Franca. Peter did not do those things. He has fought against them. He risked his life for Marianna and for our mother. You cannot keep him at bay like a plague. We are not that kind of people."

"Papa would not want me around a German soldier."

"Papa would not want you to have a romance or marry a German soldier, but he would recognize what Peter has done. And he would want us to accept his help."

"Yes, he would. And this is what we all need to talk about right now." Bruno shambled into the room with the help of Peter Weimer. "We need to discuss how we are going to run the chores and help one another." He sat down on the end of the bed and looked me in the eye. "It is very dangerous for Peter to be seen or discovered. But if we are careful, he can be of great help. We need to accept that help."

Laura had finished plaiting my hair into one long braid. I stood up, averting my gaze from where the soldier stood by the door. I pressed my back against the pale-green wall. Cracks ran through the mortar between the big stones on the outside wall of the bedroom and like wide spiderwebs in the plaster wall behind me. I gazed through the yellowed lace curtains at the window, wishing I could escape over the sloping valleys.

"We are each limited on our capacity to work; Peter for safety's sake and the rest of us because of health or just the weight of the tasks," Bruno said.

Laura sat up straighter and took Bruno's hand. "I'm not a great deal of help. But while Mother is in the hospital, and since Franca is aware of what we are doing, we should bring the radio downstairs to the parlor. I can listen to the transmissions and note anything alarming. And I'm knitting and sewing Luca's clothes for the winter. I will do that as I listen."

Bruno leaned over and kissed his wife. "That will be a great deal of help."

I perked up at Laura's enthusiasm. Perhaps she was getting stronger.

"Since you and I can do the rest of the chores, Bruno, we should let the soldier stay hidden so he will be safe from detection," I said without looking at Peter.

Bruno unwrapped the bandages at the end of his leg where his foot had been amputated, and a metallic odor, like rancid meat, filled the room. I covered my nose. "Bruno, *che cose?* Whatever could that be?"

"I'm afraid I've gotten a serious infection where they did the amputation. I've been cleaning it for days, but it will not clear up. It's giving me a bit of the shivers today."

I cupped my hand over my mouth. Bruno had been a critical help with the animals, and he'd cooked and even cut wood while he rested the knee of his shorter leg on a bench for support.

"You must rest, Bruno. I will bring hot rags to soak your leg," I reassured him.

"*Un attimo,* we have to discuss the rest of the work to be done first," he answered.

The soldier still stood beside the doorway. "I grew up on a farm. I can muck out the stalls in the barn, haul the water to the house and for the animals, and feed them before dawn or after the sun goes down. I can butcher chickens and slop the hogs from the back of their pen. Anything you need, I will find a way to help."

"We will still need you listening on the radio also, especially if Laura hears anything suspicious or in German," Bruno added.

Peter Weimer nodded his head in agreement.

We were sliding down a slippery slope. One where I would have to see the soldier or work with him on a regular basis. I pressed my hands together in front of me. "I can milk the cow and take care of the chickens, gardens, cooking, cleaning, laundry, and Luca. But I can also do the other chores until Bruno's leg is better. That is best." I glanced up at the soldier and caught his gaze. "You need to stay hidden."

Laura tsked her tongue. "Franca, that is too much for one person. You must let Peter help you."

I looked at Bruno. "I will bring hot rags to soak your leg." I moved past the soldier and out of the room.

"Signorina Franca," I heard him call behind me. He had followed me into the hall.

I made myself face him, and he rubbed his hand over his jaw and down his neck where his hair began to curl against his collar before his clasped his hands together.

His eyes focused directly on mine. "I give you my oath; I will never harm you or your family."

I wanted to avert my gaze, but my eyes stayed locked on his. The air between us warmed, and I dabbed at the perspiration on my nose and cheeks. "Thank you. But I would like to do most or all of the chores myself."

He pressed his lips together and hesitated as if contemplating a reply.

I spun around with a tug of guilt in my belly and hurried to get the rags for Bruno.

CHAPTER NINETEEN

Franca

The soldier carried the radio to the parlor, where Laura would do her sewing and knitting on the settee.

I awoke each morning with a gasp and sat straight up in bed as if the gun that shot my mother had gone off all over again. And at night, I awoke to the slightest creak in the floor or the scratch of windblown branches at the window.

A fever overtook Bruno, and his leg swelled and festered. I kept his bandages cleaned and rinsed the wound in iodine I had found in the pantry.

Three days passed in a blur as I frantically ran and cooked meals, milked Rosa, gathered eggs, fed the pigs, tended the garden, stirred boiling laundry, took food to Bruno and Laura and fed Luca. The weather had cooled, but I lived with streams of sweat rolling down my back.

Luca cried most of the next night, and Bruno talked out of his head in a delirium of fever. The next morning, Laura shook and moved slowly but insisted on cleaning Bruno's leg and feeding Luca. Luca refused her breast and cried constantly.

I tried to comfort Luca, then kissed and tucked him back in bed despite his wailing. I had no choice; only milk would soothe him now. I ran through the kitchen to the back door, the echo of my footsteps over the cellar reminding me that I needed to take food to the barn for the soldier. In my overwhelmed state, I could not be sure I had given him food the night before.

Before I could open the door, the sight of a full bucket of milk sitting on a stool caught my eye. The soldier had done the milking and left it by the door for me. I sighed with relief, filled Luca's bottle, and filled two glasses of milk for Laura and Bruno to give them strength.

After feeding Luca, it took me an hour to scrounge up enough vegetables for a few days. I put a few shrunken potatoes in the oven and slipped into the parlor, then slumped down in a chair for a five-minute reprieve.

I could not be sure how long I dozed off, but I must have slept for at least an hour. I rubbed at a cramp in my neck and discovered a pillow that someone had placed under my head. For one dreamy moment, I thought it had been my mother, until my surroundings reminded me that I was not in Siracusa. I straightened up quickly with the realization that I had been so tired I never lit the fire in the oven. The potatoes would not be cooked in time for lunch.

The clanging of dishes in the kitchen brought me fully to my senses.

The minute I entered the kitchen, my body tensed. Peter Weimer stood at the sink. The fire had been lit in the oven and water in the big black pot we used for chores and washing conjured a cloud of steam over the top.

I stopped at the bench by the table, mustering the will and the courage to tell the soldier that I needed him to leave. My back and shoulders ached, and without the soldier's help, I would have to keep pushing myself to keep up with all I had to do. But it was better than working with rattled nerves around a German.

"Perhaps you mean to be of service, Sergeant Weimer, but as I explained before, I can take care of my family. I just need to practice and to find a pattern to the way I do things. We always had a cook and hired hands at our villa."

The soldier turned around to face me, and his brows lowered. The thin scar that lined his cheek was a dark purple that disappeared into the stubble of gold whiskers. I tried to force a polite smile, but my lips just twitched.

"You can call me Peter," he said.

The water in the pot bubbled to a boil, and when the soldier checked it, I took a step closer. "I have a plan to do things a bit more efficiently as soon as I practice . . ." I cursed the wobbling sound in my voice.

He shook his head and held up his finger. "I see you go back and forth, back and forth day and night. You never stop working, and your family is ill. You need help. There is barely any food to scrape together—no chopped wood to cook food, rotting vegetables in the garden, a rooster that attacks you, a stubborn cow that doesn't like to give you milk, and very dark circles under your eyes." I glared at his raised finger, at the nerve he had to try to hush me, but his gaze just roamed over my face. "The bruise on your forehead still looks very bad. I can see you need help, and I will no longer hide like a mole in the ground. I am the oldest in my family. I am used to this work."

Fear and shame ran a relay in my head. The soldier towered over me, and my confidence had taken a plunge as he'd vocalized the tasks that had defeated me.

When I opened my mouth to protest again, he shook his head.

"I am going to help you."

I picked up a damp dishcloth that lay on the sink to scrub the table, until I noticed that he'd already cleaned it. I smacked the rag back down. "This is not your home. There is no need to come in and start cleaning and moving pots and pans around. And your hands are too smooth—I've seen no farm callouses. I have no faith in your claim about your work experience on a farm."

"You expect lies in all I say because of your prejudice against me and my country. I cannot blame you for that." One corner of his mouth lifted. "And I did not know you had time to notice my hands, signorina."

Heat rose from my neck to my ears. "I am not used to having a Naz—a German soldier so close. After that attack, my eyes must be open at all times to notice everything. I need to be aware for safety's sake."

He locked his hands together. "I do not blame you for being afraid. Our countries are at war. And I am sorry if my hands look deceiving. I am not sure how you envision farm callouses, but I do have a few from handling weapons." He ran his finger down the thin line on his cheek. "And I have a nice scar."

"You are making fun of me."

"I apologize. I only meant to use a little humor to lighten our situation."

I swallowed. "I do not feel like laughing."

"Very well. I went to university to study languages and engineering for three years before joining the military. That is where I also officially studied Italian, although I spent many weeks in the summers in Northern Italy with relatives and friends. So I lost most of my thick calluses at university, but I grew up in the countryside on a farm."

The broad width of his shoulders attested to the truth about his claim to outdoor labor, but there was no way to verify any of his claims or motives.

There were plenty of chores I had yet to do. I turned my back to the soldier and pulled a metal tub from an open cupboard for Luca's bath. Before I could reach for the pot of water, the soldier gripped the handle and poured some into the tub. He added cold water from a bucket, reached his hand in to test the temperature and glanced at me from the corner of his eye. "The baby's bath is ready. Unless you grabbed the tub to bathe yourself? If so, I will go back outside."

I wiped at what I knew were smears of dirt from my nose and cheeks and pressed my hands over my rumpled clothes. My ears kept burning as I marched from the room to get Luca for his bath.

Luca's brown eyes lit with excitement when he saw me. I picked him up and kissed his plump cheeks before I undressed him. Chubby folds of skin lined his thighs and arms, and I sighed with relief as I hugged him. Luca seemed to flourish on the cow's milk. At least one in the household appeared well and happy.

The kitchen was empty when I returned with Luca, but a towel and a bar of lavender soap that Bruno's mother had made before she left sat next to the tub. I looked over my shoulder to be sure Peter was not behind me before I lowered Luca into the water, supporting his back with my hand. I rubbed the wet cloth and smooth bar all over the baby while I cooed and talked to him.

The scent of the soap filled the room and a pang of loneliness for my beautiful clothes and for the days when my skin had been floral scented instead of covered with grime rang through me. I used one hand to splash my face with the soapy water while Luca wiggled in my other arm. One clean corner on my apron served as my towel until the squawks and shrieks from the chickens outside caught my attention. I wrapped Luca in the towel and walked over to the window in time to see Peter Weimer chop the head off of a chicken. I jerked in shock at the force of strength and the sight of blood all over his hands and arms. I had not seen such blood on a German since the night of our attack. My legs shook, and I had to sit down, taking solace from holding Luca close and kissing the top of his head.

After Luca was dressed and lay kicking his chubby legs in his bed for a nap, I slipped back to the kitchen.

The kettle of water was still hot to the touch. I opened the back door and threw Luca's bath water out into the tall green grass. I poured more of the hot water from the pot into the tub, rolled up my sleeves and scrubbed my face, neck, and arms with the lavender soap, careful as I washed over my wounded forehead. Determined, I set to work with a wide-toothed comb on the tangles of my hair that had come loose from my braid and hung down my back.

I sat down at the table to eat a piece of bread and sliced tomato and my eyes were drawn to the spot where my mother fell when the Nazi soldier shot her. The bread I had just swallowed thickened in my throat.

Streams of light from the window turned a pale yellow as they diffused through a tall bottle of olive oil on the counter, and I could swear that my mother stood in thc golden beams. I crossed myself with a prayer that it would not be her spirit sent to say goodbye, and I lay my head in my hands. "*Mamma, oh Mamma mia,* be strong, get well, get well."

The back door flung open, and I looked up, the last chunk of bread still clenched in my hand.

Peter Weimer stopped in his tracks, his gaze lingering as if taking in my cleaner appearance, his one hand gripped around the neck of the plucked chicken and his other arm full of logs he must have chopped outside. I watched in silence as he set the chicken next to the sink and loaded the logs in a bucket by the stove, a chunk of his blond hair sweeping across his forehead as he worked. He stood and looked around the kitchen, glanced at me, and pushed his hair back with the fingers of his clean hand.

I gathered clean cloths and a bucket of water to take to my sister and Bruno for their toiletries.

"*Grazie,*" I mumbled and glanced back to be sure he did not follow as I left the room.

CHAPTER TWENTY

Franca

Rosa and I were still uneasy with each other, but I was encouraged at my progress. Perhaps the idea of pulling or tugging at an udder still repelled me, and the smell of cowhide and the piles of her excrement made me recoil, but I had a job to do. The realization that Peter Weimer had been in the barn since Marianna and Massimo left, and had overheard my struggles still stung, but I would not let it thwart me now.

I set the bucket beneath Rosa and sat on the stool. "*Va bene . . .*"

I grabbed a teat in each hand and pulled.

"Signorina, you will hurt her if you do it that way," a deep voice said right over my shoulder.

I stood up and grabbed at my blouse over my heart at the sight of Peter Weimer again.

He tipped his head. "I apologize if I startled you. I came over to see if I may be of assistance. I know that you have struggled to milk the cow." He clasped his hands behind his back as if to reassure me that he would not touch me.

"Giacomo already told me what to do."

"But you still have difficulties. And telling and showing are two different things."

His words confirmed my fears; he had heard my undignified grunts and groans as I fought for Rosa's milk. I stepped away from Rosa, and when I glanced back, the soldier still watched me. He looked right into my eyes as if there were no divide between us. But my eyes had their own will, and I quickly looked away. I would never hold an enemy's gaze.

"Very well."

He gestured to the stool. "Go ahead and sit back down."

I sat on the stool and straightened the bucket under Rosa.

The soldier stepped next to me and leaned in. "First of all, you cannot grab her teat and just pull. She has to be petted and soothed so she will let her milk down. If her calf were still here, it would nudge at her bag with his nose to start the flow."

I blushed when he reached down and bumped at the udder with his hand. I scooted back on the stool and stood. "I would prefer that you demonstrate."

He took my place and carried on as if the whole procedure was natural. After a moment, I calmed down, amazed and fascinated that a soldier who was trained to kill could be so gentle and calm with an animal. He talked me through each step with ease, his deep voice almost as soothing to me as it was to Rosa.

When the soldier finished, he stood up, and I looked down at the gloriously full bucket. The frothy milk bubbles on top popped and swelled proudly.

Relief and elation flooded in. "Perhaps I have conquered my repulsion."

The soldier patted Rosa but kept his gaze on me. "You have a charming smile, signorina Franca."

I scowled. "I did not know I was . . . I did not mean to smile. I only meant to thank you. *Buongiorno.*" I blurted, and exited the barn ahead of him, leaving him to carry the bucket of milk to the kitchen.

The soldier insisted on helping me take dinner to Laura. He fed Luca his bottle while I cleaned the dishes from dinner later that evening. I went to the parlor to get Luca when I was finished in the kitchen.

"So you know how to feed a baby," I said when I entered the parlor.

He looked up. "Does that make you more or less suspicious of me?"

"It is an observation."

"When my sister, Bettina, and I were teenagers, our mother surprised our whole family and had another baby—a baby brother whom I treasured. But sadly, he died of a fever when he was only three years old."

I sat down on the settee, and my heart sank down with me. "I am very sorry to hear that. What was his name?"

"Jacob."

"That is a nice name."

"He was the sweetest boy and very clever." The soldier looked at me in earnest. "I like the name Peter too, but you refuse to call me that."

"I am merely being proper."

"I am not in the German army anymore. And we are beyond formalities. We are stuck here together."

"We are all here at the same place but not together."

He smiled and lifted Luca to his shoulder to burp him. "I did not mean to imply anything suggestive. But you could be a bit more friendly."

I watched him pat Luca.

"Very well. I will attempt to call you Peter."

Luca let out a belch and spit up profusely all the way down the front of Peter's shirt.

I locked eyes with Peter for a split second, and he actually laughed. He handed me the soaked baby, and I hurried to the kitchen, washed Luca, and wrapped him in a towel as Peter came into the room.

"That little baby has a powerful belch. I had to clean spots on the chair and even the floor," he said.

I bit my lip. "There is still some warm water on the stove if you need to wash."

I took Luca to his room and dressed him before I put him in bed. "*Sogni d'oro* my little Luca. You have dreams of gold and let that tummy rest, and you'll be nice and hungry in the morning." Luca's eyes shone bright, and he smiled at me as I laid him down. I kissed his soft chubby cheek. "*Ti voglio bene bambino.*"

I headed back to the kitchen and stopped in my tracks as I came to the doorway. Peter leaned over the tub on the table with his eyes closed as he scrubbed his face and upper body in soapy water. His shirt lay on the bench beside him—his golden skin was a shade lighter than mine, his muscles smooth and lean on his arms and shoulders and beneath the blond hair on his chest.

My legs dipped beneath me, and I stepped backwards, trying not to make a sound, and scurried out of breath up the steps to my room. I lay on my bed, staring at the ceiling, willing the image of Peter bent over the tub from my mind, and fell into fitful sleep.

CHAPTER TWENTY-ONE

Peter

SUNDAY HAD ARRIVED WITH THE usual demands for chores, and I hurried to feed and slop the animals and clean their pens before Franca could object to my help. I'd just bathed in a washtub and dressed in the barn when Bruno called for me from the house.

"We would like to invite you to dinner," he said when I opened the kitchen door.

I lifted my brows. "Is there a special occasion?"

"Yes, in fact, there is. Laura has a birthday today, and she would love for all of us to sit together and dine like a real family."

A platter of steaming pasta topped with prosciutto, tomato saucc, and sliced boiled eggs lay in the middle of the table that was fully set for dining. A fresh loaf of bread with a dipping dish of olive oil sat beside it. Even though many of the vegetables in the garden were dying, the farm and some stored food still provided enough for now.

Franca entered the room with a pink glow in her cheeks, wearing a lovely dress that tied at her slender waist, and her hair lay full and curled like a water nymph down her back. I watched her lift her full lips in a shy smile, and I laid my hand over a tug in my belly. "*Buona serata,* signorina," I managed through a tight throat.

"Everything looks delicious, Franca," Bruno said. "I'll bring Laura."

I looked at Franca and lifted my hand toward the table. "I wish I would have known to give you some assistance."

She tsked her tongue. "I wanted to prepare the meal special for Laura. I can at least manage pasta and bread."

Birds squawked and whistled outside the window, much more at ease with what to say than I was. The sight of Franca so lovely had stolen my tongue completely.

Bruno and Laura soon returned. "*Buon compleano,* Laura," I said with a nod. She kissed me on each cheek, and the four of us sat at the table like friends, taking our time eating as if the tension of war was all a myth.

I breathed easier when I kept my gaze away from Franca's long, slender neck and amber eyes, but my will gave way time and again, and I caught myself glancing at how long and dark her lashes were and the way they swept the tops of her cheeks.

Bruno helped himself to a chunk of bread and dipped the corner in the olive oil that Franca had simmered with garlic and rosemary.

"Let me tell you a little bit about our family," Bruno said between bites of bread. "Marianna, Franca, Laura, and I were best friends growing up. We fished and played hide-and-seek and swam like dolphins in the sea together." He leaned over and kissed Laura on the top of her head.

Franca chuckled and grinned at the others, her eyes shining. "Yes, we swam for hours some days. By the time summer had ended, we were all brown as berries—"

"And Laura's hair was blonde as wheat from the sun," interjected Bruno.

Laura laid her hand over Franca's. "And Franca's hair was curly and wild as a mermaid's clear down her back."

"I am sure it was lovely," I blurted. I stiffened and clasped my hands together.

Everyone went quiet, and Franca's gaze was locked on the table. "Well that is enough reminiscing for now," she said, jumping to her feet.

I picked up some of the dishes and carried them to the sink for washing, hoping I would not drop any and that my face had not turned red. Franca gathered the platter and utensils.

Bruno extended his hand out to me as he ushered Laura toward the hallway. "Everything looks quiet outside. Join me in the parlor so we can visit more."

I did as he asked, disappointed but relieved to distance myself from Franca so my eyes would behave and I could breathe.

CHAPTER TWENTY-TWO
Franca

October 15, 1943

PETER CAME THROUGH THE KITCHEN door where I was churning butter the next day. His shirt looked freshly washed, and I noticed he had shaved his face clean. The scar on his cheek was pale and thin. Barely even noticeable.

"Signorina Franca," he said as I flinched and held the churn in my hands. "I—" He must have noticed the startled look on my face. He clasped his hands together. "If I may make a suggestion, Bruno and I discussed an idea last night that may help you with your fear of soldiers."

I set down the churn and punched down a bowl of bread dough, then lathered it with olive oil before I placed it in a pan to rise.

I turned and faced Peter. "I may always . . ." The fear he had named grew bigger and sparked a fire in my gut. I raised my voice, fed up with the guilt that churned underneath the fear and the way people discussed me behind my back. "Why am I the one who needs *help,* Peter Weimer? Mine is not an idle fear of soldiers. I do not trust enemy soldiers, and there is wisdom in that."

I stuttered on my words in spite of my resolve. "I do not trust because it is a known fact that the Ger—the Nazis cannot be trusted, that they have blindly followed Hitler and tried to take over the world by destroying everyone in their path. They have attacked, murdered, and imprisoned millions, even their neighbors for having Jewish ancestry, even if they were born in Germany. They—"

"I agree," Peter interjected over my tirade. "I agree with you about the Nazis. Although it is of significant importance that you had to stop yourself from saying *Germans* instead of *Nazis.* I know about the evil in Nazism. I lived under its control for far too long and saw evil that will haunt me for the rest of my life. That is why I walked away and defied it."

"I did not mean to throw all Germans in with Hitler. But Sicily was flooded with Nazis for years, and almost all of them were Germans. It all blurred together after a while."

"As I said, I cannot blame you. War obliterates trust. But I hope you will attempt to unblur the lines. Not all Germans are Nazis or bad people. I was a soldier. But I am not and never have been a Nazi. I never wanted to follow Hitler."

My shoulders stiffened a little. "Why did you then?"

"Why did your brother-in-law fight with Germany?"

"He had no choice. Mussolini made us join the Axis. They would have killed or imprisoned our family."

"And what do you assume the Nazis would have done to my family? I have a mother and a sister. Where would they be?"

I glanced down at the floor in thought and then raised my chin. "If so many Germans were against Hitler, then why did your people not stop him? I've heard about the parades, the thousands of Germans, the entire country cheering his name."

"By the time Hitler's evil nature had become obvious to most people, the Nazi party was too powerful to stop. Most had been fooled, many still are. The rest were or are outnumbered and outgunned by Hitler's followers and allies."

"You make yourself sound like a helpless victim."

"I am a man who made his choices, and some of them have been wrong. If God can ever forgive me, I hope to redeem myself, at least from all that is possible. It is why I help intercept information with Bruno for the partisans. It is why I listen to the radio also to find the man Keillor who could very well still be in Sicily. I will do my part to help the partisans and the Allies stop Hitler and pray I do not mow down others who were constrained into service like me."

The wooden bench creaked as I sat down. "What is your idea to help me?"

"If you would like, I will give you a bit of training on how to shoot a weapon tomorrow afternoon. It may help you defend yourself. Your sister and brother-in-law asked me to train you, to help protect your family if another attack were to happen."

"I do not own a weapon."

"Bruno said you may use his."

"Very well. I will ask him about it."

He watched me carefully as he spoke. "Yes. Please ask him so you may be at ease. We will have to go a little ways from the house for safety's sake. Ask Bruno if he is all right with that as well."

The sky was an azure sea of scattered clouds, and the birds who hopped and glided from scratchy bushes to the widespread branches of the trees called back and forth to one another.

Peter held the pistol in his hand as if it were effortless, so it surprised me when I took hold of it and my hand dropped under the weight. I raised it quickly and listened to Peter's instructions, worried that my ability would be no better with a weapon than it had been with driving an automobile.

"The dangers of war have made me realize how useless my skills in art and design truly are," I said.

"They will have their use in their own time. We will not always be at war."

"The entire world seems to show otherwise."

Peter paused a moment and lifted one eyebrow. "You do not always sound Italian in your speech or your accent."

"My mother is English. I suppose the woman who raises you has a big effect on how you speak."

He smiled. "I suppose so."

He'd gathered empty bottles from the cellar and placed them along some rocks in the distance. I was to hold the gun in one hand, support it with the other, and set my focus down the barrel.

The explosion of gunshots had my ears ringing and muffled as if the whole world floated underwater. Several bullets disappeared completely into the woods, and I had no idea where they may have landed. Peter Weimer played the teacher well and did not laugh at my bungling efforts. After a few more mishaps, he stepped closer to me, his face mere inches from mine as he helped me aim.

I tried several more shots, and Peter cleared his throat. "Signorina, I see at least one of the problems; just before you pull the trigger, you close your eyes."

Only a child would squeeze their eyes shut at the sound of a loud noise. I handed Peter the gun and covered my flaming cheeks with my hands. "I could use a break. Can we rest for a few moments?"

"Of course. Perhaps we could drink some water as well."

I stepped through tufts of grass and wildflowers and sat on a wide slab of limestone. I pulled a bottle of water and two apples from a bag I had brought along and handed an apple to Peter.

He had stretched out on the grass and leaned back on one elbow. He crunched down on the apple, and his jaw muscles tightened and flexed as he chewed and squinted into a sun that shone in his hair. He turned his head and caught me looking at him. I squared my shoulders, and he pointed at the apple still gripped tightly in my hand.

"You are not hungry, signorina?"

"This is not a picnic," I said.

He sat up. "Very well. What is it then?"

"Only food. Eating." I brushed imaginary crumbs from my lap. "I thought we may need nourishment for the training."

"Very well. I will be careful that I do not enjoy myself."

I bit the twitch in my lips and stared at his clothes. "I am curious. Where did you get that shirt and suspenders?"

He looked down at the change of clothing he wore and laughed out loud. "Giacomo had pity on me living in the same clothes—the ones Massimo gave me—day after day when I arrived, so he rummaged through some old clothing in the barn and donated them to me. God bless the sweet man."

The belly of the linen shirt hung loose on Peter. "This one even leaves me room to fatten myself." He laughed as he tugged on the fabric.

The shoulders almost fit, but the front of the shirt had been stretched. "One may have belonged to Mimmo De'Angelis's brother—Marianna's father. He had wide shoulders and a rounded belly."

Peter smiled at me. "Wider shoulders than me apparently."

I caught myself smiling back and frowned at the rocky ground when his jaw muscles flexed as he took another bite of apple.

"Do not fret. I will not eat too much," he said and stood to stretch his long legs.

He had obviously cut the bottoms of his pants off below the knee and laughed when he saw me glance at them. "The relative must not have been overly tall as I am. I cut off the bottoms of the pant legs. I preferred the look of knickers to just exposing my ankles."

The hair on his legs was as pale gold as that on his head. I caught myself staring and turned to the side, gazing at the low hills surrounding the De'Angelis farm. The air was cool but sticky, and my legs bounced restlessly.

If not for the Allied invasion in July, we would not even be here. Maybe Marianna never would have left for hospital work or to do whatever partisan activity she was a part of. She would not have been captured, Peter would not have rescued her and come here incognito, and I would not be here, staring off at the landscape to make my eyes stay away from a soldier.

"I am ready to try shooting again if you are," I said too loud as I stood.

Peter jumped to his feet. "*Facciamolo,* let us begin."

Shooting practice went more smoothly after our break. When the tension in my shoulders eased, the bullets actually hit a couple targets. But I was still frustrated with my slow progress and missed several in a row.

Peter leaned in to help me aim, and the scent of soap and fresh sweat rose up from his skin. It had a dizzying effect on me, and when he clasped one hand over the top of mine to guide my aim, I took a big step backward, lowering the gun to my side. "We have—I have learned enough."

"Are you unwell?"

"I am fine," I said, turning my chin and letting the breeze carry my words away. I watched from the corner of my eye as birds flew past and a starling swooped in to nibble at the apple core Peter had left on the ground.

I knew if I looked back, Peter would be watching me. I kept my head turned away.

The starling kept nibbling at the apple on the ground, lifting its head every few seconds to watch for predators. Peter stepped quietly in front of my view, his eyes deepened to the indigo of the Mediterranean.

"We can take another break. Whatever you wish or you need," he said so gently my muscles weakened all the way down to my toes.

"That is all for today," I managed.

Peter reached for the pistol. "You need more practice."

The breeze whipped my hair, and I pushed it back down with my free hand as he eased the gun from my fingers.

"I am willing to keep helping you, Franca," he said, the depth of his voice resonating with the low hum in the wind.

My breath shook a little. "That is enough help." I ran my hands down my side as if smoothing my billowing skirt. "I need to get back to my chores." I hurried toward the house without looking back.

CHAPTER TWENTY-THREE

Peter

I WATCHED FRANCA HURRY TO the house with a knot in my gut. I had frightened her, and it was the last thing I wanted to do.

Hiding in a barn for endless days after walking away from the pledges and vows I'd made with my army gave me nothing but time to condemn myself for every sin I had ever committed and to relive every moment of anger and horror I had experienced since the war began. But a beam of light cracked through darkness when I saw Franca Chessari for the first time on the day I'd arrived in Sortino.

Franca had a terrible shock the first time she saw me the day the Nazis attacked. But I had seen her every day for weeks through the slats of the barn wall and bales of hay. I'd listened to her frustrated groanings to a cow as she strived to be comfortable and successful at milking.

Watching her gave me a calm sense of belonging that paced right beside a stir of desire. A stir of desire that was spinning faster and faster now that we could spend time together.

The war had filled me with such horror I had forgotten about the grip in the belly and the way a heart could slam against a ribcage when a beautiful woman drew near. But this was not just any woman; Franca was young, unspoiled, and innocent, yet she exuded a power she was completely unaware of—the power to knock a man to his knees.

But all the begging in the world could not make her mine. She was not only the forbidden fruit, but she also forbad me to come near her. She was right to do so.

I had known the wonder of a woman in my arms and the pulse pounding beat of attraction. But this surpassed all others, and it pulled me in like a magnet.

I should resist. I should stay hidden and leave her be. We were all in the grips of a war that hardly lent us breath. A war that stole entire lives with the pull of a trigger. It could be over that fast. I'd seen it. I'd done it. Now I lay hidden in the hay and hoped God understood that I'd never wanted to pull a trigger. That every time I did, a part of my soul drained with that bullet.

And now I was endangering people again by hiding on this farm. The threat to Franca and her family hovered like a black cloud—they were sheltering me, and if the Allies knew, they would arrest them.

I saved Marianna and drove Franca's mother and Giacomo to the hospital, but this family was risking their safety every day by hiding me here. I owed them for that and had no idea how I could ever repay them. Helping with chores and listening on a radio seemed so trivial and useless, but I had to at least try until I could either find a way to help the partisans more actively or track down Keillor.

In the meantime, I had to keep myself in check with Franca Chessari.

CHAPTER TWENTY-FOUR
Franca

Bruno sat at the kitchen table as I burst through the door. He stopped buttering his bread. "*Madonna mia,* Franca. What is wrong?"

"Nothing, I was worried about you and Laura and the baby."

I splashed water on my face at the sink and washed my hands, still catching my breath.

Bruno scooted his bench back from the table and stared at me like I was *pazza.* "There is no need to hurry. I told you I am better. Luca is lying next to Laura asleep."

I avoided his eyes and grabbed at pots and pans, clanging them against the marble countertop, and I gathered the *farina,* salt, and a pitcher of water for making pasta. "I should start dinner then." The pitcher slipped in my hand and spilled a bit over the top. I wiped at it quickly with a rag.

Bruno stood and leaned at the end of the table, his stare slowly making me uneasy. He cleared his throat. "You seem so flustered. Were you with Peter just now?"

I poured the flour from the sack into a pyramid-shaped pile and used my hands to open a hole in the top for the water and salt. "Yes, but only briefly. He showed me how to shoot. I have no idea where he is now."

"Why is your face so red?"

I moved more quickly. "I told you I hurried back, remember?" I sprinkled salt and poured water into the flour pyramid and a stream of water missed the opening and trickled down the sides.

His voice grew more insistent. "Your face is redder now than it was when you got here. It became redder when I asked you about Peter."

I shrugged and stirred the flour into the salty water with my hands. "I do not know what you are talking about."

"Yes, you do." He hobbled up closer to me, his face pinched. "How much time are you spending with Peter?"

"I hardly see him."

"Maybe you *see* him too much."

I would not look at him. "Bruno, you are being ridiculous. And you and Laura are the ones insisting that he help with chores and teach me to shoot."

"Franca, you know how dangerous it would be for you to become involved with a German, no? The partisans shave the heads of the women who get involved with any Germans, whether they are Nazi or not. They strip and beat the women."

I gasped. "Then how are the partisans any better than a Nazi?"

"Most are good and fight for our country. But some partisans are ruffians. And you know that after two major wars, there are many people with no forgiveness for the Germans."

I moved the lumpy dough to the marble slab by the stove and kept kneading it to keep myself from looking at Bruno.

"Listen to me, Franca. I know Peter is a good man. But I just found out through the radio that Italy officially declared war against Germany two days ago on October 13th. We have officially changed sides against the Nazis. No matter what Peter did for Marianna and our family or how much he helps with the chores, do not get involved with or too close to a German soldier; it could put all of us in danger. We can shelter him until he finds his way, but that is all."

I spun around to face him, my breath short, my chin up. "I am not involved with or close to him. He was teaching me to shoot . . . and nothing more happened."

"Do not let yourself even think about it. Your father would forbid it, and your mother would see you as unfaithful to your own family, country, and even her English ancestry. The Allies have taken over Sicily, but we are still in the middle of this war. You cannot even flirt with someone considered an enemy."

I threw my hands in the air. "*Basta,* Bruno. I already said it was you and Laura who suggested he teach me how to use a weapon. There has been no flirting as you say. I hear your worries already. I told you, I have done nothing inappropriate with him."

The kitchen door opened, and Peter entered. Bruno said hello to him, and I spun back around and kept my focus on the pasta I was making until I could not take the tension of Bruno looking back and forth between me and Peter anymore.

Laura called my name from the bedroom, and I slapped the dough down on the slab to rise. "*Va bene,* there is Laura." I forced myself to walk rather than scurry from the room.

Bruno's words burned. But they held truth. I'd had my life threatened by the Nazis—I'd seen them attack the charity group I ran with Marianna. They had stormed the city dance and pointed their rifles in our faces for hanging the Italian flag. And they had shot my mother and Giacomo before my eyes. The memory punched me in the stomach every time I relived it.

I would not let childish gratitude for Peter's help confuse me or create a giddy girlishness around him. He had gotten close to me for shooting practice, and I'd become uncomfortable.

My defiance grew as the minutes ticked. Thankfully, Peter kept to himself for the rest of the day. When he did come back inside the house, I stiffened and looked up at him from the kitchen table. "Thank you for helping me learn to shoot a weapon. But you need to go back to the barn and stay there. No more helping."

He set an armload of wood by the stove and looked back at me. "I did not know I was a prisoner here."

I stood up. "You are not a prisoner, and I do not mean to be rude. I am grateful. But I just feel that—"

"I know what you feel."

"I do not know what you mean."

"Yes, you do."

We stood there looking at each other, and my chest rose and fell at an increasing rate.

Peter's gaze finally softened. "No one in this room is at war, signorina."

My shoulders slumped in defeat for a brief second as I looked at him.

"You are safe with me. You were safe with me earlier today," he said.

My pulse rose in my throat. "I must have been affected by the sun and the excitement of finally learning to shoot."

"You ran."

"I wanted to hurry and tell my sister, Laura, that I could shoot."

He placed his hands in his pockets, his face sober. "Call it what you need to, Franca."

My belly did a flip when he said my name. I turned my head a little and straightened my shoulders. "I do not need any more weapons lessons. In fact, I would prefer that I did all the chores myself. I am uncomfortable because of—"

"Fear," he interrupted.

"Differences that are impossible to ignore."

"I am aware of our differences."

I gripped the edge of the table with my hand. "Yes, they make me upset, and I would rather . . . I need to work alone. You need to go. The um . . . cellar or the barn would be all right."

Peter looked at my hand where I clutched the table.

"I would never do anything to harm you or your family."

I stood taller and locked my knees in place. "I know. Thank you. But please, just go."

His brows lowered. "Very well then. It looks as though you really do prefer to do everything yourself. I will leave you to do so."

He turned abruptly and walked out the back door.

CHAPTER TWENTY-FIVE

Franca

A FEW DAYS PASSED, AND Peter did not assist me with any of the chores. Bruno's leg had swelled again when he tried to move much, so I had to do everything myself.

I was being ridiculous. I knew it, and I knew Peter did too. I only saw him in brief glimpses when I gave him food in the barn. When I milked Rosa and slopped the hogs, he stayed behind the bales of hay or walked out of the barn in silence.

The days blurred into one another. I kept Luca beside me at night as I slept, too tired to carry him to his bed or to sit up to feed him. Thankfully he peacefully drank his bottles in the blackness of night as I cuddled him.

It was hard to see in the mornings. My eyes refused to accept the sunrise and fully open. I used a wrap to strap Luca to my back and walked like the dead from one chore to the next.

"Franca, you are so pale," Laura said one morning.

"I guess I should spend more time in the garden so the sun can give me a little color in my cheeks," I replied.

"I am so sorry I cannot do more. Bring me any darning you need or let me sort through the fruit and vegetables in the basket or peel potatoes. You and Peter do the work of five servants."

Guilt nagged at me. I had kept my ostracizing of Peter a secret from Laura. She and Bruno had no idea how much I was doing myself, and I was worried my fatigue might give me away.

"I must say that I miss our dear Alma every day. I could use some of her cooking," I said a little too brightly.

"You make jokes, but I know you are tired and hurting."

I sat beside her on the bed. "Laura, can you tell me of one person you know who is not tired and hurting?"

Her eyes filled with tears. "I suppose not. We just have to stay brave and keep fighting."

A familiar rustle and the click of a crutch smacking rhythmically on wood came from the hallway. Bruno entered the room, his brow lowered as if he were frustrated. He plopped down with his back to us at the radio in the corner, the back of his hair flattened and askew from lying in bed so much. He propped his injured leg on a chair. The side of the radio had been opened and he fiddled with knobs and wires.

A loud pop made me jump. Bruno slapped his hands down on the table in frustration. "I tell you I am tired of fighting this radio. It keeps going out on me this morning." Bruno turned toward me. "So what is this I hear from Peter? That he has not been helping you with the chores because you refused to let him?"

I lifted my chin in spite of my hesitation. "I said that I could do the chores on my own."

Laura gasped. "Franca, *come mai?* You must have him help you."

Bruno grabbed his crutch and stood up. "I am going to talk to him right now about the radio. Laura, you try to talk some sense into your sister."

Laura's lips were dry, and her blonde hair lay limp on her pillow. I kissed her cheek. "Do not worry yourself about the chores or Peter Weimer. All is well."

My sister surprised me and sat up against the headboard, staring me down. "It is time you told me the truth about what is going on, Francesaca Chessari. Why are you refusing to let Peter help you?"

I closed my eyes and opened my mouth, determined to push all concerns out the window.

"No," Laura said, sitting up straighter and gripping the bedspread in her hands. "You will not push my concerns away and put on an act like everything is fine. I am fed up with that. I know that you put on a show for me every time you walk in this room to keep my anxiety at bay. But I know how difficult our circumstances are, I know how sick and weak I am, and how injured and at risk my husband is. Stop pretending to be my nursemaid and just be my sister. Do not lie to me anymore."

I covered my eyes with my hands and let out a loud, long breath to loosen the knot that had wedged itself in my throat. "I am trying to do the right things, Laura. Everyone needs me, and the war is suffocating me with its power and control. I cannot win no matter what I do, and having a German around is difficult. You know how afraid of them we have always been. Having Peter try to help just made things worse."

"Yes, we have seen the worst of things from the Nazis and have been through terrifying times. But I can see by the look in your eyes and the way you and Peter tried not to look at each other at my birthday dinner that fear is not the problem. There is only one reason that Peter's help could make things this difficult. You have attraction for one other."

"I do not, and it is impossible that he would."

"I told you not to lie to me. Now I am telling you not to lie to yourself. You are young, but you are a woman, Franca. Peter is a handsome and strong man. It is only natural that you would develop some attraction, even though it is dangerous and forbidden because he is German. Perhaps that even makes it worse."

"I have done nothing wrong. You want him to work beside me but how is that proper for the two of us to be off and alone?"

"I am sure you have done nothing wrong and what you are saying is true. But we are at war and desperate for help. We have been taught well; you can will yourself to work beside Peter and ignore the rest or refuse to let it get the best of you. Do not worry. The war will end, and then our men will return in droves, and you will have your pick. This will pass, and Peter will find his way to Germany. All will be well."

Laura's words hung like a weight around my neck when I left the room. The past few days away from Peter had not lessened my awareness of him. I had watched for him against my will, expecting to see him come around a corner to help me lift the buckets of water to feed the animals. Or to insist on milking Rosa when he heard me curse under my breath. The truth was that as much as it made my heart quiver to be around Peter, he also calmed me, strengthened me—as if the chaos and fears in my head hushed and fell into place.

But he was German. It was wrong of me to remember the way the sun highlighted his hair—the pressure and breathlessness in my chest when he stood close to me. Guilt fed on my thoughts and chewed at my nerves, but it had not helped the itch that lived under my skin.

Laura was right; I had to ignore it and refuse to let it get the best of me. In fact, I resented it greatly. I was working night and day to do what was needed and right, and these nagging interruptions were an inexcusable nuisance. But the weakness in my legs when Peter put his hand over mine to help me aim the pistol made me doubt I was the pillar of strength my sister believed me to be. I had to keep my distance if I was to keep my focus.

I entered the kitchen with doubts about my capability but still resolved to continue the chores alone.

The sight of the dishes I'd been too exhausted to wash the night before came into view, and the mound of laundry on the floor next to the stove taunted me.

First things first, the animals needed tending.

Marianna's aunt and uncle had their menagerie of animals stripped down to just Rosa, two pigs, and a brood of chickens when the Nazis had taken over. It made my job lighter but still not easy. Slopping the remaining two pigs was the biggest chore. They stood almost as tall as the walls of their pen and stuck their noses over the top to grunt at me if I passed without feeding them.

Slopping pigs appeared simple when Giacomo and my brothers did it. But filling and lifting the buckets of grains for the pigs and Rosa was not easy. Neither were the trips back and forth hauling the water. But I'd managed it each day since I'd ostracized Peter from helping and grit my teeth against the throbbing in my back and shoulders.

I headed toward the pigpen with a bucket of rotting fruit, vegetables, and table scraps as the sky darkened to a menacing black. The wind whisked around the trees and howled like a wolf, whipping my clothes and hair to and fro. I leaned over the pigpen to pour the slop in the long, wooden trough and lost my grip. The bucket bounced and rolled behind both sows. I had no choice but to retrieve it.

An earlier deluge of rain had turned the pen into a gravy of dung and mud. I hoisted my skirt up before I climbed carefully but quickly into the pen, thankful for the work boots that spared my feet. The mud sucked at my boots as I made my way to the bucket, and one of the sows squealed in alarm and slammed into my backside with her powerful snout. I fell forward and sunk down on my belly and panicked because the sow was right behind me and outweighed me by plenty. I grabbed hold of the bucket and scrambled over the top of the pen, landing on the rain-soaked ground. Out of breath and dripping, I ran off for the well, groaning in disgust with my lips closed for fear the manure that had splattered my face would dribble into my mouth.

If Bruno had seen me, he would have laughed, no doubt my little brothers would have too. But I silently cursed the sows and gritted my teeth in frustration.

I made it to the well and pulled up two buckets of cold water just as the sky opened its belly and poured sheets of rain from blackened clouds. I poured the chilly water over myself to rinse the nastiness from my face, clothes, boots, and hands, and then filled the buckets with fresh water again. My skirt and blouse stuck to me, my boots squashed water with each step, and I shivered with cold.

Whatever remnants of the pigpen remained on my clothes was washing away in the deluge of rain.

The weight of the buckets pulled on my shoulder muscles like I'd strapped a boulder to each arm as I headed back to water the pigs. I'd only made it halfway when the cramps in my arms made me stop to rest.

Thunder cracked like a cannon in the sky. I had to hurry and get back inside the house. My feet slipped and slid in the mud like I was a baby learning to walk. I blew my hair out of my eyes the best I could but missed seeing a hole in the ground until my foot had slipped inside and my ankle twisted. I sat flat and fell back with the weight of the buckets until I lay on my back. Pellets of rain pummeled my face.

I decided to stay there. The buckets had already spilled, poured down the slope of the yard like it had somewhere to go. Providence had won. No wonder I could not fight in the resistance like Marianna; I could not even feed animals and take care of four people—and one of them was a baby.

The rain, warm when it first hit my clothing, turned cold as is soaked through the layers and the wind seeped through. The ache in my ankle grew to a stabbing pain, refusing to let me get up. I wanted to surrender and sink into the mud. I covered my eyes with my arm.

I remembered Marianna's courage and faith and made myself say a prayer. "God, my family needs me. If you exist and you will spare my ankle, I promise to light one hundred candles the next time I pass a church." The rain poured harder and tried to run up my nose and under my eyelids. I covered my face with my hands and pursed my lips against the throb in my ankle.

I pulled my hands away from my face in surprise when someone lifted my leg and gently probed at my ankle. I knew it was Peter the minute he touched me—but I was too exhausted to jerk my leg away, too defeated to lift my head out of the mud and too pitiful to argue. The rain pounded on his back as he knelt over me. I had no strength left to fight him. The rain had eased just enough to let my voice be heard.

"Tell me, Peter, do you trust that God exists?"

He did not answer me. He lay my leg down, put his hand under my shoulders, and lifted me to a sitting position. I had never been drunk before, but this must be what it felt like, what giving up felt like anyway—lethargy, limp muscles, dizziness, the urge to laugh hysterically and cry uncontrollably at the same time, the lack of will to climb out of a muddy hole.

I did not protest until he tried to lift me in his arms. I kicked my legs and cried out in pain when it jerked my ankle. I looked through my dripping hair at Peter, his face so close I could see each raindrop as it splattered on his skin and ran down through the whiskers that darkened his jaw. My head swam with the urge to lay my head against his shoulder.

"I asked God for a miracle, so if He wants His candles lit in a cathedral the next time I am in town, He will heal my leg so I can walk."

Peter looked straight ahead as if I had not said a word and stalked through the rain across the muddy ground like I weighed no more than a sack of *farina.*

My breath was short. "This is not appropriate."

"This is not a picnic, Franca. We are at war, remember?"

"You do not understand."

He exhaled as he shook his head. "I understand enough."

With that, the rain died down, but Peter did not say a word or look at me. He plopped me down on a bench in the kitchen when we reached the house. He pulled the tub out and set it on the floor in front of me with a thump against the wood floor and walked back outside, slamming the door behind him. I sat on the bench, my clothes and hair dripping water on the floor. I finally rubbed at my sore ankle.

Peter stomped back in five minutes later and poured two buckets of water into the tub. He grabbed a hunk of soap and a towel and tossed them onto the table beside me and headed down the hall. Five minutes later, he came back and tossed a dress and chemise onto the table, and I blushed when I realized he had handled my underclothes.

He scowled at me. "You are acting foolish in your crusade to be some kind of hero and do everything yourself. I will not stand by any longer. I am going to help you no matter your feelings about me or what you say. If you are uncomfortable as I work, you need not speak to me at all."

I pushed my dripping hair out of my face. "I am not feeling anything about you. I am Italian and you are Na—German. I thank you for helping me into the house, but there is no reason for further discussion or speaking at all."

His face had turned red. "Very well. No discussions, no talking."

He turned as if an army officer had given him an order and marched out of the house. I waited until the sound of his footsteps faded and then bathed so quickly I could not be sure that I'd washed all the mud from my hair. But Peter did not return.

CHAPTER TWENTY-SIX

Franca

I WOKE WELL BEFORE ANY light showed on the horizon the next morning and slipped into the kitchen to start my chores before Peter could awake. His determination to help me with chores put me on edge, and I had to be sure to outwork him to keep him at bay. I'd tossed back and forth in my bed with dreams and worries about my mother and with despair that my father had been gone so long. Before the attack in the kitchen, Bruno was able to track Papa down through the radio, but there had been no recent word. Something terrible must have happened to him on his way to or coming back from our northern vineyard.

I owed God a hundred candles. My ankle was painful, and I had a slight limp, but I could get around.

Luca fussed and interrupted my attempts to fix breakfast. I tried to make coffee while Luca screamed, straddled on my hip, and my ankle spiked pain up my leg.

Peter came through the kitchen door, a bucket of milk in his hand. He set it next to the sink without saying a word.

The sound of an axe splitting wood over and over went on. Peter carried the pieces of wood to a pile by the back door. The pile grew so large we would not need any more for a month.

I took Luca with me to feed the animals and saw that Peter had mucked out Rosa's stall and slopped the pigs. In the next few days, he repaired a leak in the roof, carried Laura from her room to the parlor and back to give her breaks, cleaned the chicken coop, washed some of the dishes and even did laundry, all without uttering one word to me. Even if I'd wanted to thank him, the stern look on his face stopped me.

It freed me to help Laura bathe and to clean the bed linens and Luca's nappies. It gave me time to cook better meals, work in the garden, and to hold

Luca when Laura needed a nap. I even had time to give him fresh air outside on walks.

But in the next few days, the silence from Peter had become so loud I wanted to scream. He followed or assisted me at every task without uttering a word or looking in my direction. Tension stayed coiled around my chest.

Peter changed Luca's diaper in the bedroom while I was helping Laura bathe in the kitchen.

I passed him in the hallway later. "Chores are one thing, but you do not need to change Luca's—"

He kept walking and looked away as if he had no interest in a word I had to say. My face burned.

At times I forced myself to utter a brief thank-you, but Peter never replied.

Bruno stayed busy with the radio, and Peter stayed beside him at times, especially at night when some of the transmissions came through in German. I overheard him tell Bruno of his frustrations that nothing about Keillor's location had come through and his hope that it meant Keillor had been killed or vanished. But I did not dare ask him about it myself.

Thankfully Laura and Bruno did not notice, or perhaps they even approved of the silence between me and Peter. At least they did not comment. My nerves stayed on edge around Peter no matter the lack of speaking or my defiance, and when he held Luca gently and nuzzled his cheeks, my legs went weak again, and I had to close my eyes.

Rain poured again three days later. The pigpen flooded, and the sows snorted with joy and pranced in the mud. By midday, the rain stopped and the pigs had stirred the muck into thick clay that came up to their bellies and locked them in place. I found a shovel in the barn and dug at the mud from over the fence to set them free. But I had no leverage. I swung my legs over the side of the pen and sat atop the fence, but it still wasn't enough. I laid a long board beside them and climbed inside, kneeling on the board and working at the pig's legs one at a time. They swung their heads around and grunted and squealed at me. I stood up on the board and the bigger of the two knocked me behind the knees. I toppled over the top of the other pig.

Peter came up beside the pen with a wheelbarrow full of hay and shoveled heaps of it into the pen. He climbed in. I managed to stand up and continue shoveling at the mud around the pigs while he worked at getting each of their legs free and settled on the dry hay.

By the time we had finished, the pigs were free, and I was covered in muck up to my waist and up my arms to my shoulders. Peter had worked beside me in silence, and I was too exhausted to complain.

I was overwhelmed by my tasks, and we both knew it. I bit back tears all the way to the well where I rinsed myself off. Peter washed himself too, the mud streaming from his hands and clothes, his shirt clinging to his skin.

When we both finished, I had no patience for the silence anymore. "*Grazie* . . . for the assistance," I said and tried to look in his eyes.

He walked away without saying a word, without even a nod of his head.

"I said, *grazie,*" I called out to his retreating back.

He kept walking, never missing a step.

I poured myself a full, warm bath in a deep tin bathtub in the bedroom downstairs. Heating pots of water on the stove was a painstaking task, but the results were worth it. I'd let a bar of lavender soap soak and scent the water, and I slipped beneath the surface and scrubbed at my hair. I used a rough cloth and scoured my skin until it was pink all over and shampooed my hair. Then I leaned against the back of the tub and let my tears drip into the water.

All I had dreamed of as a young girl was going to Paris and immersing myself in the world of fashion design. Our mother had taught us some of her native English, but I'd studied French all through school. Now those pursuits were so trivial. I wanted my life to mean more, and I wanted to take a stand for what was right, but there was nothing I could do but nurse my sick family and keep a neglected farm going.

I closed my eyes and pictured my family before the war, our elegant villa and the rolling countryside of Sicily. The vision darkened and blood ran down her streets. All the dreams and wishing in the world, or protesting in my head, could not make the world safe again.

I wiped my tears with the washcloth and let my thoughts cross over the forbidden line to Peter. My muscles went limp, and more tears welled in my eyes. My unfriendliness toward him was not my fault. The Germans had hovered over and threatened our lives for years. I did not invite Peter here to my country. The coldness of his demeanor came back fresh in my mind—the day after day silence and underlying disapproval. It chipped away at my resolve and threw fuel on my frustration. And there seemed nothing I could do about it.

The next morning, I grabbed a basket from the kitchen and headed outside to gather the eggs. The rooster charged at me with his usual fury, his spurs aimed at my legs. Peter rounded the corner with a wide broom in his hand, roared like a bear, and charged back at the rooster. "*Scio, scio!* Shoo, go on!" he hissed as he waved the broom. The rooster squawked and ran the other direction.

I placed one hand on my hip and glared at Peter. He furrowed his brow as he stared back at me. And all reason snapped. I slammed the basket down on the ground. "You say more when you growl at a rooster than you have said to me in days."

Peter grunted and threw up his hand. "That is because the rooster listens to me."

"Maybe the rooster is wrong. Even *stupido.*"

"Because he listens to a German?"

"Because he does not realize he does not have to. He can stand his ground."

"What ground, Franca? What is so superior about your ground?"

I kicked the basket in his direction, and it landed at his feet. "Nothing, except that I never shot a woman and killed an old man in a kitchen. I never tried to take over a country."

"Neither did I."

"Your army did! Your . . ." I pointed at him. "Your uniform did. I see it in my nightmares."

"I do not wear that uniform, and it is not my army anymore. It never was. Not the Nazi army."

"I still see it."

"Then you are blind."

I fisted my hands and raised my voice. "Maybe I like being blind. Heaven knows my family thinks that I am—that I am not capable. Even you see me as inept. But no matter my imperfections, it is not my fault that we are at war and we are enemies." I brushed some hair out of my face and blinked back tears. "So, you can keep gathering eggs, chop wood, or change all the diapers you want as long as you still stay away from me. I will just be in the barn—shoveling dung."

Peter growled and kicked the basket back my direction. "The only war you and I are fighting is the one in your head."

I swallowed a sob, reached down, and grabbed the basket, then stomped off full speed for the barn.

I sensed rather than heard him marching up behind me, his footsteps moving faster than mine. I quickened my pace and made it through the barn doors with him right on my heels and my heart pounding like a deer on the run. He caught up and grabbed my hand, pulling me around to face him. I glared at him, ready to reach out and fight if I had to.

He backed me against the wall until his face was just inches away. "Stop," he said.

I looked at him, wide-eyed and flushed. "I cannot stop."

"Yes, you can. We both can."

I tried to steady my breathing, but I stared at him one second too long. He leaned toward me until our faces almost touched.

"No one is an enemy in this moment, Franca. I do not know who I am anymore. Maybe no one knows who they are. But I am never going to hurt you or your family or your country." He placed his hand against the barn wall right next to my cheek and slowed his breathing. "I am not your enemy."

I locked my stare with his, his eyes just inches from mine. "We are at war. You may not have a choice but to hurt people again. You said so yourself." My voice quivered.

"I have made my choice. I made it that day when I saved your friend Marianna. I am never going back to the Nazis."

"I do not believe you."

He paused a moment and then whispered, "Yes, you do."

His face was too close, his breath too warm on my skin, but I could not make myself move.

The floor became unsteady beneath my feet.

And Bruno called my name from the house.

CHAPTER TWENTY-SEVEN

Franca

Sleep eluded me for two days. Dreams of drowning and being pulled from the water made me wake with a jolt when I nodded off.

Restlessness streamed through my veins all day, especially when I caught glimpses of Peter. I could not continue going this way and still keep things from "getting the best of me" like Laura had suggested. I did not want her and Bruno to know about the confrontation in the barn—about the way Peter had drawn so close to me his breath brushed my lips and cheeks.

A constant sense of urgency kept my nerves jumping. Perhaps I needed to join the partisans, to take a stand, to be in charge of at least part of my life.

I watched for Peter from the corner of my eye as we each did our chores. He kept his distance and assisted without stepping in my way. When our paths crossed, I stopped breathing, managed a small smile, but did not dare let my gaze linger.

Two days later, Peter stopped me in the yard. "I would be willing to help you with more target practice."

I looked at him warily. "I am not sure it is a good idea."

"I honestly wish to make sure you can defend yourself. I have no other motive."

"I want to defend myself and my family but—"

"I am your friend, Franca. Nothing more."

The band around my chest eased. "Very well."

The morning had been so busy I realized I had not eaten or set anything out for Peter. I grabbed a basket, threw bread, cheese, and apples inside, and filled a jar with fresh water to go out and brave another target practice. I told Laura where Peter and I were going instead of telling Bruno so I would not have to see the concern is his eyes or endure another warning.

We traveled farther from the farm this time to more open spaces so I could practice hitting targets at greater distance.

Sloping green and rocky terrain widened before us, but I found myself looking for the long, neat rows of grapevines in our vineyard that lay just forty-eight kilometers away. So close and yet our father had insisted it was not safe there. I longed to inhale the fruity air that diffused with the saltiness of the Mediterranean.

Jackdaws fluttered their black wings and chattered nonstop like squeaky wheels needing to be oiled. They peeked out at Peter and me through the foliage, their eyes as pale and silvery as summer skies.

Whispering breezes replaced the usual calls for help from my family that filled my days. I hurried down a hill, exhilarated as the pump of fresh oxygen filled my breast.

I placed the basket of food on the ground just as Peter caught up with me. I had made up my mind to be friendlier, but the confrontation in the barn left me floundering for words. Peter looked down at the food and took the rifle from his shoulder, propping it against a tree.

I sat down on a thatch of grass beside the basket and buoyed myself for an attempt at casual conversation. "You have not eaten today so I brought you some food. It is the least I can do to thank you for training me to defend myself."

"There is no need to thank me. You and your family have given me shelter and freedom. I will always be in your debt."

"You saved Marianna and my mother."

He sat down a few feet away, and I leaned over and handed him a napkin with a chunk of bread and cheese.

"Then I guess we are eternally in each other's debt," he said with a smile. I flinched at the wave of intimacy his words conveyed, and Peter sobered. "Thank you for the meal, signorina. It is a nice day for eating outside."

"Yes. I just saw several butterflies swish by. No doubt on their way to gather nectar. The butterflies in Germany also drink nectar, no?"

Peter chuckled. "Yes, they do. Maybe our countries are not so different after all."

The butterflies in my belly settled a bit. "It would be nice to hear about your life, Peter Weimer. Your family, your childhood, anything."

"Maybe it is better to talk about other things."

"Why?" I wrapped a piece of bread around some cheese. "Is there a secret you do not want me to know?"

"You still do not trust me."

"I am curious as to why you hesitate to talk about your family."

"My family is fine. They are good." He stretched out his legs.

"Then why do you not want to talk about them?"

"I am from Germany. Born and raised there. I know that is not a good setting for telling anyone here my stories."

I reached in the basket for a piece of bread. "Give me a chance. My worries are because of war, not your family."

He hesitated for a minute. "My family is small. Because of the death of my baby brother, there is only me and my younger sister, Bettina, and our mother. My father passed away just a few years ago."

"I am sorry to hear that. Did he die in the war?"

"No, he died in an accident. He worked building the railway through the mountains. It was very dangerous, but he worked safely day after day. And then an accident on our own property took him."

My eyes widened. "How devastating. What happened?"

"Maybe we should do your shooting practice in case your family calls for you."

"We both need to eat, and Luca is napping, so I have some time. Tell me about your father and what happened."

Peter finished the bread and cheese and brushed off his hands.

"Very well." He picked up a small rock and held it in his hand, rubbing the dirt and gravel away with his fingers before he began. "The summer before the war began, my friend August and I returned from school. My father needed help building a new barn. August and I cut trees from my family's land and used the horses to pull the logs. Our horses were Belgians and very powerful. We worked for hours one day and pulled the last load home.

"The rain had soaked the ground into muddy glue that latched onto our boots as we walked. The horses stomped their way through it, but my father's foot sunk deep in a mud hole, and he fell back. It only startled the horses a bit, but just as my father made his way back on his feet, a fox dashed around between the horses' legs, and they panicked. My father grabbed onto their bridles to hold them steady, but they reared up, and he went flying up with them. The Belgians are so tall my father was several feet off the ground. He lost his grip, and when he fell, he landed against a big rock that smashed into his side. A rib must have pierced one of his lungs or his heart. He died within minutes." Peter's voice had slowed and thickened as he spoke, the rims of his eyes red.

"How terrible for your family. I am so sorry," I managed to whisper.

"You are very familiar with shock and loss, Franca." He gestured through the trees toward the house. "That attack on you and your family in the kitchen. I do know why you would fear Germans."

I rubbed my fingers over my brow and closed my eyes.

"But maybe one day you will not fear me," Peter added, his voice softer.

I opened my eyes but kept my focus on the rock that he smoothed in his hand. The birds quieted a moment, and I took a deep breath. "Like I said before, the Nazis and Germans blurred together when they moved into Sicily. I never thought there was a difference." When I got the nerve to lift my gaze, I found Peter Weimer watching me. The winds ceased, and the sun grew hot on my shoulders. A ground squirrel behind Peter scurried up a tree and darted under a leafy branch. I took a deep breath. "Tell me more about you or your family. What happened after you lost your father?"

Peter took the apple I offered from the basket and took a bite, swallowing and pausing before he answered. "I was injured the same day we lost my father. When he fell, I ran over and grabbed the horse's bridles so they would calm down and not trample him, but the biggest one knocked me down, and I fell back in the mud. He reared again and when he came down his front hoof smacked down on my leg. I heard the snap of the bone in my thigh before the pain exploded."

Peter pulled up the pant leg on the pants he wore, and I winced when he showed me a long deep scar above his right knee.

"The doctors had to do surgery and cast my leg. It ended up delaying my enlistment to military duty. Several months later, when my leg had regained most of its strength, I joined."

The vision of Peter in uniform, shooting and throwing grenades with Hitler's army chilled the wind. I rubbed my hands up and down my arms.

The Italians could make no claims to greater wisdom or valiance than the German people who had been lured in by Hitler—Mussolini had fooled the majority of my people in the beginning as well. There was no way I could lay blame or make accusations without taking much of the shame for myself. And Peter had never thrown the follies of the Italians in my face when I pointed out the blind support the Germans gave Hitler.

"You are so young and yet you have at least two painful scars," I finally managed.

Peter grimaced and rubbed at the long thin scar that ran down his cheek. "I am twenty-four years old. And are you referring to this? This scar did not come from battle either. At least not a battle in the field."

"You got that scar before military service also?"

"No, this one was a gift from a true Nazi, a man with a personal vendetta against me that he may end up finally fulfilling someday."

"One of your fellow soldiers did that?" I asked, astonished.

"One of my 'superiors,'" he said, shaking his head in disgust.

I gasped. "Why? How could an officer do such a thing?"

"Evil comes easily to some. But that is a story for another day."

The clouds cast moving shadows on the ground. I clasped my hands together. "So, we have been brought together by evil men who have made you and I enemies to one another."

"You are not my enemy, Franca Chessari. You never could be. And no matter my scars or mileage, I am thankful we have been brought together."

I tried to ignore the pulse that pounded in my throat at his words and brushed my windblown hair back out of my eyes. I placed the water jar and napkins back in the basket to keep my hands busy.

"Did you know those soldiers who came here and attacked us?" My throat tightened while I waited for his answer.

"No." He stood and walked just a couple steps in front of me. "I did not know them at all."

I exhaled in relief that he hadn't known the evil soldiers who'd attacked us, but his proximity started warning whistles blowing again. My eyes darted to the side, but Peter reached out his hand to help me to my feet. I hesitated before accepting his hand, breathing easier when he took a step back as soon as I'd stood.

"Do you know what I do when I am not helping you with chores, Franca?"

"You help Bruno with the radio, no?"

"Yes, I listen in on the radio with Bruno for any transmissions in German. I spy on my own people. I have even transmitted false messages to flush out Axis soldiers or spies. I listen for German military plans, locations, any dirty information I can find so I can turn it over to complete strangers in the American OSS or any other Allied officer who snatches it up. I stab a knife in the back of my fellow soldiers and my whole country every day."

"You are trying to stop Hitler. There is no shame in that. It is not wrong."

"It does not change the fact that I am a traitor to my country. My actions may expose good German soldiers, others who are against Hitler's tyranny. Maybe even my friends who are decent people. My friends, Franca—lifelong friends I grew up with, August and Dieter, who are out there somewhere in the midst of the chaos. I could get them killed. If what I am doing is not wrong, does that make it right?"

"Right and wrong are scrambled together."

"Heaven and hell are scrambled together," he said with a grimace.

"Marianna told me that when she thought she had lost Massimo forever, she realized there was more than one way to die in this war, but there is more than one way to live in it. You can keep your humanity, or you can let evil destroy you."

"I am not sure where my humanity lies anymore."

"Have you caused any deaths for Germans?"

"There is no way to know."

"Can you ask anyone about your friends?"

"The chances are very slim. Your father may know bits and pieces because of the work he does, but he would not know my friends by name. There are too many thousands of soldiers."

"The work my father does?"

"Yes, for the resistance. Bruno said he had told you about the radio and your family's involvement. You have heard nothing of your father, his partisan work?"

I knew my mother had contact with Papa through the radio at the house but not that he helped with the resistance. "I thought Bruno and my mother were just helping the local rebels." My eyes widened. "Papa is up in the north to work and protect our other vineyard. I know nothing of him being involved with the resistance."

"It may make your family unhappy that I told you."

My face and ears burned with anger at Bruno. After all I had said to him, after his promise to me about honesty and openness in our family, he had kept this vital information from me. Paolo Chessari was my father, not his. He had no right to keep this a secret from me while demanding that I toe a line with Peter according to his dictation. I fisted my hands in the pockets of my skirt.

"I do not care if it makes them unhappy. I want to know everything that you know, Peter. However, if Bruno told you about my father in confidence, I will not tell him you let it slip and expose you to his disapproval. You must not risk your safety in hiding here."

"Your brother-in-law never said that it was a secret. I do not share the same beliefs as your family—lack of information does not keep one protected. And I do not see you as a little sister. You are far more capable and brave than they realize, a woman who is fighting her way through the war like everyone else."

"I am fed up with being protected."

Peter reached out and pushed a loose tendril of my hair back behind my ear. "Perhaps your father demanded that his work be a secret. I cannot blame your family. I know I want you safe, Franca."

The brush of his fingers on my ear made me tremble, but I fought to keep my focus.

"I am glad you let it slip about my father. I cannot comprehend why I did not see it. Maybe I am as weak and blind as my family sees me."

"I have certainly seen your strength. I am supposed to be the fearsome one, and yet you have managed to lock me in a cellar and order me around since we met."

He smirked, and I could not contain a guilty chuckle.

A slow breeze stirred up again and seeded the air with the scent of damp earth and greenery. It lifted and lowered a tree branch overhead in a steady rhythm and blew Peter's hair across his forehead.

I put my hand over the tug in my stomach.

The tree branch lifted again, and the sunlight illuminated the even row of Peter's teeth and the fullness of his lips as he laughed along with me. I took a cautious step in retreat. "Luca could be awake by now. I should go back. We can practice shooting another day."

"Do not go yet, Franca. Just a few more moments of sanity in a world turned upside down." Peter reached for my hand and squeezed it gently before he let it go again.

His hand was warm, strong. My legs quivered, and panic dried my throat. "I do not feel 'moments of sanity' around you at all. I cannot keep my mind clear right now. It is not right for you to do things like that—to speak with kindness, to stand close to me in the sun, to touch my hand. It makes things confusing and blurs lines that are etched in stone."

"I'm sorry, Franca. I did not mean anything inappropriate. You can trust me."

"How am I to trust you if I do not trust myself?"

My words shocked me with their truth. In one afternoon, I could throw all loyalty to the wind and let myself lean against this German soldier, inhale the hint of soap and the scent of hay that served as his bed every night. I could turn my cheek and—I could not let myself go further.

Peter lifted his brows as if pleased to hear what I had said.

I frowned at him, and he put his hands behind his back. "Perhaps you are right; we can practice your shooting another day."

Gravel scratched at the soles of my leather shoes as I marched for the house. A cactus appeared between flower stalks and snatched at my sock with its spines. I did not slow down or look over my shoulder to be sure Peter followed for fear the next words that came from my mouth would expose my weakness for him completely. He was supposed to be dangerous and cruel, but he acted anything but and was more honest with me than my own family. Trust was earned, and my family was now in a deep deficit.

Peter matched my stride and caught up, stepping easily beside me. He reached for my arm and pulled me away from another cactus right before I stepped on it, and when he slid his hand down my arm and took hold of my hand I let my fingers intertwine with his. A breeze lifted my hair as the warmth of Peter's fingers and the rush of joy from his palm against mine filled my breast.

Peter smiled at me, but within a few moments, we were in view and could be seen by the others in the house. Reality dropped like an anvil, and we let go of each other's hands.

"I forgot I needed to check on the chickens before I go in the house," I whispered reluctantly as we headed our separate ways.

I walked on alone to a row of vines behind the coop and sank down on a concrete bench. Peter did not follow me, and disappointment pressed down on my chest until I panted for breath. I stared at the sprouts of grass and soil on the ground as if seeing the earth for the first time. I wanted him—I could no longer deny the fact that I wanted Peter and he wanted me—but the war held us in its claws and would never let go.

I could not defeat Hitler; I could not make the world safe or even keep my family safe. And I had to face the truth that my heart had been captured by a German soldier, and perhaps I wanted it to be. I got up from the bench and lay back on the spongy grass, watching the clouds drift across the sky with complete freedom. Even when war planes shot through them or explosions hit the air, the smoke always cleared eventually. The debris fell away. The clouds kept moving.

The war may control my circumstances, but it could not control my heart. I had been shrinking away from Peter because of the horrific actions of others. But a voice buried in the deepest part of my soul knew Peter Weimer was not my enemy, and I was finished with fooling myself.

CHAPTER TWENTY-EIGHT

Peter

Bruno beckoned me into an extra bedroom moments after Franca and I had returned and I'd gone into the house to return Bruno's weapon.

"There is word from the hospital. Laura and Franca's mother has died," Bruno said, his face red and eyes teary.

The words hit me with a punch. "That is devastating. I am very sorry."

Bruno stared off in deep thought. "One of our connections said there was someone, a man who seemed suspicious, who had gone to the hospital and inquired after her before she died. He even said her name, Elisa Chessari."

I looked at Bruno, dumbfounded. "How is that possible? How would anyone know who she is and that she was there?"

"I contacted Lieutenant Bianco and told him about the man. Bianco was in Messina but said he would be at the hospital by tomorrow to pick up his wife and take her somewhere else just in case this man was up to no good. But she must have died before he could get there."

"What you are saying? That the man slipped into the hospital ward and killed her?"

"I am saying nothing for certain. I am in shock and trying to contemplate telling Laura and Franca this news. My wife may not survive it."

He covered his brow with his hand and then wiped at his wet eyes, and even though I had no right, I patted his shoulder.

"*Forza,* Bruno. You are strong, and you will be your wife's strength."

"And Franca's. She will be devastated."

"I will continue to help her with the chores any way I can," I answered.

"Lieutenant Bianco says he knows it is risky for you but wants to know if you will go into town. Take a look around for this mysterious man who asked about his wife and see if there were any other Axis hideouts that you knew of or heard about. See if anyone looks familiar—any Nazis, Fascists, Axis soldiers trying to mingle incognito with the people in town."

"I will get ready right away and go."

I hurried to the barn to change into more presentable clothes that would be the least conspicuous in town. Thankful again for the clothes Giacomo had given me before he'd been shot, I slipped on the pair of pants that seemed the likeliest to cover my ankles and found a wrinkled but clean button-up shirt. It was the end of October now, and the weather had cooled, so Giacomo's old hat and a scarf from the bottom of the pile would not look out of place and would give me more cover.

When I came back into the house, I found Franca at the table. Her eyes were swollen and red from crying. I longed to take her in my arms and comfort her.

She stood straight up and squared her shoulders. "I am going to town. I want to see my mother's body, and I am bringing her back with me."

Bruno came into the kitchen and opened his mouth to speak to Franca, but she held up her hand in defiance. "I said I am going to town. I am bringing my mother back where she belongs with her family. I will not let a group of strangers at a hospital bury her in a cold, unmarked grave. She is my mother, and you cannot stop me."

Bruno tried to speak again, but Franca ignored him and marched past me and out the door.

"I will go with her and follow what Lieutenant Bianco asked me to do as well. I will bring her back safely, Bruno. And your mother-in-law's body. I will help you bury her here. At least for now."

"Yes, go."

I hurried outside before Franca left me behind.

She had already opened the big side doors of the barn and was pulling on the bales of hay that concealed the truck.

"Why do we always bury this truck in hay? Do people still steal them? All these emergencies, and we cannot even get away," she said, her voice lifted in anger as she brushed new tears from her cheeks. She tugged at the bales that refused to move and let out a growl of frustration.

"I will take you to the hospital," I told her when her voice quieted.

Franca stopped and stared straight at me, looking determined and fragile at the same time. "Italy is officially at war with Germany now; it was declared two days ago. You cannot go into town or you will be taken prisoner."

I knew better than to argue or to offer too much sympathy or she may attack me or fall apart. Neither reaction would do at this point. "That declaration is redundant. Italy has been at war with the Nazis since the Allies arrived on Sicily. I realize it is risky for me to go into town, but I have been asked to go by Marianna's partisan leader, Lieutenant Bianco," I told her.

"Very well." She climbed in the truck and waited in silence while I used a gas can to fuel the tank and cleared the rest of the hay.

We sat in silence as we traveled across the countryside, Franca's face blanched white and stoic as she let the wind whip her hair out the window, and strands of it flew around her face. There would be no way she could go into the hospital in such shock and near crumbling. When we drew close to Siracusa, I pulled over by the same copse of trees where she had left me the last time.

"Franca, I do not want to go into town without telling you how sorry I am about your mother."

"I did not even go back to visit her," she finally said out the window.

"You had no choice. Your family members have been desperate for your help every day."

"I never told her goodbye."

"She knew you loved her."

"I was not affectionate enough with her. She was loving but reserved, so I was reserved."

"You followed her lead, Franca."

"But I always wanted to show her more. I always planned to, but the war came, and everything started to move fast and became so difficult."

"It is not your fault. Everyone we know has been trying to stay alive."

"Everyone has been telling me where I have to be, and what I must do or not do. And I have allowed it. I could have gone to see her, at least one last time."

"Your mother would understand and—"

Before I could finish, Franca turned to me and slid over against my side. With deep sobs, she buried her face in my chest. After a moment's hesitation, I wrapped her in my arms, and she molded against me.

At times, I dared not move around Francesca for fear I would let the boundaries of war be damned and pull her against me like this. My arms were strong and weak at the same time as I rubbed her slender back and whispered reassurances into her ear, in awe that I could.

Minutes passed before she sighed between sobs and took a deep breath. Thankfully, she kept her head on my shoulder and did not pull away. I wiped at the tears on her face with my handkerchief.

"I wish I could take your pain away, Franca."

She fit against me as if we'd been carved from the same stone, her eyes bottomless, her lashes wet. She reached up and brushed her fingers across the whiskers on my face and joy grew into a fire so compelling it was all I could do not to lift Franca's chin and kiss her mouth like I had wanted to from the moment I'd met her.

"You have kept me strong from the moment you rescued me in this truck. And I have been terrible to you. So cold. So selfish," she almost whispered.

"You have been true to your country and family. You are braver and stronger than you realize."

"I am not brave." She kept her head on my shoulder, looking up at me and still rubbing her fingers lightly back and forth along my jaw. "I was too afraid to go back to town to see my mother if I had to go alone, so I missed out on telling her goodbye. I was too afraid to speak up and go to work in the hospital with Marianna when she left the first time. I was even too afraid of a ridiculous rooster." She leaned in closer to my face. "And I have been too afraid to do what I want to do for myself. To do this . . ."

Franca moved in completely and, in one fell swoop, pressed her lips against mine with full measure. I knew her pain had made her vulnerable and her tears had made her weak, but my mouth moved against hers of its own volition, and I drank her in with a thirst she'd stirred in me for weeks. She tasted salty from her tears, and I kissed her again, more fully, as if the waves of the Mediterranean had swept us away from every threat that stood in our way.

Minutes later, reality lifted its terrible head, and I made myself ease back. "Franca, I know you are too distraught right now for me to keep kissing you. You have had a terrible shock and need time."

"Life does not wait for us to be ready or brave. It will move on without us if we do not grab on. I told Marianna that when she was afraid to hold on to Massimo. No matter how fear has taunted me, a yearning to kiss you has been consuming me so long I can barely breathe when I'm near you. I am not going to be afraid or let the war control me anymore."

She reached her arms up around my neck, and I brushed my lips over her beautiful face, the curves of her cheek, her jaw, even the tip of her nose, and then stoked the fire with the fullness of her mouth.

But I held myself in check. Newfound courage or not, Franca had suffered a terrible shock and heartache. She needed time to take care of her mother and grieve. I put the truck in gear and pressed on the gas.

Franca stayed curled against me the rest of the way to the hospital, and I wished I could go inside with her, but the risk was too great. My Italian was good, but anyone who listened closely would detect my German accent. Plus, my height made me tower over most people, and my hair—if anyone saw it beneath my hat—was exceptionally light.

"I'll be right here waiting for you," I said as I pulled the truck up in front of the wide stone steps.

Franca bit her bottom lip and held tightly on to my hands until she had to get out of the truck.

CHAPTER TWENTY-NINE

Franca

The same foul odors and yellow candlelight greeted me at the hospital door. I could not help but look down row after row of the patients for my mother's face. The last time I'd been here, she'd been alive, and I'd laid my head on her bedside just to be close to her. I bit down on my lip to keep it from quivering.

It took almost an hour before the nurses at the hospital escorted me back to speak to Donatella. She frowned when she saw me, and I clasped my hands together on my knees when I sat down across from her at her desk.

"Thank you for seeing me, Donatella. Perhaps you remember me? I am Franca Chessari, daughter of Paolo and Elisa Chessari. You were so helpful the day I brought my mother and hired man in."

She stiffened in her chair when I mentioned my parents, but her face stayed blank.

"You have a lot of patients, but perhaps you remember that my mother just died? I was hoping you could tell me how or why and then let me take her body back with me to be buried at our church."

"I know of her passing, and I am very sorry, signorina." She lifted her head and met my gaze, her eyes almost black and veiled by formality.

"I'm sure you did all you could to save my mother's life, and the day I brought her in, I did not have the presence of mind to thank you enough."

Donatella ruffled through the pages of a clipboard and did not look at me. "We all must do what we can, no?"

She focused on her paperwork, and I dabbed at the corners of my eyes with my handkerchief.

At last she looked up. "I am sorry, but I just checked my records, and we cannot release your mother's remains. There has been a typhus outbreak for the past few months, so your mother's body has been taken to a designated gravesite outside of town."

"What do you mean? Did she have typhus? Is that how she died? Where is this grave? It must be blessed and sanctified."

Donatella lit a cigarette and looked out the window. "The public cannot go to this site. It is where all patients must be buried for safety's sake. The risk is too great."

I stood, the handkerchief gripped tight in my hand. "No, no, you cannot do this. You cannot keep her away from her family, from a church burial." The smoke from her cigarette rose above our heads, making the sunlight from the window murky.

"It is what we must do, signorina. No one is happy about this. I am very sorry, but there is nothing I can do. It is the law."

She stood and called to someone in the hallway. A man came in the room and gestured for me to follow him out.

"After the war, there may be a chance for families to find relatives and bury them properly," Donatella called as I was ushered out of the hospital, my voice locked behind the knot in my throat.

CHAPTER THIRTY

Peter

FRANCA CAME RUNNING DOWN THE steps, new tears pouring down her face as she reached the open window of the truck.

"What am I going to do? What am I going to do?" she repeated, gasping for breath through the window. "My mother's body is gone. Typhus. They put her in a mass typhus grave. I do not know where it is, where she is. They will not tell me."

When she climbed into the truck, I grabbed hold of her hands and held tight. "Look at me and listen. We will find her. We will find someone to help us."

She quieted her sobs, but I kept her hands grasped in mine. "Franca, I suspect they are hiding the truth. A partisan leader directed me to come with you today to look for anything or anyone suspicious."

A man in a long trench coat walked past the truck and glanced inside at the two of us. I stopped talking and watched him closely, ready to grab the pistol I had hidden in my pocket. But a woman and child came up the sidewalk from the other direction, and they all embraced.

Stone buildings abutted one another in a semicircle next to the church hospital. An alley in between a towering brick banca and the library appeared empty. Traffic was light, but a jeep full of Allied soldiers sped past, and a fruit vendor pushed his cart down the other side of the road, his voice echoing off the buildings as he shouted for customers and ambled along. When things appeared safe, I continued.

"There is more; have you heard anyone speak of a Lieutenant Bianco?" I asked.

She looked at me, questions in her eyes. "Yes."

"Before we left the house, Bruno referred to Bianco sending orders, and then he referred to your mother as Bianco's wife. I did not want to interrupt him at such a difficult time to ask him to clarify, but he sounded sure in his wording.

Lieutenant Bianco may be your father using a code name to protect his identity. I knew your father was involved in helping the resistance, but if he is Bianco, then your father is a very important man in the partisan movement. He is the one giving Bruno, Marianna, Massimo, me, and many, many others our orders."

Franca gasped, her eyes widened in shock. "That is why he has been gone so much?" She stared out the window, her eyelashes still wet from crying. "My parents have lived in an entirely different world than me. A secret world."

"Because your father is a high-ranking partisan, it also puts a target on his back, maybe even on everyone in your family."

She covered her eyes with her hand and then raised it in the air. "Of course. That must be why he has insisted we stay in hiding in Sortino. But what good is that knowledge now? How can this help us find my mother—her body?" Her voice caught when she said the word *body.*

"Your father was upset over the report that a man at the hospital had been asking about your mother. Perhaps the threat changed their plans, and they hid her body from the strange man."

Franca gasped. "Or maybe he had something to do with her death. Peter, what if he was there to kill her?"

I let go of Franca's hands and started the truck. "We need to search the area for anyone who looks out of place. And I know of a few locations where Nazi soldiers have hidden before. I picked up on someone's voice as I have listened to the radio. I'm almost sure it is the lieutenant I told you about—Keillor, the one who gave me this scar." I pointed at my cheek. "He could be involved with your mother's death and could very well have caused it. The first place I want to check is the basement of an abandoned palazzo."

The tires on the truck squealed as I whipped us around the corner. "We will not have far to go."

"Wait here for me no matter how long I take," I told Franca before I skulked my way to the back entrance of a three-story abandoned palazzo and headed down the stairs.

The basement was empty—cleaned with no trace that anyone had ever been there. I and two other soldiers had been ordered to hide out here after the Allied invasion until Keillor ordered me back to the catacombs. But no one could be found now, and I had seen for myself that the catacombs had been cleared out by the Allies when Massimo's group and I went looking for Marianna.

There was another possible place I needed to check. I passed through shadows and crossed the street, tipping my hat at Franca to reassure her all was well.

I hid behind the pillars of a bank building, peered out, and a pair of hands gripped me around the throat from behind. I reached for my pistol in my pocket, but it was empty. The captor squeezed his grip tighter around my neck, cutting off my air as he pulled me off balance. Then he dragged me around a dark corner before he shoved me to the ground facedown. He jumped on my back and pounded his fists into my ribs. I gasped for breath and tried to buck him off my back. I kicked and twisted, trying to flip over so I could see his face, but he grabbed me by the throat again and squeezed. Just before darkness closed in, the man let go, and I rolled onto my back on the cobbled ground, wheezing and gasping for air.

The man stood straddled over me with a pistol pointed at my head. He lit a cigarette with his other hand as if taking a break. The lighter illuminated his face. Jurgen, one of the soldiers who had hidden in the basement and the catacombs with me. He bent over and blew his cigarette smoke in my face.

"Guess what, pretty boy. I know you are the traitor who told the Allies about our hideout in the catacombs. I bet you thought they killed or captured us all, no? Well, I am too smart and too quick for them. And now that I found you, my work is almost finished here. All I have to do is turn you over to Keillor, and maybe he will be so grateful to me I will get new orders to go back to Germany. I just hope that after I am gone, the führer will get back here soon and blow up this entire country." He kept his pistol pointed at my head and flicked his ashes in my face. "I am so fed up. So disgusted by your betrayal of our country. You deserve to be punished by someone like Keillor. He knows how to make traitors pay." He leaned down and brought the flame of his cigarette within an inch of my face. "Now do not be afraid; I will not mess up your pretty face." He chuckled. "I know Keillor will want to do that."

I managed a breath. "I did not know you thought I was pretty, Jurgen."

The roar of passing vehicles echoed from the front of the building. We were tucked around a corner behind a wall, out of sight. Jurgen took a long, slow drag from his cigarette and then kicked me in the ribs. He sneered and kicked me on the other side so hard it shot all the air out of my lungs.

"I spotted a woman waiting in a truck across the road. Is she with you?" he asked. "I bet she is pretty, and I can show her what a true German man can do for her. I'll handcuff you in a minute and go introduce myself."

He sat down on the edge of a wall just a couple feet away, the pistol still aimed at my head. I slowly got my breath and eased to a sitting position. If I could get my feet under me while he talked, I could lunge forward and get a hold of his throat and shut his filthy mouth once and for all. I made it to my knees.

Jurgen stood up and kicked me in the stomach, and I toppled back down to the ground. He tossed his cigarette on top of my shirt, lifted his right hand, and snapped his fingers as if summoning someone. Several seconds passed, and he looked over his shoulder.

"Hiegle, Vigor, get over here now," he called. Still no one came, and he stiffened in anger and aimed the gun more steadily at my gut. "We are going around the corner to see why my friends have been delayed. Step carefully in front of me, or I will blow a hole through you."

I made it to my feet and walked like a hunchback in front of Jurgen to the pillars in front of the bank, watching for the men who were supposed to have answered his summons. No one was in sight.

Jurgen pressed the gun into my back. "Keep walking, *stupido.*" He grunted. "*Stupido.* I guess I learned one useful word from these worthless people."

"What about *porco* or *scemo*?" I asked. "You should know the words *pig* and *fool* in all languages."

He punched me in the back, and I lost my breath again, but it pushed me ahead of him by a couple of steps. I took advantage of the movement to slip around a pillar and stopped in surprise at what I found; Franca Chessari braced with a rifle at her shoulder, aimed at two German soldiers. These had to be the men that Jurgen had tried to summon. I stopped in my tracks as Jurgen rounded the corner to stop me from running away.

Franca gasped when she saw us and moved the aim of the rifle straight at Jurgen. He smiled. "Oh, I see. You must be the woman who was hiding in the truck. Yes, you are very pretty. Go ahead and pull the trigger on that rifle, signorina, I will kill this soldier before your bullet reaches me."

The two Germans she'd held at bay stayed pressed against the wall.

She didn't flinch. "Go ahead. He is just another German to me."

"I am convinced otherwise, and I will prove it to you if you do not drop your rifle."

I looked at Jurgen. "I will back away with the signorina and let you and these two men go. And you can run and hide wherever you want to. Maybe we will meet another day."

Jurgen shrugged and stuck out his lower lip. "I have to turn you in to Keillor for your execution. Or maybe the Allies will kill you first. That would really be disappointing, but I can see several *Americani* over your shoulder coming our way, and I have an escape route while you do not." He cocked his head at the other two men, and they dashed around the corner. I looked around and saw no Americans. Jurgen ran off behind his minions.

Franca lowered the rifle and looked at me in frustration. "Why did you let them go? I had the rifle pointed right at them."

"You could not have gotten all three of them before Jurgen had killed you." I took a step toward Franca. "May I hold the rifle now?"

She lifted the weapon again to give it to me, but her fingers were locked so tight around the handle I had to pry them free.

"I want to hear just how you got the best of those two men, but we have got to get out of here and back to the farm."

I spotted movement over her shoulder and grabbed hold of her arm. "We had better hurry. I see the American soldiers now, and they may be headed our direction."

We hurried across the road when the Americans had entered a nearby building. Perhaps they had gotten word that some Germans had been spotted nearby and were searching for them. We had to get back to the Sortino farm. But there was no real safe place.

I knew nothing would stop Jurgen from telling Keillor he had seen me. And there was no stopping Keillor from his vengeance. The time of hiding like a useless prisoner had passed; I had to find Keillor before he found me. I wanted to get Franca back to Sortino, and I wanted to get a hold of Lieutenant Bianco to tell him about his wife's missing body and about Keillor. And, God willing, Bianco may have more information.

I climbed in the truck beside Franca and started the engine, roaring down the road as far from the area as we could get.

When we were far enough away from the bank, she let out her breath. "I saw that man just before he grabbed you, Peter, so I went for the rifle under the seat and darted behind the pillar like you had just as the other two men went running up to the building. I am so glad you came up when you did because my arms were shaking so much I thought I would drop the rifle any minute."

"Your fingers were like granite around that rifle. I doubt you could've dropped it. And I am amazed at your backbone. You could command an army." I reached for her hand as I whisked the truck around the corners of the city. "You are still shaking. Move up next to me so you can stay warm."

The moon threw light through the truck windows, casting Franca's face in an ethereal glow, and I realized her teeth were chattering. As soon as we were in the countryside, I stopped the truck and rubbed my hands up and down her arms to warm and calm her. "You are in shock. Take slow, even breaths. We are safe now. Those men are hidden away and have no idea where we are staying."

Franca kept her eyes focused on mine and breathed in and out carefully as her chin slowed and finally stopped quivering. I pulled her into me and pressed her cheek against mine. "We are safe now. In a few minutes, we will be at the farmhouse and can lock the doors behind us."

"*Si, si,* I will be fine," she whispered against my cheek. I reluctantly let go of her, put the truck into gear, and pressed on the gas. Black clouds covered the moon. There would be no affection allowed once we arrived at the farmhouse. No partaking of forbidden fruit. A lingering look between us, a suspicious touch in front of her family or anyone else could upend Franca's world and put her at risk. Any danger for me was superfluous—I already walked with a noose around my neck. But I would do all in my power to keep Franca safe, be it from scorn or danger.

The house was a black silhouette at the end of a long, tree-lined road in the distance. Franca's family must have gone to sleep. Before I made the last turn, Franca squeezed her hand over mine on the steering wheel and looked at me beseechingly.

I pulled the truck over and took her in my arms. She cried again for a few moments against my chest, and I kissed her tears and held her against me. "We will find your mother's body, Franca. I promise you I will do everything that I can to help you."

She sniffed and laid her head on my chest. "I know you will. And I will have to learn to live without her no matter what we find."

I pressed my foot down on the clutch, ready to go.

But Franca lifted her head. "Not yet. Once we return, we cannot be this way."

"I know."

"Let's give ourselves one minute more."

"I would give you a thousand minutes, Francesca."

Even in the moonlight, I could see her eyes soften. "You have never called me Francesca before."

"You have never captured three armed soldiers before."

"Maybe I should have learned to shoot sooner to gain your respect."

"You have had my respect since the day I met you, signorina Chessari."

I turned off the engine and lost myself in Franca, memorizing the sweetness and warmth of her kisses as the sands in the hourglass trickled down.

CHAPTER THIRTY-ONE

Peter

November 1943

I WOKE JUST BEFORE DAWN after a night packed with nightmares and looked up at the rafters of the barn with relief. The wooden beams were still intact, the aged stones and wood plank walls were not pocked with jagged holes where bombs, grenades, and bullets had blown through, like I had seen in so many places I'd sheltered in the past.

While fighting in North Africa, I woke to the coppery smell of drying blood, sweat, and decay every morning. I might have died and gone to hell in my sleep every night without knowing the difference. I'd wake and move my eyes back and forth, glancing at my surroundings without moving my head, ease my hand over my rifle, and finally risk looking around to be sure only fellow soldiers were nearby and that no one had crept up to kill me in my sleep.

The peace at this farm was surreal, the house simple but warm and beautiful with its stone and plaster walls and wooden floors. I took deep breaths to clear the nightmares away, grabbed clean clothes, and made my way to the well to wash up.

The time with Franca in my arms the night before had given my life new meaning—and suffocating fear. I could close my eyes and relive the taste of her lips, but the rising sun and the war pushed us apart and held us prisoner.

"Did you know the soldiers who attacked you?" Bruno asked when I entered the house and sat at the table across from him. He looked haggard this morning, his eyes shot with red and his brows pinched and lowered.

Franca came into the kitchen and smiled at me behind Bruno's back. It was all I could do not to jump up and pull her to me. We had both determined that the risks were too great; we would stay back from one another after our time together the night before. She took a chair beside Bruno, and I had to avert my eyes and thoughts from focusing on her lips.

Bruno set a glass of water in front of me with a rap against the wooden table. "There has been no more information on the radio from the hospital this morning," he said. "And now it has quit working." He turned to Franca when she sat down beside him. "I am sorry I have no update about your mother's body, but I have fixed the radio before; I should be able to do it again."

"I am no expert on radios but will be happy to help find the problem if I can," I interjected.

"I would welcome the assistance," he said with a nod of his head.

Franca had bowed her head and kept it there when there was no report about her mother. I held my focus on the gravity that surrounded the situation, tamping down my desire to hold and comfort her. She rose from the table, dabbing at her eyes, and retrieved a plate laid out with bread and fruit.

"I knew one of the attackers last night," I finally answered Bruno. "The main one who grabbed me is named Jurgen. I was ordered to stay here in Sicily when the Allies landed and after our Axis soldiers retreated. A few of us holed up in a basement together in Siracusa and briefly in the catacombs until Keillor had his puppets capture Marianna and bring her in. I did not recognize the other two men last night."

Bruno leaned back in his chair. "Keillor is obviously an evil, sick man, especially when it comes to women. Was he your commanding officer?"

"His full name is Vasyl Keillor, and yes, he was my commander. He is a merciless killer. And, unfortunately, he is very effective at torturing prisoners for information. The Nazis revere him for it, and he wears their approval like a crown of glory. I'd hoped he had been killed or captured when the Allies raided the catacombs, but the things Jurgen told me last night indicated that Keillor is still hiding somewhere here in Sicily. That is not good news for any of us. I knew him before the war, and if he were to track me down, it would be extremely dangerous."

Bruno opened his hands, palms up. "How did you know this Keillor before the war?"

"It is a very long story and not a pleasant one," I answered, taking a sip of water and wishing I would not have to relive the memories.

"If he is so dangerous, we need to know all we can about him."

"*Va bene*," I said, rubbing my fingers over my eyes with a sigh of resignation. "I knew Keillor as a young boy in Germany; he was the school bully—known for cruelty. Rumor was that his father was a criminal and his mother did shameful things on the side to get by."

Bruno lowered his brow and Franca's eyes widened as she tsked her tongue. The bread and fruit on the platter went untouched.

"No one liked Keillor, so I pitied him at first. But he tripped the girls and spit in their hair. I backed him in a corner one day and told him he'd better leave the girls alone, and he ran away. But after that, he called me 'altar boy' and wolf whistled when he saw me coming.

"When we were about twelve years old, he spit in the hair of the girl I liked, and I punched him in the gut. He curled up and yowled like a wounded animal just as a group of girls came around the corner. A few of the girls spit in Keillor's hair just like he had done to them. His hatred for me tripled after that.

"Thankfully, Keillor's family moved away a few months later.

"Years passed, and then after the war started, I overheard my seventeen-year-old sister, Bettina, telling our mother about a Lieutenant Keillor that she'd met at a military dance. When I asked her, if he had lived in town when he was boy, she smiled and said *yes* as if it was good news.

"I held my tongue at first. Bettina was as fiery as her hair, and I knew she would only run the other way if I tried to pull her back too quickly.

"Bettina gushed over Keillor in the next few days, so I finally told her about his past. She was convinced I was just remembering boyhood pranks and that he had changed.

"I attended the dances with her from then on. My gut told me Keillor was still the bully I'd known, but I decided to watch carefully and see if he deserved a second chance."

"You were not in the military at that time?" Bruno asked.

"Not yet; I'd broken my leg pretty seriously the summer before, so it delayed my military duty until 1940. My leg still dragged a bit when I went with Bettina to the dances, so I sat on the sidelines. It gave me a good view of what was going on.

"Vasyl Keillor laid on the charm and led my sister on. I watched him slip out the door with a couple other girls when Bettina was not looking, but when I tried to tell her, she claimed I was just holding old grudges.

"Then one night Keillor offered my sister a ride home from the dance, and I followed a little behind. He drove her to a remote area thick with trees and winding roads. By the time I located where he'd parked his car, it was empty. I heard screams and hurried as fast as I could with my limp, trying to find Bettina."

Franca had covered her mouth with her hands, so I paused my story, questioning how to convey the next part. She must have sensed my hesitation and lowered her hands to her lap. "*Sto bene,* Peter. Go ahead."

I took a drink of water to wash the nasty taste out of my mouth before I continued.

"I found Bettina. Keillor had pinned her down beneath him on the ground. Bettina saw me over his shoulder and screamed my name just as I grabbed Keillor by his hair and yanked him off my sister. She scrambled up and ran toward me, but Keillor came at me first with his fists raised.

"Even though my leg was weak, I was bigger than Keillor and a lot angrier. We exchanged several punches, but I finally stopped him with an uppercut to the jaw, and he flew up like a kicked dog and landed out cold on the ground. We left him there unconscious.

"Bettina cried all the way home. I never asked her how bad Keillor's attack had been, but she never went to a dance after that night. I hated to see the spark in her die, but in time, she seemed to recover, and her stubbornness turned into strength and bravery. I've been proud of her."

Bruno shook his head in disgust. "This Keillor is what we call a *scemo,* a jerk and a fool."

"How could Keillor get away with such horrible things?" Franca asked, her hand laid at her throat.

I shrugged and held out my hands in frustration. "By the time Keillor attacked Bettina, he was revered by his superiors for his skills in interrogations. He had a reputation for extracting the most information from prisoners. I filed a report against him, but it was dismissed." I paused in my narration and lowered my brow when I looked at Bruno. "His talent for torture is like an obsession for him now. We cannot let him ever find us, especially Laura and Franca. Keillor's rage against me will never stop."

Franca's eyes were open wide, shining with rapt attention and fear. I longed to pull her into my arms.

Bruno grimaced and twisted a napkin in his hand. "Perhaps I am barbaric, but I wish that you had been able to kill him that night when he attacked your sister. When he sent his men out to capture Marianna, they almost killed her with that blow to her head. And if you had not been there to intervene in the catacombs . . ."

"You have no idea how many times I wish he had rushed me one more time or pulled a gun on me that night with Bettina so I could have stopped him for good."

Franca put a bowl of apples on the table. "You told me that Keillor gave you that scar on your face, no?" Franca said, her face pale when she sat back down.

I hesitated.

"That scar came from a commander?" asked Bruno, pointing at my cheek.

The kitchen chair screeched beneath me as I pushed myself back a few inches from the table. "Yes, shortly after I joined the army, Keillor requested that I be put in his squadron. He ordered me to do all kinds of disgusting things and put me in danger out in battle at every turn. But one day he ordered me to clean his boots. He took them off, rubbed them in the mud, and then ordered me to lick the boots clean. I'd reached my limit and refused. Keillor repeated the order and then ordered me to kneel down. The second I did, he reached in his pocket for his knife and sliced it like a razor blade down the left side of my face."

I traced the line of my scar with my finger, and Franca covered her teary eyes with her hands.

"I will spare you any further details and only add that the hell of war was doubled because of Keillor with the assignments he gave me at the front lines and other horrors he thrived on exposing me to. He did some of the same to other soldiers who defied him.

"Keillor kept me in his division when we got to Siracusa last year and made me sit in the room for every interrogation he did while men were beaten and women assaulted.

"I silently celebrated liberation when the Allies invaded Sicily and Mussolini was arrested. But on August 11, when the German army retreated to mainland Italy, Keillor ordered me to remain behind in the catacombs in secret. We were to plan sabotages against the Allies and intercept the intelligence necessary to overtake them and recapture Sicily. For Keillor, that meant he interrogated prisoners night and day to find his way back to power over Italy.

"I'd dodged the horrors of interrogations day after day by taking guard duty, but after a while, Keillor noticed I had not been around. The day Keillor ordered me to beat and assault Marianna, I'd had enough. I had discovered the cave and remembered where it was in case I would need to hide myself or one of the female prisoners there. When Keillor was distracted by a skirmish in the main cave, I knew what I had to do. I hurried Marianna out and hid her in the cave in the ceiling. I wanted to take her with me, but the guards at the door would never have let me pass. I made my escape and reported to the Americans for my surrender. I told them about the catacombs and the hidden young woman with hopes that they would rescue her."

"You gave up your freedom and risked death just to save Marianna," Bruno said.

"I saved Marianna and my own soul. I had no freedom until I turned myself in to the Allies. But I have to find a way out of here and back to Germany soon."

"The Allies control Italy all the way to Monte Cassino. From there north is German occupation, but I see no way for you to make it that far without being killed or captured," Bruno said.

"And if the Germans realize who you are and that you quit the army, you will be shot, no?" Franca asked.

"Possibly. At times, that does not seem so unjust. I have pulled the trigger on many men, even though I recoiled at what I was doing. I did it because I thought I had no choice." I looked right at Franca. "I have realized since then that we always have a choice, so perhaps I have condemned myself."

Bruno dropped his jaw open and shook his head. "Do you believe God blames you or holds you guilty?" he asked, his face grave.

"He does not have to. I do enough of it for Him."

I paused and did not look either of them in the eye. "I have to stop Keillor. He will never quit until he has killed me and my family. There is no doubt he will brutalize women and murder even after the war. There is only one way to stop him once and for all, and I just hope God will grant me one more drop of mercy and open the necessary door."

CHAPTER THIRTY-TWO

Franca

To everyone's surprise, Laura regained some strength and sat in the parlor holding Luca that evening. She and Bruno insisted that Peter join us. Laura asked me to play the pianoforte, but I had no desire. When she pled with me, I relented.

The music actually soothed me as my fingers remembered the notes and rhythms. I played a slow waltz, and Bruno passed Luca to Peter and helped Laura to her feet. They were too weak and injured to dance, but they swayed to the music and held on to one another. I watched my sister's slow movements, the way her head rested on Bruno as if all the hope in the world was stored in his shoulder.

Peter held the sleeping baby against his chest and watched me. I could only manage glances in his direction, but his gaze radiated over me like a wand of fire.

He pressed Luca's head against his cheek and kissed him on the top of his head. Tears pressed behind my eyes, and I held my breath until the need for air burned in my throat. How did I ever see this man as a Nazi, an enemy, a danger? I knew all along, even the night I saw him for the first time and he drove me, Mama, and Giacomo to Siracusa, a part of me sighed with relief that he was there.

Before long, Bruno and Laura went back to their room, taking Luca with them. I walked over to Peter on shaky legs and looked into his eyes. Peter stood up, and a few of my tears gave way, their warmth blending with the flush on my face as the candle on the table burned down to a tiny flame floating on a puddle of wax.

I reached up and traced Peter's square jawline with my fingers as we swayed to music that only played in our heads. I brushed my tears away with the back of my hand and then ran my finger across Peter's lower lip. Imaginary drums beat softly as I stepped in closer and slipped one hand around his neck. I stopped swaying and lifted my chin.

Peter leaned down and glided his lips over mine like a slow-moving dance. I basked in the scratch of his whiskers on my lips and chin, the strength of his arms as he slid his hands up my back. I was drowning and floating at the same time. Falling and racing through the clouds. I'd never danced this way before—never disappeared into another human being.

Peter pulled me against him and pressed his lips against my cheek as he whispered. "You are so beautiful, *carina.*"

I leaned back slightly to look up at him.

His eyes were blue as deep twilight. His mouth—I'd looked at the firm fullness of his lips for weeks without ever letting myself admit it. I'd even watched the muscles of his jaw when he chewed his food and wondered why my belly ached a little each time. Now I knew. Peter was no village boy I'd danced with in the past. I had woken up as if I'd never been awake before when I kissed him on the way to Siracusa, and all I wanted was this dream.

He kissed me again, and I closed my eyes to savor the taste and fervor of his mouth. My legs almost buckled, but I clasped my hands around his neck and, for just a moment, blocked out all the warning whistles that Bruno or Laura may catch us.

Minutes passed, and I half moaned, half cried in my throat. It had to end or I would be consumed in this fire.

"We cannot do this," I whispered against his lips.

Peter inched back, and his eyes searched mine. "We cannot do what?"

"This. This . . . we said it was too risky, that last night would be the last of it." I dropped my arms from around his neck. "Bruno could walk in any minute. Nazis are after you. It is too dangerous."

He took my face in his hands. "It may be dangerous, but it is not wrong."

One second of happiness sparked in my chest before it imploded. I looked into his eyes and the hope that floated across oceans that waited there, and then remembered the power of the war that could pull us down until we drowned.

I drew away from Peter. "I'm afraid. Afraid for you, for my family. The network of the Nazis is so widespread they may have sent a man to find my mother in a hospital. For revenge? Did he kill her to get to my father?"

Peter stepped closer to me and stroked my cheek. "We will find the answers."

I put my hand over his. "I do not know what to do or if I can do it."

"You are braver than you know."

"But brave enough for what? Others risk their lives to end the war, and I put you and my family at risk just to touch you."

Peter's eyes lowered before he spoke. "I will stay away. I do not want you worried or upset like this."

Tears slipped from my eyes. I whisked them away and waited until I could speak calmly. "I am upset over my mother and scared of who could be watching us. Allies, enemies, whatever we are, we are both prisoners of this war."

"We have the right to our own beliefs and feelings, Franca. No one can take that away."

I shook my head. "But they can punish us for them. You know they can and they do. The partisans sometimes take the women who become involved with Germans and beat them. They shave their heads. They strip them and parade them down the streets. And you would be shot or hung."

I pressed my fingers over my eyes to stop the flow of tears, and Peter stroked my cheeks with his thumbs as he held my chin in his hands. "The last thing I want is to bring you more danger and threats." He dropped his hands but held his gaze locked with mine in the pale-yellow light.

His hand grasped my fingers. "This will be the last of it then. But kiss me, Franca, one last time. And then I will leave you alone."

"If I kiss you again, I will not have the strength to let you go." I wiped at the tears that gushed again.

Peter reached his arms around me, slid his hands to my lower back, and eased me against him. The candle flickered out, and I was the wax and Peter the flame that melted me.

I knew that if Peter let go of me, I would fall to the ground. He sat down in the rocking chair where he'd held Luca and pulled me onto his lap. I fell against him and cried on his neck. "You cannot leave me alone, Peter. You cannot be my enemy."

He pressed his finger against my lips like he had the first time I'd seen him. "Shh . . . Francesca. No one is an enemy in this room."

CHAPTER THIRTY-THREE

Franca

November 30, 1943

THE VEGETABLES WERE DYING. I had no idea how to stop the decay, and I could not find any new seeds to plant. Thankfully, the apple and fig trees still bore some fruit, and the citrus would be ready in the winter if we were still here. A few squash and tomatoes kept us going, along with a supply of flour, oil, and bottled tomatoes from the cellar. On my hands and knees, I tugged at weeds, keeping the worst of the rotting vegetables for the pigs.

Peter worked in the barn and took care of the animals while I hoed and raked the dead vines and plants. November was much cooler than the summer had been, but the sun beamed straight down on the top of my head and my hair lay like a blanket down my back. Sweat trickled between my shoulder blades.

I had spotted a pond down one side of the hill behind the farmhouse and remembered the bar of soap that was still in my pocket since Luca's last bath. I hurried through the trees and bushes to the edge of the pond. Even out alone, it did not feel proper to take my clothes off outside. I jumped into the pond with my clothes on, determined I had enough time to let most of the water drip from my dress before I got back to the house so I would not make a mess.

I soaked and scrubbed with the soap until my fingertips puckered and held my breath under the water as I swished my head back and forth to rinse my hair. My scalp tingled in the cold, but the shivers brought me more energy than I'd had for days.

Trees surrounded the pond, but they were sparser on one side. I could look out at a hill that cut against the horizon like the profile of a robust woman lying asleep on her side. Clouds floated over her figure like puffs of breath. Rounded hills covered the entire landscape like the sleeping woman's family had lain down for a nap near her, and the grass grew up and over the top of them.

I was surprised that the water went all the way over my head in places, although I could only manage two or three swimming strokes before I reached each edge. Pebbles scratched at my feet when I stood, while tiny fish bumped their lips against my ankles.

My hair floated on top of the frigid water. My toes and fingers were tingling in the chilly water, but I did not care—I relished the moments of freedom and the fresh sensations that cleansed my mind and numbed the longing that lingered on my skin for more caresses from Peter.

Kissing Peter had opened a world before my eyes, a world of breathlessness and yearning—of peace and frenzy. The longing for home ceased when I was around him, as if I'd already arrived, while my pulse beat like a drum, all the way to my fingertips.

Two birds shot up out of the bushes farther up the hill. I froze in place with the soap still gripped in my hand. I did not dare move or make a sound for a full minute in case someone had followed me.

Another snap and scratch of movement tensed my muscles again. I carefully kicked my way over to the edge of the water.

Peter stepped out from around a tree, a big smile on his face. "So, signorina Chessari thought she would go for a swim?" He looked down with a smile, and his eyebrows raised.

I ran my arms back and forth over the top of the water to keep it rippled. "You have no business sneaking up on me, Peter Weimer," I said, barely containing a smile.

"I have no business being anywhere I go these days. But I am actually here on a valid mission. You took off all by yourself, and someone has to stand guard."

I blushed. "And that someone had to be you."

"I may have had more than one motive when I took the job," he said with another sideways smile.

I cupped a handful of water and flung it in his direction, splashing the front of his clothes. He wore the loose shirt and cropped pants with suspenders again. "I hope that will help keep you cool while you are working."

He looked down at his wet shirt and pants. "No, that wasn't enough to cool me off. It's still too warm out here." He slipped off his shoes and clothes down to his shorts and undershirt and slipped all the way under the water.

I yelped as Peter came up for air, a huge grin on his face.

"You look really cold, Francesca. Your lips are almost purple."

"This water is freezing."

He glided his way closer. "Let me see if I can help you warm up a little."

I wanted to argue, to remind him of our decision to stay away from one another. We had strived to keep our affection to a minimum for weeks, but his eyes reflected the blue of the pond, his wet undershirt outlined the muscles in his shoulders, and the ache in my belly was a magnet that pulled me toward him.

"What about the danger of being caught together?" I finally managed.

"There is nothing more dangerous than you at this moment," he said with a smile. But his eyes held mine for a moment, growing more serious. He looked away. "You are right; I should go. I am sorry." He turned around and moved toward the edge of the pond.

I came up behind him and touched him on his back before he could climb out. "Wait," I whispered.

He turned around, and I floated up against him. My teeth stopped chattering when our lips came together. Peter tasted like fresh, clean water and salty skin. The scratch of his whiskers on my lips and chin stirred a longing that knotted my insides. My arms recovered all sensation, and I slid them up his back, losing my breath all over again at the strength of his shoulders.

"You are the one making me shiver now," I whispered with my lips pressed against his.

My head spun as our lips slid together. Peter held me close, his arms around me the only thing keeping me afloat.

I inhaled and pulled back a couple feet, needing to catch my breath before I drowned in sensations. "Perhaps I was right all along. You are dangerous, Peter Weimer."

I splashed water in his direction, and he splashed me back before he grabbed my hand and pulled me against him.

"Do not worry. I am a gentleman," he said, raising one eyebrow and smiling. He leaned in closer until his mouth was an inch from mine. "But I will enjoy another kiss while I am here. It is the only payment I get for guarding you."

He kissed me quick before I could respond and then lay back, floating in the water. "I am beginning to like this job."

I smiled but tsked my tongue. "You may be fired for inappropriate behavior."

He looked at me and lowered his brow. "If you think that was inappropriate, you should see what I have planned next."

"We are not—"

He swam back over and stopped my words with his mouth, and in spite of every lesson my mother ever taught me on proper etiquette with men, I melted into Peter until I was as liquid as the water we floated in.

We spun in circles for a few brief moments, kissing, laughing, kissing again as if the world was normal, and we were free and safe. Shivering as much from the danger as the chill of the water, we settled in for one more long, deep kiss, the soft rustle of the mourning doves in the bushes cooing in approval.

"*Weimer hier sind wir wieder mit einer Fraulein zwischen uns,*" someone said from the side of the pond.

Peter pulled away in an instant, and while I could not understand the German the man in the Nazi uniform had spoken, I had no question what the pistols he held in each hand meant.

CHAPTER THIRTY-FOUR

Peter

Keillor chortled. "This time I have all the power in my hands. Come out of the water and do what I say, or I will shoot your woman just for fun."

He stood at the edge of the pond, a sneer on his face.

I spun around, keeping Franca behind and up against me to block her from his view.

"Very well. Like you said, Keillor, you have all the power, so shooting will not be necessary."

Franca gripped me tighter when I said the name *Keillor.*

We inched our way to the edge of the pond and climbed out. I kept Franca behind me and faced Keillor.

"Go ahead and get dressed. I do not wish to kill you in your underwear," Keillor said, using the pistol in his right hand to point at me.

I tugged the shirt and pants on over my wet skin, buttoning them with shaky hands and watching Franca from the corner of my eye. Except for a small gasp of fear every time she glanced up at Keillor, she slipped her shoes on and stayed silent.

"You are not very smart, Peter Weimer. Jurgen followed you almost all the way here the night you attacked him in Siracusa. I have been occupied or I would have come sooner. It was not so hard to find you today." He looked at Franca. "Thank you for laughing and having a good time. When I could not find you at the farm, I just followed the echo of your laughter. Now we can all laugh together." He sneered.

Reason trumped the rage that burned in my throat. I had to think fast and clear before Keillor lost his sense of victory and unleashed the demon that lurked inside of him.

I pulled up my suspenders and then reached down as if picking up my shoes. I gripped my hand around a large rock and came up quick, pitching the rock at Keillor with the snap of my arm. It hit him in the forehead, and he fell back on the ground like I had hoped. But I had not hit him hard enough, and he still held the pistols. He growled in frustration, struggling to get back on his feet without dropping his weapons. If I lunged at him now, he could aim and shoot in a split second.

I grabbed Franca her by the arm and pulled her behind two boulders for cover before we took off in a sprint through the trees. I glanced over my shoulder at Keillor just getting to his feet. The blow to his head must have dazed him more than I thought or he would have been up and after us by now.

Wind whipped through the trees as fast as we did, and birds squawked and whistled in alarm as we passed, causing such a racket I could not hear if there were footsteps behind us.

Franca kept her hand gripped tight in mine, her breath coming fast as she matched my pace. I took us through the trees in a roundabout route to the far edge of the De'Angelis property, hoping Keillor would lose sight of us. If we could make it to the house first, I could get Bruno's rifle and stop Keillor. We ducked behind a broken-down tractor so I could look behind us.

I pulled Franca in close. "*Silenzio.* Stay silent and do not move." I steadied my breath and pointed at a thicket of shrubs and hedges growing at the foot of a copse of cypress trees closer to the house.

"Keillor may hide and wait for us to come out in the open, and he may not be alone. Do not move or make a sound. Stay here behind this tractor." I crouched down and made my way around a couple old tractor tires, a dilapidated wagon, and a watering trough, watching the tree line around the farm for movement before I came back to Franca. "I did not see him, but I know Keillor is out there somewhere. We need to return to the house, quickly."

I grabbed Franca's hand, and we ran as if the enemy snapped at our heels. We'd made it to the side of the barn when Keillor stepped out from behind the well just twenty feet away, his pistols pointed at Franca.

"Do not try to fight me or the girl is dead."

I lifted one hand in the air and pulled Franca behind me with the other one.

"What do you want, Keillor?" I asked.

"You are a traitor. Lower than a dog. I would enjoy seeing you hang, but I do not have a rope, so I must settle for shooting you. But I want the radio—the one I know you use in your betrayal of our führer."

"I do not have a radio."

He narrowed his eyes. "You are a liar as well as a traitor. You sabotage your own army. I am convinced you killed the men I had scouting this area. Those men were working on my orders while looking for you and any other dog who lies with the enemy like you do." He pointed one of the guns toward Franca. "Does your little harlot know you ran away from the catacombs like a coward because you could not be a man?"

"She knows enough."

"Maybe I should teach her more—show her some things I am sure you are too afraid to do like a normal man."

"You are not a man. You are a sick animal."

"Careful, Peter. If you make me angry, I will just kill her."

"Leave her alone. She has nothing to do with the hatred you have for me."

Keillor smirked. "She has everything to do with it. I saw your amateur romance in the water before I spoke to you. You are quite besotted with this little signorina, so now I may have to get to know her too, just like Bettina. But back to business. If I did not have to take you in for questioning, I would kill you right now. I know you spy on fellow Germans, and you reported my work and location in the catacombs to the Allies. Almost all of your comrades there were killed."

"Those men were Nazi puppets who loved torture as much as you do. I would not call them comrades. You were the one who stayed behind when you had your chance to flee this island with the others. But now you are stuck."

"Maybe I will kill you and take your girlfriend prisoner. She is more to my liking."

"I am surprised, Keillor. You've hated me since we were children. This is your chance to see me tortured. You do not need the girl. Let her go, and you can take me."

Keillor sneered. "If I take you back to our camp, it will be for one reason only, so that the other men can enjoy watching you die for treason after we torture you for information." He pointed at Franca. "And no, the young woman cannot go. She is coming with me. My comrades will be glad that I brought her. They are not afraid to be men like you were in the cave with the prisoner. You were so scared of a woman you ran away like a dog with his tail between his legs."

"It looks like you know me pretty well. But I will only come with you if the girl goes free. Otherwise one of us has to kill the other one."

"So the farm boy believes he can fight better than me, huh?" He lifted his pistols higher. "And how will you do that without a weapon?"

My hands had balled into fists, but I did not move. "I know how we can find out. Give me one of your pistols, and we will have an old-fashioned duel. Unless you are too afraid?"

Franca leaned up closer behind me.

Keillor double blinked and stared at me as if startled by my words. He shrugged with exaggerated and feigned nonchalance and aimed the pistols more directly at my chest. "I changed my mind. I'm not sure I can wait any longer to have your little princess or to get you back to camp to see you die. I definitely want to be the only one who gets to pull the trigger.

"But before I kill you, I want you to know my plans, and I want you to hear me well and clearly, Weimer. The moment you die, it will be with the knowledge that as soon as I rip your girlfriend here to pieces, I will make my way back to Germany and I will find your sister, Bettina. As you mentioned, I have unfinished business with her—our romantic interlude that you interrupted. She will be glad to be reunited with me at last, and you will be dead, unable to run to the rescue again. I will enjoy myself even more knowing that you are watching from hell while she and I make up for lost time."

It was all I could do to stop myself from running straight at him and smashing his filthy mouth with my fists. A low growl emitted from my throat, and my hands clenched and flexed over and over. "You will never touch them, Keillor. Even if I have to rise up from the grave and send the hounds of hell to rip out your throat."

"Okay, that is enough small talk for now," he said with a shrug. "You are dead." He pointed the pistols straight at me, and the crack of gunfire burst through the air.

Keillor ran toward the well as I spun around, shocked that I was not wounded.

"Run back behind the barn, Franca," I yelled. But she had grabbed my hand, and we both sprinted for cover as more rifle fire exploded.

With bursts of gunfire behind our backs, we dashed around the corner of the barn. I looked back and spotted Bruno shooting at Keillor from a bedroom window. A bullet splintered the wooden roof that covered the well, and Keillor ducked under the cover like a trapped rabbit. The bedroom window was almost directly above the well. Keillor fired his pistols up in the air over his head, but if he moved in any direction from under the roof, he was a sitting target.

Bruno paused to reload, and Keillor rolled down the hill at the edge of the house behind the well and crouched behind a stack of rocks.

"You may convince yourself you are victorious today, but you are trapped here, Peter Weimer," he yelled. "I am leaving now, but I promise you I will make my way back to your sister. And when I am through tearing her apart, she will die."

Keillor ran like his tail was on fire away from the farm. Bruno dropped the rifle down to me from the bedroom window, and I chased behind Keillor. But he jumped from a ridge where he must have stashed a jeep, and he escaped across the landscape.

CHAPTER THIRTY-FIVE

Franca

I RAN TO PETER WHEN he returned from chasing Keillor, and he grabbed my hand.

"We all have to leave this place," he said. "Now."

We hurried to the house and gathered in the bedroom with Bruno and Laura.

Bruno glanced at my wet hair and clothes. "Are you wounded? Who was that Nazi? Where were you?"

"That was Keillor. The one who is after Peter," I blurted.

Bruno looked at Peter's wet clothes and scowled.

"Like Franca said, that Nazi was Keillor, the one from the catacombs who ordered me to torture Marianna."

"I know who he is," Bruno shouted, pushing his hands back through his hair in frustration.

"He just vowed to find my sister, Bettina, and kill her in revenge against me. But I know him; he will come back here, probably with others to kill all of us first."

Bruno grimaced. "We have to go back to the Chessari villa in Siracusa now and hope it is safe. There are more supplies there, and it's possible to find medical help for Laura." He looked back and forth between me and Peter. "There may be contacts in town that can help you too, Peter. Both of you grab what you can, quickly. We will leave immediately for Siracusa."

"But what about Dominic and Damiano?" I blurted. "They will come back here sometime and will not know where we are. It could be dangerous for them."

"I will go and tell them," Peter said, his face grim.

Bruno grunted in frustration. "There is no time; we need to go to Siracusa now."

"Yes, you do," Peter said.

My eyes widened as the meaning behind Peter's words hit me; he would not be coming to Siracusa with us.

"Keillor will not give up." Peter grimaced. "I've been the worst kind of fool. I never should have come here and endangered you all like this. And it is too risky for any of you to travel with a German."

"But what will you do? Where will you go?" I asked through the thickness in my throat.

"After I find your brothers and warn them, I am going to find and kill Keillor."

"Do you know where he could be hiding?" Bruno asked.

"No, but I will go all the way back to Germany if that is what it takes to find him and to save my sister and mother. I've been hiding long enough, too long. I have put you all in danger. I hope your family can forgive me for that."

"You saved our family more than once. We will always be grateful," Bruno said.

Their words sounded final, like a permanent farewell. The walls were closing in and squeezing my breath.

I held out my hands. "But wait, Keillor does not know our names or where our vineyard is in Siracusa, and there are a lot of people traveling on the roads. There are Italians with blond hair, and we can disguise you."

Peter looked right at me, the grimace gone. "Keillor found me here today. He will find me again and will kill me and anyone I care about—or love." He headed toward the door. "I will get the truck uncovered and ready while you pack."

Bruno rattled off a list of what we should take with us and how we could transport Laura. I ran to the barn to find Peter.

He was pulling bales of hay out of the way for access to the truck. I stopped right in front of him and put out my arms to embrace him, but he stepped around me.

"I am leaving, Franca. I almost got you killed today."

I stepped in front of him again, but he twisted to the side and kept working.

"You are killing me now," I said through the thickness in my throat.

The bales flew through the air as he tossed them off and away from the truck one by one, never meeting my eyes. "I am saving your life. I have had no business being near you. You were right to avoid me, and I was an idiot for . . . for coming here in the first place."

"We never would have met."

"That would have been better for you. I will never forgive myself for this, for all I have done."

"*All* you have done? So now you condemn yourself for meeting me?"

Anger shot out of Peter's eyes. "Yes. I regret that you could have been killed today—that you still might be because of me."

I had not stopped shaking since kissing Peter in the pond and since Keillor had tried to kill us. It was hard to speak. "I regret nothing. I will go with you to warn my brothers and to lead Keillor away from my family, to find him or go with you to Germany to warn your family—the two of us traveling together will not look as strange or suspicious as you would alone."

Peter took me by the shoulders. "Franca, you have not seen how brutal and dangerous this war is in the battle zones. And your sister could be dying. Bruno is crippled, and they have a tiny, defenseless baby. Can you leave them helpless to run off with me?"

Luca was crying so hard and loud in the house that the sound carried over the yard like a siren.

"Take me with you, Peter," I sobbed. "I cannot do it anymore, to stay behind watching my sister die while you leave to face a monster, and I wait for word of your death."

My shoulders weakened in his grip, and he squeezed tighter.

"We both know what you have to choose. I will not let you risk your life to travel with me."

The wind slammed the barn door shut with a bang, and I jumped and cried out as Peter let go of me and threw another bale of hay from in front of the truck.

He looked back over his shoulder. "Keillor could double back here any minute. You have to grab any supplies you can and go. Now, Franca," he said with a grimace.

I shook my head and followed his every footstep right behind him, refusing to let his words penetrate my ears. "I am going to find a way to come with you."

The truck door creaked as he yanked it open and leaned on the frame with a frustrated sigh. "*Basta,* Franca. Stop this. Neither of our countries will ever accept the two of us being together, and we cannot change that reality. I will tell you what is real: hatred, threats, bullets, bombs, grenades, and torture."

I tried to put my arms around Peter again as he spoke, to grab onto him and refuse to let go, but he pushed my arms down.

"Even if or when this war ends, no one will accept us being together, and you know that is the truth. You need to go, to go on and live a beautiful life someday—one that I can never give you. And if our paths ever cross again, you must act like you do not know me or it will endanger us both."

Gas cans lined the wall beside the barn door. Peter grabbed one and used a spout to pour the petrol into the tank. He'd used three cans before he finished and brushed the last remnants of straw from the windshield of the truck.

I watched him, my mind spinning desperately for an answer—anything I could do or say to block his words and make him listen to me. "But why are you surrendering now? We can all get away. You can come to Siracusa with us to take Laura and her family back, and then you and I can find my brothers."

The truck keys hung on a hook that had been hidden behind the hay. Peter marched over and snatched them in his hand, and I stepped up behind him.

"You used the word *love* in the house just now," I whispered to his back.

He stayed still, his head bowed toward the ground, his shoulders slumped. Seconds ticked, and my hope rose. But he turned around and gripped me by my shoulders again, his eyes wide. "It does not matter what I feel or what I felt or even what you feel. We both knew this was wrong."

I grabbed his arm, despair coiling up my throat. "No. You said it yourself when we were together in the parlor. Our feelings may be forbidden and dangerous, but they are not wrong." I swallowed and watched him for any sign of hope.

Peter stared me down and then grimaced as he pushed my hand away from his arm. His eyes glazed over. "I was a fool, and this is over. You were right from the very beginning, Franca. We are enemies. Now go."

CHAPTER THIRTY-SIX

Franca

Reeds and grass whipped and stung my legs as I sprinted toward the house in a haze, numbed by Peter's last words.

Bruno and I threw food, diapers, and clothes into a suitcase and baskets as if the house were on fire.

Peter drove the truck up to the house, and within minutes, we had loaded most of the essential supplies inside, including the radio. He carried Laura and laid her on the mattress in the back of the truck with nary a glance in my direction, and I did not dare let my gaze lock on him for fear the pressure in my chest would burst.

I hurried inside the house to fill canteens with water, and when I came back outside, there was no sign of Peter.

Bruno, already seated in the truck, held Luca. "Come, Franca. We have to leave, quickly," called Bruno. "There is an automobile approaching from across the fields that could be Keillor. Peter ran to the other side of the property for a better look and to get ready. Come quickly. He said for us to hurry ourselves and go."

Bruno pointed at the dust cloud rising from an approaching vehicle.

Laura lay pale as the moon on the mattress in the back of the truck. Luca fussed in Bruno's arms. I held my breath one last time and turned in every direction, but there was no sign of Peter; the property stood motionless and empty, the trees dark and looming. My head spun fast as the wheels of the encroaching vehicle, but my legs did not move.

Laura finally called my name. "Franca, Franca, please."

I jumped behind the wheel of the truck and stomped on the gas while we could still get away.

"If we cut across by the olive trees to the road, we won't intersect with the Jeep," Bruno shouted over the roar of the truck engine.

I gripped the steering wheel, keeping it steady as we rumbled as fast as the truck would go over brush and rocks. We left the De'Angelis farm and Peter Weimer behind in a cloud of dust.

Miles passed, my fingers blanched white on the wheel.

Bruno rested his chin on Luca's head while they both dozed. Laura appeared quiet in the back. And I stared at a road that drained my soul with every mile we drew farther away from Peter.

I wondered if it was a blessing or a curse that I had been so self-aware, so sure about what I wanted just when everything conspired against me and wrenched it away. I wiped the tears from my face before Bruno could open his eyes and see them.

Luca wiggled and rubbed his face into Bruno's neck, and for a moment, I begrudged the love I held for that tiny baby and his parents and all of my family who carried me away from Peter and the chance to pull the fragments of what we had back together.

The tenderness Luca's cries stirred up in me and the bond that kept me bound to my sick sister held me hostage. My birthright, my nationality, stole my ability to love whom I chose. The freedom soldiers were fighting for would never truly reach me—war between Italy and Germany would leave a permanent scar, a wall that dammed my freedom no matter who won the battles. I laid my hand on Luca's back, grasping for bitter solace while tears dried on my cheeks.

The forty-eight kilometers home seemed to stretch across an ocean as we made our way. I was torn in two by a riptide that pulled me toward our villa and back for Peter.

I'd never been a nature aficionada like Marianna, but when we arrived and the rows of grapevines came into view, a part of me came alive again. The smell of the Mediterranean was an old friend, and the leaves on the grapevines waved in the breeze in quiet salutation. At last, I brought the truck to a stop.

"Wait just a moment," I told Bruno. "I will go check the house to be sure we are safe."

The rooms of our villa were too quiet, the air heavy with loneliness until the click-clack of footsteps echoed down the hallway from the kitchen. For a quick instant, I dreamed that it could be my mother. But there was no place for dreams. I hid around a corner where I could see the hall through a crack in the door, and my heart lurched with joy when I recognized our old housekeeper.

"Alma," I cried. I ran down the hall and wrapped my arms around her soft frame. Her embrace flowed into me like it had from the time Alma had bandaged my blisters and knees as a child. I lifted my head from her shoulder, and she held up her apron for me to dry my eyes before she lowered her brows, the usual pleasantness drained from her pale face. "Why are you here, Francesca? You were not to come back at all; it is not safe."

"Why are you here, Alma? You left to take care of your relatives in Ragusa."

"*Si, si, si,* I know, but when the good soldiers came, my sisters and cousins acted safe and happy. They did not need me. I came back to take care of my plants and kitchen. Soldiers came through and left everything a mess."

"I am grateful you are here." I dipped water from the bucket on the table and gulped it down quickly before I returned to the truck for the rest of the family. Bruno smiled when he saw Alma. She hugged him tightly, and then we helped Laura and the baby into the house.

Tears poured down Alma's cheeks when Laura and I told her about the attack in Sortino, Giacomo, and finally about our mother's death. Mama and Alma had worked side by side in our home since before I was born. We sat around the kitchen table and held each other's hands while we wept together. After a time Alma washed her face, straightened her apron and fussed over our family, and especially Luca, like a hen over a nest of eggs.

That evening when things had settled, she stopped me in the hallway. "Signorina Franca, you must go back. Go back to the farm in Sortino. Your papa would be very, very upset to know you are here."

"I know about my papa and his worries, Alma. *Non ti preoccupare.*" I patted her shoulder. "You have always been a blessing to our family; I can never thank you enough."

Alma walked over and hugged me to her bosom.

"*Grazie, carina,*" she said softly.

"You would be content to help with Laura and the baby while I go into town in a couple days? I need to return to the hospital for information."

"Oh, yes, but if you plan to go to town or back to the hospital to see about your mother's body, you must have a man go with you. There are soldiers everywhere, and it will be much too dangerous."

"It is only a few miles away and right in town. And you know it is not a heavily traveled road. Maybe life will always be dangerous. I am not running from it anymore."

The picture window in the kitchen beckoned me outside, and I slipped out the door to escape Alma's warnings.

Row after row of grapevines lined our land like a giant had taken a comb and parted the soil and vines in perfect symmetry. Grape leaves flashed green, yellow, and red in the sun and many of them drooped or had shriveled up and died. Plump clusters of dusty purple grapes hung from the vines, some of them overripe and spoiled, some still awaiting a harvest that would not come this year. I longed for the chaos of gathered workers and the scent of grape juice that soaked the air as the birds dived for a taste of the banquet we laid out for the celebrations.

A breeze hummed a soft tune through the branches and eased the tourniquet that squeezed around my heart. I wanted to run carefree down the rows of grapevines as I had as a child. I wanted Laura to be strong enough to run with me. I wanted the tug of war in my heart to be won and to see Peter standing here beside me.

CHAPTER THIRTY-SEVEN

Franca

December 3, 1943

I WENT TO CHECK ON Laura and found her propped up in bed, a blue blanket across her legs. Her yarn and knitting needles lay on the nightstand untouched. We'd been back for a few days, but this was the first time Laura had sat up. I clung to hope and tried to dismiss the blue coloring in her lips.

"We should take you outside in a chair every day just so you can sit in the vineyard, Laura. Being back at the vineyard has stirred my memories of our young and carefree days running through those rows and dodging behind the vines. Remember playing hide-and-go-seek with Bruno, Marianna, and the boys when we were young?"

"I miss the boys so much," she said softly.

"I do too. I'm glad they can be of help to the widow women, but I hope Peter found them and that they are on their way here."

"That is what I am hoping for," Laura said with a sigh. "I need to see them." Her skin appeared like it was coated in wax, and her eyes were ringed with the same bluish hue as her lips.

I swallowed hard. "Would you like to go sit outside now, Laura? We could take Luca out there with us on a blanket."

She gazed through the curtains out the window like I had not even spoken. "You've done the right thing, Franca," she finally said.

"What right thing?"

"You got us home. This is where I longed to be, where I wanted to rest."

I searched the top of her bureau for her hairbrush and then raised it like a beacon of hope in my hand. "I'm glad; you can regain your strength on our own land now. Let me brush your hair for you and pin it up."

"I will not get stronger, Franca. You know that. I knew it before, and then when that Nazi soldier came back and Bruno shot at him from our window, my heart stopped and hung there like a weight pulled it down. Bruno called to me, so I said a silent prayer, and my heart started beating again. I wanted the comfort of home; Bruno will need that, and I want Luca to grow up here."

"Stop talking that way, Laura. It will only make you more tired," I said, though my throat had locked tight.

"You know I am telling the truth. We have always known that God only granted me a short sojourn on earth, but you will have to help Bruno accept it."

She reached for my hand, and I set the hairbrush back on the bureau slowly before I made my way beside her. I refused to let her words sink in. "You are just too tired and need rest most of all." I kissed her on the forehead. "And you will see; you will get stronger."

Two days later, we stood at her graveside. I wondered where the breeze had gone, why the sun had a filter over it, and the twitter of birds seemed miles away. I stood like a statue while Bruno and a neighbor boy named Elio lowered Laura into the ground. None of us wanted to track down a priest for a church burial where Laura would be miles away.

Alma wept and bounced a fussy Luca in her arms. I wanted to hold Luca and comfort him, but my arms stayed limp at my sides.

Bruno and Elio finished filling the grave, and then Bruno fell on top of the mound of dirt, sobbing like a child.

My sister's heart had always been weak, but the war had killed her—Hitler, his army, Vasyl Keillor, complications after Luca's birth. Weak heart or not, terror and pain took her away years before she was supposed to go.

The war killed her, but I had failed her. If I had not distracted Peter in the pond, he could have stopped Keillor before he got to the house and gave Laura that final shock to her heart. But I'd been busy laughing and kissing a forbidden man.

Peter's parting words chopped their way through the wall I had built around my heart and lay it wide open. "*We are enemies.*"

After we buried Laura, I walked the mile to Marianna's property and found my way through the debris and destruction the war had left in its wake. The De'Angelis home was nothing but charred beams and blackened stone. I lay on the ground next to the stagnant pond, wept, and tried to imagine that the world still existed without Laura. Memories comforted and devastated me. If I closed my eyes, Laura, Marianna, and I would be braiding and coifing each other's hair, wearing each other's clothes, trying the newest cosmetics that we'd ordered from a catalog from Milano.

I returned to our villa and sat in the vineyard, listening to our childhood banter and Laura's laughter dive and sweep in and out of the grapevines and dance on the clouds before they floated away.

CHAPTER THIRTY-EIGHT

Franca

December 17, 1943

Two weeks passed. I sat at the kitchen table, staring at the calendar on the wall. Christmas would be next week. The Mediterranean infused itself in the swirling winds, a clammy cold that seeped through the cracks in the house and my layers of clothing, all the way to my bones. We kept a fire in the fireplace, and I clung to Luca to keep him warm and to comfort him and myself at the same time.

At night, I shivered under my covers and dreamed about running through a fog to find Peter just like I'd read in romance books and seen in daydreams. There had been no word from him and no sign of my brothers, Dominic and Damiano, since we left Sortino. I dreaded telling them about Laura, but their vivacious spirits would do much for Bruno and the rest of us.

Bruno held a bundled Luca the next day—kissing him and holding him clasped in his arms on the rise where we had buried Laura. It took a moment for me to wipe the blur of tears from my eyes and see that Bruno had stood and was calling my name. He pointed toward the road, and I spotted a military truck coming toward our villa.

Our encounters with Keillor had made us leery. I grabbed two rifles from the pantry and held one out to Bruno after he'd made it back to the house and passed Luca to Alma.

"I told Elio to be on watch from behind those trees just in case," Bruno said, pointing at a group of olive trees and hedges on the side of the house. "Allied soldiers do not just stop by, but perhaps this is just a routine check for Nazi or Fascist strays."

"I'll wait behind the bushes in the courtyard," I blurted as I gripped the other rifle and hurried away.

Alma scurried out of the kitchen and down the hall with Luca.

I placed the rifle behind a flower box and sat in a porch chair behind a thick bougainvillea. The roar of the truck lowered in pitch and wound down in its approach. I picked up a book to read as if I'd been lounging for the afternoon and waited for soldiers to come my way.

The vehicle came to a stop right in front of our villa. The doors creaked as they opened and closed, and I detected three separate voices—three very familiar voices. I set the book down and stepped around the hedge, then took off at a run, right into the arms of Marianna De'Angelis Scalvone. We both wept and twirled in circles as we hugged and kissed each other on each cheek. I greeted Massimo and, finally, Marianna's mother, signora De'Angelis, the same way. It seemed an impossible dream that they were here. The last I'd seen them, they were headed to Foggia on the mainland, and it could have been months before we'd see them again.

"What are you doing here?" I asked all three at once.

Their faces became somber, and Marianna spoke first. "The bombings in Foggia are horrendous; the city is almost destroyed. But we also came back here because we needed to do some work in Siracusa. Especially Massimo. He is here on assignment." She looked up at him as she spoke, and Massimo put his arm around her.

"How horrible for the people of Foggia; they must be devastated and frantic." My voice quivered as I fought to keep our own tragic news quiet for at least a moment.

Marianna and I looked at each other as we had a thousand times in our lives. But she had healed from her injuries, and now I looked at a beautiful woman, her dark hair pinned halfway up in back before it fell down in spiraling waves. Her eyes like her mother's, brown as freshly upturned earth with an edge of sorrow that had been planted by the war and the loss of her father.

We leaned forward and hugged each other again before she gripped my hand and our tears flowed.

Shadows of fatigue underlined signora De'Angelis's eyes, and I had nothing but more pain to give her. I took her hand. "Please, please come inside and see Bruno. He may have seen you out here by now, and there is news—" My voice faltered.

Massimo spoke up. "Marianna and her mother have been so anxious to see you."

I gazed at his handsome face. "I am so grateful you made it all the way here safely." I repeated and swallowed the lump in my throat as I looked at the three of them. "Before we go inside, I have to tell you." I pressed my hands over my eyes, willing the tears to let me speak. "Laura became too weak in the past month. She died just two weeks ago."

Signora De'Angelis grasped her throat with her hand. "No, no, no, Franca. It cannot be true. Where is Bruno? Take me to Bruno," she cried.

The door in the courtyard opened, and Bruno stood leaning against it with his crutch, his eyes hollow, his expression lifeless, until we stepped inside. He fell on his mother's breast, and they wept openly in each other's arms.

Minutes passed before the world started turning again.

I would have to tell them what happened with my mother also, but for a moment, I did not have the strength. I guided everyone to a seat and called to Alma to please bring us all a fresh drink.

Marianna held onto my hand. "Franca, I do not know how I can endure this loss. I am in shock. Even though we knew she had a weak heart, I never expected Laura would go so very young."

When Alma walked in with Luca in her arms, signora De'Angelis immediately reached for him, kissing his face over and over and crying anew.

The fire needed stoking, but I was hesitant to leave Marianna's side. Bruno sat beside his mother, his eyes red but his demeanor more peaceful.

Signora De'Angelis wiped her tears. "Have you gotten word about Laura to your mother? And your father?"

I pressed my hand against my heart. "We lost our mother too. She died in the hospital after her injuries from a Nazi attack at the farm. They had told us she was healing, but then she was gone. There is no word on where we can even find her body."

I expected a new wave of sorrow, but everyone sat there silent, their eyes wide.

"No, Franca, you are misinformed," Marianna said, a look of shock on her face. "Your mother is not dead."

I drew back. "Yes, she is. I went to the hospital, and they told me directly."

"Massimo was told before we left the mainland that your mother's death was faked to get her out of the hospital alive and safe."

My ears rang as I looked back and forth between Marianna and Massimo and tried to make the whirl of her words make sense. "I went to the hospital. The woman there, Donatella, said she was dead. They had even put her body in a mass grave because of typhus risk."

"That must have been a cover story. Word was that your mother was in danger, so I am sure the partisans got her out of there," Massimo said.

"But how could they? The nurse, she had a record of her passing. Details." Reality hit me like a cold wave. "The nurse, Donatella, she must have been in on a cover story."

"Your parents were in Messina, and then they were supposed to go up the mainland," Massimo continued.

"My father had been that close? In Messina?"

Bruno had stood as he followed our conversation. His red-rimmed eyes opened wide.

"You look like you need to sit back down, Bruno," Massimo said. He looked back and forth between me and my brother-in-law. "Both of you seem to be in shock."

Alma hurried into the room with glasses of water for everyone. "Signora Chessari is alive?"

"*Si*, it is true. Elisa Chessari is alive. But we must keep all of this quiet, to ourselves," Marianna said. She held a glass of water up to my mouth. "Drink this. Take a deep breath."

I drank the water, my hands shaking.

I longed for the relief Marianna's words should have given me, but new pain and confusion burned and consumed my thoughts like a fever. "Why did my father take my mother away without coming for the rest of us? Why was there no word to us that she was alive, her own children? Her death was one of the final blows that weakened Laura. If she had been told the truth, it may have given her strength to carry on, to heal."

"The radio had quit working the night you went to find her body, remember, Franca?" Bruno said. "There would be no way for him to signal us."

"He could have come for us. He could have sent a messenger."

"A Nazi had been asking about your mother, so maybe he thought it was too dangerous to go to Sortino," Marianna said, grasping my hand.

"I am not sure of anything anymore," I said, standing up. "I did not even know my father was a partisan leader until recently. He never bothered to tell me."

Signora De'Angelis came over and put her arm around me. "*Capisco e mi dispiace.* I understand your confusion, *carina*. And most of all, I am so very sorry about beautiful Laura."

Hearing Laura's name spoken with such compassion almost choked me. The joy over my mother being alive stayed locked in my gut, churning and held hostage by the lie about her death that may have shortened Laura's life. Even our mother had not found a way to reassure us.

The air closed in around me. I marched out the back door and made my way to the graveside to find Laura. The sun died on the horizon while I relived the horrifying moments in the kitchen when the Nazi soldiers had attacked and shot our mother. The gunshots echoed like cannon fire in my head. Laura had begun a downward spiral into her grave that day, and I had refused to accept it. I crushed a handful of dirt in my hands and screamed at rows of silent, skeletal grapevines.

I washed my face from the well behind the house and sat in the parlor to rest my eyes. The front door opened, and Dominic and Damiano casually walked in, huge grins on their faces. I jumped from my seat with a cry of relief and wrapped my arms around them, roughed up their hair with my hands, and kissed their cheeks over and over.

"You have grown a foot each," I said through my tears. I kissed them again.

"We walked all the way here," Damiano said as he plopped down in his filthy clothes on the settee.

"And pushed a cow the whole way," added Dominic. "We were like hobos or vagabonds, and it took us days to get here, but there was no transportation available."

"Rosa? The cow is Rosa?" I asked, surprised at the spark of happiness that gave me.

"Yes, Rosa. Peter insisted that we bring her with us."

My heart dropped to my feet at the mention of Peter's name, but I held my smile in place.

"Were you afraid of Peter when he came for you?" I asked both of them.

They shook their heads with a tsk of their tongues, and Dom jumped in first. "He left a note for us tacked to the barn door to tell us who he was and the whole story and situation. Then we met him out under a tree—"

"We could tell he was the real thing," bragged Damiano. "You just get a feel for some people, no?"

My brothers had better instincts than I did. "So you returned to the farm first?"

Dominic laughed. "Yes, it was on our way anyway and we had to turn the pigs and chickens loose so they could forage for food. Those pigs were mean. They charged right at us when we took the side down for them."

"Ungrateful swine. Dom barely made it over one of the walls before one of them ploughed him over."

I smiled at the image of my brothers running and dodging the pigs. "How did you have enough food for the journey? You must be starving."

Damiano lifted an empty bag that was slung across his shoulder. "The widows loaded us up with bread, fruit, and cheese. We found water along the way."

"And when we went back to the farm, we found a bit more food there," Dominic added.

I finally asked, "And Peter? What happened to him, did he come with you?"

Dominic shrugged. "No. He told us goodbye as soon as we got back to the farm. He said he had to get back to his family in Germany."

Before I could react, Dominic quipped, "Where is Laura?"

I put my arms around both of my brothers. "Sit down, *fratelli miei*; I have something I must tell you."

CHAPTER THIRTY-NINE

Franca

December 21, 1943

Marianna and I sat across from each other on my bed like we had hundreds of times before. Two days had passed since the boys returned, and I knew Mari's time here was limited.

She leaned back on the cast-iron footboard and pulled the edge of my bedding up over her lap, playing with the white fringe on the edge of the bedspread like she had in our youth, tying the long strings together or braiding them. Today she brushed the fringe distractedly with the fingers of one hand. I was grateful that in the three months since I had last seen her the bruises on her face and legs had faded and she had regained color in her cheeks.

My room had not changed—its curtains, although worn with age, still warmed the room in floral pink. The armoire and dressers stood regal in deep mahogany with gold trim, and the white, marble floor was elegant with its veins of black and gray. I sat on a pillow in one of my lace-collared blouses and green skirt, almost feeling out of place in my room and the clothes I had missed so much in Sortino.

"How are the boys?" Mari asked, squeezing my fingers. "I saw them out by Laura's grave this morning. They are buoyant and brave, and I know they will help comfort your family."

I hoped she was right and watched her fingers straighten the fringe evenly.

"You know what is strange?" I asked, looking in her eyes. "I still want to pray for God to spare Laura's life, even when I know it's too late. I've been reciting prayers for her my whole life, and I do not know how to stop even though I hardly believe in God anymore."

"Keep praying. Light candles for her at the church. I will go with you."

I tsked my tongue. My faith was as faded as the curtains.

Mari still held me by the hand, her eyes shiny with emotion. "It does not seem real that she is gone. In Foggia, I found myself picturing you all here as usual—happy and together. I cannot fathom the horror you went through when those Nazis attacked you in Sortino. I am glad we were sent back here to Siracusa so we can be with you now. As soon as I heard about the attack, I told Massimo we had to come back, but of course, we had to wait for his orders. I have missed you so much, Franca. And I have been missing my father terribly. I wish I had time to take our boat out if it is still there. I long to be on the water."

I sighed. "I long for our simple, happy days. Life was an open book, an unmarked map laid out before us. But the whole world is bombed and full of holes."

"War is chaos and confusion. We are all trapped in a web, trying to survive."

"A web of deceit, where you cannot tell your daughter who and what you really are? What you are doing? That you are even alive? Laura needed to know my mother was alive; it would have given her hope and reassurance."

"Maybe they tried to send you word."

"It frightens me because maybe they tried and were thwarted by danger."

The clanging of dishes and aroma of garlic simmering in olive oil told me that Alma was at work in the kitchen. There were a lot of us to feed now, especially with my two lanky brothers back home. I needed to see if I could help—a task I never would have thought of before Sortino. I climbed off the bed and changed my blouse for an older one.

"Massimo has gone into town to search for some answers about your parents."

"I need to see them; I have to see my mother with my own eyes. Everything keeps turning upside down. Mama will be devastated to hear about Laura."

"I am so sorry. I am sure your parents will find great comfort in Luca when they return."

I could see her vision—my mother nuzzling Luca's cheeks, my father smiling and holding Luca on his lap. But a wall of fear came up in front of my eyes. Hope could be a dangerous thing during a war.

I sat back down on the edge of the bed and tipped my head back, staring at the ceiling and letting my tears run into my hair. "It was my job to care for Laura—to save her. And I failed."

Mari climbed off the bed and stood beside me, her brow creased in worry as she held me by my shoulders and locked her gaze on mine. "You must stop blaming yourself. It is not your fault that Laura was born with a faulty heart. And you did save her—you saw her through a lifetime of difficulties and limitations. You gave her weeks of care in Sortino after Luca was born and got her home. You've become the strength for everyone in your family, Franca. You even saved your mother's life."

I shook my head. "Doctors did that. I could not even drive the truck to the hospital."

"Yes, you could and you did. Bruno said you dropped Peter outside of town and drove the truck to the hospital in time. Then you saved Peter by picking him back up, even though I know you must have been afraid of him."

Mari sat back down beside me and took my hand, but I slipped it away and turned toward her. "You are my closest friend, Marianna, even closer than a sister in some ways. But you did not tell me you left a German soldier hiding right under my feet when you left Sortino."

"I wanted to tell you. The words almost burst from me before we left. But our partisan leader forbade me. Everyone else agreed, and I knew it was dangerous for anyone to know Peter was there in case of an attack or interrogation."

"I know that now. And I know who your partisan leader is—my own father, Lieutenant Bianco," I said with an edge of resentment and raising my hands toward the ceiling in frustration.

"You know about him?" Mari asked with a deep exhale. "I am so relieved. I hated keeping it a secret. I am so sorry, Franca."

"Do you know where Peter is now?" I asked, holding my breath.

She slowly shook her head. "I asked Bruno where Peter was shortly after we discussed Laura and your mother, and he said he had stayed behind to find the boys and see if he could get back to Germany."

"It will be impossible for him to return to Germany alive. He is an enemy everywhere he goes," I said, pushing my hair back with my fingers and staring up at the ceiling.

Frustration still had me by the throat, and I frowned at Mari, throwing my hands up. "I have known about partisans for years. Why all the dishonesty and the secrecy about my father?"

"Because he is one of the top organizers and leaders. He works directly with the American OSS, so exposing him is too dangerous. The secret of who he was could have been discovered by the Nazis anytime, and he did not want them searching for him here or using any of his family as a pawn or a punishment."

"So that is why he had us stay away, in case the Nazis were trying to track any of us down."

"Yes."

She had confirmed my belief, but angst still gnawed at my gut. I walked over to the window and looked outside to take a deep breath. Dominic held Luca in the courtyard. The baby was almost five months old now, his eyes still a deep blue and his cheeks dimpled. Luca grinned when Dominic leaned down and blew a kiss on his cheek, and he grabbed onto Dominic's curly hair with both hands. My brother laughed and carefully pried his hair from each of Luca's fists.

I turned back to Marianna and sat down on a high-back floral chair. "All of this has made me realize I must make my own life, my own decisions, my own way. I've let others protect me for far too long. I waited and longed to be home, but now that I am here it is strangely empty, even with all of you here. I wake up at night staring at the ceiling as if I have never seen it before."

"Perhaps it is you who is different and not the house. You have changed, Franca. You are so serious and . . ." She walked over to me and turned my hand palm up. "There are calluses I never thought I'd see on Franca Chessari."

She pulled her skirt over her knees as she sat on the footstool in front of my chair and smiled. "There are many ways to be a hero."

Memories of how I fumbled and stumbled at the Sortino farm came back to me. I shook my head with my eyes closed. "I have been so pampered, Mari, even lazy and selfish."

She tsked her tongue and frowned. "That is not true. You are talented, educated, and gifted and have always worked hard. Do I need to show you your hundreds of fashion designs and creations in your art books?" She gestured toward my ample bookcase with her hand. "And that is not all. Your heart is one of compassion, and you have sacrificed so much for your family, Franca. You have kept everyone alive and well for months. Remember our charity group and our deliveries to the families in Siracusa? You have helped many people."

I shrugged my shoulders, unimpressed with her list. "*Grazie*, I have learned *tantissime cose*, but you were the brave one who started our charity group and has worked as a spy. I helped our charity group, but back then, I never would have been courageous enough to do it on my own."

"And now?"

The weight of her question pushed down on my shoulders, and I hung my head and stared at the floor, unsure of what to do and how to do it alone now that Mari was married, Laura was gone, and Peter had disappeared.

The call of the jackdaws outside my window caught my attention and took me back to standing beside Peter in the fields of Sortino and learning to use a weapon. I'd missed the targets more than once, but in the end, I had hit them.

I lifted my chin. "Now, I would do it. Even though I may be terrified. There is nothing for me to help with here except chores and watching Luca, and Alma and your mother are here for him, even the boys now too. I have done all I could for my family, and something is beckoning me."

Marianna climbed back on the bed and tucked her legs up beside her with a smile. "Or perhaps someone is beckoning you. That leads me to some questions I have—questions about Peter Weimer."

My face flushed, and I stood up and slipped on my leather shoes. "I should go help Alma with *pranzo*. We will need to eat soon."

"I heard my mother in there working with her."

"Luca may need me."

Marianna pointed through the curtains outside where Dominic still sat in a patio chair holding Luca.

I sat back down on the edge of the bed and gripped my hands tight together on my lap, resigned to my fate. "What do you mean? What about Peter?"

"You have avoided saying anything about him. Did you get to know him at all?"

"He is . . ." I rubbed my hand over my forehead, avoiding her scrutiny. "He was very helpful with the chores at the farm."

"How helpful?"

I looked at her, and she lifted her eyebrows. I knew I could confide in her, but I also knew how hard she had worked for the partisans. She may be worried over any involvement with a German.

"I tried to resist his help for a long time, but we were desperate, and he was persistent," I answered.

Marianna's gaze bore into me, pressing me to say more.

I finally relented. "And what else did you want to know? If I ever noticed his handsome face?"

She grinned. "I know you too well, *amica mia*—you noticed his handsome face."

I tsked my tongue, seeing Peter's clear, blue eyes and strong jaw before me again and steeling myself against the wound that threatened to burst open.

"I have said nothing about him."

"I know. The truth is in what you do not say."

I lay back on the bed with my hands clasped over my stomach and stared up at the ceiling so I would not have to meet Mari's eyes. "There is nothing more. Even if I had noticed him as you say, or he noticed me, it is forbidden."

"It may be forbidden, even dammed, but that does not stop a flood of attraction and true emotion," she said.

I clasped one hand over my brow, unsure where her questions were leading. "Do I look like I am drowning?"

She huffed out her breath. "I am not a stranger, Franca, or an interrogator. Stop hiding your real answers. I can hear and see them in you whether you say them or not. I thought of this when we departed for Foggia and left Peter behind, that there was a distinct strength in Peter. There may be more than one reason he came into our lives. You once lectured me about Massimo when I thought a future with him was impossible. Now it is my turn. Peter is a good man, and someday this war really will end."

Her words sounded positive, even hopeful. It twisted a knife in my belly as I relived the last moments with Peter in the barn again—his scowl and the tightness in his jaw before he coldly spoke his parting words. *We are enemies.*

The shock over Keillor's attack and losing Laura had kept my thoughts tumbling and churning. But sitting here with Marianna again, unable to keep the pain of the last moments I'd had with Peter at bay, brought a new memory and realization to light; in that last second, the last instant before I had run to the house, I glanced at Peter one last time. And when I did I glimpsed a shadow of sorrow pass over his eyes.

The truth rose up like a tidal wave and took my breath—Peter did not mean the things he had said to me—he said them to make me get away safely. He knew I would not leave him or that I may come back again and try to find him, and it would be too dangerous.

I wanted to fall on Marianna's shoulder and cry with relief, but the tidal wave of realization still held another truth; no matter Peter's intentions at that moment, no matter the reality that his feelings for me had been real, his goodbye had also been real. My countrymen had held bias against Germans since WWI, and now their wrath was an inferno. Peter's eyes had said it all when they clouded over as he looked at me—he severed everything between us because he knew a future for us was impossible.

Peter was gone, lost in enemy territory and finding his way back to Germany for good. He had said goodbye to all of us and set out on his own with the mission to find Vasyl Keillor or to reach his family first. He would not be working with Bruno or my father's partisans anymore. He would not be coming back to Sicily. There would be no way to trace him on his journey. He could be killed by Keillor, hung by his own army or one of my fellow Italians, and I would never know.

Half of me had stayed behind the day we left Sortino, a ghost of myself haunting the barn, the house, the pond, searching for Peter, waiting for him to deny the things he'd said and return to me. But he was no longer there, and he had made sure to sever our ties completely before he left. I had to summon this ghost of myself and move on. But there was one thing more I had to do before I let him go.

Marianna sat watching me, waiting for me to share Peter's and my story. But I could not make myself relive the pain. I clasped my hands tighter over the wrench in my belly, beckoning the ghost and putting myself back together.

"I may have noticed Peter but nothing . . . anymore. Do not worry; there will be no danger because of me. Peter comes from the Nazi army. I cannot change that."

Mari let out a huff of breath. "Hitler was Peter's leader until Peter saw the truth. And Mussolini was our leader until we Italians saw the truth. Did that make us all Fascists or Nazis?"

"Maybe it just made us all fools," I answered dully.

"So what are we now? Are we still fools?"

I turned my head and looked directly at Marianna in her black skirt with a white blouse tucked into it, a dark scarf at her neck and a belt at the waist that was designed to hold ammunition and a weapon when needed against the Axis—the Germans. I fisted my hands until my nails dug into my palms as I looked at the strength and confidence Marianna exuded. I had found some of that confidence in Sortino, and maybe I could find a way to use it to help my parents and to help Peter one last time.

"I will not be a fool," I said. "But there is an emergency that we must help Peter with."

Before Marianna could respond, Massimo came into my room, his dark eyes serious as he looked at me.

I sat up quickly.

"I went to town to get an update about your mother and father, Franca. I have checked with contacts, and they say they were last seen in Napoli, but then we hit a brick wall. I am sorry and very frustrated, but there are no more details. Wherever they are and whatever they are doing, it is incognito."

My pulse kicked against my ribs. "Could they be in hiding? Have they been captured?"

His eyes looked sympathetic as he shook his head. "*Mi dispiace*, I am sorry, but at this point, I am out of answers."

Marianna had climbed off the bed and moved beside Massimo. He put his arm around her and held her close as she whispered in his ear.

He nodded. "Marianna assures me we are free to tell you everything now. Your father and my father have been working together as partisans against Mussolini and Hitler since the war began. Your father as Lieutenant Bianco and my father as Gregorio. I work close under my father's direction, but until we arrived here, I did not know that contact with your father had been lost. If I had known, perhaps I could have found out more before we left."

I held my hand over my chest and looked down the black veins and patterns that meandered their way to nowhere in the marble floor as I tried to gather my thoughts. "Did you radio your father about Lieutenant Bianco when you were in town?" I asked, my voice rising with hope.

"I sent a message to him through our contacts, but because of where my father is, it could take a long time to reach him."

Mari and Massimo both looked at me with sadness and concern in their eyes, but that did me no good. I did not need sympathy; I needed answers.

"So what do we do? How do we find out where they are? And there is another situation I must tell you about; Peter Weimer's family is in danger." I grabbed Marianna's hand. "The Nazi leader that had you captured has a personal vendetta against Peter with a long history since before the war. This man, Keillor, is the one who attacked us just before we left Sortino. He vowed to find Peter's family and torture and kill them in retaliation for Peter's actions. Is there any way you can use your connections to send word and warn Peter's mother and sister? Peter said he is going to find a way back to Germany to get them to safety, but we know how impossible those odds are."

Marianna had gone pale, and she and Massimo stared at me, their eyes wide as they contemplated my words.

Massimo grimaced. "Keillor must be stopped, and I am compelled to help. But as you know, half the world is at war, and everyone is in danger. I honestly do not know if we can get word into Germany. The odds are totally against it. The other obstacle is that another urgent assignment just came in, and Marianna and I have to leave as quickly as we can for Catania. I hurried back here to tell you." He looked at Marianna.

"How long will this urgent assignment take?" I asked, my chest constricting. If Massimo and Marianna left, I had no idea how to find more answers about my parents or how to help Peter.

"Several days, maybe even a week or two. But if I know your father, he has holed up somewhere safe, so do not panic, Franca. And I promise I will send word to Peter's family if at all possible. But although we are very grateful to him, I am afraid there will be little we can do. "

Marianna put her arms around me. "I will help find your parents and see if we can help Peter also—as soon as we can."

I could not unlock my fingers from my throat or hug Marianna in return. I knew that my parents were in danger, and a sense of urgency to help Peter rose in my throat. I'd heard reassurances my whole life while other people moved forward and took action.

"I will grab our things," Massimo said as he left the room.

I turned to Marianna, grabbing her hands to hold her full attention. "How did you become involved with the partisans?"

"I talked your father into letting me help. It was not easy."

"I am not waiting for word about my parents. I lost my mother and now my sister, and I will not sit back and lose my mother all over again and my father as well. It is eating me up inside. I can search for them and maybe get others to search more deeply."

"But Franca, your father is not here to connect you with good people, and our best team members are all in the Puglia now. Some rebel army members are ruthless and violent."

I rejected her warnings with a shake of my head. "I will go back to the hospital for information. I am convinced that the nurse, Donatella, recognized my father's name the night I took my mother to the hospital. I am convinced she will have information or know someone who can help me."

Mari squeezed my hand and lowered her brow. "You are right; waiting a few days can be the difference between life and death, and I see no reason why you should not ask for help. But step softly if you can. Donatella does know who your father is, but you will have to be careful to get her to admit she knows him or anything about your mother. She was a partisan three years ago along with her fiancé. The two of them were captured, and during questioning, they broke both of Donatella's legs and killed her fiancé. She is bitter and very hesitant to admit she knows anything about partisan members or what they do. Use my name if you need to and . . . if you must find out more, see if Donatella will help you connect with her brother, Lello, in Napoli. I know him, and he may assist you."

"Thank you, Mari." I put my arms around her, drawing on her strength and courage. "I will try to be careful."

CHAPTER FORTY

Franca

I'D WAITED FOR OVER AN hour at the hospital, breathing through my mouth to stave off the reek of seeping wounds and urine and sure that Donatella hoped I would become discouraged and leave her alone.

I finally opened the door to her office on my own, drawing the scent of lemon oil and stale cigarette smoke into my lungs as I took a deep breath and planted myself in front of Donatella's wide oak desk.

She lifted her head from studying paperwork and frowned. "I am busy."

"I can see that. Forgive my interruption, but I need more information about my mother and where she really is," I said to the top of Donatella's head when she lowered it back down in dismissal. "I could see your hesitation to take my mother and our hired man in the night I brought them here, but you still did. Why?"

"You were just a young woman; you seemed so helpless," she answered without looking up.

"But in the beginning, you refused to take them. You were adamant about it. It wasn't until you heard my name, or actually, it was when I told you my father's name that you agreed to take care of them."

"I assure you it was to help you because of pity. Nothing more."

"Then why will you not help me now? Tell me what really happened to my mother. I know she did not really die." I grabbed hold of the edge of her desk. "*Ti prego, Donatella, aiutami,*" I begged.

She still refused to look up at me, and my spine stiffened. "I asked you once before. Is this the only hospital for soldiers in Siracusa? My friend volunteered as a nurse at one, but it may have been closer to the edge of town."

She lifted her chin and glared at me. "What was your friend's name?"

"Marianna De'Angelis."

Her eyes darted back and forth, and she fidgeted with her papers, then stuffed them into a filing cabinet that squeaked as she slammed the drawer.

"*Va bene*, yes, we do have another hospital on the southern edge of town, and I worked there until recently."

"You were Marianna's supervisor, no? She worked there just a few weeks. Did you not know her well?" I bit the inside of my cheek and gathered my nerve. "Some called her *Siara*."

Donatella smacked a file she had taken from the drawer down on her desk. "Why are you really here again, and why are you asking about this woman?" she quipped.

I dug my nails into my palms. "Because my friend Marianna or Siara or whatever you called her said you might help me find out where my parents are."

Donatella headed straight for the door. "This Marianna? Siara? No, I do not know what you are talking about. She must have had a different supervisor. I apologize but I must get back to work. Please go."

She opened the office door, her jaw locked tight. But I stood stock-still.

"I am not leaving. My father is missing, Donatella. You know him. You know what he does. And you know that my mother did not really die. And now he and my mother are missing."

Donatella cursed and pushed her fingers back through her hair. "*Madonna mia, non c'e la faccio piu.* I cannot do this anymore." She gripped me by my elbow and shoved me toward a chair. "I am fed up with being pulled in with you rebels no matter what I say to keep you people away. I will tell you some things, but I swear on the head of Santa Lucia that if you ever come here again I will turn you over to the authorities as a spy for the Nazis."

"I do not care," I said, refusing to sit where she had shoved me and staring her down. "Tell me what you know."

Her eyes were daggers. "Yes, I know your father, and I knew when I heard your mother's name the night you brought her here that he would want her saved. I felt like I owed him a favor because he directs my brother's partisan group. So I told the doctor to help you and take your mother in. Now I regret it. And I do not know why your parents are missing or where they are." She pursed her lips. "I have told you enough. You need to leave, signorina. I am sorry I do not have all the answers."

"I am not leaving until you tell me where they may be or who can help me find them. I am sure you know a lot more. Paolo and Elisa Chessari are my family, not yours, and you have no right to keep information about them from me. You are going to tell me now. You said your brother works under my father. If I had information about your brother, I would tell you. We are at war, but we are still human beings."

I was astonished at the volume of my own voice. Anyone in the hallway would have heard me. But I did not care if Hitler heard me. I was finished with secrets.

I glared at Donatella when she remained silent. "I said I am not leaving."

Donatella threw her notebook on the floor and threw her hands up once again. She sat down on a leather chair, lit a cigarette, and blew a full breath of smoke out her nostrils.

"I will tell you more. But I forbid God and the saints from holding me responsible for other people's secrets anymore."

I wanted to grab her by the shoulders and shake her until she finally said something that helped. "Donatella, I do not care about your feelings. Tell me what you know." I glowered at her. "Now."

She raised the hand with the cigarette in the air and whipped it around in a small circle in surrender. "Yes, like I said, I know your father . . . Paolo Chessari. He is, eh, not just a vintner. He is also someone who helps in secret to end the war. Your mother has assisted too."

"I already knew this. Tell me more."

She scowled and sucked on her cigarette, a deep crease forming in her forehead. "Some Germans know about your parents too, and they planned to find and kill them. We got a warning here at the hospital that a Nazi named Keillor was searching for your mother. We did not know what to do. We used the radio to contact Bianco, and he came and took your mother out in a coffin as if she was dead. I helped them. There. That is all. The end of it."

I laid my hand over my chest. "Keillor? A German soldier named Keillor?"

"*Si*, Keillor," She said before she faced me again. "I do not have more details. I try to stay out of it all I can. When you brought your mother here, shot in her belly, and I heard her name, I knew we had to try to save her. As I told you, your father has helped my brother and many, many others for years."

"I have to find them. I will not stay here hiding while my parents are missing or fighting in a war. I will not do it, Donatella. Tell me where my parents went that night. Tell me where to go and what to do. I will not stop asking you until you do."

She shrugged and took a deep breath before she exhaled and put out her cigarette. "I have come this far and broken all my silence, so I will tell you all I know once and for all. The last I heard, they were on the mainland. I am not sure where they were headed. My guess would be Napoli because of activity I have heard of up there. The partisans may kill me for even telling you that much, so I might as well tell you the rest, and then I hope that is the last I have to see or hear of you or another partisan."

She lit another cigarette while I bit down on my lip to keep from yelling at her to hurry and speak up. She crossed her legs and looked out the window.

"Napoli was liberated from the Nazis because of a huge rebellion by its citizens at the end of September, so partisans are probably still there. Perhaps that is where you parents were headed when they disappeared. Word is a few squads were there, but it is not easy to arm, clothe, and feed them when the cities are half starved, so who knows where they may be camped or traveling. It takes a whole division of rebels to do any real damage against the Nazis, so I do not know if your father would still be there or not. It may not do him much good."

"I told you my father and my mother are missing. They may have been captured. I have that information from two of his squad leaders themselves."

"I hear you, but maybe your parents do not want to be found because it is too risky. If you want to try to find them, it will be very dangerous."

"I do not care if it is dangerous. Give me names or information to help me find them."

She took another drag from her cigarette and shook her head in disapproval. "You are a fool, but so are most of the people I know, so here it is. No one is supposed to be on the water but the military, but in two days, there will be a boat that leaves for Napoli, and it is including a few passengers that need to escape from Sicily. If I give you a ticket to show the captain and tell you the password, he will let you on this boat. If you do not find your parents or more information in Napoli, you may go look farther north, closer to the fighting, if you do not mind being killed. But I have no idea where you would need to go outside of Napoli. The partisans and your parents could be anywhere, and the Nazis will be everywhere. They control the entire top half of *Italia*, so it will do you no good to risk your life. Your father is an expert at staying out of sight, and you cannot trust anyone to seek information about them."

I sat on the edge of the chair. "You will not thwart me with your warnings. I will do what I need to find help. Tell me, do you have any more information about connections in Napoli? More names?"

She shook her head in disapproval. "You really want to die."

I stared her down, and she rolled her eyes. "I have changed my mind. I have already said too much. Your father may shoot me himself when he returns. I know he would not let me give you that ticket and password so you can just jump on a boat on an impossible quest. I cannot do it. And I swear on the head of Santa Lucia that I do not know anything more."

"I want that ticket and password, Donatella. I need it."

"I cannot do it," she said, folding her arms tight.

I stood up and kept my gaze locked on her face. She wouldn't look back at me as she shook her head in refusal.

"It's getting dark, and I have to go. Give me the information and password now, or I will come back a hundred times or hold you captive until you do, Donatella."

Her eyes widened. "*Madonna mia*, *ragazzaccia*, maybe you are an evil girl or more courageous than I thought."

"I am not evil or courageous. But I will not give up."

Donatella cursed under her breath, but I left the hospital with the ticket for the boat gripped in my hand, the password replaying over and over in my head, and an address where I may find help when I got to Napoli.

I kept my plans a secret, knowing full well that my family would worry too much if I told them I was going to the mainland to search for my parents alone. I placed a note on my pillow and left in the wee hours of the morning on horseback on the day the boat was scheduled to leave. I'd eased my bedroom door shut behind me so they would assume I was just sleeping late. By the time they found the note, I would be in Siracusa and would keep myself hidden down by the boat docks.

> *My beloved family,*
>
> *Please do not worry yourselves about me. I have obtained vital information that I must act on, and I will be gone several days. I have help and am well and safe with competent people. I promise I will contact you with good news soon.*
>
> *I love you all,*
>
> *Franca*

I'd cringed as I left, knowing they would worry about me no matter how I had tried to reassure them. But there was nothing I could have told my family or Alma about my plans that would have made my departure any easier, and I knew they would do all in their power to make me stay. I could not endure their pressure and worries on top of the anticipation of the journey that took my breath every few minutes.

I paid a young boy to return the horse to our villa when I arrived at the dock that evening, promising to pay him double when I returned if I found that he had followed through on my request. The odds were against him returning the horse, but I would have to chance it.

Boats bounced on the water like giant fishing bobbers as the wind whipped up the sea. The briny air filled my nostrils and dampened my coat as I watched for a long, white boat with red trim and the name *Buona Fortuna* painted on the sides. When it came into view, I stood and waited, locking my knees so they would stop shaking. I tied a scarf over my hair and across the lower half of my face to ward off the icy fingers of the wind and to conceal my identity. The boat docked, and I stepped forward, already racked with seasickness.

CHAPTER FORTY-ONE

Franca

December 23, 1943

THE BOAT ROCKED LIKE A seesaw, and my head bobbed no matter how I fought it. It was crowded, the seating belowdecks already full when I came onboard. I sat on a long bench between two men on the main deck and kept my gaze on my shoes. I'd brought some bread and water in my knapsack, but the thought of trying to drink or chew made my stomach flop like a fish.

We would have to stop in Messina, and from there, going incognito across to Napoli could take up to twelve hours depending on how many times we needed to slow back or change course if a threat appeared. Any boat out on the water ran the risk of being targeted by the Axis or the Allies. I had no idea who specifically arranged this transportation, but I knew we were on the Allies' side and the Axis would blow us out of the water if they had a chance. I rubbed my hands together to keep them warm and channel my nerves.

After a brief stop in Messina, where more bundled passengers shuffled quietly on board, we were on our way again. My neck throbbed, and I was in great need of a bathroom. I tugged on my coat and scarf to be sure my face was concealed enough and chanced a glance at more of my surroundings.

Several women and men, all as hunkered down and quiet as I had been, sat on the benches in front and behind me. I stepped carefully past my neighbors and made my way around, looking for any kind of bathroom, and my eyes locked on the familiar silhouette of a man on the upper deck. My breath froze and I covered my face with my hands, spinning around and looking for a place to hide.

Peter Weimer. It had to be a dream. I thought he would have left Sicily long before now. I tugged on the hood of my coat and wrapped my belt and arms around myself tightly, willing myself invisible and trying to calm my spinning thoughts. If Peter saw me, he may try to thwart my journey. The coldness in his dismissal in Sortino still haunted me no matter Peter's motives.

I hurried back to my seat, quietly bouncing my legs because I had not found a bathroom and to prevent myself from running to Peter. Seeing him brought it all back again, the burning in my breast when he was near me, the fear and exhilaration that pulled my belly in a tug-of-war.

Peter wore civilian clothes like everyone else, and in order to be on this boat, he must have made contact with someone who gave him the ticket and password.

If we spoke and he tried to intervene in my plans, I would make him understand I could not sit back watching the walls move closer and closer until they swallowed me. I could not look at Bruno's empty eyes and hear Luca's cries for Laura anymore or I would die myself. But most important of all, I had to find my parents to make sure they were safe and alive, to see life and breath in my mother.

And then the other part of my plan—when I found my parents, I would ask my father to use his connections to warn Peter's sister and mother about Keillor. I could not tell Peter the last part of my plan in case he refused to let me risk my safety to protect his family.

I slowed my breath and laid out the options before me, glancing every few seconds for the silhouette I longed for on the upper deck. I caught another glimpse of Peter and wanted to curl up and weep for what I'd lost. Any hope between us had died the day Keillor found us at the pond, replaced by the realization of what we had to choose—the safety of our families and even ourselves.

Several hours passed, and the sun came up in a silver haze on the horizon. It was late when we docked in Napoli, hours later than we had anticipated because of stops we had to make to cut the engines so we would not be detected by the enemy.

The bell atop the boat clanged, and I grabbed my duffle bag. I wormed my way ahead of where I thought Peter may go and kept moving. The minute I stepped onto land, I would dart around a corner so he would not see me.

The crowd moved in tight on all sides to disembark, and a woman in front of me bent over several children who fussed and wiggled. Two of them boxed at each other and tripped, slowing my descent down the gangplank.

Despite the frigid wind, I was sweating under my scarf; Peter could be right behind me. I glanced up, surprised when I spotted him on the shore; he must have gone down another gangplank. And he was not alone; two American soldiers stood with him, and Peter reached in his pocket and pulled out papers.

I made it around the children and pulled the hood of my coat snug against the sides of my face. The shore was crowded, and I was pushed along like driftwood in a river. Seagulls screeched and cried overhead, their clamor mixing with the chattering crowd. In a moment, I would pass within inches of Peter. If those soldiers who were questioning him discovered he was German, he would be put in a prison camp or shot.

I could take Peter by the arm and pretend to be his girlfriend or even his wife, but perhaps he already had another cover story that I would invalidate. I kept my hands clenched tight, my eyes stinging in the wind, and scurried past.

I had no idea what to do. It seemed wrong to leave Peter behind, but I also knew if he got away from the Americans and saw me, he would come straight away to try to stop my quest. I gripped my coat over my heart with both hands, and when I peeked back around, the soldiers and Peter were headed my direction. I slid around to the other side of a building as they passed and bit my lip until I tasted the coppery tang of blood to keep myself from calling Peter's name.

After he was gone, I tipped my head back against the wall. The sky was slate gray and spit tiny needles of freezing rain on my face. I had to find cover before my coat soaked through, and I had to find the address Donatella had given me to find assistance.

Footsteps echoed quickly up beside me, and someone grabbed my arm. I stifled a scream as a tall, lanky young man with curly brown hair pulled me around to face him.

His eyes were opened wide, his jaw set as he stared down at me. "Franca, no? What are you doing just standing in the rain?"

I pulled my arm from the young man's grip. "Who are you and how do you know my name?"

The young man smiled, exposing big, square teeth with a sizable gap between each one. "I am Lello. Donatella did not tell you I would be here to meet the boat? She radioed that you would be wearing a dark-green wool coat and that you were very pretty. She was correct on both points."

I caught my breath and tsked my tongue. "She said nothing about anyone meeting me. She gave me an address."

He glanced in each direction before he took me by the elbow and pushed me down a steep walkway at a brisk pace. "We need to get moving. The address Donatella gave you is compromised, so we need to find a place to lay low."

He hardly seemed older than a kid, yet his tone and manner were very direct and sure.

"You have to be crazy to travel off the island alone, signorina. Why is no one with you? And where are you going?"

"I have to find my father and mother. They are missing."

He snorted. "A lot of people are missing. A lot of people are dead and dying as we speak. How do you plan to find two people in this mess and why did my sister have you connect with me?"

"I would assume she would have explained."

"Not on a radio that can be intercepted," he said, pulling me through the cobblestone streets. Cars and horse-drawn wagons passed. Exhaust filled the air with acrid smoke from rumbling military trucks that honked their horns endlessly at numerous pedestrians, the groan and grinding of their gears like snarling beasts.

"You know Lieutenant Bianco?" I yelled over the din.

He laughed out loud but kept me marching quickly beside him. "That is a definite yes."

"He is my father, and he and my mother are missing. I am worried they are in grave danger, and I need to find them."

He guided us around an old woman pushing a wheelbarrow before he answered. "I am not sure I would call them missing."

I stopped in my tracks, refusing to let him push me farther. "Do you know where they are? Why they have been out of communication so long?"

"We have narrowed down the area where they may be held, but getting to them to free them is another matter."

"Why?" I demanded, unable to move.

He leaned in to shout over the roar of another army truck that splashed through puddles in the pitted cobblestone. "Because we are almost sure they are prisoners in German hands on the other side of the Gustav Line. It is impossible to break through there right now. And when Bianco passed through here, he gave orders that if he were ever missing or captured, we were to complete other missions instead of risking ourselves to find him. So I am afraid you have wasted your trip."

The constant burning, the urgency that vibrated in me day and night to find my parents and help Peter steeled my nerves against the confirmation that they had been captured. I'd heard too many tales of how the Germans treated their prisoners. I almost chortled in Lello's face at the implication that I was mistaken in coming.

"I am going to find them with or without your help, Lello. If you do not want to help me, I hope you know others who will."

"And what will you do if you happen to find where they are being held? Are you going to go storming into the middle of a German prison camp and snatch them up?" He threw his head back as if shouting to the sky. "Why would my sister let you come here?"

"I did not give her much choice." I marched away, unsure of where I was going but determined to get at least a few steps away from his criticism. An old man wobbled past on a bicycle, leaving a trail of cigar smoke behind him and almost running over me.

The buildings were towering sentinels that lined every roadway with banks, churches, and stores. Clotheslines roped one building to another down the alleyways where clothing and linens hung like dripping flags that grew heavier and wetter in the icy rain.

Lello caught up with me and pulled me to a stop on the sidewalk. He bit his lip before he spoke. "We all want to save Bianco and have tried to get more information about him. There is no way you will ever make it to your parents. There is a line, the one I just mentioned. The Gustav Line cuts all the way across Italy—the Germans are on one side and the Allies are here below. Trained soldiers have been trying to blow through that line for weeks. The Nazis will not just bow to a woman and let you pass like a princess. Every Nazi above that line will kill you or worse." He stared straight into my eyes again. "You have to go back. Let us keep trying to find your parents. You must return safely to Siracusa."

Cars moved past, splashing water on our ankles. I ignored them and glared at Lello.

He sighed and shrugged in defeat. "Like I said, a situation arose. We cannot go to our normal hideout until we know it is clear tomorrow. Today and tonight we can hide out somewhere here in town—a church or a barn where you can get some rest. I am guessing you did not sleep much on that boat."

Every bone in my body ached with exhaustion. "I would be grateful for a bit of rest."

We found an empty storeroom behind an abandoned *pasticceria*, and I lay down on a dirty mattress, letting my mind slip in and out in snatches of sleep in spite of the chaos of the city.

Lello disappeared for several hours, and when he returned, he brought me a *panino* for dinner. I gobbled my food, suddenly starving. Lello was snoring within minutes, lying beside my mattress on a pile of rags.

CHAPTER FORTY-TWO

Franca

The inner city swallowed us in an even greater swarm of roaring traffic and scurrying civilians the next morning. American and Canadian soldiers drove or marched by and grimaced at everyone as if they were the enemy. Lello's arm looped through mine as he pushed and pulled me through the city like he had the day before. Misty rain soaked my hair in droplets, and my feet slipped on the wet cobblestones, twisting and jerking my ankles to the sides. I regretted leaving my rain boots behind, but I kept moving.

"I know you have worked with my friends Massimo and Marianna, and that is why Donatella thought you might help me find more information," I explained to Lello while we waited to cross a busy road.

He let out a stream of foul words. "I am going to thump my sister and her big mouth. And stop throwing names out like free *dolci*."

"No one told me I could not use names since we are on the Allies' side now and the Germans are all up north. But I do not care how angry you are with me. I care about my parents and I will follow you everywhere you go until you help me or find someone who will."

He shook his head in exasperation and then pointed at a bench in a corner park. "Wait over there. I have to meet up with some people *uno minuto*."

Lello ran inside a bar across the street and did not come back for thirty minutes. He returned with a bag in his hand and a smirk on his face. "Looks like your luck has improved. A few members will be searching for your parents after all, and they will let you go with them, at least as far as Campobasso. There are rumors your parents were seen there before they disappeared." He held a calzone in his hand, tore it in half, and offered the bigger piece to me. "Eat this. I'm not sure if there will be much to eat in Campobasso; it's been heavily bombed. Someone will be coming to pick you up soon."

I almost jumped in his arms with joy but kept my seat and chewed on the soft, doughy bread of the calzone as if I had composure, amazed and grateful to find a tiny piece of prosciutto and melted *formaggio* in the middle. I was so happy an effort was being made to find my parents and so hungry that I did not care that the rain trickled down the neck of my coat and my fingers shook with cold.

A mammoth-sized army truck pulled up beside us an hour later. Lello grabbed my bag and threw it in the back behind the canvas-covered sides.

"Climb up front, signorina," Lello directed. "I am sorry if I have seemed rude. Tell your friends I said hello if you see them again. And good luck in Campobasso." He smiled, his big teeth making his lips stretch wide, and his eyes lit with mischief. "When you get to town, follow Enzo. And if anyone asks who you are, tell them you are Ivo's girlfriend."

"Who is Ivo?"

Lello held his hand toward the truck. "Get in and you will see." He winked.

I hoped that the filthy bearded man who frowned at me and grunted when I climbed inside was not Ivo, but no one else was in the truck. He smelled like old fish, and his hands were black with grime. His shirt looked like he'd wiped his hands on it a hundred times. He said nothing more as the engine grumbled its way out of town.

After a while, I worked up my nerve. "You are Ivo, no?"

He grunted in the affirmative and chewed on a stick he had used to scratch his scalp just a moment before.

"And we are going to Campobasso?" I asked, keeping my gaze from the debris in his bushy beard.

He glanced at me and bobbed his head. "So they are sending lambs to the wolves now, eh?" He grinned, exposing a row of rotten teeth, chuckling to himself, and tapping the wet stick he'd been chewing on the steering wheel.

And that was the end of our conversation.

Hours later, we made it to Campobasso, and my hopes plunged. There was almost nothing left but burned-out buildings and tumbled walls that blocked the streets. The people here must have died by the thousands.

The truck squealed to a stop. "You need to get out now," Ivo grunted.

I searched the ruins for any sign of survivors, but except for a couple old men and stray dogs, there was no life in sight.

"I am supposed to find someone named Enzo," I said, trying to keep the panic out of my voice.

Ivo laughed and rolled his eyes as if I was the most ignorant woman he had ever met, and in that moment, I agreed with him.

"Enzo will find you, *bambina.* Just get out and turn around."

I stepped out and headed to the back of the truck, hoping Ivo would not pull away before I could get my bag. I hurried to the rear of the truck and gasped at the sight of two men climbing out of the back. One of them must be the Enzo I was supposed to "turn around" to meet, and the other one was Peter Weimer.

The glint of anger in Peter's eyes shook me more than the surprise of seeing him. He did not say a word to me or expose that we knew each other. I could hardly breathe.

The other man stepped in front of Peter. He was tall, dark haired, and cleanly shaved. "*Mi chiamo* Enzo. We will be traveling together."

"*Grazie.*" I raised my chin, faking composure. I was relieved that Enzo sounded polite after the grunting Ivo.

I struggled to keep my eyes averted from Peter, gripping my hands together tightly.

"This is Peter," Enzo said with ease as he held his hand toward Peter. "Do not worry if he seems foreign. He's here on approval."

The truck belched black smoke as Ivo pulled away, leaving us behind in a city of desolation.

Enzo had said Peter was "here on approval." The information surprised me, and I wondered if Massimo and Marianna had somehow connected with Peter and helped him after all.

The city was eerily quiet after the din of Napoli. We walked past a few people who ambled down the roads. Some dug through the ruins, and others gripped a loaf of bread or a blanket in their arms, their children clinging tight against their sides.

A steep set of stairs abutted the ruins of a large apartment building. The stairs had been bombed out at the second floor, but they led down to a basement where we met up with six other men who looked like they had lived on the lam for a long time—ragged piecemeal uniforms, bearded stubble, and a young man with hair like an un-sheared sheep. But all of them looked to have a decent coat, rifles, belts lined with bullets, shells, and pistols. They sat around on the debris-strewn ground or on dilapidated furniture that reeked of mildew.

The three of us stood at the front of the group, and Enzo pointed at Peter. "This is a German who is anti-Nazi. His name is Peter. He is here because of longstanding approval from Bianco, and he will help us with the Germans and the language."

He pointed at me. "And this is Franca. She is here to assist and is hoping to help in our search for Bianco."

I hugged my bag to my chest and held my chin steady while the whole group scrutinized me. A couple of the men smirked, but no one uttered disapproval. I sidestepped my way to a chair as Enzo pointed at each of the other men. "This is Vincenzo, Marino, Carlo, Davide, Giuseppe, and Andrea. All of them are *ragazzacci*, but we will put up with them," he said with a wink.

"*Va bene*, as you all know, Lieutenant Bianco instructed us to move on with other missions and leave him be if he disappeared. But Gregorio himself contacted me and has instructed us to find Bianco, and I, for one, am grateful. Bianco has saved people by the hundreds, and I'm relieved we can stick our necks out for him in return."

Enzo pointed at a map divided by lines and arrows behind him. "The last sighting of both Bianco and his wife was here in Campobasso. After the last battle, they disappeared. The city and rubble have been thoroughly searched with no sign of them, and there has been no word from Bianco since that time.

"Now we're hearing rumors from outside the city of Cassino. The Nazis have control of that city, the monastery—Monte Cassino—on the mountain, and the eighty miles beyond it to Rome. The Germans are thick as fleas all through there. But our contact in the area said he heard of a highly sought after husband and wife who were being held somewhere outside Cassino, and Gregorio wants us to get up there, see if it's Bianco and his wife, and get them out."

Hearing my hopes and fears meshed together slammed me in the chest—my parents had possibly been located, but they were being held by the Nazis. Everyone knew about the brutal interrogations performed by the Nazis.

Enzo paused, and the men talked back and forth about the new information. All the men, except Peter, occasionally tossed glances in my direction.

Enzo had been studying the map and then stood in front of the group again. "Incidentally, *Buon Natale*, everyone."

My eyes opened wide. I'd completely forgotten the date. Christmas had been a suppressed affair for four years, but I'd never completely overlooked it before. But a holiday hardly seemed to matter; I had made it all the way to Campobasso alive and well, and I was on my way to find my parents. God willing, we could be together for Christmas next year.

Enzo stepped over to talk closely with a couple of the men. My eyes refused to follow protocol, and I caught glimpses of Peter's profile. He spoke with the other men when they asked him questions, or he looked up at the sky through a jagged hole in the roof but never at me. But even with the dam the war had built between us, just being near Peter still calmed and reassured me—as if water flowed over the top of the dam and quenched an aching thirst.

CHAPTER FORTY-THREE

Peter

December 25, 1943

"WE'RE GOING TO TAKE A truck as far as we can toward Cassino. If not for the broken roadways, we would have less than a hundred miles to traverse and could get there quickly. But we will encounter many obstacles, and I'm not sure how long we can drive before we have to go on foot," Enzo said to our group.

We'd studied the map for an hour since Enzo had introduced me and Franca to this group of rebel soldiers in this bombed-out basement. Marianna had told me before she and Massimo left me in Sortino that if I ever needed help, I could go to her connection at the Hotel Grande in Siracusa and use her name as a reference. Marianna's graciousness knew no bounds, but I could never repay her for helping me find a way back to Germany. I'd made it to Campobasso because of her and Massimo's connections.

But when Lello came into the bar in Napoli and announced that Lieutenant Bianco's daughter would be coming with us to Campobasso, I jumped in shock, hiding the extent of my reaction from Enzo and Lello. Perhaps Marianna had given Franca the same information and pass to get on the boat to Napoli. Or perhaps the nurse, Donatella, had. But one thing was certain—Franca Chessari had proved that no matter anyone's warnings about danger, she would not be thwarted.

Lello confirmed that Donatella had given Franca the ticket and password to come to Napoli. I almost exploded with anger. Franca had no training, no skills, and as far as Donatella knew, no one to protect her.

All the way to Campobasso, I tried to deduce why Franca would take such a risk and how I could convince her to go back to Siracusa. By the time we arrived, my fear for her safety turned into anger, and I wanted to shake her and I cursed that more than half of the railway system had been sabotaged or derailed, so there was no way to put her on the next train for home. I climbed out of the truck, exploding with frustration, but when I met the steel that masked the fear in Franca's eyes, I knew my efforts to send her back would fail.

I held my angst inside and watched the eyes of the men when Enzo introduced Franca and amassed our team in the basement of the bombed-out building. No one seemed to stare at her in a threatening way, but I would be on silent lookout.

I recognized two of Enzo's men from Massimo's group in Siracusa: Andrea and Davide. I had to keep my distance from Davide; he'd made his anger toward my German race very clear when we were searching for Marianna De'Angelis Scalvone, and his manner had not warmed.

Andrea shook my hand when Enzo introduced us, but Davide held back. They were friendly to Franca, but I tensed when Davide's gaze roamed over her the minute she turned her head.

Frustration and worry gnawed at my stomach every time I looked at Franca. The absurdity of her presence made me livid, but the anger helped me keep my distance. I had meant it when I'd severed our relationship in Sortino. I had almost cost her and her family their lives. I had been a fool and would never cross that line again. When dreams betrayed my will and haunted me with memories of Franca—of hearing her laugh and seeing her courage beneath the vulnerability in her eyes—I woke to the reality of her folly and latched onto my anger like a life raft.

And that was the core of it. The fact that she had put herself in such danger. Beneath my anger was fear, fear that something would happen to her and I would have to suffer the loss of her all over again.

Three days into our journey, we'd had to abandon the truck and travel on foot because of bombed-out roads. We camped without a tent the night before, and I only slept once I'd seen from the corner of my eye that Franca looked safe between the campfire and Enzo. I'd only met Enzo in Campobasso but sensed a nobility in him like I'd seen in Massimo Scalvone.

Our food was frozen bread, jerky, and cheese, very hard on the teeth, and we had to melt snow for water, but Franca never complained. Everyone was subdued and trudged through fields of snow, up mountains patched in ice, or in muddy ravines on our way to Cassino. We took turns carrying the radio in our backpacks, and Franca insisted on taking her turn.

I followed her when we stopped for lunch and she made her way off the trail, I assumed for personal toiletry. The men were focused on eating or lay back in the snow for a quick nap and did not seem to notice me or Franca wander away.

When we were out of sight, I grabbed Franca's arm and pulled her behind a group of hedges.

"Do you realize the danger you are in out in the wild with a group of renegades and underneath the eye of the Nazis? What are you doing? Why are you here?" I growled, already knowing I would not like her answers.

She shook her arm out of my grasp and lowered her brows. "You know why I am here—to find my parents."

"Did you follow me?"

"No," she answered in a huff. "Why would I do that? You pushed me away, and I have had no idea where you were. I was as surprised as you were when I saw you in the back of the truck."

"Why can you not leave danger alone, let the people who are trained for this find your parents? Why does it have to be you?"

"It had to be me because . . . because no one was looking for my parents when I was in Siracusa, and I knew I had to come," she said, her eyes wide.

I checked behind the snow laden-hedges to be sure no one was coming and then threw out my arms in frustration. "And how will you find your parents when the Nazis capture and imprison you?"

The sun came from behind a cloud, lighting her eyes as she glared at me. "You have so little faith in me. You see me as such an imbecile. It is a wonder you ever cared for me at all. Why did you follow me out here and bother to ask me anything?" Her voice came out raspy, her eyes shining bright with tears.

My anger retreated, and I reached for her arm, holding onto it more gently this time. Franca's hair hung in a messy braid down her back, and her cheeks were bright red with cold.

"I have made it clear between us, that I . . . I regret the way I let my judgement lapse with you, and it put you and your family in danger, Franca. I hope you will forgive me." I let go of her arm, took a deep, slow breath, and stepped back. "But I cannot bear to think of anything happening to you. Please go home. I will find a way to free your parents before I return to Germany."

I almost choked on the words that rose in my throat, the ones I could not utter to profess the undying affection and longing I still held for Franca. I would bury those words forever to keep her safe.

She wiped at her eyes with gloved hands before she put them back in the pockets of the military pants Enzo must have given her. She wore canvas boots and a jacket too, but her teeth still chattered in between some of her words.

"There is nothing to forgive you for, Peter Weimer. Contrary to your deep regrets, I cherish our time in Sortino and do not view this war and its insanity as somehow your fault. We may never have a chance to talk this way again, so I want you to know the truth. I came here to find my parents, but I have another reason as well. I know it is impossible for you to make it back to Germany, at least on your own. So that is the other reason I am here. I am the only one who could convince my father to help you. I realized after talking to Marianna just how many connections my father has with the Allies, and I know he will have a way to save Bettina and your mother."

I leaned back on a large rock, overwhelmed by her admission, and covered my eyes with my hand. "Franca, no. I would never want you to take risks like this. Never."

I reached for her hand, but she pulled herself away just as I heard the crunch of footsteps in the snow. "Someone is coming. Quick, head back toward the camp."

Franca scrambled away from me, and I jumped into motion and headed back to join the others. Davide stepped from behind a tree.

"What are you up to, Nazi?" he growled.

"I saw that the young woman went to relieve herself and thought someone should stand guard."

He glared at me. "That someone is not you. Let her own countrymen take care of her."

"By the way you look at her, I am not sure she would be the safest with you, Davide."

He stomped up, pointing his finger in my face. "You have no right to her or anything. You had better watch what you say and do."

"Do you think you have a 'right to her'?" I asked, staring him down.

He raised his fist and shook it in my face. "I have a right to what and whom I choose; this is my country." He poked my chest with his finger. "You are the enemy and had better find your way out of here soon."

"That is the plan." I refused to anger him further and made my way back to camp with glances over my shoulder to be sure he followed. I sighed with relief when Franca returned.

I found Enzo going through his ammunition and squatted down beside him. "I realize I have no authority here, but I have to say I am concerned about Davide's behavior toward Franca."

He paused and then kept working without looking up.

An hour later, I noticed Enzo and Davide had disappeared. When Davide returned to camp, he had a bloody lip and stared at me with pure hatred in his eyes. Enzo soon followed and sat down with a slight nod of his head in my direction. I slept easier that night.

We climbed over hills and through valleys in freezing winds, icy rain, and snow, making our way toward Cassino, hardly resting for days at a time, but Franca never complained or wavered. We searched through towns and villages for any pockets of Nazis and any hiding place where they may keep Lieutenant Bianco and his wife hidden. There was no sign of soldiers from the Axis or the Allies this deep in the mountains, so we carried on.

Several days in, we stopped under a gray bank of clouds at the base of a wide mountain range. We were well into January now—1944, and the war had been slogging on since '39.

"We should make camp here under that ridge," Enzo said, pointing. He grabbed his binoculars, aiming them at the closest mountain. "Wait a minute. I see a whole group of boulders up on that high ledge. It could be the perfect lookout for the enemy. Let's set up behind some trees, get some food in our bellies, and try the radio again."

Andrea tried the radio, and we all stopped eating at once and stared at the metal box when he detected voices. Enzo signaled me over, and I held the handle to my ear. The snap and scratch of static distorted the voices, but it was clear they were speaking German.

My nagging misgivings were back again—the knots that lived in my gut because as I helped the Allies defeat Hitler, I could betray or endanger my friends. There was nothing I could do for my country now; we were lost to the rule of a madman, but I had no desire to hurt those I knew to be trapped in the war like me. I could only hope to save my family, try to avoid hurting friends, and maybe someday I could help rebuild a life from the ashes, if the soul of Germany survived at all.

I listened further without breathing and then reported to the group. "There are definitely Germans up behind those boulders, maybe a thousand feet up the side of the mountain, and they're receiving orders from somewhere nearby. Sounds like they plan to attack us as soon as the sun comes up."

"We will sneak up from behind them and shower them with grenades before their eyes flutter open in the morning," Davide hissed. "Blood-sucking Krauts."

Enzo glanced at me before he addressed the crowd. "We will attack them from behind before dawn, but only on my command."

Evening approached, the sky glowing orange and red over the mountains and oblivious to the fact that men slit each other's throats and bombed one another beneath its splendor.

I listened to the transmissions from the hideout behind the boulders again, and when a familiar resonance came over the waves, I froze. It seemed impossible, but I detected the deep rasp of August's voice. If I was correct, it could mean Dieter would be with him.

If I let the partisans attack that ledge, August and Dieter would be doomed. Theirs was a small group of Germans. Not even a real threat in the whole scheme of things. But they held the upper hand in their position and would pick us off like ducks lined in a row if we tried to pass.

I knew Enzo's plan; we were going to climb up the backside of that ridge and drop grenades behind those boulders. But if I stopped Enzo or lied and said the Germans had retreated, then our group and even Franca would come out in plain sight and be obliterated when we tried to pass.

I couldn't tell Enzo or the others that I had heard a friend's voice among the Germans. They had no loyalty to me and could choose to kill me alongside my buddies if I tried to stop them from attacking. Even if Enzo cared, he would see no way to spare my friends when they held such a critical position on the mountain and we were in danger.

I had no choice; I had to break away and climb up the far side of the mountain by myself, hoping the Germans would not see and shoot me before I could surrender to them and try to get Dieter and August and the rest of them out of there. Once they were out, I would double back and tell Enzo it was safe for them to pass.

But I had no idea what I would do with August and Dieter once I had warned and stopped them from attacking us. If I told them I had joined up with the partisans against the Nazis, their comrades would have to capture or shoot me. August and Dieter could be shot along with me if they tried to protect me from their comrades. I could not coerce my friends to betray the German army and join the partisans with me against their will if they were loyal to the führer. My only choice would be to lie and say I had been caught long ago by the Allies and finally escaped and hope that word of my desertion had not spread. Then I would find a way to keep them from attacking the partisan group.

Franca may think me a traitor and a liar when I left to warn my friends, but I could not compromise her by telling her my plan.

I had no real answers, but I was going to do everything in my power to save August and Dieter, and I would not let them attack the partisans.

Vincenzo passed out chunks of bread and jerky to everyone for dinner, and while they were eating, I made the excuse that I had to go relieve myself. I dashed out the far end of a gully where no one could see me and climbed through the bushes and trees up the side of the mountain. I had insisted that Franca wear my uniform coat to keep her warmer, so I only wore civilian clothes. But if I could make it up and around and close enough for Dieter or August to recognize me before anyone let off a shot, then maybe I had a chance.

My plan worked. I came from the side, but instead of rushing up behind the boulders, I leaned around a tree and called out Dieter's name.

Dieter darted around the tree and looked at me, his eyes wide in shock before he grinned. "What are you doing in the middle of nowhere, Peter?" he cried as he put his arms around me and slapped me on the back.

"I have broken away from the enemy. My squadron was wiped out in Siracusa and I have been a prisoner. Now I am making my way back." He pulled me in behind cover. August, Dieter, and I rejoiced in seeing each other and patted each other on the backs for surviving. We burst into questions about where we had all been and what we'd been through.

They and the other three soldiers with them believed my story—that I'd escaped and come here to the mountains to make my way back to the Axis side.

"I dodged dozens of Americans and Italians down there," I lied to keep them from starting a volley of fire with the partisans. "We'd best head over the top of this mountain and find more comrades. We're vastly outnumbered."

August and Dieter vouched for my integrity to the other soldiers, and we made our way over the mountain. I realized there would be no way for me to double back to the partisans. Enzo and the others would question what had happened to me when they discovered that I and the Germans behind the hideout were gone, and Franca would be in distress. But there was nothing more that I could do but get my comrades as far from the partisans as possible, for everyone's sake.

Dieter led us over several hills and a large mountain range before we came to a deep and long gulch between two mountains outside the city of Cassino. A low cliff hung over the top of one side, obscuring the gulch almost completely. Two wide, towering peaks flanked the sides, and I assumed they were lined with hidden lookouts occupied by more Germans.

The hideout ran the full length of the mountain. A full nest of Nazis, dozens and dozens of them, part of the massive Axis army that controlled the whole north of Italy. Keillor may even be here, and if so, I had to find him before he found me.

CHAPTER FORTY-FOUR

Franca

Peter had been gone too long. I followed his footsteps in the snow and then jumped when I looked up and saw Davide step in front of me.

"Where are you going, Franca?" he asked with a smile that made the hair at the back of my neck rise a little.

The others had told me that Davide helped Massimo rescue Marianna, but instinct told me I should watch my step.

"I need to find privacy for toiletries, so I came behind these bushes. So if you will, please return to camp." Sweat gathered under my scarf around my neck.

Davide stepped in close. "But we finally have a few moments to ourselves. I cannot help but notice how brave you are as well as beautiful." He leaned in and I could smell liquor and poor hygiene on his breath.

I stepped back, and he frowned. "I believe you favor the Nazi, Peter. You may find you favor me more, signorina, if you give me a chance."

I tipped my head back. "I can smell alcohol on your breath, Davide. You know that Enzo would be angry about that and if he saw us alone. We must return to camp right away."

He grunted. "You act all high and mighty, but I am not sure you behave yourself with that German."

"You have been drinking, and it is altering your perception. And your judgement."

He frowned and then reached his hand around my neck and pulled me in, mashing his mouth against mine until it crushed my lips against my teeth. I held my mouth shut tight to ward off his kiss.

I jerked and jumped back out of Davide's grasp and fell on the ground; and my right hand landed right on a big piece of a broken branch. I did not want to yell at Davide and alert the others that Peter was gone from camp. And judging by the abundance of alcohol on his breath, I knew Davide's sense or reason was gone and yelling would do no good.

He loomed over me where I'd fallen on the ground, the broken branch still under my hand.

"I risked my neck to save your friend Marianna," he said. "I have been a good man, a faithful Italian. You owe some allegiance to your fellow partisans and can spare a few kisses."

He lunged to land on top of me. I swung the branch around full force and hit him across his face with a wallop.

He fell facedown in the snow and did not move.

I wasted no time in darting away, running along the side of the mountain until my breath burned like fire in my throat and there was no sign of Davide behind me. I stopped and rested on an embankment until my pulse stopped pounding in my temples and I'd scrubbed my face and mouth clean with handfuls of snow.

I got my breath back and looked around. Davide must not have followed me, and my concern and focus was on finding Peter. I had to get my bearings.

I hoped it was not too late to find where Peter had gone. If he planned to spy on the Germans or attack them himself, he may need back up. I made my way up the far side of the mountain, where his footsteps led, and stopped to check my surroundings. The low murmur of voices carried on the wind, and I halted in place, stunned as I watched Peter slip from behind the boulders and climb side by side with a group of German soldiers until they disappeared around the other side of the mountain.

My legs refused to move. My voice was frozen in my throat. Either Peter had known the soldiers, so he warned them, or he had been captured by them. If I told Enzo and the others what I had seen, they would find Peter guilty of betrayal because he was German.

I sat in the snow, my mind more numbed than my fingers and toes. I had no idea what to do and waited for some type of guidance to arrive. I finally realized I had no choice but to return to our camp and made my way down the mountain to the copse of trees where we'd hidden, ready to tell the men that I'd been gone because I'd felt ill. But our camp was deserted.

Dozens of footsteps in the snow went in all directions, and a snowdrift was filling them fast. None of the men were anywhere in sight. I searched the area carefully, concealing myself behind bushes and trees, but there was no sign of the men.

I was all alone.

I had to think fast; twilight was slipping away, and without cover, I would freeze to death. I came upon a tiny shed in what seemed the middle of nowhere. The shed door swung open, and I found a few animal blankets hidden in a pile of hay in the corner. I wrapped the blankets around my legs and body, pulled my arms against my chest inside Peter's military coat, and tucked my face into the collar.

The hills would be covered in snow or frost in the morning, but at least I had shelter. The gray twilight disappeared completely, leaving me in such darkness I could hardly tell the difference when my eyes finally closed, and I fell asleep.

The high-pitched whine of an icy breeze whipped around the shed and woke me to the milky light of morning. A low vibration of voices put me on alert, and I scrambled to hide beneath the straw. The voices grew louder, and I shook with fear. Germans could kill me, torture me, fascists too. Villagers would run me off or beat me because I wore a German coat, but if I took it off, I would freeze to death.

The shed door slowly squeaked open, and two men came in. They talked rapidly in Italian about the gardening tools that hung on the walls. It did not take long for me to realize they were military deserters, because they talked about hiding out from the Allies and the Axis. If they found me, my chances of going unscathed were dismal at best.

One of the men walked around, knocking the rakes and shovels off the wall and jarring my nerves. I wanted to curl into a tighter ball, but I didn't dare move. The man's footsteps thumped as he kicked at the ground and then at the hay all around me. I held my breath.

Someone snatched my foot and pulled me out from under the hay. I let out one shriek and then forced myself to be quiet. Anyone outside the shed could be just as dangerous or even more so.

The shed door opened, and a woman entered. She looked me up and down before addressing the men.

"So I see you've found a little traitor hiding like a dog in a doghouse. She's obviously a German's mistress. Look at her coat. Where is your boyfriend, *fraulein*?" the girl asked me and then laughed at herself. "Did he go to find you some bratwurst or schnitzel for your breakfast?" She lit a cigarette. "Omberto, give me that scythe. Our little *fraulein* needs a haircut so everyone will know what a back-stabbing pig she is to us faithful Italians."

"If you are faithful to Italy, then why are you here in a shed and not with your troop or fighting with the partisans?" I asked.

The woman blew more smoke in my face. "And why aren't you, my little *fraulein*?"

"I got separated from them, and I'm trying to find my way back. I stole this coat off a dead German so I wouldn't freeze. I need to find a partisan by the name of Bianco. Lieutenant Bianco. Have you heard of him?

"I do not tell German whores anything." She sneered and leaned so close to my face I could smell the stale tobacco on her breath. She grabbed hold of my hair and pulled on it. "Omberto, the scythe."

"Let me do it, Lena," the one named Omberto said.

"No." She sneered. "This is woman's work."

I screamed, but the two men held me down, and the woman used the scythe to lob off my braid. The men laughed and let me sit up, and I looked in shock at my dark, braided hair lying against the yellow hay.

Lena smirked. "You are lucky I do not have a razor or I'd shave your whole head. Now get out."

Omberto huffed. "Now wait a minute. I don't want her to leave yet. You had your fun with her, and I want mine." He grinned and scratched at his beard.

I scrambled to my feet and grabbed a shovel. Before anyone could move, I swung the shovel around and hit Omberto on the side of his head. He howled and grabbed his ear, and I ran out the door in a blind panic.

My feet slipped on icy patches as I stumbled on. I didn't dare look back until I'd made it down the side of the hill. I gasped when I glanced over my shoulder and realized the second man was right behind me. He was tall and heavy, and I was light on my feet, able to jump over big rocks and land several feet away. But he still somehow managed to stay behind me.

My face ached in the freezing gusts of wind as it rushed past. The grunts and gasps for air from the man kept my feet moving faster and faster until my lungs were on fire. Within seconds, I would fall to the ground, and the man would have all power over me.

I ran into some trees, and the next thing I knew, I was pulled into a ditch and shoved down by someone with strong, rough hands.

"*Stai zitta,* signorina," said a woman's voice. I stayed silent as she'd asked and gasped for breath. She covered me with branches, and I heard the rustle of other leaves around me. I didn't dare move.

A few minutes later, things had gone quiet, and the woman moved the branches from off the top of my head.

"What are you doing out in the middle of nowhere, signorina? You are either after someone to kill them or after being killed yourself."

The woman glared at me and sneered. "Are you looking for soldiers? Trying to make a little money? The Germans don't have to pay, and the partisans don't have any money. Like I said, you are after being killed."

"No, no, signora." I tsked my tongue. "I am searching for my . . . searching for a man that may be in this area. His name is Lieutenant Bianco."

"Ha." She brushed some leaves from my hair. "You want to find a specific man in this mess? People are shooting at each other from rock to rock and hill to hill. Everyone is a killer and a liar. No one has a name anymore."

"I am not either of those things, and I gave you the name of the person I am looking for because you are a fellow Italian. I thought I could trust you."

She kept her gaze locked on the coat I wore and then yanked on my hair where my braid had been cut off. "I am not a fellow anything to anyone." She jerked her chin, then stared at my coat again, and I held my breath. "You were a German's little girlfriend, huh? You will be beaten to death very soon. The hills are crawling with partisans, and they will eat you for breakfast."

"Not all partisans are brutal. I've heard Lieutenant Bianco is good."

She laughed out loud. "No one is good."

"What side are you on?"

"The side that keeps young girls like you, so you can make yourself useful." She grabbed me by my wrist and twisted it. "Now give me your other hand."

CHAPTER FORTY-FIVE

Franca

January 16, 1944

I WANTED TO SCREAM, TO run. But the others who had chased me would still be close by. I reached my free hand out to slap the woman, but she punched me on the side of my head, and my vision turned dark and blurry. She grabbed my hands and wrapped them together with rope, and I did let out a scream.

The ground teetered and swam under my feet. I threw myself against the woman with my shoulder to knock her backwards and tried to get my footing on some exposed roots sticking out of the side of the ditch.

A man appeared at the edge of the ditch, yelling in dialect to the woman. He pushed my head back with the palm of his hand as the woman grabbed me around the waist. I lost my footing on the roots and fell backward. I screamed as loud as I could. At this point, anyone else in close proximity that would hear me could not be any worse than the two who held me now.

The man jumped in the ditch with us. Oily dirt and food stains covered his shirt, and he reached out to touch me with long, skinny fingers. The woman smacked his hand down and growled at him. "Leave her be. She's for me, not you."

Hope drained. These were not allied partisans. In fact, I realized they may be working for the Nazis. And I had jumped right into their hands.

The man jerked on the rope that bound my hands and pulled me out of the ditch, and I fought to keep my arms from being wrenched from my shoulders. He lifted his rifle and pushed me to walk ahead of him.

The woman lagged behind. "Take her to the stake behind the food tents and tie her up. Get your chain for her ankle and stake it behind the tent so no one will see her."

The man poked me in the back with the rifle and growled back. "I will. I will, Pina. *Lasciami stare*. Leave me alone."

A deep ravine in the side of a mountain opened on the other side. Dozens of Germans had spread out down inside, and the far end looked like it wrapped around the mountainside and disappeared. Camouflaged tents and piles of supply boxes and food lined the encampment.

The man pushed me up and over the top of the mountain where a huge cliff hung over the ravine and no one would notice us pass. A plane could fly over this place and never see it. We ended up descending into the ravine behind a massive tent. He pushed me back against a post where he lifted my hands over my head to a big hook.

No one could be seen back here, and panic burned my lungs.

The filthy man leaned against me, smelling like a dog that had rolled around in its excrement. His breath was hot on my cheek, his lips almost touching mine. "One of these days, Pina won't be looking," he sputtered. He licked my cheek, and I turned away and gagged.

Pina came around the corner and chased the man away with a knife.

Half of Pina's teeth were eaten away, leaving crusty, black spikes poking out of swollen, red gums. Thick ropes of saliva strung between her lips as she spoke. "Now you listen here to me," she grunted. "I am a slave just like you."

"I am not a slave," I spat out.

She laughed. "You are now. I have to cook for dozens and dozens of these Nazis every day, and they do not treat me any better than a dog. I need some help, and you are going to give it to me. You are young and strong. You will get up before dawn and cook and clean until I tell you not to. And if you complain about it, I will beat you until you shut up," she boasted, raising her thick fist.

She pointed the knife at the disgusting man again. "Riccardo will be watching you. And if you do not want to be treated worse than I treat you, you will listen to what I say."

She walked away, her squat figure rocking back and forth to keep her corpulence in balance, then turned back again. "If you try to escape, there are at least fifty soldiers on the other side of this tent who will have you for dinner in five minutes, or I'll shoot you myself before you reach the edge of this ravine." She pulled a pistol out of her apron pocket and held it up to her cheek with a rotten-toothed grin. "I know how to use this."

So do I, I thought to myself. Fear had me in its grip, but I would find a way to escape.

Riccardo returned and shackled a chain around my ankle that he then fastened to another thick stake in the ground. The stake must have been here since summer in order for it to be so deeply embedded in the frozen soil.

I would have no chance of getting my hands on that pistol while I was chained to a post. The metal around my ankle was so rusty I guessed it came from the Middle Ages, but it was heavy and sturdy and chafed my skin. I tried cutting through it with a sharp rock all through the first night, but it barely left a scratch.

I did all of the chores Pina told me to behind and inside of the tent, still shackled with a six-foot chain that Riccardo moved from stake to stake depending on where I was needed. At least the Nazi soldiers could not see me back here, and if they did, I told myself they could not carry me away to do the worst harm with my foot chained. But I searched the ground in the circumference the chain allowed for the largest rock I could find to defend myself and also dropped a small stone in my pocket.

During the day, Riccardo shackled me to a post inside the food tent. I boiled potatoes, kneaded bread, and cooked pasta. After the meals, I washed endless piles of dishes that Pina and Riccardo brought to me. The bitter cold air bit at my skin, so the warmer tent and hot fires for cooking were a welcome relief at least.

I shivered all night long, chained behind the tent without a canopy and only ratty blankets to cover myself with. I often woke with a thin layer of icy snow over me and shook it off quickly before it soaked through my covers. Pina had let me keep Peter's coat, and the heavy wool made the difference between life and death.

Two weeks into my captivity, Pina surprised me and brought me a straw mattress that kept me off the frozen ground. I still shivered with cold but could finally slip into fitful sleep. Pina slept in the food tent, her snoring as loud as the planes that buzzed in the air night and day. But it was Riccardo who kept the key to my chains, and I had no idea where he went every night.

The commotion in the camp never ceased. Planes flew overhead, and horses neighed. I found a tiny hole in the tent and watched soldiers scream orders and scurry like rats strapped with heavy weapons and belts lined with bullets. Explosions cracked the air, and I shook like a rabbit, anticipating that a bomb would find me and set me free once and for all.

I stayed hidden and had not been approached by any Germans. Like she had told me, everything Pina ordered me to do was done in or behind the food tent. I had no desire to be seen by Nazi soldiers, but the urgency to escape kept me twitching with nerves or choking back tears.

Every night, I tossed and turned and wondered where Peter had gone, why he had left our resistance group and walked away with a group of German soldiers, and if I had been as blind as the stars behind the wall of smoke that obscured the sky. The doubts and devastation turned to anger, and I imagined myself free and able to confront Peter, to tell him I had seen his suspicious departure and demand answers. But every morning, I awoke with my hope and defiance chained to a spike.

Days passed, and I fought for strength; I'd come all this way and accomplished nothing. Peter and my family had been right; there was no way to find my father and to help anyone. I had done nothing but slow Peter down, lead him back to the Nazis, and become a slave.

I had no idea what week or time it was except when Pina kicked me awake or hit me on the head to make me cook or clean faster to have the meals ready on time. She had not learned to trust me any more than the first day and never came up beside me where I would have a chance to reach in her pocket for the pistol. The rock in my pocket was too small to knock someone unconscious, and my hands or my feet were always chained or tied.

"Pina . . . it's getting colder every night. Could I sleep closer to the firepits where we cook the soups?"

Pina stared at me, her eyebrows raised in surprise that I would ask for anything. After a few minutes, she answered me. "I'll have Riccardo hammer a stake over there tomorrow."

CHAPTER FORTY-SIX

Franca

February 1944

THE DAY CAME THAT I saw Peter through the hole in the tent wall and watched in devastation as he came and went day after day with a smile on his face and weapons in his hands. He saluted officers and laughed with the men. He played ball with his comrades. And did nothing to get back to Germany and find his sister.

After watching Peter acting happy with the Nazis, I had no strength left. I peeled the potatoes so slowly that Pina made a habit of slapping me in the head. It was the only time I felt anything. The only time I could let the tears sting my eyes.

The soup was late. I'd taken too long to get it ready. Pina woke up to the sound of soldiers banging on their bowls with their spoons in demand of their meal. Riccardo filled up the bowls as fast as he could and ran from the cooking tent into the mess tent to serve the men. The yelling and banging from the German soldiers grew louder.

Pina grunted in frustration and slapped me across the cheek. She had Riccardo unchain my foot.

"Take a tray out there," she barked. "Hurry, before they come back here to get it themselves."

I wiped the blood that ran from my nose with the back of my hand before I picked up the heavy tray and ran into the huge mess tent lined with tables full of soldiers. None of them seemed to notice me at first. I kept my eyes downcast and hurried to set the bowls before the men before I ran back for another tray.

On my third trip back, I hurried too fast around the corner of the table and slammed my knee on the sharp edge of a bench. I leaned down in pain and sensed the pressure of someone staring at me. I lifted my eyes and met the gaze of Peter Weimer. His eyes widened in recognition for just a second, and then he pointed at me and said something in German that made his comrades laugh. I hobbled back to the cooking tent and fell back in a chair, the pain in my leg minimal compared to the way Peter and his laughing Nazis had gutted me.

Pina noticed I had sat down and slapped me in the head. I got to my feet, let the blood run down my leg where I'd cut it on the bench, and filled more bowls with soup. When I returned to the mess tent, Peter was gone.

I lay on the mattress that night looking up at a frozen sky and wiped at my tears before they could freeze.

Peter was a German. I knew that in the beginning. I told myself, told him so many times, that I could not feel or show affection for an enemy. And all the while, he had looked at me and reassured me that he was against Hitler—that I could trust him. Now he sat with them, ate and served with them, and wore a Nazi uniform once again.

The thought of Peter's sister and mother in danger from Vasyl Keillor still made me worried and sick inside, but I questioned if his story or anything he told me was true. And if it was, there may be nothing my father could do to help them anyway. My father was a man of honor and decency and had enormous tasks to attend to. I could not ask him to help Peter's family anymore with so many doubts and questions.

I did chores mindlessly for the next two days, unable to think or feel beyond the way Peter had looked at me, made some kind of joke to his comrades, and laughed in my face. My plan to find my parents and to help Peter Weimer had turned into the biggest joke of all. A skinny slave chained to a spike had nothing to offer.

Two nights later, I awoke with jerk when a hand clasped over my mouth. Peter had slipped around the tent and found where I was chained. I glared into his eyes as fear, rage, and devastation spun and collided. Peter leaned down to say something in my ear, and I pushed and slapped him away as warm tears flooded my eyes.

Peter stayed hovered over me, not even flinching when I slapped at him, and sobs racked my chest. His expression was somber, his gaze piercing under the light of a bright moon as I cried. I tried to remember what it had felt like to trust him, to long for him. But my body ached with exhaustion, and my heart had frozen over.

Peter took my face in his hands, and I stared at him, muted and spent.

He leaned down and whispered in my ear so softly I could barely hear him. "I am going to get you out of here. I know where there is an empty, broken-down tank at the bottom of this mountain for you to hide in."

I shook my head back and forth against the mattress. "I do not trust anything you say," I declared too loudly.

Peter pressed his finger over my lips. "Yes, you do. You have to. We cannot argue now or that wretched woman may hear."

I raised my head, almost pressing my nose to his, but kept my voice at a whisper. "I've seen you laughing and talking with soldiers here like they are your friends and you are happy to be fighting with Nazis."

"The day I left, I thought I heard August's voice on the radio. I climbed the hill behind the boulders and found Dieter and August like an apparition right there in front of me. What could I do to my best friends? Kill them? I knew the partisans would not spare them or trust me if I said they were good men. I had no choice but to get them out of there. I told them I had been a prisoner of the Allies and had escaped. Thankfully there is so much danger and chaos that no one is taking the time to check my record."

"But you are shooting at my people, my country. Every time you go out with those soldiers, it is as if you are shooting at me or my friends and family."

"I do not fight with my comrades against Italians. I told the leaders here that the mountains and hills around us are full of hundreds of soldiers, so they won't try to attack until backup arrives. I have stalled them, and it is buying me time to strategize. I have been trying to convince Dieter and August to fight against Hitler and the Reich. They are afraid to leave, but I swear it to you, my friends are not Nazis. None of us want this war."

The band around my chest eased, and tears of relief replaced the bitterness that had flooded me just moments before. Peter wiped my tears with the sleeve of his uniform and then looked down at my chained foot. He gritted his teeth.

"I will shoot that woman for doing this to you. How did you get here? Why are you held prisoner? She is an Italian, no?"

"Yes. She claims she is a prisoner here, but I have seen an officer give her money. She captured me the day after you left and makes me do almost all of her work. An old man named Riccardo is the one who chains me and has the key, but he comes and goes at odd times and does not stay with Pina."

Peter shook his head in disgust. "I will get you out of here as soon as I can find that old man and get the key. The Allies could launch an attack on this hideout any day. If I don't find a way to unchain you quickly, you'll be stuck in the middle of the battles." He ran off into the dark, and when he came back, he placed a palm-sized rock in my hand. "I do not have an extra weapon to give you, but if the bombing and fighting get too close before I can get the key from Riccardo, at least use this on anyone who tries to attack you. Hit the enemy in the nose or the temple. If you get free, run away from the worst of things down to the end of the ravine. I heard rumors three days ago about high-ranking prisoners being held down there but have not found a way to check. There is a chance your parents could be among them because I heard one of them may be a woman, but I have not been able to get any names."

I sat up in surprise and was overcome by a grain of hope. "I have to get out of here. I have to see if there is the slightest chance my parents are there."

Peter gripped the chain on my ankle in his hand and pulled at the spike in the frozen ground, but it did not budge. "I am going to track this Riccardo down. I will come for you the minute it is safe."

The moon illuminated the angle of his cheekbones, his square jaw, and full lips. He leaned down and kissed my cheek before he ran off, and I cried myself to sleep with hope and fear at war in my dreams.

CHAPTER FORTY-SEVEN

Franca

February 10, 1944

DAWN SHOT ITS FIRST RAYS behind the mountains, and the world burst open. The Allies were attacking the camp, and a thousand rounds of ammunition whizzed through the air from machine guns somewhere, while bombs dropped from the sky and exploded like crashing waves. The ground rumbled and shook, and I marveled that the earth did not crack open to its core. I was still chained and scrambled to hide under a nearby table, but it was too far away. I was out in the open, my only shelter the bare branches of a nearby bush that hung over my head. I curled up on my side and covered my head with my hands.

A wave of pain smacked me in the back of the head, and everything went black.

My head refused to move and I couldn't open my eyes. Acrid smoke burned my nostrils, and my voice stayed trapped in my chest. A high-pitched ringing filled my ears, and I twitched with the urge to cover them with my hands, but my arms stayed limp at my sides.

A piercing pain in my stomach grew unbearable. I tried to move, to roll over. The muffled sound of gunfire and bombs burst like distant fireworks. I managed to ease myself to the side and landed like a rag doll on the ground. A bomb must have exploded, and I had landed belly-side-down over the stake that kept me chained.

Pina came rumbling over, screeching my name. "They're still coming and on foot now. We will be killed by our own people." She shook me by the shoulders. "*Madonna mia*, we are all going to die. Killed by our own people."

She leaned close over me, her eyes darting frantically, her sour breath wafting in my face. As if I would help her—as if the danger of the moment suddenly made us allies. I had never intentionally hurt another human being, but I gripped the rock that Peter had given me and smashed Pina in the temple. She fell to the ground, and I looked down at her bloated, unconscious face. "You are not my people."

I reached in Pina's pocket, grabbed her pistol, and used it to shoot the chain close to the spike to free myself. I ran to the other side of the tent, the chain dangling from my ankle, to see if I could find Peter. But all I could see were soldiers crouched behind barriers or lying dead on the ground.

One of those dead men could be Peter. I wanted to scream his name, to beg God that none of those bodies would be his. I headed at a run toward the end of the ravine, away from the Germans, away from the Allies who would assume I was the enemy, and hoping to get away from the ear-bursting blasts of machine guns and bombs to find my mother and father.

The ravine seemed to wind forever around the mountain, and my strength ebbed quickly. At last I came upon a large tent where the pathway wound around a corner, but no movement or sound stirred the camp. I held my breath and latched onto the hope that I could still find something, someone, anyone who could lead me to my parents if they were not here.

Cots, papers, dishes, a radio, and military rations lay askew inside the tent as if the occupants had escaped in a hurry. The nasty swastika marked the supply boxes against the far wall. It was definitely a German camp, but no one was here.

I sat down on a cot and hung my throbbing head in my hands. Thirst burned like a fire in my throat, and I looked around, relieved to find a canteen with water. I gulped it down, relishing the cool, metallic flavor. I looked at the scattered papers and ransacked the boxes looking for clues or mention of my father—a note about a Lieutenant Bianco or Paolo Chessari. Nothing. I scooted the cots to the side to look beneath them and stopped abruptly at the sound of someone coughing outside the tent.

I stepped carefully outside, the rock I'd used to hit Pina clasped in my hand. I stole around the back side and stared in surprise at another smaller tent I had not seen. I eased the flaps back, and my knees almost buckled. Papa and Mama looked up at me from where they lay on a ratty mattress on the ground, their eyes wide with astonishment. I cried out their names and ran to them.

They were covered in bruises and wounds caked with dried blood, and I fell to my knees beside the mattress and gently pulled my mother into my arms. Her cheek was cool and smooth against mine in spite of her disheveled appearance. I reached for Papa's hand as I sobbed on my mama's shoulder. She pushed my hair back from my face and stared at me as if I was an apparition, and I clung to her like she had risen from the grave.

"How is this possible? You cannot be here," my father said. "Elisa, do you see her? Do you see Franca?"

"Yes, Paolo. Yes, I see her. She is real," she answered, holding my face in her shaking hands and weeping.

Months and weeks of wondering blindly where my father had been, the anguish of believing my mother was dead, and the days of searching through frozen mountains before being held captive had come to an end at last. Mama's hair was matted, and my father was far too thin, but when I touched each of their faces, they were real and alive. Papa reached for me and kissed my cheek before he pulled me into a trembling embrace.

The threat of the enemy returning cut our rejoicing short. "I cannot explain anything now," I said. "We have to get you out of here. The Allies are attacking the German camp where I was held captive, and the combat is so fierce I am sure they will win the battle. By the time we make our way there, the camp may be occupied by the Allies and safe for us."

"We have heard all the explosions in the distance, and our captors sprinted out of here with their arms loaded with weapons and ammo. I am relieved you did not encounter them," Papa said.

"The Allied attack may be the thing that has saved us all. I am not sure how I could have freed you otherwise."

I stood and reached my hands out to help my parents get up from the filthy mattress and grimaced in anger and frustration when I pulled back the blankets and saw that their ankles were chained to spikes like mine had been.

I searched through several nearby boxes until I found a key that unlocked the shackles around all three of our ankles and sighed with relief. I was free. My parents were free. But we were not out of danger.

I led them back to the place where I had been held captive to see if the battle was still raging. We hiked for what seemed like hours at the fastest pace my parents could tolerate, stopping frequently so my mother could rest. Papa held onto my shoulder to keep himself moving, and I held Mama's arm on my other side. My head still ached from the explosion that had flipped me in the air, but finding my family gave me new strength.

When we reached the camp, the fighting had ceased. Allied soldiers combed the grounds, carrying the bodies of the German soldiers away in bags and on stretchers. More bodies covered in blood and blasted to pieces lay scattered on the ground, the whole camp and human life obliterated. Acid burned in my belly and up my throat.

I kept my focus on my parents, petrified to look for Peter among the dead. The possibility of discovering his body hummed and shivered just under my skin, and I blinked back tears each time I glanced up.

One of the commanders recognized my father as we approached, and he sent men over to meet us with stretchers to carry my parents the rest of the way to cots under a makeshift tent.

The Allies had triumphed and now occupied the camp—what was left of it anyway. The German tents looked like a sharp-clawed animal had ripped them to shreds. Some were burned and still smoldered. The huge mess tent was a broken-winged bird, the poles and canvass askew and fractured. Trees and bushes were reduced to blackened skeletons. And the real skeletons of men littered the ground.

It seemed no one could have survived this onslaught of destruction. I found a place behind a tree, fell to my knees, and vomited. I refused to give up all hope that Peter was alive, but my stomach refused to stop coiling into knots.

CHAPTER FORTY-EIGHT

Franca

UNDER THE TENT, I LAY my hand on my mother's shoulder, sickened at how thin and bony she had become. Papa looked the worst; some of his teeth were missing, his eyes were sunken, his jaw was swollen and bruised, and his skin had grown whiter than my mother's. We spent much of the evening crying over Laura together and then holding on to the relief that Dominic and Damiano were with the family and that everyone else at home seemed healthy. Mama's tears slowed when I told her Camilla De'Angelis had been living at our villa to take care of Bruno and the baby and that Alma had returned.

The Allied captain walked over and shook Papa's hand where he rested on a cot. The captain's hair was combed perfectly, and his face was clean shaven even though his uniform was splattered with grime and blood.

"So good to see you and your wife alive, Bianco," he said. "We were just about to send a search party down the ravine to find you, and low and behold, here you came walking right toward me. You look a bit haggard and broken, but we'll take care of that."

Papa tried to smile, and the captain looked around at the debris all over camp.

"We stopped this nest of Nazis with bombs and machine guns that were strategically and secretly placed above this ravine. By the time the enemy gave up the battle, only a few of them were left—some from the foxholes and a few who may have held you captive. When you feel a bit rested, I'd like you to point those men out."

"Very well," Papa answered the captain, and I gasped out loud before I could contain myself. Peter could be one of those captured soldiers. The chances were bleak, but I grasped onto the grain of hope.

The Allies let my parents and me sleep on cots in one of their tents. I slept warmer than I had in weeks but tossed and turned, envisioning Peter locked up with the other prisoners or stashed away forever in a black bag.

The next morning, I followed my father and the captain to the barbed wire enclosure where they held the prisoners. A dozen or more soldiers sat huddled together on the ground for warmth, their uniforms blending them in a blur of green and gray as I scanned frantically for a set of wide shoulders, stark blond hair, and the long, purple scar that distinguished Peter Weimer from all others.

The men looked over at us a few at a time until the last soldier removed his hat and lifted his head, revealing the features I had longed to see. He met my tearful gaze, and my heart lurched in my throat. Peter was alive. He was a forbidden prisoner I could not reach, but he was alive. I bit my lip until I tasted blood to keep myself from crying out his name. Our gazes stayed locked together.

We were interrupted by a ruckus of shouting voices. I spun around and watched a ragged band of seven or eight people waltz into camp with their weapons propped over their shoulders and grins on their faces as if they were special guests. My gut churned when I recognized Lena and Omberto, who had attacked me and cut off my hair. I'd hardly had a moment to think about the braid Lena had lobbed from my head; a haircut had been the least of my concerns since then. But seeing her again made my hackles rise, and I reached back for the hair that was no longer there.

The ragged band stopped in front of us, and Lena looked at me and smirked.

An American officer walked out to greet them, and Lena stepped forward. "We are a dynamic group of Italian and Polish partisans at your service," she said with a salute. She pointed at me. "But why is she still here? None of you have discovered her secret? That she is a little *fraulein* for one of these German soldiers? I found her wrapped in a German coat like it was her lover's, and she never denied it. She is a traitor, and now she is walking around free in this camp like she is royalty."

"She is royalty," my father said from behind me. "And who are you?"

"Her name is Lena, and she is nothing but a criminal," I answered. "A thief and a kidnapper." I stared into Lena's face. "It took me a while, but I finally put it together. You are friends with Pina and helped her and Riccardo kidnap me and keep me like a slave."

Lena snorted. "That slob Pina was not my friend. I would rather be shot than help her."

"A shooting can be arranged if needed," my father said. He surveyed Lena through narrowed eyes and then turned his attention to the American captain. "If my daughter says that these people are criminals, I would take her at her word and question them."

Lena cursed and hissed like a cat when soldiers took her into custody. Omberto tried to run before he was caught. But they were outnumbered, and my breathing eased when they were finally led away.

Papa went with the captain, and Mama and I were invited to eat with the Allies. The men had scrounged up two unbroken chairs for us to sit on, and I thanked them profusely for sparing us from the frozen ground. Mama sat beside me but said very little as she nibbled her food. Her fatigue and trauma would take time to heal. I patted her leg softly, and her returning smile reassured me. She went back to the tent to lie down, and I decided to find my father and tell him about Peter.

But when I came around the corner, Peter and the other prisoners were being led out of the camp and the ravine with their hands tied behind their backs.

"Wait—" I shouted and turned to the American captain beside my father. "Where are you taking these soldiers?"

The captain lowered his brow at me. "To Cassino, where we have a more functional prison camp."

"But I have special information about one of the prisoners. Please, please, let me explain."

The captain did not look pleased with my interruption. "Some of these men captured and tortured your parents." He pointed at Peter. "And one of them pretended to be a partisan but was actually a spy."

I looked at the captain in shock. "The information about the spy is not true. Who told you this?"

He pointed to a few soldiers and partisans nearby, and I gasped when I spotted Davide in the group.

"Did he tell you this?" I asked, pointing to Davide.

"Yes, he said he witnessed it," the captain said.

I grabbed my father's arm and looked at the captain to be sure they were both listening. "Papa, I know this man you say is your witness. His name is Davide, and he has a personal vendetta against one of these men. He is lying."

I pointed at Peter. "This man is German, but he changed sides and joined the partisans long ago. He traveled with us to find you, Papa."

I scowled at Davide. "Where are Enzo and the others?"

"When you chased your boyfriend up this mountain, we had to escape and hide before you sent the Germans to find us."

"That is not how it happened. Tell me where the others are," I demanded.

He sneered and shrugged. "Enzo and our loyal partisans are fighting with the Americans outside Rome. I came here under Enzo's orders to report your German boyfriend for double-crossing our army."

I knew that Peter's decision to save Dieter and August would seem like betrayal, but Davide's bitterness toward Nazis and his jealousy were the driving force in his efforts.

I turned to Papa. "Please, can I explain to you and the captain in private?"

We sat in chairs by a firepit while I told my parents and the captain about Peter—that he had saved Marianna, that he had saved Mama when he drove us to Siracusa, that he had helped the resistance by translating German radio broadcasts and tracked my little brothers down to get them home to our villa.

"He is against Hitler and even traveled with me up here to find you and Mama," I said, out of breath from rattling the long list.

Papa looked back at me, his eyes creased in confusion. "I know of Peter and can validate that he saved Marianna De'Angelis if this is the same man. But Davide said that Peter was supposed to clean out a nest of Germans. Instead, he warned them and then left with them to rejoin their army."

"That is not true. He wants to stop the Nazi army. I was with him that day. When he went up the mountain to attack the Germans in a hideout, he discovered that two of them were his closest friends. He has known them since they were children, and there was no way he could kill them. And he did not turn against the partisans or rejoin the Nazis. He told the leaders here that the mountains were packed with Allied soldiers so they would not attack the partisans because they were too outnumbered."

"Why would Davide lie?" the captain asked.

"Davide's brother was killed by the Germans right in front of him. He hates Peter and all Germans and was bitter that Peter was trusted by the partisans and allowed to travel with us." I hesitated with the last bit of information, but I had to make them believe me. I took a deep breath and looked down at the ground. "Davide also accused me of sleeping with Peter and vowed revenge."

My father bristled at my words, and the American captain got to his feet. "I will leave this situation up to you, Lieutenant Bianco. It appears it should be your call."

"I appreciate that," Papa answered and then looked at me. "I will have Peter brought to me so we can talk this over."

Papa and the captain walked over to the prisoners and left me and Mama alone. She placed her hand on my back, and I looked at her through the pool of tears in my eyes.

Her eyes were steely gray, and she lowered her brows, looking worried. "Franca, you love this man, Peter. You love a German. You cannot love a German."

I gasped in shock at her discernment. "I never said that I loved Peter." I brushed my hands over my eyes and could not look at her.

"Your voice quivers when you say his name." Her eyes softened, and she held her hand on my cheek. "You must be so careful, *carina mia.* We are at war with his people."

"The war forces people to hate each other."

"It is terrible, but hatred drives people to madness and puts you in terrible danger."

I sat straighter. "You are English, and Papa is Italian."

"Your father and I were not mortal enemies when we met and married." She wiped a tear from my cheek. "Be extremely vigilant that no one sees or knows how you feel."

I lay my hand over the top of hers, strengthened by her loving concern as Papa walked back to the two of us. "Peter is safe. I told Davide to join in with the American soldiers if he wanted to be useful, but he stormed off."

I stood and embraced my noble father. "*Grazie tantissimo*, papa. I am so grateful and relieved. But now I must tell you about Peter's family right away. It is a long and horrible story, and I do not have time to tell you every detail, but his mother and sister are in grave danger. We owe him help because of all he has done for us."

Papa frowned and waved his hand at me to stop my story. "I am grateful to Peter also, but that does not mean you should have risked your life to come here on his behalf."

I shook my head. "I came to find you most of all. But yes, I also came because I hoped you would help Peter. The reasons are compelling; a German soldier named Keillor vowed to make his way back to Germany to Peter's home to seek vengeance because Peter stopped him from diabolical deeds against his sister. Keillor is going to torture and kill Peter's sister and probably his mother too. If Peter does not get back to Germany to warn and help his family escape before Keillor gets there, they are doomed. Keillor is a demon. He is the one who captured Marianna and would have assaulted and killed her. He was stationed as a spy in Sicily when the Germans retreated, and he revels in capturing and torturing people."

Papa stood and rubbed his hand over his brow. "All this time I believed you were safe and tucked away in Sortino. You have immersed yourself in the middle of the worst kinds of danger."

I hardly heard his comments as I searched my mind for a solution. The answer came to me as the words flowed from my mouth. "Let Peter go to his family, Papa. At least look away and let him escape. As I told you, he has been a partisan for our side for months. If he is taken away with the other Germans and they find out what he has done for the Allies, he will be killed. Davide may even tell them just so they will kill him."

The scowl had not softened on my father's face, but he nodded. "I will decide what needs to be done."

The prisoners were moved back to the holding area, but I kept my distance from Peter, not wanting the men with him to suspect our connection.

Papa came and went from the tent, resting in between whatever errands he made. I made excuses to do tasks in the camp to reassure myself that the prisoners had not left. But I did not tax Papa's patience and mar his judgement with further pleadings for Peter. Papa was a reasonable and honorable man, and I had to put Peter and my trust in his hands.

The next morning after breakfast, Papa called me back inside our tent. I was surprised and relieved when Peter joined us a few minutes later.

"I have good news, and then a possible solution for the danger your family is in," Papa said, looking at Peter.

"Perhaps this man Keillor has been reassigned from Sicily and is planning to go north to find your sister. Perhaps not. But if you will give us the location of your home in Germany, we can evacuate your family. It may take a while, so I cannot promise anything, but we will see what we can do."

Peter gripped his hands together. "Yes, yes, sir, I will give you the exact location."

Papa lifted the corners of his mouth. "Good. I have formulated a plan to pick up your mother and sister and have them flown back to Italy. The Allies have plane routes for carrying supplies from Sicily to Russia. They sometimes fly over Germany for assessment on their way back to Italy. I will arrange a landing in Germany one time for a brief window of time so the soldiers can pick up your mother and sister and bring them to Italy. They will land in the south on the mainland and have to travel from there over to Siracusa if they can."

A smile lit Peter's face. An expression I had not seen in weeks. "That would be most appreciated, sir. I would never ask for such a thing."

"You have saved our family in more than one instance. If we can pull this off, it would be to repay you for saving my wife and for Marianna as well." He paused. "Now as for you and our daughter Franca." He stopped and looked back and forth at the two of us and then settled on Peter. "I am asking that you leave here and travel with Franca to see her back to Siracusa safely." Papa looked at me. "Will that suit you, Franca? Are you willing to return to Siracusa now that your mother and I are free and it looks as if Peter's family will be rescued?"

My father sounded so formal and so official that I had the urge to salute him. I smiled instead. "Yes, that is an acceptable plan, sir. But considering your poor state of health, I assumed you and Mama would go back to our villa to heal. Please, Papa."

He kissed me on the cheek. "Franca, there are doctors on hand right here, and your mother refuses to leave me. She is not well, so I will not insist upon it. As for me, I can rest in this camp all I need. We are just about to break through the wall to kick the Nazis out of Italy, and there is no time for me to take a vacation."

I knew further argument would be futile, so I held my tongue and kissed my father in reply.

He patted my back. "*Allora*, since you are content, I will ask for a few more minutes alone with Sergeant Weimer."

I slipped out of the tent. I was nervous about what my father may be saying to Peter, but I also had a hope and peace I had not experienced in many months.

CHAPTER FORTY-NINE

Peter

Lieutenant Bianco kept a sharp gaze on me. "Sergeant Weimer, your Italian is very good. In your journeys anywhere in Italy now, you need to tell everyone that you are Italian. Choose a small town on the border of Italy and Switzerland to tell people you are from, and that will explain your German-slanted accent. But be sure you convince people that you are Italian."

"I will follow that plan completely. And I can never express my gratitude for your help with my family. This will probably save their lives."

"I am counting on that." He lowered his brow. "But one other thing; it is my impression that there has been affection expressed between you and Franca. She is my daughter, and you know the grave danger to her if people conceive the notion that she is involved with a German. If I could spare the extra man, I would send a third person with you for propriety's sake.

"We owe you for what you have done for our family. Nevertheless, in honor of your mother and sister's return, I ask that you do not touch Francesca or have any romantic connection with her at all as you travel and even after. Once the war is over and Keillor is no longer a threat, I am sure you can return to Germany safely, and Franca can carry on with her life and plans."

"Understood sir. And if I may ask just one more thing?" I hesitated when he lifted his brow. I knew he was surprised I would ask for anything more, but I had to. "Sir, the group of us that was almost sent to the prison camp yesterday . . ."

"Yes . . ."

"Two of those men are my lifelong friends. I would not ask for their freedom, of course, but if I dare, I would ask if they are truly being taken to a camp and not to be executed?"

"Give me their full names, and you have my word that your friends will be kept in a decent camp and not targeted for execution. I cannot say the same for those who captured my wife and me and tortured us."

"Of course, sir. Thank you, sir." I let out the breath that had been choking me and left the tent with renewed hope for Dieter and August and a sense that my mother and sister would be safe at last. I would keep Franca safe through the entire journey and keep my vow to her father.

CHAPTER FIFTY

Franca

February 13, 1944

My nerves twitched by the time Peter came to my tent and said he was ready for us to leave. I held on to my mother's hands as I backed away until only our fingertips touched. She had insisted that she stay to help Papa since everyone was safe at our villa and my father was not well. But Mama herself looked frail and exhausted.

Neither of my parents would tell me what torture the Nazis had put them through, but the bruises all over them were still deep purple and green, and my father walked with a heavy limp, his foot dragging a few inches before he could move it forward with each step. They were both too weak for travel.

Most of our journey would be on foot, and our map showed that it was hundreds of miles to Siracusa. Many people traveled without maps because the roads, buses, and railways had been blown up and sabotaged—the maps seemed obsolete. But we needed some way to keep us on track.

Food was scarce, but we packed what we could into backpacks. Clothing was even more scarce, but we each found an extra shirt or two that soldiers had left behind, and I found a heavy blanket in a trunk, surprised that it had survived all the bombings.

Peter and I each had a bedroll and a canteen, so now our journey could begin. We wanted to make it back to Siracusa before Peter's family members arrived, but Papa reassured us he would send word ahead so Bruno and his mother would know to expect them if they arrived first.

The terrain made for constant climbing and descending over rocks, hills, and mountains. The sky stayed covered in a blanket of gray, casting a muted light over the frozen morning frost. Peter and I plodded on steadily, but the breathlessness from climbing made conversation difficult.

Nighttime came, and I gathered wood for a fire. I sat across from Peter, captivated by the way the yellow flames flickered in his eyes and cast gold in his hair. It had been weeks since the day we tumbled in the pond in each other's arms and shared the kisses that made my belly quiver.

"Peter?"

"Yes?" he finally answered without lifting his head.

"The day I left Sortino . . . the day we'd been at the pond together and Keillor came . . . do you ever think back on that day?"

He hesitated. "Our paths have divided since then."

I picked up a stick and poked at a log that had rolled to the side. "And yet, here we are. Do you remember the time we spent together?"

His gaze flashed past mine before he focused on the fire. "I remember, but then I move my thoughts on."

I dropped the stick to the ground and watched him keep his gaze locked on the fire. "So they are bad memories for you?"

"No, just mistaken and forbidden."

"That is the same as a bad memory."

"No." He shook his head and exhaled loudly. "We both need to forget about those days."

"So you see our time together as a mistake?"

"The world we live in forces it to be a mistake, and that is how I will remember it."

"So you hold nothing for me now? You do not want to touch me?"

He clenched his jaw and looked away. "It's better if we do not talk about it anymore."

"Why?"

"Being close to you before made it impossible to use reason; I lost my head, my common sense, and my self-control."

"And now?"

"Now I know what I am and am not allowed to feel, to think, to do. I have to follow my duty."

"What if I refuse to follow my duty? What if I reach out and touch you and show you what I feel?"

"Franca, stop. You cannot talk that way. I cannot hear it."

"So you would push me away?"

He climbed in his bedroll and turned his back to me, answering over his shoulder.

"I would walk away."

I lay awake on my side, longing to move over and press myself against Peter and unwilling to give up. No matter his stoic behavior, softness like a caress crossed his eyes when he looked at me. I watched him from the corner of my eye, fully expecting that if he turned over and caught me looking in his direction, he would move farther away.

"Have I offended you, Peter?" I asked after a silent morning, and we stopped to eat lunch the next day.

"Of course not. You have saved me from imprisonment and are the whole reason my mother and sister will soon be safe and that I can see them again. I am very grateful."

We'd brushed snow off fallen logs and sat down across from each other. His smile was polite, his words spoken slow and formal.

"Do you resent accompanying me?"

"No, why would I? Your father is saving my sister and mother; I would do anything for him. And I want you to be safe. This way I know you will be."

"So this journey is all in gratitude to my father. You will get back together with your family, go your own way, and say, *Thank you, Franca, it was so nice to meet you. Have a happy future.*" I could not keep all the bitterness out of my voice.

"What choice do I have, Franca? What do you want me to do? Put your life on the line? Endanger everyone we know? Betray your father?"

"You would never betray my father."

"That is true, and that is best."

"You talk, you use words, but you do not tell me anything. Only half truths."

He stood abruptly and put his hands on his hips. "Do you really think that your father sent us on this trip alone without making me commit that I would never touch you or compromise you? Your father is very protective; he has seen the atrocities right before his eyes that have happened to women who have involvement with Germans. Before we left, he extracted a promise from me that there would be absolutely nothing between us."

His words cut me off like a guillotine, and I covered my eyes with my hand so he would not see my tears. "So there is nothing I can say. And there is nothing I can do."

"There is nothing either one of us can do."

We acted like practical strangers for days. Peter was always several feet away unless he noticed I needed a hand over some rocks or up a hill. He dropped my hand immediately after each time and marched ahead. Loneliness was my constant companion, and the dreams I once had floated away and never looked back.

It would do us no good to be together if we were ripped apart, tortured or killed for it. Marianna had been right when she told me there was more than one way to die in this war, and it was time for me to surrender to the truth.

The cold lived in my bones, sent icicles up my spine and kept my heart frozen. All my choices in life had been bombed or derailed.

I sat beside a stream in filthy, wrinkled clothes, trying to get a drink and clean my teeth with a rag. My hair only touched my shoulders since Lena had cut off my braid, and now the curl made my hair so full I had to let it go, let it float on the chilly wind, or try to tuck it inside my scarf. I longed for a bath. I'd worn the same clothes—men's pants and a button-up shirt—and soldier's boots for weeks.

Peter sat far away from me, looking the other way. I finished my toiletries and drank my fill of the icy cold stream that chilled my chest and belly.

A rabbit darted out from its den, its long fur coat like angel hair and its light-colored eyes flashing. It dashed over the ground frantically, stopping for one split second to look at me. I wanted to scoop it up and lay my cheek on its soft fur. I wanted to take it with me to keep me company. A shot rang out, and I jumped in alarm, then spotted Peter, his rifle in his hands. He walked to the dead rabbit and picked it up by its ears.

He built a fire and roasted the rabbit, handing me a leg quarter when it was deep brown and smelled delicious.

"I do not want it," I said flatly.

"You are not hungry?"

"Not anymore. I was until you shot the rabbit I had been watching."

"Are you opposed to me hunting for our food?"

"That gunshot echoed all the way through me."

"I thought you would be used to gunshots by now."

"I will never get used to them," I answered through a wall of tears.

The journey rolled endlessly, hours and days of walking, climbing, stumbling. The quiet in the valleys, the buzz of fighter planes crossing the sky, and the click and rumble of people passing by in wagons or pushing wheelbarrows full of their belongings when we passed through towns became commonplace.

We passed through a ravine, careful to keep a steady watch in each direction for anyone who might question Peter's presence. The air whispered through the mountains, accompanied only by the occasional cry of a bird or snap of brittle branches when they grew too heavy with snow and lost their battle with gravity.

Peter led the way and had gotten too far ahead. I leapt over an icy brook to catch up and screamed when the ground gave way beneath me.

I strained to lift my eyelids, surprised to see that the mountains had all been tipped on their sides. I questioned why someone would do such a feat. It would be much more difficult to climb over them now, and I was tired. Maybe if I went back to sleep and tried to wake up again, the mountains would stand back up.

When I opened my eyes again, the mountains were gone, and everything had turned gray. I wanted to sleep on, to float and float until my head stopped circling around and confusing everything. But the spinning got worse when someone yanked me by the shoulders and pulled me backwards over muddy, icy ground.

I did not fully reach consciousness until the back of my heels had bumped over a long stretch of land. Someone was taking me away. I shrieked and tried to wrench myself free of my captor. He stopped and laid my shoulders back onto the ground and knelt beside me. I looked up into Peter's face, confused to see it had turned red.

He covered my mouth with his hand. "Can you run? Walk? We have to get out of here as fast as we can."

I forced myself to ignore the stabs of pain in my head and let him help me to my feet. I had no time to ask questions. He wrapped his arm around me and helped me hurry past trees and through brush and branches.

We found our way around the side of a mountain, but the crack of gunshot bounced off the rocks and pinged past our heads. There must be German snipers scattered through the hills we just passed. Peter grabbed my arm, and we dived into some bushes and crawled through the terrain, sliding into a cave-like shelter under a rocky ledge at the base of a mountain. We crawled deeper and deeper until a cavern opened before us, and Peter spread his coat on the ground and helped me lie down.

"You have blood on your face," I said.

"Yes, just a little bit of blood. But how is your head, Franca? You flew up, and your head hit a rock when you landed on your side."

I rubbed at my temples, wincing when I found the large bump on one side. "That seems to be a pattern for me. I was knocked unconscious when the Allies attacked us in the ravine too. My head is pounding like an exploding grenade."

"That is what was lobbed at us, a grenade. Luckily it landed behind some rocks, but the percussion still got us. There should not be any Germans this far south, but we came across a renegade soldier or a lost sniper."

"Tell me why your face is bleeding."

"A bullet grazed the side of my forehead, but it's just a scratch."

The pounding in my head made me nauseous. My stomach heaved, and I vomited to the side of the blanket. Peter used his handkerchief to wipe my mouth, covered my vomit with dirt, and sat where he could hold my head in his lap. He slowly stroked my face with his fingers, and I closed my eyes, letting tears relieve the pulsing pain behind my eyes and soaking in the comfort of Peter's touch.

"Will the soldier come here looking for us?" I whispered.

"I am guessing he fled the moment he saw us run well out of his way."

"I hope that is true; I am not sure I can move or keep going yet."

"We will stay here tonight. This is a good cave far behind a ridge, and I can make a small fire to keep us warm. I'm going to double back in a bit and see if I can find our bags."

I hated to have him leave me, but we needed our supplies.

Peter returned quickly with our bags and brought a ball of snow he'd wrapped in a handkerchief and held it against the bulging knot on my head. I leaned back against his chest and fell asleep. Hours later, I awoke curled up against his chest by the warmth of a fire.

We rested a few extra days in the cave because my head refused to show me mercy, and my stomach protested each time I moved. Peter kept fresh snow in the handkerchief for my head and fed me bites of food. I did as he directed, too weak to protest. I laid my hand over his when he held the ice pack on my head and was relieved when he did not move his hand away.

The food had run out. It took two days before we came upon a town again because I slowed us down. Even my arms and legs ached with hunger, but my head had greatly improved.

The weather had warmed a bit, and we came upon a villa with shutters at the windows, a barren garden, and a chicken coop where the fowls squawked and clucked as if it were springtime. Peter and I stood side by side, watching for any suspicious activity. A small stream of smoke twirled out the top of a rock chimney, and a chicken escaped the coop and ran in circles around the yard.

"We need food. Maybe we can give this place a chance," I whispered.

"It is probably best that we lead them to believe we are a married couple. It will help them to be less suspicious about my German accent, and they may find it strange that we are traveling together otherwise."

I smiled. "I agree. Signore and signora Chessari. Franca and Pietro."

CHAPTER FIFTY-ONE

Franca

"The Germans have been all around this *paese*, but by the grace of God, they have never come to our home," the old man said after he and his elderly wife had welcomed us and sat us at their table.

"We have stragglers and the wounded who come here for help, so we consider ourselves servants for Saint Christopher," interjected his wife with a huge grin that made her eyes disappear.

The woman placed a plate of pasta in front of each of us. "You look like such a pretty couple and like you have had a very rough time. You can eat, take a long special bath, and sleep here until you're ready to leave. We keep a room in the back for the weary."

The old woman introduced herself as Anna, and she held my cheek in her hand. "*Poverina*, what is your name?"

"Franca." I gestured to Peter. "This is my husband, Pietro."

"Ahh," the husband and wife exhaled together.

"This is just like Santo Pietro," the old man said. "I knew it. I tell you, Mama, the saints are working together, and they know who to send to us."

Anna stroked my cheek again. "You have come to the right place indeed. The tubbing room in the back of the house is built right on top of a hot spring, and the water can heal anything that ails you. I am going to get the room ready for your big, hot bath to soothe and warm your tired bones. You eat, and then I will show you your room while Papa gives Pietro a bit of wine before his bath."

I ate the *tortellini* hungrily and washed it down with a glass of cold water from their well.

"Your bath is ready," Anna said when she came down the hall a few minutes later. I followed her with great anticipation.

Minutes later, I sank into the giant tub, closing my eyes and letting the warm minerals in the water fill every one of my senses. I slid under the surface, the soft fluid soothing my sore head and aching bones. At least half an hour passed as I soaked and floated, letting every worry and drop of sorrow seep into the liquid.

The soap Anna had given me had a light vanilla scent, and I held it to my nose, relishing the sweetness as it filled my nostrils. I let myself linger and only started when Anna came in with a fresh pot of steamy tea. "This is an herbal tea that I drink when I bathe. You will sleep like a baby tonight." She sat on a chair near the tub, a huge grin on her rosy-cheeked face.

After I finished the tea, she grabbed a plump sponge and soaked it in the water. She rubbed the soap all over it until it bubbled up and then proceeded to scrub my back. I let out a squeak of surprise, but the rough scrubbing actually rejuvenated me and eased the stiffness in my muscles.

After scrubbing my hair and scalp with the same enthusiasm, taking care around the wound on my head, she then went to the side of the tub, reached into the water, and yanked my foot and leg into the air with gusto. It pulled me forward, my head and body sinking all the way into the sloshing water. I was relieved the tub had a layer of bubbles over the top to keep my modesty intact, but the woman was so focused on scouring my foot and toes I doubted she would notice anyway. When she had finished with both feet, she stood.

"There you go, signora. Papa and I have run these springs for years, helping people bathe and soothe their pains. I have some lotion there on the dresser. Would you like me to return later and help you with that as well?"

I blushed at the idea of this lady lathering me all over with lotion.

"I will be fine, but I thank you very much."

"Before the war, this business even made us money. People came from all over just to stay here and have our bathing service from our hot spring. I am so glad the Nazis never heard about it."

She nodded briskly as if we had completed a business agreement. "*Va bene.* Very well. I will go and get your husband to join you for his turn now."

As soon as she closed the door, I got to my feet, water dripping like rain as I grabbed my towel, wrapped it around me, and scurried behind a dressing screen where the woman had placed my bag of clothes.

I covered myself liberally with the lotion she had offered, relishing the clean scent and silky smoothness on my skin even as I hurried. I'd slipped on a clean chemise and a long flannel nightgown just as Anna pushed the door open and nudged Peter inside.

"There was no need to get out of the tub so soon, signora. There was plenty of room down on the other end," Anna told me and Peter as she pointed to the tub. "We have had nine children at a time in this tub before. Papa built it for all of our children many, many years ago, and then we used it for our little business." She sighed, her cheeks lowering in sorrow. "Maybe someday the war will end, and we will be in business again. But we help who we can."

She started unbuttoning Peter's shirt for him while she talked. His face went red as a beet, but she did not seem to notice.

"Sometimes Papa and I sit in this tub for hours, drinking wine and praying to the saints." She sighed.

Peter reached for the buttons himself, and Anna caught the hint. "Very well. I will leave the two of you alone for a while."

She shut the door behind herself, and I could not contain it anymore. The image of the gray-haired Anna and her husband sitting in the tub drinking wine and praying was too much for my tired mind to resist, and I burst out laughing.

Peter lifted his hands in the air. "This is not so funny. How can we get out of this situation without exposing our lie? She will be back any minute and expect to see me in the tub."

"Then you'd best climb in," I said, still struggling to control my giggles. Peter's face glowed red again, and the absurdity of the situation was too much. The bath had dissolved my worries, and I had no strength to keep from laughing again.

Peter tried to glare at me but gave in and chuckled. "Stop laughing, Franca. What are we going to do?"

"Do not panic; I will simply head to the bedroom."

I picked up my bag and looked at Peter one more time. He had his hands hanging on to the front of his shirt again, as if still guarding his buttons, and I covered my mouth to stifle one more giggle as I went out the door.

I found the bedroom and climbed up on the bed under layers of thick quilts and curled up on my side.

Peter and I had laid close together the last few nights since we'd been attacked and injured, but this seemed completely different. We would share a bed, a soft mattress with crisp linens and feathered pillows meant to loosen the aches and pains of the day and let one sink into a dreamlike state—a bed for a husband and wife, not for a single girl and a man Anna and her husband would call the dreaded enemy.

My cheeks flushed with errant thoughts of how it could be if Peter and I really were husband and wife. This bed was not for us, not for who we were now and forced to be. But I could not help but shiver in anticipation that Peter would be so near, that my dream would hover just behind a silver cloud.

Peter had followed his vow to stay away from me so perfectly it seemed apparent that all of his passion for me had dried up and blown away. But that did not mean that mine had, and I had to tuck the blankets tight around my shoulders and turn on my side, to feign sleep when Peter returned from his bath and lay down beside me or I might let myself take a risk and reach for him.

When Peter finally did come into the room, I stayed on my side and kept my eyes closed, resigned to the distance that would be between us no matter how enchanted the bed was.

I had left a candle burning on the dresser and expected him to extinguish it shortly, but I heard him rummaging through a closet instead. The room finally went dark, but Peter had not said one word to me or climbed on the bed. In a moment, I realized he must have been looking for extra blankets and made himself a bed on the floor. Propriety should have prepared me for his arrangement—it was the decent thing for Peter to do. But in spite of the logic, my cheeks still burned with the humiliation of rejection, not because he had done the proper thing, but because he had not even seemed tempted to do otherwise. Perhaps I was easy to resist.

When I rolled over on my back my arms ached with emptiness at my sides, but Peter had quickly made his bed and retired without so much as a word to me. We both lay silently in our separate beds in the dark.

"So did you get a brisk scrubbing in the tub like I did?" Peter asked in a loud whisper, breaking the strain of silence.

I gasped in surprise and sat halfway up. "Anna scrubbed your back too?" Despite all my burning and torn emotions, I burst into giggles again. "I am shocked that she would do that with a man."

Peter laughed hard, his hand over his mouth to keep from being heard by the old couple. "Apparently, she does not have your sense of propriety. If I hadn't intervened, she would've scrubbed me head to toe. I had to reach for the sponge and tell her I would be fine cleaning the rest of me after she washed my whole backside so quick and thorough there was no stopping her."

We both rolled with laughter.

"I only got my back, hair, and toes done. I think I received the cheap end of the deal," I whispered.

"More like the less shocking version, I would say."

We laughed even harder, lying beneath the vaulted wood beams of the ceiling.

Our laughter subsided, and the chill in the air had me pulling the quilts higher over my shoulders.

"Are you warm enough?" I asked him. "How many blankets did you find?"

"Just one. But I will be fine," he said, his voice more formal.

I sat up again. "You will not be fine. It will be freezing in here before morning." I peeled two layers of my covers off my bed and tossed them to Peter.

"Thank you," he replied before awkwardness grew in another silent pause. "Franca, do you know why I am down here on the floor?" he finally whispered.

"I understand propriety very well. But we have been closer than this sleeping beside campfires. I trust you."

Peter sighed loudly into the darkness. "Perhaps I do not trust myself . . . *Buona notte*, Franca."

I covered my mouth with my hands to stifle my gasp—thrilled that he had admitted to at least a hint of attraction for me no matter the futility. I wanted to say something, to tell him it would be difficult for me to be close to him too, but for once, words escaped me.

No matter how much I ached and yearned to be close to Peter, to press my mouth against his and slide into the headiness of his kisses, I knew I could not stand the rejection or loss that would inevitably follow. My hopes and wishes were nothing but a dream I must dampen with more courage. The war had poisoned the world against us being together, and there was no antidote. I had to stop acting like a schoolgirl and respect Peter's efforts to be honorable and to keep us safe.

But I would take these last moments, this doomed opportunity to be close enough to inhale the scent of the vanilla soap mingling with the musk of his skin that I detected in the air, and soak in the healing minerals of being near him.

We ate a breakfast of *calzoni* filled with homemade ricotta with Anna and her husband. They gave us bread and dried fruit in a knapsack, and we thanked and kissed both of them on each cheek before we left.

March arrived, and spring was spreading its wings over the countryside. The road wound endlessly, green weeds and shoots of grasses lining the way. A reflection of light caught my eye in some bushes beside the road, and I went to inspect. A motorcycle—a green American army motorcycle without the official insignia. Peter tried to start it, but the tank was empty. We pushed it along beside us. If we could somehow find some petrol, we could travel so much faster. Pushing the bike over bumpy roads and terrain slowed us down, but it could be worth it.

Peter and I stayed a day at a widow's home outside of a village where she was caring for two wounded children and had been shot in the leg herself. Only three of the walls of her villa remained, and most of the furniture had been burned, but it had begun to rain, and the roof of the villa still remained.

The woman's leg was painful, so I fed and bathed the children and bandaged an old gash that had remained infected on the little boy's head while Peter made a sling for the older girl's arm that was swollen. The children thanked us shyly and rested on their beds, fussing in pain only in their sleep because when they were awake, they knew it was futile to call out for help from a wounded mother.

The next day, Peter chased a chicken in the yard to butcher it for the widow and her children. He followed the chicken over a hill, and when he came back, he had it by the neck and had a huge grin on his face.

"I found an abandoned army jeep over that hill. The engine is gone, but it has petrol in the tank. We can syphon it for the motorcycle and get a lot farther tomorrow."

The soreness and fatigue in my feet had made every step almost unbearable the past few days, so the discovery of the old jeep was a miracle. I jumped up from a damp chair and hugged Peter in celebration. His arms enveloped me, and he swung me around until my feet came off the ground. He tipped his head down and brushed his whiskered cheek against mine before he pulled away.

Peter cleaned the chicken, and I made a big pot of soup, adding vegetables I scrounged up from their garden, and then boiling pasta they could add to the soup. We all ate heartily and left enough for the widow and her children for the next few days.

Peter syphoned the gas, and much to our joy, the motorcycle started.

Two things gave me the greatest joy: the speed we were able to move on the motorcycle after walking so many miles, and the comfort that emitted from Peter as I kept my arms locked around him. It was still cold, the wind making the chill almost unbearable at times. My face ached, and I buried it in Peter's shoulder for relief.

The motorcycle rumbled and roared, the sound familiar because of all the soldiers who had traversed every road around Siracusa on motorcycles for many years. Only this time, it was I who rode on the seat. It was I who relished the power and the whip of wind that thrashed my hair. I did not care how messy my hair was. If I could stay behind Peter like this, I would travel circle after circle around the world.

The bleakness in my future grew and darkened as we traveled toward Siracusa. Peter's mother and sister would hopefully arrive soon if they had not already, and the dread and joy in that grew in contrast. A sick ache in my gut told me that Peter and his family would not stay for long and that, when they left, the true devastation of war would possess me.

At last, when we finally arrived, our villa stood before us like a beautiful painting. I longed to be able to open the doors and find every family member, including Laura, waiting for me. But it was not to be. Peter and I drove up on the motorcycle, and my young brothers rushed out to meet us, followed by Bruno's mother and Alma. I hugged them all, tears streaming down my face, and picked up Luca when he crawled over and lifted up his arms to be held. I covered his cheeks in kisses, comforted by a surreal and warm connection with Laura.

Luca was eight months old now. He crawled all over the house with his chubby legs when we went inside the house.

Bruno was in the study, and he embraced me and shook Peter's hand. We all gathered in the parlor where I explained why I had left in a hurry and the details of everything that had happened since I'd left Siracusa.

Evening approached, and Alma fed us all boiled eggs, grilled fish my brothers had caught, peppers, and hunks of bread. I insisted that Peter eat with us. My brothers told jokes and stories about the widows and children they had helped, and Luca gnawed on a chewy hunk of bread on Signora De'Angelis's lap.

Peter made his new home in the cellar beneath the winery, where I and my mother and brothers and Marianna and her mother all hid for weeks when the Allies first invaded Siracusa.

I fell into bed exhausted, the space beside me where Peter had been for days on end like a hollow void. I missed my parents, and I missed Marianna. I cried over Laura. Then I sank into deep, troubled slumber.

CHAPTER FIFTY-TWO

Peter

April 1944

AN ARMY TRUCK CAME UP the drive. I watched from the barn, nervous and hopeful that my family would be inside.

A tall Italian man climbed out of the truck first, followed by a slender young woman with curly red hair and a silver-haired older lady—my mother and Bettina. Franca brought them to the barn, and I grabbed both of them in my arms, weeping and holding my hands to their wet cheeks to look at them and rejoice that they were really here.

Franca watched from the doorway, and I gestured for her to come. She walked up to us slowly, as if she were hesitant to interrupt. When I introduced her to Mama and Bettina, my mother held her arms out, and Franca stepped right into the embrace, crying on my mother's shoulder. Bettina hugged the two of them, and I joined in, all three women in my arms.

"I spent hours, days, and weeks so scared and worried for you. I am grateful you are here and safe. Seeing the joy on your faces and the happy tears proves that hope and family can flourish, even in the middle of war," Franca said.

The sweet innocence in her words gripped me in the belly, and I longed to reach out and hold her, to kiss every inch of her face and lips. I glanced down at the ground to gain my composure.

"We have to keep your presence here a secret," Franca continued. "Our neighbors could misunderstand if they discovered the two of you and Peter. They may try to attack us or report your presence. There is some danger, but with all that Peter has done for us, we want to keep you safe and show our gratitude. You are welcome here."

Mama grabbed Franca's hands and smiled. "*Si*, we follow all you say."

Bettina smiled. "I apologize. Our mother does not speak but a few words of Italian. You are beautiful, Franca, so kind. We thank you so very, very much."

Franca blushed, her eyes like infinite pools of gentility. "*Grazie*, Bettina. You are very welcome."

I had to glance away again and clear my throat. "Franca and I planned ahead for your arrival. Mama, Bettina, the three of us will need to stay in a large cellar beneath the winery where Franca's family keeps cots, supplies, and even a stove—"

Franca's eyes lit up. "But with time, if the countryside looks very quiet, we may be able to bring you into the main house. Do you like to sew, bake, paint, or read?"

Bettina grinned and clapped her hands together in response. "Oh, yes. I enjoy art the most and to sew and to read also."

"Perfect. We are going to have a marvelous time."

In spite of the relief that my mother and Bettina were safe, I tossed and turned on the cot in the cellar that night. In the journey back to Siracusa, I had to keep Franca safe and see her home. The focus kept my guard up, my duty engaged. Now that we were back and my family was here with me, the wall I'd built between Franca and me tumbled down with the power of an earthquake. I had known the fullness of Franca's soft lips. I had tasted the sweetness and knew the satin smoothness of her skin. All the desire I'd held in check for Franca flooded in, and I felt like I was drowning.

I could not keep my end of the agreement with Franca's father if we stayed here very long. I needed a place where my mother and sister and I could reside, at least until the war was over or I could receive word that Keillor was no longer a threat and that we could return to Germany. Until that time, I would have to be very careful to keep my distance from Franca Chessari, and it twisted like a knife in my gut.

CHAPTER FIFTY-THREE
Franca

May–June 1944

Peter's mother watched me with blue eyes that had softened to a warm gray with age. She smiled and patted my shoulder every few minutes at the table. Time had passed without mishap, and the Weimers came up from the cellar for dinner. We left the door to the wine cellar beneath the kitchen open in case they needed a quick escape.

Alma had made a fire in the parlor, and we gathered together after we had eaten. Bettina held Luca, and he grabbed onto the tendrils of her curly hair and tried to chew on them. She laughed and played with him, bumping her nose against his and kissing his cheek.

"I see why you adore this baby, Franca. He is cute," she said in choppy Italian. "It is too long since our home had a baby."

Bettina's blue eyes and pale skin glowed in the firelight and the red in her hair burned like the flames. She was beautiful, and she kept Luca enraptured with tickles and little songs in German. Peter joined in on one of the songs, and his mother's face glowed with joy.

"It is a song our mother always sang to us as children," Peter said when they'd finished.

The furrow of stress around his eyes had vanished, replaced by an ease I had never seen before. I could not look away. Peter raised his eyes and saw me watching him. Instead of jerking his head the other way, he let his gaze linger, and my chest burned with longing.

"No more singing. It is bedtime for Luca," Bruno said. His scrutiny darted between me and Peter before he stared at Bettina holding Luca. "Franca, would you put Luca to bed this time?"

I winced at the abruptness in Bruno's tone. I knew he condemned a connection between me and Peter, but he need not be cold to Bettina.

Bruno looked more rested, and while I had been gone up north, his mother spent her days sewing clothes for him and Luca and helping Alma with the cooking. But he lowered his brow when he looked at Bettina.

I jumped to my feet. "Of course I will put Luca to bed. Bettina, would you help me?"

Bruno murmured as we left the room, but I ignored him.

Later, I climbed into bed, contemplating the way Peter had watched me in the parlor. Hope rose and fell with each breath as I lay alone beneath the blankets. But his family was out of danger, and that relief eased the frequency of my nightmares about bombings, gunfire whisking past my head, and freezing to death night after night with a chain around my ankle.

My brothers cared for the animals and worked as much of the vineyard as they could, hoping to harvest at least a small part. They had turned thirteen while we were all apart, and their energy and high spirits strengthened us all. They hovered around Bettina, spent time in the cellar with huge grins on their faces and competed over who would carry meals to the family.

June arrived, and Bruno burst into the parlor with news that the Allies had driven the Germans back and had taken over Rome. At long last, after months of slaughter, the German line had been broken, and Germany was forced to retreat out of Rome. Soon they would be out of Italy altogether. I hurried to the cellar to tell Peter and his family the news and cried into my handkerchief with relief, not wanting to show too much jubilation; Peter's family may be worried for their friends and family on the German side.

"I am sorry for any of your dear ones who are suffering in the war," I told them.

Peter put his arm around his mother. "I believe this is the beginning of the end of the war. It will take a long time for Hitler to see he is defeated, but he is losing more of his hold every day. He must be stopped and overthrown—even executed. We can only hope the Allies can accomplish this without destroying all of our people as they go."

I put my hand on Bettina's shoulder. "Yes, I hope that the Germans who may have been trapped like you or are innocent will not have to suffer, just like I hope for the Italians."

My words fell flat inside the cramped quarters of the cellar. We all knew what a fleeting hope my wish conveyed. The innocent suffered the most on both sides of the war and in the greatest number.

I pushed a lighter tone into my voice. "Maybe you can come outside a little more. The neighbors may be defensive or suspicious about you, so we need to be cautious, but the threat of the Axis taking Italy back should be over, and if Keillor is still doing spy work in Sicily, he must be seeking a way out of here."

"Yes, the victory in Rome gives us all a surge of confidence that the end is in sight. Hitler has been pushed back like never before," Peter said to his mother and Bettina.

His mother wiped her eyes and pressed her cheek to Peter's.

After the sun had set, I found Frau Weimer crying out in the garden. I sat beside her and she patted my hand. Her sorrow did not need words. We had all lost family and friends in the war and lived in fear, and even with the victory in Rome, we knew Hitler would not stop killing until the bitter end.

Crickets rubbed their wings together in the bushes and played their evening music as if the world was safe and free. I picked up a handful of soil and let it trickle out of my fingers. The pungent scent of damp earth softened and restored the air with its promise of fertility.

Peter found us, and after a quick glance in my direction, he sat beside his mother. He took her hand in his, and they spoke quietly to each other in German.

At times, I caught a gaze from Peter that rippled the air between us and hinted that, in spite of his restraint, a deeper stirring still haunted him. But those moments died quickly. Hearing his quiet conversation with his mother in a language I could not understand was a harsh reminder that we came from very different lands. I slipped away to let them have time together and wept on my bed. Perhaps the war would end soon, but I had lost my battle.

My parents returned home months after Peter and I had left them behind. Dominic and Damiano jumped and cheered and opened the doors of the truck before it had come to a full stop in front of our villa. My heart sank when my father climbed out. A man from the back of the truck came forward and put his arm around Papa to give him support as they walked inside. Mama walked on the other side of him with her arm around his shoulder. The limp in his leg had worsened, and he dragged it behind him like a useless appendage before he could pull it forward. He had thinned to the point of a skeleton, and if my mother had not come with him, I was not sure I would have recognized him.

I waited until they had helped him to bed before I leaned down and kissed his forehead. He patted my cheek with his hand. "Do not worry. The Germans denied me food, but I will grow fat in no time."

Mama told us the story around the dinner table. Papa had again been captured by the Germans in Rome and starved to the point of dying before the Allies had taken over the city. His leg had been broken and had not healed.

"We will find a doctor for him immediately, Mama Chessari," Bruno vowed.

My mother's eyes were sunken and ringed in dark circles, but she looked far better than my father. Camilla De'Angelis and Alma fussed over her and Papa, bringing them soup and soft bread. Worry for my parents' health burrowed its way into my heart, but my parents were safe and alive. I would place my focus and faith on that.

Bruno had long since repaired the radio, and he used it to find a doctor who could treat my father. The doctor splinted the fracture in Papa's calf, but it had already begun to heal improperly, so without surgery, Papa would always have a limp.

CHAPTER FIFTY-FOUR

Franca

July 1944

THE AFTERNOON WAS CLEAR, AND a breeze blew over the tops of the grapevines. I longed to take a deep breath and go for a ride in the countryside after days of worry over my parents. I hitched our horse to our wagon. Peter was anxious to go with me for protection because so many Allied soldiers were still around, and Bettina longed to escape the cellar and come along. They would ride in the back of the wagon, between bales of hay in case we crossed paths with anyone.

With the reins in my hands, the click of my tongue keeping the horses steady, and the squeak and scratch of the wheels on the dusty road, my muscles relaxed. The sun warmed my skin; the wind lifted my hair; and my senses were on high alert with Peter so close behind me in the wagon.

Bettina had told me about her love of mosaics, so we stopped at the abandoned church I knew so well. "There is no one here or even close by. You should be safe," I said to Peter and Bettina when we pulled up front.

They climbed out, carefully looking around before they walked through the open doorway where the splintered wooden doors hung loose on the hinges.

I told them all about Marianna and our group, "*L'Amici di Carità*" or "Friends of Charity" and how we had met here at this church to organize our gathered food and fresh water to take to the poor families in the city.

The church ruins looked the same as the last time I'd been here, and I expected to see my friends arrive any moment as the three of us walked through the wide chapel and gazed up at the mosaic of St. Peter on the ceiling. Part of St. Peter's face and his hands clasped in prayer were absent, but much of his robes and the letters of his name in gold still remained.

"I would guess there are catacombs beneath this church just like the ones closer to Siracusa, no?" Peter asked.

I pointed at a stairway on the opposite end of the chapel. "Yes, there are deep catacombs, but I've never seen graves or tombs in them."

"I want to make sure no one is hiding down there." He disappeared down the steps.

"Be careful," Bettina and I both called after him.

Bettina ran her hands along the tiles of another mosaic on the wall, the depiction of cherubs surrounding *Il Bambino Gesu* like a puzzle with half of the pieces missing.

I took a drink from a flask of water I had brought along and handed it to Bettina. "You must be thirsty," I said with a reassuring smile.

She took the water and drank. "*Grazie tanto, amica mia*," she said, bowing slightly in case she had fumbled the words.

"*Prego, amica mia*." I winked. "Do not worry; I told you that you speak *Italiano* much better than you think. I understand all you mean to say."

"*Da vero?* That makes me very happy." She placed the flask on one of the tables where Marianna and our group had sat and planned our trip to the city just the year before. Those poignant days had faded away when Marianna left to join the partisans. I brushed the dust from a chair and scooted up to the table with a knot in my throat.

Bettina focused on the mosaic again. She wore a green dress today, a deep green that matched her brilliant eyes. No wonder my twin brothers were captivated by her beauty.

She ran her fingers over the tiles that made baby Gesu's face. "I want to create mosaics like this." The awe in her voice rang like a prayer. "I paint on canvas, but this, this is *celestial*—"

The low drone of an engine echoed through the chapel and grew louder by the second. I leapt to my feet as Bettina spun around to face me, her eyes opened wide in panic.

"Peter," I called out, "someone is coming."

If he was deep inside the tunnels, he would never hear my warning.

Car doors slammed, and I grabbed Bettina by the hand. We darted up the steps at the front end of the chapel and hid, huddled together behind wide pillar.

Footsteps echoed off the walls, and I froze with fear when a man spoke in German.

Bettina grabbed my hands in a vice grip and mouthed the name *Keillor*.

I held my breath to keep myself from screaming. Bettina had to be wrong—it could not be Keillor. No German officer would dare remain in Sicily and drive in the open now that the Allies completely controlled Italy—he would be shot, killed, or captured. But Bettina knew his voice too well, and reality slammed me in the chest. Perhaps Keillor had never left Sicily at all.

Another man answered Keillor in what sounded like choppy German. His voice hinted at familiarity, but I could not hear him well.

The footsteps stopped. The talking ceased. Silence choked the air for several minutes, but we did not dare peek around the pillar for fear of being seen.

"*Ciao*, Bettina. At long last we are reunited."

Bettina shrieked and spun around, clearing the way for me to see Vasyl Keillor had crept up right behind her.

He held a pistol aimed at her belly and grabbed her by the throat with the other hand, spewing something guttural in German. Panic ran through my veins like icy water.

Bettina screamed again, and he pistol-whipped her across the cheek. "*Nein, nein, nein*," he said with a sickening lilt in his voice.

He glanced at me and switched to speaking Italian. "We will take care of you in a moment. I have something special in mind for Peter's harlot."

My stomach heaved, and panic flooded over me like icy water. The man was more twisted than I had ever realized, and we were at his mercy.

Bettina staggered, and Keillor prodded her with the pistol down the stairs and over to a chair. As soon as he yanked her away, I dropped down and crawled behind a dilapidated communion cupboard, looking for anything I could use as a weapon.

The walls behind me were the most intact, and no doorway was near. I chanced a glance to see what Keillor was doing to Bettina, but there was nothing I could do to help her with my hands empty.

Keillor pulled a rope from a bag at his hip and tied her hands behind her back as he talked and taunted her in German. I had no way of knowing what he said, but Bettina's whimpers and cries told me enough.

Bettina's head bobbed, and I knew she must be trying to stay aware after that blow to her cheek. There was no sign of the other man with Keillor and no sign of Peter.

I wanted to berate myself for going out unarmed, for assuming everything was safe, but it was too late now. Perhaps I could make a distraction so Keillor would look my way again and Bettina could at least try to run.

I stood up behind the pillar again where I could see Bettina better, and someone grabbed me from behind. I jerked and twisted, trying to break free to no avail. The man pushed me against the pillar face-first and tied my hands with rope behind my back just like Keillor had done to Bettina.

"Move it, and do not try to run. I do not want to shoot you."

I gasped and managed to look over my shoulder at a filthy, bearded face. "Davide. How did you get here? Why would you—?"

"Stop talking. I quit the resistance and came back to Siracusa."

I spun around, my wrists burning where the rope was cinched tight. "You are helping a Nazi? Why? How could you?"

"Because Peter should not be free, and I knew Keillor would help me get rid of him. I found Keillor hiding in the catacombs. He just wants Peter and his sister and swore you would not be harmed."

I glared at him, nausea swirling in my gut. "I will not be harmed? You are pointing a gun at me."

"Only so you will not try to help the others until Keillor takes them away."

"Are you *pazzo?* He will kill all of us, even you. We were in the resistance together, Davide. How could you betray your friends and country like this?"

His eyes squinted into slits. "You and your father are the traitors. I joined the partisans to fight the Germans, not to fall into their beds and save them like you and your father have done. I can hardly bear to look at you, Franca."

Realization hit me like a blow to the belly. "You told Keillor that Peter and Bettina were at my family's villa."

"Someone needed to tell him—to get them out of our country. I cannot believe your father would rescue Germans."

"So you stayed around long enough in camp to hear about my father's plan for Peter to get me home and to rescue his mother and sister. You must have been standing outside our tent like a pathetic spy."

Davide grimaced and lifted his chin. "So what if I overheard? Someone has to keep the enemy out of Italy. They have no place here."

"Davide, I know the Nazis killed your brother, but Peter and Bettina are not Nazis—Keillor is. Peter has helped—"

"Stop talking." He glared and raised his hand to hit me, but I saw hesitancy and even sorrow in his eyes. He shoved me down the stairs to a chair near Bettina.

Davide's bitterness had possessed him, but he had stopped before hitting me. And he had sought out Keillor to get rid of Peter rather than just killing Peter himself. Davide was enraged with bitterness toward the Germans and misled in his infatuation with me, but perhaps he was not a cold-blooded killer. Perhaps he would change his mind and help us get away.

Peter was still missing, and I was terrified for him to find us here with Keillor and terrified that he would not. I had not seen a weapon on Peter, and he was outgunned by two men.

Keillor pulled Bettina's head back and ran the side of his knife blade up and down her cheek while he whispered in her ear.

I had to stop him from cutting Bettina. "You are nothing but a coward who hides in caves and brutalizes women."

Keillor sneered at me. "I was left in Sicily to spy on the Allies. An assignment I have flourished in. And do not underestimate me; I enjoy torturing men as much as women—although I still have not had enough chances to torture Peter. He has been taunting me since we were children, but his day has come." He shrugged and pursed his lips. "I have been watching all of you. Waiting until your guard was down. And today is the day."

Bettina stopped crying and looked at Keillor in disgust, spewing words in an angry tone and spitting in his face.

He leaned down and kissed her on the lips. Bettina jerked her head to the side and spat on the floor.

Keillor looked at me. "I know your paramour is here somewhere. And I know he abandoned his army and exposed our location in the catacombs. It was the final straw as the saying goes, and he will pay for it today. I wish he would hurry and play the hero so I can tie him up and let him watch me punish the women. Peter is so afraid of being a man that he has to try to keep others from it too. Oh well, we can take care of both women before they die, can we not, Davide?"

Davide frowned. "You never said anything about harming the women."

Keillor scowled with disgust. "Cowardly Italians. Keep your gun pointed at these two while I procure a surprise from the jeep."

As soon as Keillor walked away, I looked at Davide. "You can stop this. We have been comrades against the Nazis—"

"I keep telling you to stop talking, Franca." He came close and glared right in my face, his nose almost touching mine. "You knew I cared for you, but you degraded yourself with a German—a disgusting Kraut that has no right to live."

Keillor came back carrying a box in his arms that he set on the table. He pulled out a bottle of wine and some glasses, his eyes opened extra wide with an exaggerated smile on his face. "Anyone thirsty besides me?" He looked back and forth at each of us. "Wine is just what we all need. I want to celebrate our special occasion." He poured two glasses and handed one to Davide.

Davide was red in the face, his brows locked in a scowl as he gulped several swallows.

Keillor slapped the glass from Davide's hand, and it shattered on the floor. "Wait, do not gulp it down like a dog; let us be civilized. I want to make a toast."

Keillor raised his glass toward Bettina with a grin and continued in Italian so we could all understand. "To my beautiful Bettina. Mine, all mine, at last."

Davide stared down at his broken glass of wine. His eyes widened, and I knew he realized he had made a pact with the devil.

Keillor poured another glass of wine, stood before Bettina, and drizzled it over her head.

Bettina inhaled sharply and closed her eyes as the wine dripped and streamed red down her neck and dress.

"Hmm . . ." He pressed his face into Bettina's neck. "Now you smell delicious."

"My brother will kill you if you touch me."

"Oh? Did you think I came here with only me and Davide? I expect our other comrade to find and bring your brother into the room any minute."

My breath came in short spurts. Peter could have been trapped or killed in the catacombs by this other man.

Keillor poured another glass of wine and pressed it against my mouth. I held my lips closed tight, and he stepped back. "Now, signorina, I am being very gracious here. I am bonding us all together. Show your Italian hospitality and drink this wine."

Davide had shown me no mercy with the tight rope around my wrists; I had little sensation left in my hands and fingers, but my legs had not been bound. When Keillor stepped back, I jumped up and smashed him in the groin with my knee. He doubled over and dropped the glass of wine.

Davide came right up behind me and grabbed my arms. I snapped my head back with full force and rammed him in the nose. The crack of bone echoed off the wall, and Davide dropped to his knees with his hand over his face while Keillor stood doubled over in pain.

Bettina and I both ran for the doors of the chapel with our hands still bound behind us, but a gunshot exploded, slammed me in the shoulder, and sent me flying. I had no way to catch myself and fell flat down on my belly. Breath burst from my lungs, and my chin smacked the ground on impact. I gasped for air as the room swirled and telescoped into a tunnel.

Angry voices brought me to my senses. Pain burned and pounded like a hammer in my shoulder, refusing to let me lie still. I opened my eyes and managed to roll to my side just enough to see Keillor point his pistol toward Davide.

"I told you what we were about today," growled Keillor.

Davide fisted his hands. "There was no need to shoot her. You can take your anger out on Peter and leave the women out of it, Keillor."

Keillor sneered. "I am tired of your cowardice."

Davide grabbed his pistol and aimed it at Keillor, but he was too slow. A gunshot rang from Keillor's pistol, and Davide fell back on the floor.

The fire in my shoulder made me want to cry out in pain, but I bit my lip and stayed down. I'd caught a glimpse of a second gun tucked in the back of Davide's pants before he fell. If I could get my hands loose and crawl over . . . but my mind kept sliding in and out of consciousness.

Keillor reached down and took the pistol from Davide's lifeless hand, and someone slammed into Keillor's back and knocked him down. I recognized Peter before my head swirled again and a black tunnel shut out the light.

CHAPTER FIFTY-FIVE

Peter

A WOMAN'S SCREAM REVERBERATED THROUGH the tunnel of the catacombs, and I jumped like a grenade had detonated. Franca and Bettina were in trouble. I tore through the main hall on my way back to the chapel, and someone slammed into my side and knocked me off my feet. I rolled to my side, shaking my head and caught a glimpse of the man who'd knocked me to the ground.

Grunting and panting, the man jumped for the gun that must have flown from his hand when he hit me.

I rose up and punched him in the jaw before he could reach his weapon. He unleashed a stream of curse words in German, condemning me in the name of the führer and confirming my suspicion; he was disguised in civilian clothes, but my attacker was a Nazi.

I had seconds to spare and a muscled soldier to get past before I could help the women. He punched me with both hands in the gut and ribs with fists of iron. The man was taller and stronger than me, but the urgency to get up the stairs and find Franca and Bettina kept me on my feet.

I bent at the waist, gasping for air, and dove straight into the man's stomach, knocking him off balance. I struck him in the belly, sucked in a quick, stabbing breath and hit him with an uppercut to the jaw. The man's head snapped back, and he fell to the ground.

I grabbed the pistol from across the cavern, and when the man came to his feet and barreled straight for me, I pulled the trigger several times, but only one bullet fired. It was enough; the man fell lifeless to the floor.

Out of breath and gripped by the pain of more than one broken rib, I clamored up the stairs to find the women as angry voices echoed up above, and gunshots cracked through the air.

I glanced around a pillar to make my plan of attack. Bettina was gone, and Davide lay dead on the ground in front of Vasyl Keillor. Franca lay facedown on the chapel floor several feet away, a stain of blood growing on her back.

Keillor had his back to me and had pointed the gun back at Franca. I gritted my teeth, ran and jumped, flying through the air before I slammed into his back. Keillor hit the ground with me on top of him, and I growled in his ear. "You are dead, Vasyl Keillor. Dead."

The fight with the other soldier and dash up the stairs had left me in pain and winded, but I pounded Keillor in the kidneys before he could move a muscle. He bucked up and rolled to the side, knocking me to the floor beside him and pointing his gun in my face. I whacked his hand to the side, scrambling to get up and grab for the gun, but Keillor spun himself around on the ground and knocked my feet out from under me with his leg. I landed on my back but managed to kick the pistol from Keillor's hand.

The pistol few across the floor toward Franca, and Keillor jumped up and grabbed it. I expected him to shoot me then and there, but he stopped long enough to hold the pistol up to my view and grin before he ran and disappeared outside. Dread flooded in; he did not want to shoot me before he had made me watch him terrorize or kill Bettina.

I glanced at Davide; he was dead, no gun in his hands. I stopped long enough to see that Franca was breathing, and the gunshot was in her shoulder. I gritted my teeth, hoping it was above her lung. I kissed her on the head with a command, more than a prayer, that she stay alive and scrambled for the door to find Keillor before he could murder my sister.

The walls around the gardens were crumbling. I ran to the closest courtyard and spotted Bettina, her eyes wide open in panic and her hands still tied behind her back. The front of her dress had been torn open to her chemise, and blood ran from her nose. Keillor had her gripped by a handful of her hair and held her over the opening of a large well.

I crouched behind a wall where Keillor could not see me and darted along the wall to get closer.

"Peter," Keillor shouted. "I know you are hiding. I am happy we have finally come to the reunion I have dreamed of. You are not armed, and fortunately for me, and for Bettina, I am. There is nothing you can do to stop me because if you come one step closer I will drop your dear sister into this dried-up well. It is at least fifty feet deep, and when she hits the rocks at the bottom and her head is cracked open, you will know I have won and that cowards always lose. Because that is all you are, a coward and a traitor."

The man sounded like the demented schoolyard bully he'd always been, bragging and threatening his schoolmates. I would not give him the satisfaction of a response and saw him nervously glance around the courtyard. I had to get my hands on a weapon of some kind, but except for large rocks, there was nothing within my reach.

My mind raced. The vision of Franca weak and bleeding on the chapel floor kicked me in the gut over and over, and I knew in that moment that if she died, my life, my joy, my future, would float away with her, and I would be left a ghost in chains. I would not care if I died, but if I could save Bettina, she could go back to our mother, and the two of them would have a chance to make a life for themselves.

I made my way around the wall behind the well, hoping that the element of surprise would be enough and that I could grab Keillor from behind with one hand and push Bettina away from the well with the other before Keillor could aim and shoot me. It was a weak plan, but it was all I had.

I crouched down just a few feet away, waiting for Keillor to sweat long enough that his guard would be down and I could pounce. He twitched and jerked his head back and forth, trying to find me. The collar of his civilian shirt was soaked with sweat. He wore torn pants held up by suspenders, and his shoes were covered in mud. Gone was his shiny Nazi uniform. Gone was the vehicle where he had trapped and victimized women. Gone were the puppet soldiers who had always done his bidding.

I sprang, but Keillor had heard a noise behind me at the same instant I jumped, and he spun around and looked me right in the eyes. He aimed past me and pulled the trigger on his pistol, and two shots went off, exploding in the air.

Keillor lost hold of Bettina, grabbed his right shoulder, and dropped his pistol. Someone rushed past me, and I recognized Franca from the corner of my eye. She had shot Keillor in the shoulder and was rushing past him now, reaching for Bettina to keep her from falling in the well.

I lunged for Keillor's gun on the ground, but he kicked it out of my reach. I charged him, gripped him around the throat with both hands, and pushed him backward as he tried to grab at my hands with his left hand, his other hand limp and bloody, hanging down at his side.

He spit at my face and missed, and as much as I longed to strangle and kill him once and for all, I knew I needed to get his hands tied and turn him in to the Allies. "You've lost, Keillor. This war is over for you."

He squirmed and tried to jerk free. "Not quite over," he breathed in my face and thrust his hand at my side. The cold steel of a knife blade gored me in the ribs.

I staggered and lost my breath but kept my grip around his neck, shoving him back with the last of my strength.

Keillor stumbled backwards and tripped over the wall of the gaping well. He fell, eyes wide open in terror, and grabbed for the bucket that hung by a piece of rotten rope over the opening. The old rope disintegrated into dust, and Keillor's screams ended abruptly at least fifty feet down on a bed of dry rocks.

Franca was with me suddenly, holding my head in her lap. Her shoulder was bloody, and her chin swollen where someone or something had hit her. She was the most beautiful woman I had ever seen. I could barely breathe through the pain in my chest, but God was merciful after all and let Franca's face be the last thing I would see in this world.

CHAPTER FIFTY-SIX

Franca

The doctor was back again. "You look much better, signorina Franca. Keep spending a few minutes sitting outside for fresh air each day."

"*Grazie, dottore*. I am much better," I said, leaning back on the pillows of my bed and forcing a smile.

He tsked his tongue and patted my leg. "You must be so careful. The infection in your wound is almost gone, but you took a long time to heal. Do no chores or anything that can make you tired."

"Very well," I said, relieved when he left so I could stare out the window of my bedroom and hope that an automobile would show up and a certain German man would return.

"It has only been three weeks. The doctor said it could take longer because of his lung. Do not give up hope," Bettina said as she entered my room with a tray of *biscotti.* She had helped my mother tend to me night and day.

I breathed easier, and Bettina set the tray on the table next to my bed. As long as she and her mother were here, I still had a connection to Peter—even if that connection was fragile as a brittle twig.

"Three weeks. It seems like a year has gone by." I sighed.

She handed me a saucer with a cup of tea and a few of the *biscotti.* "Indeed. But the nurse there tells Bruno that Peter is improving now. They hope he is past the danger."

"I almost wish my wound would have been more dangerous. As long as I was at the hospital, I was closer to him."

"You came close enough to death with your infection. Do not scare us like that again."

Later, Dominic helped me to a chair in the courtyard, and I breathed in the salty air of the Mediterranean. The sun glowed on the horizon, orange as a peach ready to be picked from the sky. It made me hungry for the first time in weeks. But maybe my appetite was returning because Peter was out of danger. At least the danger from his stab wound. A couple inches over and Keillor would have gotten his heart as well as his lung with that knife. The memory of seeing blood coming from Peter's mouth when he coughed flashed again, and I curled my toes under the blanket Dom had laid over me.

The bullet had gone clear through my shoulder when Keillor shot me, but the shortage of medication in the hospital left me unprotected, and infection flared up in my shoulder and then spread to my whole body. I hardly remembered some of the time at the hospital, looking up at the ceiling through the hazy fog of raging fever, my mother beside me speaking to me as if we floated beneath the surface of the Mediterranean. No matter what Mama said to me, I cried Peter's name in reply, convinced that he was dead and that no one would tell me the truth.

Everyone took a turn reassuring me that Keillor was really dead and could not come after us again. Even Davide had died when Keillor shot him in the head just because he was finished using him.

Bettina and I had loaded Peter into the vehicle that Kiellor had driven to the church and drove him straight to the hospital. Donatella looked me in the eye when we arrived and did not even question who he was before she took Peter in for surgery. They had saved him just in time before his lung had completely filled with blood or he would have bled to death.

Now that I was free of my fever and delirium, I could see the honesty in my family's eyes when they reassured me Peter would survive and that there was every reason to hope.

But hope was a ribbon that only reached so far before it snapped. Peter would live, but that changed nothing of the war that still raged on the land and seas and in the souls of men—the hatred and bias in my world that kept Peter and me apart.

The Gustav Line had been broken, and the Allies and our country were in control of Italy. But nothing had changed, and nothing may ever change between the Italians and the Germans.

Hatred incinerated people like an erupting volcano, reducing everything to ashes before it crusted over the land with a blackened shell. Under that shell beat my heart that could see no way to find the light again.

I'd been too weak to see Peter at the hospital when I was there. And when it was time for me to come home, the doctor had forbidden any visitors for him. Papa told me it was because Peter's presence at the hospital was a secret to almost everyone. They had given him a fake identity, but it would not be hard for the other patients to see he looked foreign, and in his delirium, he may speak in German.

Days passed as I asked everyone, even Dominic and Damiano, if word had come that Peter was healing and stable.

Every time the doctor left my side, he stopped in to check on my father's progress and to report to him about Peter. I could not get my breath until word came that they both were going to be all right and had improved.

When I returned from the hospital, my father had gained enough strength to spend time beside my bed reading to me.

"You look a bit better today, Franca," Papa said as he sat in a nearby chair in the courtyard and patted my hand.

"That is what the doctor said." I managed a smile in spite of the fact that I could hardly breathe until he said the words I needed to hear.

"And the doctor also said that Peter is much improved. He may be able to come back here soon."

I puffed out a breath of air and blinked to stave off my tears. Even though he had expressed many times that he was so grateful Peter had come to our rescue that day at the old church, I knew that the fact that Keillor had attacked us because of Peter only solidified my father's belief that it was far too dangerous for there to be anything between Peter and me. And Peter would not want to defy or disrespect my father.

CHAPTER FIFTY-SEVEN

Franca

August 1944

I WENT UNDER THE WARM water of the bath, luxuriating in the soft lavender scent of signora De'Angelis's soap before Alma came in and washed my hair for me because it still hurt to raise my left arm. "*Grazie,* Alma. It has been many years since you bathed me like a baby." We both laughed, and when I finished, I slipped a dress on instead of another nightgown.

Another week had passed and still no Peter. The walls of our villa were a cage, and I had walked the halls a hundred times to build up my strength. The outside air called to me, so I settled down in a porch chair behind the house. I gazed at Laura's grave on the hill and sobbed.

I looked toward the cellar under the winery where I knew Peter would be resting when he finally returned from the hospital. His strong jaw would be soft in slumber each night, his blue eyes dark as the evening sky. I wished he were here, that I could envelop myself in the warmth and strength of being near him.

The horror of constant suffering may ease now that the reports stated that Hitler and the Axis were officially losing the war. But Hitler refused to give in and forced his bedraggled army on. It was all so futile. Millions were dead, millions were wounded, and millions lived shattered lives. I laid my head back, watching the clouds float by like an overhead parade. The world moved on, no matter what we did to it.

Sunlight receded, darkening my mood with its shadows. I lit a lantern and ambled my way to the barn, settling down on the milking stool beside Rosa, content that my brothers had brought her to our villa. I'd struggled at her side so many times in Sortino, never dreaming what lay ahead in the rest of my journey. And most of all, never dreaming Peter lay hidden in the hay only steps away and that he would change my life no matter the outcome of the war.

I leaned my forehead against Rosa's side. "Hello, old friend, I hope you are—"

The barn door opened and closed, and I hunched down lower behind Rosa; fear of the unknown was a habit now.

"Do you need help milking the cow, signorina Chessari?" said a deep, familiar voice. "As I recall, you had some difficulty in the past."

Peter came into view like an apparition. He stopped at the end of Rosa's stall and leaned heavily on the post, and I held back the urge to jump to my feet and rush into his arms. He'd come to find me as soon as he returned from the hospital. I hardly dared move.

His hair had grown longer, curling behind his ears while a few strands fell forward on his forehead. The lantern light cast his skin in pale gold with a trace of purple still haunting under his eyes.

I finally spoke. "I've become confident in milking a cow. I had a really good teacher if you remember."

"Oh, I remember very well," he said, one side of his mouth lifting in a smile. "I would be willing to give you a refresher course, but I still find it quite painful to bend."

I swallowed the sob in my throat. "I thank God every day that you are alive. The saints are weary of my prayers."

"Yes, the pain in my chest reminds me constantly that I am alive. Thank you for your prayers, Franca. I have no doubt that you saved me, physically and spiritually."

It was hard to breathe, and I came to my feet. "You must be crazy to come out to the barn when you need your rest."

"I am definitely crazy." He swallowed hard. "But I had to find you. Even though, now that I am here, I realize I am quite weak and helpless."

"Perhaps if I came over to you, you could tell me what to do to help you." I walked over and stood in front of him. Then I reached up and brushed the loose strands of hair off his forehead. My fingers were shaking, and my voice caught in my throat. "I thought you were going to die. And I would die right after you because there would be no reason to—"

"Shh . . . Francesca," he whispered, brushing his finger softly back and forth over my lips. "No one is going to die in this room."

"And no one is an enemy in this room," I whispered back and took a step closer.

He eased his hands around my waist and drew me close until our cheeks pressed to one another's.

I closed my eyes and skimmed my nose across the stubble of his whiskers, savoring the scent of his skin.

Peter glided his lips over my jaw and down my neck before he came back again and closed his mouth over mine. I gave back in turn, drinking in the familiar taste of his lips, surrendering to the gentle demand in his kiss and the strength in his hands.

"I love you, Francesca Chessari," he whispered in my ear.

I wanted to answer, but he kissed me again, and joy overpowered my ability to speak. I took his lead and let the world disappear behind kisses, the flicker of the lantern and the soft chirrup of crickets.

Peter's feet shifted, and he stumbled. I grabbed him by the waist. "You need to lie down."

His breathing was labored, and his steps unsteady. I took him by the hand and led him over to the hay, grabbed an old blanket out of a chest, and helped Peter lie down.

"You are still too weak. We need to get you inside."

"Let me rest a bit, and we'll make our way back. I told Bettina I wanted to see you alone first, before I went down to the cellar."

I smiled. "So that is where Bettina went today, to the hospital. I asked about her, but no one knew where she was."

"I wanted her to bring me home instead of bothering any of your family again. And I did not want you to be nervous or worried about my return."

"I have been watching and longing to see you for weeks."

He put out his hand. "Here. Come lie beside me."

I lay down with my head on his arm near the top of his shoulder, making sure I did not put any pressure near his chest and that my injured shoulder was not compressed.

"We are a fine pair," I said with a chuckle.

"Like two ninety-year-olds trying to have a tumble in the hay."

"Is that what this is? You are just after a tumble?" I teased, managing to lean over his face.

He smiled and played with a tendril of my hair. "I would tumble with you every day for the rest of my life."

"I love you, Peter."

He cupped my neck in his hand and pulled me in for a kiss. A kiss and kisses that lasted far into the night.

I woke the next morning to find Peter lying on his side watching me. "Have I ever told you that you look like a goddess when you sleep?"

I wanted to melt into him and his words, but my disheveled appearance got the better of me; I knew my hair must be a mess and full of straw. "The goddess of haystacks, I suppose."

I chuckled and lifted a heavy quilt that had been laid over us. "Where did we get the extra covers?"

"I suspect Bettina was our benefactor. She was the only one who knew we were here together."

"And she must have told my family or they would have come looking for me."

Peter kissed me again, but I hesitated. "I must smell and taste like a barn."

"You are delicious anywhere, anytime."

I grinned and kissed him back. "And so are you, my forbidden lover."

He sat up carefully, his eyes gone sober. "I will never deny my feelings for you again, Francesca. I vowed that every day in the hospital after I almost lost you. But it does not mean the way will be easy."

I moved around and sat right in front of him, leaning in until our noses almost touched. "We will find a way. I know we will."

He reached up and held my cheek with his hand. "I want to marry you, Francesca Chessari."

I pressed my hand over his, letting my tears flow onto our fingers. "And I want to marry you."

CHAPTER FIFTY-EIGHT

Franca

We held each other up, both of us weak and exhausted, and made our way back to the house. I did not know what my family would say when we walked in together, but I braced myself for the worst.

Bruno and his mother were in the kitchen with Alma, and Luca was giggling on Bruno's knee. We asked them to join my brothers and parents with us in the parlor.

Peter and I stood side by side before them, and Peter took me by the hand.

"You both look so tired," Alma said. She pulled up two chairs, and Peter and I sat down next to one another before Alma left the room.

Peter glanced at everyone in the room and spoke to my parents first. "Signore and signora Chessari, I know I have little to offer at this time, and you have many concerns. I have kept my vow to you about Franca. But I realized as I lay on the verge of death that there is no reason for this war—no reason we have risked our lives for months and years—if there is no love at the end of it. I love your daughter, and I realize there is great opposition and even danger in that. I will do whatever it takes, even if we have to leave the country for a while, to keep Franca and the rest of you safe. But I cannot deny what I feel for her anymore."

"I feel the same way. I love Peter," I said, elation swelling in my chest as the words tumbled out so freely and real. I could hardly stay seated.

Bruno got up and left the room. I knew it would take more time for him to accept what we were saying. Laura's last bout of weakness hit her because of Germany's invasion and Vasyl Keillor. It could take him a long time to heal. Bettina got up a moment later and followed Bruno outside. I glanced out the window and saw the two of them standing beside one another at Laura's grave.

Perhaps Bruno would heal sooner than we thought.

Everyone except Peter's mother and my parents slipped out of the room. Signora Weimer's lips quivered as she dabbed at her eyes with a handkerchief.

Alma peeked at me from around the corner where no one else could see her, smiled, and pressed her hands over her heart.

Papa looked at the floor as if deep in thought. "We lost Laura sooner than we would have because of the war." He looked up at both of us, his eyes still sunken. "And we do not want to lose the only daughter we have left. But when a Chessari heart is locked onto love, it does not let go. So it seems the only way we can stay close and keep you, Franca, is to accept Peter."

Mama sat up straighter. "I have known how you felt in spite of our efforts to keep distance between you. Your eyes were full of tears every time you asked about Peter these past weeks. We know you are a good man, Peter. We have only been afraid."

Peter winced. "I sincerely apologize for bringing you worry and fear. I have tried my best to keep Franca safe, and I realize she was harmed and almost killed at the old church because of me. I'm not sure when I can forgive myself for that."

"It was because of the evil in another man, not you," Papa said.

Mama lifted her hand in reassurance. "Perhaps God saved the two of you for a reason."

Papa bowed his head in agreement. "We understand and will accept your decision to be together."

If not for my weakened state, I would have leapt with joy from my chair. I went over to my parents, and we embraced one another, kissed each other's cheeks, and then Peter and I put our arms around his mother, and she pressed her hands on our cheeks. "I am so happy. So very happy."

Dominic and Damiano had been listening at the door and ran back in the room jumping and cheering. "Does this mean that Bettina will be staying around too?" asked Dom before Damiano tackled him to the floor.

Peter and I both laughed, and Mama tsked her tongue at the boys. "Go on now. This is about your sister, not you."

"We know," said Dom, and both brothers hugged Peter and me before heading out of the room, still cheering.

Peter and I sat back down, and my parents looked at each other before Papa spoke again. "We suspected this was coming. We are willing to do anything we can to help keep the two of you safe. I have a connection in Switzerland, a comrade there who would be able to take you in. He is a liaison, and we need him for other work in the near future. He told me last week he would need a couple to stay at his farm and work his dairy if he is to fulfill our need. Would the two of you be willing to do such a thing?"

Peter's eyes glistened as we looked at one another, our eyes open wide. We grinned with excitement, squeezing our hands together.

"Yes, sir." Peter nodded to my father. "I will rest and recuperate, and as soon as possible, I will be on my feet and ready to go."

"And me, Papa. I want to be with Peter wherever it needs to be."

Peter stood, still holding onto my hand. He looked soberly at my parents. "In order to take this position, I need to ask permission to marry Franca. I promise to keep her close, love her, and care for her all of our lives."

Papa carefully rose and extended his hand to shake Peter's. "I believe that covers it, son. If Franca says she is willing to marry you, I give you my permission."

I cried out with joy and came to my feet beside Peter, wrapping my arms around his waist and pressing my lips to his. Peter took my face in his hands and kissed me back as if no one was in the room.

Mama wiped at her tears, and Papa raised his brows. "Franca, you grew up on a vineyard in a villa with servants. Are you sure you can work a farm and take care of a dairy?"

I looked into Peter's eyes and smiled before I answered. "Of course. I am very good at milking cows."

ABOUT THE AUTHOR

MELINDA S. SANCHEZ, GREW UP spellbound by the characters of wonderful books from Pippi Longstocking, Laura Ingalls Wilder, and Kit Tyler to Scout and Scarlett O'Hara.

She wrote her first book in second grade, was a poet by age twelve, and began writing stories and novels by the time she reached adulthood.

As an adult, Melinda lived in the picturesque country of Italy and fell in love with the people, language, landscape, and history. She met her husband there, and together, they have five beautiful grown children, six perfect granddaughters, and one handsome grandson. They also have a house full of dogs, cats, exotic lizards and creatures, and birds—plenty of love and characters to keep Melinda inspired and writing, writing, writing for a long time to come.